* * *

The Intus Invasion

Book One of the Battles of the Republic

* * *

By James Rosone
and
Brandon Ellis

* * *

Illustration © Tom Edwards
Tom EdwardsDesign.com

* * *

Published in conjunction with Front Line Publishing, Inc.

Manuscript Copyright Notice

©2025, James Rosone and Brandon Ellis, in conjunction with Front Line Publishing, Inc. Except as provided by the Copyright Act, no part of this publication may be reproduced, stored in a retrieval system or transmitted in any form or by any means without the prior written permission of the publisher.

All rights reserved.

ISBN: 978-1-961748-92-7
Sun City Center, Florida, United States of America
Library of Congress Control Number: 2025900243

Table of Contents

Chapter 1
No Safe Harbor

Year 2086
Manzanillo, Mexico
Earth

Ripley Willis Lee took a step over a severed hand. It still clutched a rosary, its fingers charred. Lee didn't want to know why a person had lost their hand, or how it had ended up here. He looked away as he continued to walk down the sidewalk, doing his best to push the image out of his mind.

Three blocks away, a hover-SUV with tinted windows and a mounted .50-caliber machine gun drove past a group of children kicking a crushed can over a shabby grass field.

When the children glanced at the vehicle, they scattered. The SUV revved its engine and accelerated around a corner, disappearing from view.

These days, if someone walked alone in Manzanillo, Mexico, they'd find themselves either dead under a bridge with their organs stolen or kidnapped for auction into slavery in the underground Perbudakan networks. Yet now, Ripley Willis Lee strode down those very streets.

The city, also known for its drug trade and cartel presence, had a great view of the Pacific Ocean. Lee had to give it that much. As he walked down the broken sidewalk, the waves rumbled in the distance.

After his Olympic gold medals in sharpshooting and yet another rejection from the military, he didn't care about playing it safe. Not anymore. The gig he'd drummed up down here in the slums would pay him the money he needed to help himself. Supposedly, the job guaranteed his safety too.

Lee touched the crinkled edge of the military rejection letter folded in his pants pocket. He remembered opening the email on his data tablet nearly a year ago—the words were burned into his mind: "...disqualified from service due to retinitis pigmentosa, with visual acuity below acceptable standards..."

He'd printed it off and carried it with him wherever he went. When the paper would wear down, he'd print off another one. His eyes had failed him—the very tools he needed to pursue his military calling.

Something needed to fuel his drive, and this letter did it for him. He'd sacrifice every luxury until he could afford the corrective surgery. Still, it didn't make sense. He was a perfect shot, even with his eye problems. The gold medals proved as much.

Lee fished out a plastic card from his other pocket. In dark ink, someone had scribbled his contact's address on the back.

I'm almost there, he thought.

The narrow street stretched before him. He'd been on foot for almost twenty minutes, ever since the taxi driver had refused to venture further, saying something about this neighborhood being under new management. It was a thinly veiled warning that the cartel had recently muscled their way into this forgotten corner of the city.

With a Higgs 92X Compact pistol in his hand, he walked around a loose slab on the sidewalk. He halted to rest his shoulder against a building with a hanging sign above the entrance—the Calle Libertad—while he looked at the card again.

Another two blocks.

Before he'd made his way down to Mexico, his soon-to-be new boss had told him over a comm call to carry a weapon, though he'd promised Lee would be safe. Lee had taken the counsel seriously.

In front of him, weeds burst through cracks in the uneven pavement. Bordering the sidewalk, rusted lampposts blinked. Stray dogs prowled the empty storefronts across the street, their fur dark against the flashing neon of a lonely cantina.

This area is sketchy as hell.

As he started to walk again, two men headed in his direction. Lee tucked the card back into his pocket. When he attempted to pass them, one man in a gray sweatshirt stood in Lee's way.

"Wallet and anything else valuable." One of the men spoke with a definite Texan drawl, the guy no doubt from Texas. The other individual looked local.

Lee took a slow step back and tipped his head toward the Higgs 92X in his hand. "I'm good. How about you guys?"

The local threw his arms out to his sides. "Are you threatening us?"

"Be careful making quick movements like that, my friend," Lee said. "Some trigger-happy tourist may take your head off." He kept his focus trained on the two men in front of him while also maintaining awareness of his peripheral vision for anyone else who might approach from the sides of the deserted street.

"Who you callin' friend? Give me your money," the Texan replied.

"Look, fellas, I don't want any trouble. Just let me go on my way, please."

The local man sneered. "Give us what you got, or you'll find yourself someplace you don't want to be."

I'm kinda already in that "someplace." "I'm an expert with my weapon."

"We know." The man from Texas laughed. "But we're asking nicely."

Neither person carried a gun—at least, not in plain sight. Still, they exuded an air of confidence. Too much confidence. To Lee, it meant they probably had armed friends somewhere nearby. He kept his gun low. If he raised it, someone would likely send a bullet through his back.

Lee relaxed a little. He remembered his new employer had pledged to keep him safe. "I'm here to see Miguel Ángel Treviño." Maybe saying the man's name would do the trick.

They exchanged looks. "Miguel Ángel Treviño? You're lying, bro."

"I'm not." Lee frowned. "I'm his private security contractor."

The local man chuckled. "Nice try. Look at you, all skinny with glasses. How do you know Miguel's full name, man? You look and sound, and kinda smell"—he sniffed a few times—"fishy to me."

"He's hired me. That's all I can say."

The Texan looked behind him. "They'd have had Arturo come and meet you and guide you to the compound by now. You're trespassing. Give me your damn money or die. Either way, I'm still rich."

Lee's pistol hand twitched. One squeeze of the trigger and he could end this confrontation fast.

Across the street, a large dumpster caught the corner of his eye—potential cover if he played his cards right. Behind the Texan, an alleyway gave him a quick escape route if he could outmaneuver his adversaries, who might be more than just these two hostiles.

"I've got no money," Lee said. "None. So walk away."

The local man spat at Lee's feet and eyed him for a good five seconds. "You're Ripley Willis Lee, famed Olympic star. With whatever endorsements you have, you've got money. Hand it over."

They didn't want him for just his wallet. If they kidnapped him, they could garner tons of money via holding him hostage.

Have I been set up? Was this my new employer's plan the entire time? Lee wondered.

The Texan raised a fist. "When I open my hand, you die. I'm giving you three seconds to hand over your wallet and—"

"The endorsements pay lousy. I'm barely getting by as is, hence why I'm down here. And if I hand over my wallet, you'll grab me. I look away, even for a millisecond, you have the advantage. Simple as that."

"You're a confident guy, aren't you?" the Texan said.

Lee shook his head. "Confident? No. But if you take a step in my direction, I'm confident I *will* kill you." Without moving his head, he glanced at the local man. "And you too. So leave me be."

One way or another, if he lowered his weapon, fished for his wallet, or even budged a millimeter, they'd take him to the ground and wrestle his pistol free.

If I die today, I take one of these guys with me.

The Texan continued to hold his fist in the air. For a brief second, he took his eyes off Lee. In a flash, Lee raised his gun. Two shots rang out, and both adversaries fell to the sidewalk.

Lee dashed toward the alleyway a moment before a bullet ricocheted off the wall and dust clouded in the air. Gunshots reverberated throughout the street. The pounding of heavy feet, perhaps of a dozen men, entered the vicinity. Men hollered while Lee turned down the side street. A bullet sank into the concrete near his heel. Without looking, he returned fire.

Lee leaped over a pile of crates before he found cover behind a crumbling brick wall. The dozen men chasing him sprinted close behind. Their shouts echoed through the narrow alleyway.

As he scanned his surroundings for an escape route, a fire escape ladder leading to the rooftop of an old apartment building presented itself. Without hesitation, he ran toward it. A bullet whizzed past his head and sank into a wooden eave, cracking it in half.

Lee gripped the rusted metal rungs and climbed the ladder. His muscles burned as he moved as fast as he possibly could. He reached the top of the building. His expression dropped. It was a dead end.

Sheer walls rose several stories higher on all sides. Concrete stretched out before him. Ten meters in front of him stood a solitary apartment window caked in cobwebs.

He looked down the ladder. Several men climbed after him. Lee's breaths came quickly as he turned and faced the window. He charged forward. Once he reached the glass, he threw his shoulder against the window with all his might. The glass shattered, and he tumbled into the empty apartment. Shards cut into his skin as he rolled across the dusty floor.

Two of his pursuers rushed onto the roof after him. Their guns were drawn as they burst through the broken window. Lee reacted in the blink of an eye, his own weapon already in hand. He fired off two quick shots, the bullets finding their targets.

The first man dropped right away. Dead. The second man—Lee gasped. Young. Too young. The boy's eyes widened with shock. The kid reached up to touch the crimson blossoming on his chest. He couldn't have been more than sixteen, maybe seventeen. For a fraction of a second, they stared into each other's eyes. In the next instant, the life drained from the poor kid's face.

Shouts drew closer. Lee bolted out of the apartment and down the hallway, raced down several flights of stairs, and broke through a door leading to a wide, empty street.

He forced down the vomit rising in his throat. He had to move. Had to run. Questions about why they'd send a teen after him could wait.

Three more individuals appeared from around the corner, their weapons raised. Shots pierced the air. Lee dove behind a dumpster, his pulse pounding. Bullets ricocheted off the metal.

I need to act… now!

He popped up from behind his cover and rapid-fired three rounds. Each one hit its target. The men flopped backwards.

Seven down. A handful more. I'm an idiot and got myself in deep crap. How did I not see this when I signed up for this gig? Lee asked himself. *Stop thinking! Move, move!*

Bullets whizzed through the air. Lee ducked down after squeezing the trigger to an empty magazine. He slammed a fresh mag into his weapon, racking the slide to chamber a new round. "Lord, help me… please, please. It's not my fault," he muttered under his breath. "I don't want to kill any of these guys." He crawled toward an overturned car, using it as a makeshift barricade.

A fiery pain burned his shoulder as a bullet nicked him. Lee gritted his teeth. He pushed through the discomfort as he rounded the side of the car for better cover. Blood dripped.

He grimaced as he eyed a few men strutting down the middle of the road. They wore heavy overcoats and clutched rifles. Either those were stolen and reprogrammed old Synths, or those individuals had a death wish.

With a burst of adrenaline, Lee charged forward, his gun blazing. One assailant fell. Another fired but missed wide, the shot slamming into a light pole. Lee's bullet caught the man square in the middle of the forehead. The guy went to his knees, the weapon falling from his listless grip. The third person moved to the left, no doubt trying to find cover. Lee pivoted, his weapon tracking the man's movements. He squeezed the trigger. A round tore through the attacker's chest and sent him to the ground.

Lee held his breath. *How did I live through that?*

He surveyed the hellish sight around him. The street was littered with bodies.

I have to keep moving. Gotta stay one step ahead. Ten down. Where's the rest?

Lee bolted down the street to put as much distance as possible between himself and the scene of the firefight. He didn't know where he was going or exactly where he was.

Holding his wounded shoulder, Lee made his way through the winding streets. As sirens in the distance grew louder, Lee wandered into an old industrial warehouse. Rusted metal walls surrounded the area. He could tell the building had once manufactured advanced propulsion engines for large navy space vessels as he passed by one of the massive engines lying on the asphalt. Beside it, a hatch showed.

With a grunt of pain, Lee pulled open the heavy metal door and lowered himself into the tight space. Musty air carried to his nostrils as he pulled the hatch closed, plunging himself into darkness.

He pulled out a lighter from his pocket and flicked it to life. The small flame sent a dim light over the area. He was in a small storage room filled with rusted tools and spare parts.

Lee glanced at his throbbing shoulder. He peeled back his shirt, wincing as the fabric stuck to the blood. The bullet had taken a chunk out of his flesh.

Searching the storage room, he found a small knife. With a quick motion, he sliced off the sleeve of his shirt and, using his teeth and his good arm, wrapped the fabric tightly around the bullet wound. The intense pressure helped to dull the pain. He needed proper medical attention, and soon.

As he stared at his blood-soaked sleeve, a soft whir sounded close by. In the corner of the room, a small surveillance drone hovered. Its blinking red light focused on him. Lee cursed under his breath. If it was the attackers or their cartel masters watching, he only had seconds to decide his next move.

Chapter 2
The Offer

Lee froze, not daring to move. The drone's unblinking gaze moved over him. Lee's mind went into overdrive. If he smashed the drone, they'd know he was aware of its presence. If he hid deeper in this room, they'd no doubt keep watching. Quickly, he slipped through the hatch he'd used to get into this space. His arm ached, and he grunted through the movement. The gunshot wound throbbed. Who knew a flesh wound could hurt so much?

In the middle of the warehouse, he searched for a place to hide. After eyeing the exit—considering just leaving instead—he noticed stairs. They led to something similar to a loft, an area he'd not seen before. He sprinted up the metal steps. On the upper level, and right there across the way, stood a faucet. Thirst had been burning his dry throat for the past hour. Once he crossed the room, he turned on the water and drank. Rust. Metal. The taste practically stained his mouth, if that was possible. Immediately, he regretted drinking it, but he needed something to tide him over.

Voices came in from outside. Lee crouched low and crawled to the window. People milled about in the large disused parking lot below. He slid down, his back against the wall, his head under the windowsill, and curled his fingers into fists. If anyone came through the front door—any door—he'd fight.

He grimaced as his wound screamed at even the idea of it all, of a fight, of running, of anything. By the minute, his body became heavier. *Fighting? Not now. I can't do this. I need sleep.*

He slapped his face. "Stay awake."

Just wait it out, he said to himself. *Just a little longer. They'll leave.*

His eyelids grew heavy. The pain, the exhaustion, the blood loss—it all caught up to him at once. He closed his eyes, and his head drooped forward as consciousness fell away.

When he jerked awake, evening shadows filled the warehouse.

Where am I?

In a split second, he remembered. He'd fallen asleep only to wake up to the nightmare he'd walked into not long ago.

How am I going to get out of Mexico?

Outside, the sound of engines burst through the air. People yelled orders. He looked out from his hiding spot. An AT-70 Osprey Assault Transport had landed, and a group of armed soldiers surrounded the building.

There's no way I can fight my way through this alive. The authorities have found me. He checked his magazine and peered around for a higher vantage point. Just as he was about to formulate a plan, he froze.

The drone was hovering half a meter away from him, its red light beaming directly on his chest.

How did it get out of the storage room?

A voice filled the night. "Ripley Willis Lee! This is the Republic Navy. We know you're in there. We tracked you and observed what you've done on video surveillance."

Lee stiffened. *The Republic Navy?*

With all he had, he yelled, "It was in self-defense! It's on the videos!"

"You're surrounded by a team of Delta operators," the man said. "We don't have much time, son, so listen carefully. If you come out now with your hands up, no charges will be made against you. You have my word."

Lee's brain spun. He knew he couldn't outrun or outfight the Deltas, and the idea of no charges being filed against him was more than tempting. Was it true? The Republic Navy in this area of Mexico made little to no sense. Was it really the Republic Navy?

I'm too tired. They've got me. Time to meet my fate like a man.

The Delta operators moved in quickly, several busting through different entrances into the warehouse. They trained their weapons on him as he walked down the stairs to the warehouse's main level.

Lee stood motionless as a big older man strode into the building. "Ripley, I'm Commander Elijah Jones. I'm a part of Republic intelligence. We've been conducting operations against the local cartels in this area of Mexico for some time. But when I spotted you here, a former Olympian sharpshooter gold medalist who was being chased through streets by sicarios—well, I thought it might be time to pay you a visit."

Lee wasn't sure what to think. "It…it was in self-defense," he stammered.

"The local authorities here don't care." Commander Jones smiled. "They're paid by the very people you're trying to evade."

Lee grabbed at his throbbing shoulder. It sure hurt a lot for such a small injury.

Jones directed a medic to tend to Lee's wound before he continued. "Look, here's the deal, Ripley. You don't belong here. So, when you popped up on my radar as some new gun-for-hire to protect a particularly unsavory character, I started looking into you and observing your actions in your new bodyguard role. I wanted to see if you would become another sicario, using your skills with a gun to hurt people, or what would you do.

"Here's the thing, Ripley—you clearly have skills and know how to handle yourself in a tough situation, but this—" he waved his arms about, "—this doesn't have a future, at least not one that will keep you alive and out of the sights of law enforcement."

Lee wasn't sure where this was going or what his angle was. "Let me guess, you have a better idea?"

Jones smiled. "It's funny you say that, because I just might. One of my jobs is looking for people with above average IQs, street smarts, and the ability to think quickly on their feet. Those are all traits you seem to possess in abundance, and if given a little guidance, might benefit the Navy."

"Oh? The Republic military turned me down twice. That ship has sailed; hence, why I'm here in Mexico," Lee countered, unable to hide the bitterness and disappointment in his tone.

"Correction, Ripley—the Republic *Army* has turned you down. I looked into your file. That untreated eyesight diagnosis you have disqualified you from the Army, but guess what? The Navy doesn't have the same rules. We have this thing called a waiver that would allow you to still join. And if you play your cards right, the Navy might help you with that surgery to fix your eyes…that *is* why you're down here, isn't it? To save up the money to have it fixed?" Jones asked pointedly.

Lee felt exposed. *How long have they been following me?* he wondered. He slowly nodded. There was no reason to hide the truth at this point. "It is," he confirmed. "I only wanted the gig long enough to save up the money I needed to find a specialist and pay for it. So, are you offering me a chance out of here if I join the Navy—is that what you're saying?"

Jones smiled broadly. "See, that's what I like about you, Ripley. You think on your feet. But to answer your question, yeah—I'm offering you a chance out. But not to join the Navy as an enlisted spacer. I got bigger plans for you than that. You see, I'm also an instructor from time-to-time at the Academy. I teach advanced intelligence operations and tactics. I help the Academy spot individuals who could excel in leadership roles within the Navy if given some proper guidance. I believe you've got the right skills and the grit to become the kind of officer the Navy's going to need as we expand into the stars.

"So what do you say, Ripley? You want to get out of here?"

"What if I say no?" Lee found himself asking.

Jones laughed. "Well, if you'd like to stay here and take your chances with the cartels or eventually the courts…"

"Commander, we need to move," one of the Delta soldiers said just loud enough for Lee to hear. "Local law enforcement is five mikes from our pos. Alpha team just finished clearing the area. All objectives complete."

"Very well. Let's clear the area and get out of here," Jones ordered, then turned to Lee. "You coming, Rip? It's now or never."

"Oh, what the hell," said Lee. "Yeah, I'm coming. If what you said about the Academy is true—count me in. My whole life, I wanted to serve. When the Army wouldn't take me—"

"Come on, let's get out of here," interrupted Jones. "You made the right call, Ripley. You're with us now, and we take care of our own." Jones guided them out of the warehouse to a waiting Osprey.

As they climbed aboard and took their seats, the pilot lifted off, and they were gone.

Jones looked at Lee. "Life's about choices and opportunities, Ripley. It's what you do with them that matters."

Chapter 3
Fresh Start, Old Ghosts

A Month Later

Year 2086
The Academy
Colorado Springs, Colorado
Earth

Stepping off the transport shuttle, Lee squinted. The morning sun reflected off the glass buildings. The Republic Naval Academy spread out before him—a modern campus hugging the Colorado Rockies. In the short distance, cadets marched in unison across courtyards.

For the past month, Lee had recuperated in Commander Jones's Colorado home while he worked his contacts to get Lee into the Academy. During that time, Lee had rarely seen Jones. His bullet wound had been treated by top military doctors using nanite therapy, and he'd had access to all the food he could want. Mostly, he'd waited alone, expecting at any moment to be told his past would preclude him from getting into the Academy. It all felt off, especially the being safe part. He still couldn't quite believe his luck. Even now, standing at the Academy, part of Lee was waiting for the other shoe to drop.

It was strange how life worked. Growing up in his small Mennonite community, he'd never thought he'd end up here—of course, he'd never thought he'd end up in Mexico either. Once Lee had shared with his parents his desire to pursue a military career, they had stopped speaking to him—they were devout pacifists, and serving in the military was more than their small community was willing to accept. He'd felt his calling had been too strong to ignore, like the Lord himself had planted it in his heart when he was born. He was given his perfect aim with a pistol or a rifle for a reason, wasn't he?

Lee adjusted the strap of his duffel bag, aware of his worn jeans and casual shirt. Compared to the cadets around him, he might as well have been wearing a neon sign screaming, "Outsider!" Nonetheless, he started toward the main entrance.

Fate, he realized, worked in mysterious ways. After being rejected by the Republic Army due to his eye condition, he'd channeled his frustration into Olympic shooting. That had morphed into winning multiple gold medals. Still, even those achievements hadn't turned heads in the Army. Yet here he was, the Navy seeing a bright prospect where the Army hadn't.

Commander Jones strode beside him. Everyone they passed looked at the guy with respect. Cadets snapped to attention, saluting, which Jones returned with a simple nod. Whispers trailed them, curious glances assessing the newcomer in civilian clothes escorted by a high-ranking officer.

"Keep your chin up," Jones said.

Lee straightened his back. "Yes, sir."

They entered the administrative building. Portraits of decorated officers lined the walls. Lee eyed one portrait for the longest—Admiral Harrison Mandell, the first commander to lead a fleet out of the solar system.

Jones watched Lee. "Great man, Mandell. Led with his gut and his heart."

Lee nodded. "Big shoes to fill."

"Nobody's asking you to fill them. Just focus on getting through today, and then the next day, and so on." Jones pushed open a set of double doors leading into a large auditorium.

Rows of cadets filled the space, their attention on an instructor at the front. Lee and Jones made their way down the central aisle. The instructor paused, eyeing them.

"Don't let me interrupt, Commander," Jones said.

The instructor cleared his throat. "Of course not, Commander. You haven't missed much. We just started orientation."

Jones faced Lee. "This is where we part ways. I've informed Commander Lonklin of your arrival. She'll reach out after this talk with your assignment details."

"Thank you, sir."

"You'll do fine. Remember why you're here. Life is about choices and opportunities. Yours is here and now; make the most of it." Jones quickly turned and left, leaving Lee standing at the front.

But why was he here? He'd avoided being captured down in Mexico and found himself in the Academy. None of it made a lick of sense, but he wasn't going to complain. Without Jones and the Academy, Lee might be dead for all he knew.

The idea of the Army had always filled Lee's heart. The thought of boots on the ground to defend Republic Alliance borders… well… it felt right. Now, looking around at his fellow cadets, he wondered—would the Navy be a better fit? Well, they'd saved his life, so that was a good start.

The Republic faced threats beyond Earth's surface, so the Navy could take him on plenty of adventures. While the Army did its best on the ground, warding off potential attacks and keeping civilians, and the Republic, safe, Navy crews protected humanity's forays into the unknown as Earthers developed into a spacefaring society. They defended colony transports from pirates near Mars, along with keeping important mining facilities in the Belt safe.

The instructor motioned to an empty chair. "Take a seat, Cadet…?"

"Lee."

"Very well, Cadet Lee. Join us."

Lee sat next to a tall cadet with sandy-blond hair. The cadet leaned over. "Late on the first day? Bold move."

"Rough morning," Lee replied.

"Name's Jack Hannigan."

"Ripley Lee."

"Welcome to the show, Lee."

The instructor resumed his lecture about Academy expectations, speaking of the schedule and the high standards they were all expected to meet. Lee tried to focus. It wasn't that long ago that he'd been hiding in a warehouse, and now he was here, among the best of the best, so they said.

"Feeling overwhelmed yet?" Hannigan asked.

"I guess my poker face needs work."

"Little bit. Don't worry, we've all been there."

The instructor stopped midsentence and stared at Lee and Hannigan. "Something you'd like to share, Cadets?"

"Crap," Hannigan said under his breath while adjusting in his seat. "No, sir."

"Then perhaps you'd both like to demonstrate your physical conditioning since you find the orientation… unengaging."

Hannigan's jaw dropped. "Excuse me, sir?"

"Did I stutter? Do I look like someone who enjoys repeating himself?"

"No, sir," Hannigan said.

The instructor's expression tightened. "Outside. Now. Twenty minutes of corrective PT."

Hannigan stood. "Aye, sir."

Lee's stomach hardened. *Is the guy serious?*

"Report to the training yard in five minutes," the instructor ordered. "Let's see if your actions can speak louder than your words. And since you two are so similar, let's find out which one of you is truly dominant, shall we?"

Lee raised his hand. "Sir, I think—"

The instructor's face steeled. "Go, now."

Lee and Hannigan gave each other a look before walking out of the building. Lee followed his new friend to the training yard, where the sun bore down without a tinge of shade. The instructor made them take positions on the hot pavement. Other cadets gathered around.

Great, Lee thought. *First day... no, first hour... and I'm already in trouble.*

"Push-up position," the instructor said. "Now! Get down. Hot asphalt be damned."

Lee and Hannigan dropped into planks, arms trembling slightly as the instructor circled them. "You'll hold this position until I say otherwise."

Sweat beaded on Lee's forehead. Beside him, Hannigan maintained a steady breath, his plank posture just about perfect.

"Flutter kicks," the instructor ordered. "Begin."

Their legs lifted fifteen centimeters off the ground, kicking in alternating motions. The burn built in Lee's core. For a split second, the hot pavement beneath his hands transformed into the rough concrete of that warehouse floor in Mexico. The memory flashed—lying still, breath held, listening for footsteps while blood trickled down his arm. A second later, another flash—the surprised look in that young man's eyes as Lee's shot found the kid's chest. The boy crumpled before he sprawled out, dead, onto the concrete. How quickly life could just... stop. It was one of many kills down in Mexico. Lee hadn't wanted to do it—any of it—but he'd had to if he wanted to live. *Why were they after me? Was I really worth all that money to them?* The boy's face still visited him some nights, in his dreams, in his nightmares, the image fading from Lee's vision the moment he woke up.

Lee blinked hard, forcing himself back to the present. The training yard. The Academy. Safety. He matched his breathing to Hannigan's, grateful no one seemed to notice his momentary lapse.

"Faster," the instructor said. "This isn't nap time, Cadets."

Minutes stretched like hours. They moved through mountain climbers, more push-ups, and air squats. Lee's muscles screamed, but he didn't show weakness. Hannigan caught his eye, giving a slight nod.

"You still want to chat during orientation?" the instructor asked as they struggled through another set of flutter kicks.

"No, sir," they replied in tandem.

After what felt like an eternity, the instructor called out, "Recover."

Both cadets stood, shirts soaked with sweat. The gathered crowd had thinned, the entertainment value of watching PT apparently not as great as whatever else had stolen their attention away.

The instructor stepped forward. "Let this be a reminder that discipline and focus are expected at all times." He hesitated for a second before saying, "Dismissed!"

As the rest of the crowd dispersed, Hannigan wiped his forehead. "Well, that's one way to get acquainted."

"Didn't mean to get us into trouble," Lee said.

"Trouble? Nah, that was the most fun I've had all week."

"Glad one of us enjoyed it."

They headed toward the barracks. Hannigan pointed out various buildings, offering bits of information. "That's the mess hall—the food's decent if you get there early. Over there's the simulation center. We'll spend plenty of time there."

"How long have you been here?"

"A week. Got here early. Still getting my bearings, but it's starting to feel like home. And a little advice, don't take everything too seriously. They say they try to break you down to build you back up, but hold on to who you are."

"Sounds like you've seen a few folks lose themselves," Lee said.

"Nah. I'm new. I guess I just am good at asking a bunch of questions to get some pretty decent answers. I've got a feeling you'll be just fine."

A voice called out behind them. "Cadets!"

They turned to see an officer walking toward them, eyes shaded beneath the brim of a hat. "Care to explain why you're out of uniform and loitering?"

"No excuse, sir," Hannigan said.

Lee followed suit. "Apologies, sir."

The officer looked them up and down. "Names."

"Hannigan, sir."

"Lee, sir."

"Cadet Hannigan and Cadet Lee, consider this a warning. Report to me at 0500 tomorrow for disciplinary duty."

"Yes, sir," they replied at the same time.

As the officer walked away, Hannigan shook his head. "First day and you're already on Skyles's bad side."

"Who's Skyles?"

"Him. That's Commander Skyles. Let's just say he enjoys making our lives interesting."

Lee sighed. "Great."

"Look on the bright side—we'll get to bond over scrubbing floors or whatever task he assigns."

"Can't wait."

They continued walking. Lee glanced around, taking in the Academy. Despite the rough start, a part of him felt good. This place was a chance at something new, at something unexpected, at something close to his life's goal… but not quite. Still, he'd wanted to be in the military for so long, life had turned on a dime. So, the Navy… here it was. And, it had slapped him in the face on day one, but what better way to start a career?

Hannigan broke the silence. "So, what brings you here, Lee?"

"It's a long story."

"We've got time."

Lee tried to figure out how much to share. "Let's just say I ended up here unexpectedly."

"Man of mystery, huh?"

"Pretty much."

"You look familiar, though."

"I do?" Lee asked.

"Have I seen you somewhere?"

For a year after Lee had won gold medals in the Olympics, he'd been on the holovision and in advertisements a few times. That was no doubt where Hannigan had seen him.

Those days were another lifetime now. The interviews, the sponsorships, all while carrying the stress of his family's disapproval. He still thought about them on a daily basis—his mother's sweet voice, his father's strength. Sometimes he dreamed of going home, explaining how this path was God's plan for him, but he knew they wouldn't understand.

Hannigan smirked. "All right, I'll let it slide—for now. But sooner or later, you'll have to spill."

"Maybe after we've survived Commander Skyles."

"Deal."

They reached the barracks, a massive building. Hannigan led the way inside, weaving through the hallways.

"What bunk are you?"

"Jones told me twenty-seven," Lee replied.

"Well, that was quick. Here it is," Hannigan said, stopping at a door. "Looks like we're neighbors."

"Convenient."

"See? The universe is already on our side."

Lee opened the door to his room. It was meager—a bed, a locker, a small desk. A standard-issue uniform lay folded on the bed.

Hannigan leaned against the door frame. "Didn't Commander Jones tell you to meet someone for your assignment?"

"Oh, yes. Thanks."

"Anytime. And, hey, don't worry about today. We'll figure out this place together."

"Appreciate it."

As Hannigan walked away, shutting the door behind him, Lee sat on the edge of the bed. He picked up the uniform. This was real. He was here, in the Academy, with a new path laid out before him.

He stood and moved to the small window. The campus sprawled outward. Somewhere out there, Commander Jones had seen something in him worth bringing here to the Academy.

A knock on the door pulled him from his thoughts. He opened it to a cadet holding a clipboard.

"Cadet Lee?"

"That's me."

"From Commander Lonklin," the cadet said, holding out the clipboard. "Your schedule and orientation materials. Formation begins at 0600 sharp."

"Thanks."

The cadet handed over the items and moved on. Lee glanced at the schedule. It was packed—physical training, tactical courses, leadership seminars. No room for error. He had to get this right.

"Hold on to who you are," Hannigan had said. Good advice, but who was Lee now? A fugitive given a second chance? Or an actual cadet, worthy of this incredible Academy?

Chapter 4
Qualified with Limitations

Year 2087
The Academy
Colorado Springs, Colorado
Earth

Naomi Love adjusted the harness straps across her shoulders and settled into the Osprey simulator's pilot's seat. Holographic displays came to life. A year at the Republic Naval Academy had honed her skills somewhat well, but her sessions in the simulators gave her a brand-new challenge just about every time.

Love had earned her place at the Academy differently than most. The Global Flight Response Initiative had changed everything—she'd dominated every category, setting new records in crisis response scenarios that even veteran pilots couldn't touch. And she had just been eighteen at the time. The final round had pushed her hard, requiring ridiculously intense atmospheric maneuvers through an electrical storm while managing multiple system failures.

The Navy scouts had approached her right after, impressed by how she'd handled the tough emergency protocols. It was her ticket out, and Love's alcoholic mother had insisted she take it, despite Love's reluctance to leave her mom by herself. "Dreams don't come twice," her mom had said through tears, pressing the acceptance letter into her hands. Love's father had been gone for years, lost to synthetic opioids when she was younger, and she'd watched her mother struggle to keep them afloat ever since.

Now, every success in the simulator reminded her of those long nights practicing on borrowed civilian flight rigs in her run-down neighborhood, her mother passed out on the couch but having somehow managed to scrape together enough money for Love's competition entry fees. Some nights, Love still lay awake wondering if she'd made the right choice. She'd left her mother behind to chase this dream, and the lump in Love's throat remained. Her mom's last words before Love had boarded the transport resounded in her mind: "Show them what a girl from the streets can do."

Beside her, Tim Hastings fumbled with his console. She'd seen him around the Academy, but hadn't had him in any of her classes until this year. Hastings seemed more confused than anything. "Uh, how do I initialize the preflight sequence again?"

Love glanced over while suppressing a smile. "Button on your upper left. It's labeled 'Init P-Five.' Can't miss it."

"Right, got it." Hastings tapped the button, and his screens lit up. "Thanks."

"Anytime." She turned her focus back to the mission parameters. Today's simulation involved a standard troop transport through a simulated war zone. Rumors spoke of unexpected complications thrown in by their instructors. Who knew, though? She'd heard the gossip from a fourth-year, and they were notorious for hazing.

The pod's cockpit door opened, and Troy Alden stepped in. His uniform was slightly wrinkled, and his hair looked like he'd run his hands through it one too many times. "Mind if I join? Lieutenant Daigle thought I could use a refresher and wants me to observe." He slid into the seat behind them without waiting for a response.

"Make yourself at home, Alden." Love adjusted the thruster settings.

Alden leaned forward. "Just here to watch you two either nail it or crash and burn. No pressure."

"Thanks for the vote of confidence," Hastings said.

Love pressed on the comms. "Control, this is Cadet Love initiating simulation sequence with Cadet Hastings and observer Cadet Alden."

"Copy that, Cadet Love. You're cleared for takeoff," the instructor's voice crackled in their earpieces.

The virtual landscape unfolded before them—a large desert with jagged mountain ranges. Love lifted the Osprey off the ground.

After a few minutes of ascent, Love clicked on the communication link. "Altitude steady at one thousand, five hundred meters."

Hastings monitored his instruments. "All systems nominal. Troop compartment secure."

"Good. Keep an eye on those wind shear readings. This sim area is notorious for sudden shifts."

"Noted."

As they flew toward the first waypoint, an alert flashed on Love's display. "Incoming bogeys on our six," she said. "Switching to evasive maneuvers."

"Wait, we're under attack during a transport mission?" Hastings asked.

Alden chuckled from the back. "I like you, buddy, but get with the game, man."

Love banked the Osprey hard to starboard. "Hastings, deploy countermeasures. Let's shake them off."

Hastings manipulated the controls. "Flares away."

Love pushed the engines harder, scanning for a clear escape route. "Terrain's getting rough. We need to fly lower."

"Dropping to six hundred and ten meters," Hastings confirmed.

A warning blared through the cockpit. "Engine one is overheating." Alden eyed the readouts. "We might have a coolant leak."

Hastings froze for a moment. "Wait, I'm supposed to report that."

"Sorry," Alden replied.

"Hastings, initiate engine diagnostics." Love checked the thermal readout interface on her dash. "And reroute the cooling system."

Alden leaned forward between their seats. He pressed holo buttons on the auxiliary engineering console. "Give me a sec..." He looked over the Osprey's subsystem controls and pulled up a holographic display of the cooling network. He traced the virtual coolant lines, identified the compromised section, and input a bunch of commands to redirect the flow through secondary channels. "There. Bypassed the faulty lines, but it's a temporary fix."

Love almost slapped Alden's hands aside. "You're interfering with Hastings's job." She sighed. "Adjusting thrust to compensate."

The Osprey shuddered as they descended between rocky outcrops. The wind whipped around their craft.

"Watch your pitch," Alden said. "We're getting too close to the cliffs."

"I see it," Love replied. She leveled the Osprey. "Hastings, how's our engine status?"

Before Alden could speak out of turn, Hastings put his finger up to cut him off. "I'm stabilizing them now. But we're not out of the woods," Hastings said.

A new alert sounded. "Missile lock detected," Alden warned.

"Deploying chaff." Hastings reached for the defensive systems panel mounted on his side console. He flipped the chaff deployment switch upward.

Love steered the craft around a large rock jutting out from the ground. Up ahead, a gorge came into view. "We need to find cover. There's a canyon dead ahead. If we can make it there, we might break their line of sight."

Two fighters emerged from the clouds above them, their swept-forward wings and pointed nose making Love curse internally. She should know this model—had studied it in tactical analysis class just last week. The design was foreign and had to be from the Asian Alliance, but she couldn't put her finger on the exact designation. She'd have to review those specs again after the simulation.

The fighters closed in fast. Love yanked the controls hard, diving toward the canyon. Those pursuing ships were faster and more maneuverable than their Osprey. Heck, all jets were. Their only chance was to use the terrain.

"They're closing the distance." Hastings kept his eyes on the tactical display.

Love zigzagged their bulky transport through the narrow canyon walls. Those fighters might be quick, but they'd have a harder time following through tight spaces.

"There's barely any room," Hastings said.

"Do you have a better idea?" she shot back.

Hastings shook his head. "Keep going."

Love adjusted their course. "Hang on!"

Walls towered on either side. Love weaved the Osprey through bends and turns.

"Multiple targets ahead," Alden said. "Looks like automated turrets."

"Of course there are." Love sighed for a second time. She wanted to curse at Alden for backseat driving, let alone talking during the simulation, but kept her mouth shut. No time for that now. "Hastings, can you take them out?"

"Uh, yeah. Hmm. I'll try." He looked around, unable to find the right controls. "How?"

"Right-side panel, hit the weapons control," Alden said quickly. "Toggle to the chin-mounted blaster, then press the red button under your thumb stick to arm."

Hastings found the panel. "Got it."

"Now switch to manual targeting," Alden replied. "The autotracking's useless in these canyons—too many echo signatures. Use your helmet display for visual lock."

Hastings flipped the targeting switch. "Ready."

"Wait for the tone," Alden said. "You'll hear it when you've got a clean shot."

The first turret came into view. Hastings fired. The blaster shots hit their mark. "One down!"

Love banked hard around the next bend. "Wow! Nice shot! Two more at ten o'clock!"

Hastings swung his head to align the reticle and squeezed the trigger. The Osprey's blaster roared to life, taking out the remaining turrets as they zipped through the narrow passage. The Osprey emerged from the canyon, the open skies a welcome sight.

Hastings had great aim—so good, it impressed Love to the core. She held her tongue but couldn't help but think, *Holy crap! Wow!* An expert would have a hard time with that shot, but for Hastings, it seemed easy. "Enemy fighters disengaging. Looks like we're clear."

Alden smiled. "Not bad, team."

"You're on our team now?" Love asked. She liked Alden, but in all honesty, the guy was weird. He was supposed to watch, not help. The idea was to let Hastings learn, not to take over like Alden had attempted to do. At this point in their training, no one did well in the sims. It was part of the process—these early attempts were meant for mistakes, for understanding limitations, for learning the hard way. Every cadet stumbled through these first simulations. It was how they developed into proper pilots and gunners. In this portion of the training, success would teach them nothing.

"Hold on," Hastings said. "Controls aren't responding."

She checked her console. "We've lost hydraulic pressure. Must've taken damage back there."

"We're losing altitude," Hastings pointed out.

Love's mind spun. "We'll have to execute an emergency landing. Hastings, switch to backup systems."

Hastings shook his head. "They're not activating."

"Alden, any ideas?" she asked.

He bit his lip. "There's a manual override sequence. Hit your diagnostic panel, enter code seven-seven-one-nine, then force-purge the system. It'll dump the contaminated fluid but leave us enough to limp home."

"Do it," Love said. *OK, maybe it was good Alden joined our simulated flight today.*

Alden leaned between Love's and Hastings's seats again. He punched in several commands. "All right, doing so now."

The Osprey leveled out slightly but continued to descend. Love gripped the yoke. "It's not enough. We're going down."

Panic flashed in Hastings's eyes. "What else do we do?"

"Stay calm," she said. "Focus on preparing for landing—deploy landing gear manually if you have to."

Hastings nodded. "Understood."

Love flew the Osprey toward a flat stretch of simulated terrain. Klaxons blared, but she tuned them out, concentrating solely on the descent.

"Landing gear engaged," Hastings confirmed.

The ground rushed up to meet them. Love pulled back gently, easing the Osprey into as smooth a landing as possible. They hit the ground. The sim pod created an impact to mimic the real thing, and Love's head whipped back and jerked forward. The transport bounced, and the cockpit jolted, the craft skidding across the dirt before coming to a halt.

For a moment, only the sound of cooling systems and their heavy breathing filled the pod. The simulator's screens blinked repeatedly before giving way to a steady display, showing their mission results in bold holographic text:

MISSION STATUS: COMPLETED

CASUALTIES: 0

AIRCRAFT DAMAGE: MODERATE

PERFORMANCE RATING: QUALIFIED WITH LIMITATIONS

"Qualified with limitations?" Love said. "We kept everyone alive. I think that counts for more than qualified. I did a damn good job at keeping us in one piece."

"And we destroyed three automated turrets." Hastings unbuckled his restraints. "And fast."

"They probably knocked us down for the rough landing. And someone's backseat driving," Alden said.

The cockpit canopy opened. The training room and the observation deck came into view above, where Lieutenant Commander Richardson stood beside Lieutenant Commander Daigle, both with their arms crossed, watching them.

"Oh hell," Hastings muttered under his breath. His posture stiffened. Love noticed his change in demeanor immediately.

She understood why. Lieutenant Commander Ezra Richardson was a legend both in and outside the Academy. His real claim to fame was as a commander of a squadron of Ospreys that had come under attack by pirates in the asteroid belt beyond Mars. His actions and revolutionary combat maneuvers had reportedly saved all of the Republic soldiers while clearing out a major pirate stronghold. His presence here, watching a basic simulation run, seemed out of place. Love wondered what could possibly bring someone of his caliber to observe mere cadets.

"Well," Love said, climbing out, "at least we didn't crash and burn like you predicted, Alden."

"I didn't predict that."

Love shrugged. "You kinda did."

Hastings followed Love out of the sim. "Thanks for the help back there. Both of you."

"Don't thank us yet," Alden replied, jumping down. "Tomorrow's scenario involves orbital reentry. And I heard they're adding meteor showers."

Love looked at Hastings. "Listen, get some simulator time in before next class. You've got good instincts—just need to build that muscle memory. Your shooting, though… unbelievable. I've never seen anything like it."

Before Hastings could respond, Lieutenant Commander Daigle's voice boomed from the observation deck. "Hold position, Cadets!"

They froze as the chief made his way down, leaving Richardson inside the observation room. The instructor strode down the stairs and then toward the pod, his expression stern.

"Cadet Alden, dismissed. Cadets Love and Hastings, back in that pod. Now."

"Sir, yes, sir!" they responded. Alden departed as Love and Hastings climbed back into their seats.

Daigle stood by the simulation pod's entrance. "We're going to run this until Cadet Hastings can operate every system without assistance. Then we'll move on to shuttle ops, Reaper configurations, and Orion protocols. Clear?"

"Crystal clear, sir!" Hastings said as he reinitialized his console.

"And cut the civilian chatter in there. I want proper comm discipline and standard operating procedures. You're Republic Naval cadets, not cargo haulers."

"Affirmative, sir," Love said, strapping back in.

"Outstanding." Daigle stepped back. "Control, reset simulation parameters. Let's see if these cadets can earn better than 'qualified with limitations' before sunrise."

The pod sealed shut, screens coming back to life. Love glanced at Hastings. "Ready on your mark, Tango Two."

"Roger that, Tango One. Running preflight checks."

The desert landscape materialized before them once again, and this time, Love knew it was going to be a very long night.

Chapter 5
The Path Chosen

Year 2087
The Academy
Colorado Springs, Colorado
Earth

The mess hall thrummed with the noise and chatter of mealtime at the Academy. Lee had come to find it was always like this, which he enjoyed. Cadets moved between tables. The smell of roasted meats and freshly baked bread permeated the place.

Lee balanced his tray—full with meatloaf, mashed potatoes, and a side of steamed vegetables—as he walked through the crowd. Spotting Hannigan waving from a corner table near the large window, Lee made his way over.

"Thought you'd gotten lost in the line," Hannigan said as Lee slid onto the bench opposite him. Troy Alden sat beside Hannigan, a chicken sandwich in his hands.

"Where'd you get that?" Lee asked.

"Made it," Alden replied.

Hastings made a face. "But… how'd you manage to get—"

Alden shrugged. "I have my ways."

As Lee was about to ask another, more pertinent question, Hannigan waved him off. "Don't ask. You won't get an answer. I tried."

Alden took a bite of food. "The chicken's as dry as a desert out there."

Hannigan grinned. "So, how about that ARCOM session today?"

"ARCOM?" Hastings asked, picking up his fork.

"You haven't done it yet?" Hannigan asked.

Lee shook his head. "That's a negative."

"Augmented Reality Combat Operations Module," Alden said. "Field simulation with the VR helmets and inert weapons."

"Oh, right." Lee nodded. "I've heard of that."

"You'll probably be doing it soon," Alden said.

Hannigan threw up a fist. "Today's simulation was intense. We won. Felt like I was actually in the middle of a battlefield. You know, in the real thing."

"The haptic feedback is incredible." Alden chewed while talking. "The rifles feel real, even without ammo."

"Yeah," Hannigan replied. "The weight, the recoil—just like the real damn thing, fellas. The place is immersive enough to make me trip over a virtual log."

Alden laughed. "I saw that."

Hannigan shot him a look. "How?"

"Watched in the spectator lounge. One second, you're charging ahead, the next you're flat on your face."

"At least I wasn't the one who forgot to take cover during the turret fire," Hannigan said.

"What? OK, then, how'd you see that?" Alden asked.

"Spectator lounge."

Lee gave each one of them a look. "You spying on each other?"

Alden smirked. "Comparing, I guess. I'm better. It's as simple as that."

"Sure you are," Hannigan said. "Trying to figure out how to one-up me?"

They shared a laugh. As they dug into their meals, Alden glanced around. "On a different note," he began, lowering his voice a little, "ever wonder how we got here? Not just us at the Academy, but humanity in space?"

"What do you mean?" Lee asked.

"Like, fifty years ago we were tearing ourselves apart. The Great War nearly wiped us out. The Synths, AI, all of that—it could have been the end."

Hannigan nodded. "Yeah, my grandfather fought in that war. Said the Synths forced humanity's hand."

"That's what united us, though," Alden continued. "Well, sort of."

"United is a strong word," Lee replied. "From what I learned in History of Modern Warfare, the power blocs only formed because half the world was starving and desperate."

"True," Alden said. "The Asian Alliance pulled together what was left of China, India, and the Koreas. Japan joining them was the real surprise, though, considering their history."

Hannigan stared at him. "You're just mimicking what the books say."

"I'm not. And us—the Republic," Alden added, "rising from the ashes of the old United States, Canada, and Mexico. Britain jumping ship from the EU to join us raised some eyebrows."

Lee picked at his remaining food. "Then you had the European Union aligning with Russia of all places. Strange times make strange allies, I guess. And, yeah, I read the same text."

"OK, well, I'm on that subject now in my class. Reading about the African Union siding with Asia against us," Alden said. "After everything the Republic did for them…"

"At least the Space Exploration Treaty got everyone looking up instead of at each other," Hannigan replied. "First piece of real global law. Got us to Mars, didn't it?"

"Yeah, but even that was just politics." Alden shook his head. "Keep people focused on the stars so they don't fight on Earth. Anyway, have you guys ever heard about ancient aliens?"

"Boom, just like Alden, saying random crap whenever he gets the chance," Hannigan said. "Seriously? You believe in that stuff?"

Alden shrugged. "Just curious if you've heard of the theory."

"Can't say I have," Lee said. "Coming from a Mennonite community, we didn't have much exposure to that kind of thing. Holovision was banned, so no documentaries or shows. Didn't even get corrective eye surgery until a few days before I joined the Academy. Thank the Lord the medical treatment heals fast—like, real fast."

"Wait, you've been wearing glasses all your life?" Hannigan asked.

"Pretty much. It was frowned upon to alter what was considered God-given."

Hannigan made a face. "That's… different."

"So you missed out on all the conspiracies and speculative history?" Alden asked. "Too bad."

"Seems that way," Lee said. "But I'm not sure I missed much."

Hannigan chuckled. "Trust me, you didn't. Just a bunch of people with too much time on their hands."

Alden gave a half smile. "Some of it is based on interesting archaeological findings."

"And a lot of it isn't," Hannigan said. "Anyway, why the sudden interest?"

"Just thought it was an intriguing topic." Alden took another bite of his sandwich.

Hannigan eyed him skeptically but let it drop. A moment of silence settled over them as they chowed down on their food.

Hannigan cleared his throat. "By the way, do you guys know if it's… OK to date while we're here at the Academy?"

Lee looked up. "Dating?"

"What's on your mind, Hannigan?" Alden asked.

"I just… wasn't sure what the rules are," Hannigan said. "Can cadets date each other?"

"I think same-class dating is usually permitted." Lee pushed some meat to the side. "We have to maintain professional behavior during duty hours, no public displays of affection while in uniform, and it can't interfere with training or duties."

"Sounds about right," Alden said. "The key is not letting it affect our responsibilities."

A grin spread across Hannigan's face. "That's good news."

"What? What's on your mind? There's gotta be someone in particular you're thinking of," Lee said.

Hannigan glanced around before gesturing with his chin toward the far corner of the mess hall. "See the girl sitting over there by herself?"

Lee followed his gaze. Sitting alone at a table was a cadet reading a thick manual, her short hair tucked behind her ears. She ate slowly while scanning the pages.

"That's who you're interested in?" Lee asked.

"She's in a couple of my classes," Hannigan said. "There's something about her."

Alden squinted in her direction. "Hold on—that's Cadet Love."

"Naomi Love," Lee added. "She's in my Aviation Systems and Tactics class."

"Her name's Naomi?" Hannigan repeated. "What else do you know about her?"

Alden leaned forward. "She's the best pilot I've seen. Handles the simulators like a pro. Even the instructors are impressed."

"She's definitely skilled," Lee said. "Always ahead of the class. You can tell she's got something to prove. Or it's just… talent."

"Think she'd be open to talking?"

"She's pretty focused," Alden responded. "Doesn't socialize much from what I've seen."

"Doesn't mean she wouldn't," Lee said. "Couldn't hurt to say hello. But since when are you the shy type, Hannigan?"

"Since I saw her. But maybe I'll introduce myself after dinner."

"Bold move." Alden picked up a forkful of mashed potatoes. "But, hey, fortune favors the brave."

Lee admired Hannigan. Approaching someone like Cadet Love was something he couldn't imagine doing. "Good luck."

"Thanks. You know, you guys should think about putting yourselves out there too."

Alden shook his head. "My girlfriends are vehicles and aircraft. No time for anything else."

Lee smiled. "I think I'll focus on my training for now."

"Suit yourselves. More opportunities for me," Hannigan said.

As the conversation shifted to lighter topics, Lee's thoughts drifted. The idea of dating stirred something uneasy in him. His parents had strict views about relationships outside their community. Even being here at the Academy was a point of contention. A huge point. The biggest, actually.

Lee pushed his tray away and stood. "I should get going."

"Where are you off to?" Alden asked.

"I've got a comm call to make." Lee smoothed his uniform.

"At this hour?" Hannigan said.

"Time zones. Need to catch a few people while they're available."

"All right." Alden waved. "See you later, then."

"Yeah, see you, Lee."

Lee turned to weave his way back through the busy mess hall. The conversations faded into the background as he ambled to the corridors leading to the cadet quarters.

****

Entering his small room, he closed the door behind him. Friday, 1900 hours—his designated weekly comm window. Like every other cadet, he got one hour for outside contact per week. He crossed to the wall-mounted comm unit, hesitating before making the call.

Lee picked up a small wooden cross and turned it over in his hands. The grain was uneven. The edges of the makeshift cross had been sanded down by time and touch. A single notch on the upright beam caught against his thumb—the place where his knife had slipped when he was twelve, carving the thing in his family's barn. It'd been Lee's first attempt at woodwork—messy, but earnest. His father had called it good when Lee had presented it to the church after Sunday service.

Now he kept it with him everywhere. He hadn't planned on bringing it to Mexico, but when he'd shoved his belongings into a battered pack at the last minute, he'd found it lying on his dusty dresser, untouched for years. He'd almost left it where he'd found it. Something had stopped him. Remembering the day he'd carved it, and all the things he'd had to leave behind when he'd walked out of his parents' home all those years ago, he'd shoved it into his bag as well.

He held the cross up to the light, the edge of its shadow stretching across the office's bulkhead wall behind his desk. His thoughts turned to the day he left. The arguments circled like vultures around his mind despite it happening all those years back.

They'd gathered in the living room. His parents. His minister. Even his younger sisters huddled on the stairs, their tear-swollen faces poking out between the wooden balusters. He'd paced in front of them, explaining himself again and again.

"You can't just leave like this," his father had said. "There's work here. Honest work. Something worth doing. Family, Ripley—you don't just walk away from family."

It wasn't a question, though it felt like one. He answered anyway.

"I have to, Dad. There's more for me out there than chores and Sunday service. I'm eighteen, for God's sake—"

"Watch your mouth when you talk about Him."

Lee clenched his fist at the memory of that reprimand. He sat in the quiet corner of his office aboard *Poseidon*. Even now, his father's steel-gray eyes followed him wherever he went. Judgment. Disappointment. Shame. Rejection.

The past moved like a tide. Lee didn't fight it as it pulled him deeper. That night, after they'd exhausted every word, quiet had rested in the house. No blessing given. No forgiveness offered. At two in the morning, while the Wyoming wind blew across leafless trees, Lee sneaked out. The wooden cross was in his pocket, a cheap wristwatch on his arm.

He'd tied up his running shoes and walked to the truck stop two miles out of town. A greasy diner there had had paid comm units for decades, and in its corner booth, he'd booked a taxi to meet an Army recruiter one state over later that morning. He'd arrived home at dawn and hadn't caught a wink of sleep, knowing a cab would pick him up in mere hours.

He remembered the sound of his boots crunching frozen gravel as the taxi arrived. Lee had hawked his saddle and related gear for the cab money he didn't dare ask his family for. How he'd twisted in the seat and seen them stepping onto the front porch—his mother, her apron streaked with flour she hadn't washed off. His sisters, clutching the dog's collar, and his father with arms folded tight enough to crush granite. The tears in their eyes. The way his mother waved. How his father didn't.

Lee shut his eyes. Right now, the air in his quarters was a tinge too muggy. The image came to mind, the one lasered into his brain, the one of his family shrinking into nothing as the cab sped down the road. It still hurt his heart. He *knew* why he'd done what he did—the fire in his bones had been unstoppable, uncontainable—but it didn't make the leaving hurt any less.

He placed the cross down beside the Bible on his desk. That Bible. The leather cover was cracked, the edges of its thin pages smudged dark over two decades.

Lee had been so sure back then. So sure that breaking away was what God wanted for him. He still believed that. The military was his calling—he'd always known that—but the guilt at abandoning his family lived deep. It bothered him daily.

"Why can't *You* just let me forget?" he muttered to no one.

Lee shook off his old memories and attempted the call. The screen remained dark—a standard for his family's preferences—displaying only a simple connection interface. After a few rings, the line clicked open.

"Hello?"

"Dad? It's me," Lee said.

A heavy pause sat between them.

"Dad, I wanted to check in. See how you and Mom are doing."

Silence.

"I've started new classes," Lee continued. "They're challenging, but I'm learning a lot."

No response came from the other end.

"Dad? Can we please talk? Look, I'm sorry."

A faint rustle was the only reply.

"Dad, please say something. I really miss you guys."

After a long moment, a sigh came through the speaker. "You've chosen your path, Ripley. There's nothing more to say."

The line disconnected.

Lee stared at the blank comm unit. The monotone hum lingered in the room. He sank onto the edge of his bed, elbows resting on his knees. His palms found their way to his face, fingers pressing against his temples.

The weight of his father's words—or lack thereof—pressed like the weight of a preacher's sermon on him. He sat there, grappling with the rift that had formed between him and the life he'd once known ever since he'd let his family know he'd decided on a military life.

Lee took a deep breath. The path he'd chosen came with sacrifice. He only hoped that, in time, he'd bridge the divide. For now, all he could do was move forward.

Chapter 6
Finding His Wings

Year 2087
The Academy
Colorado Springs, Colorado
Earth

Hastings worked on the controls like it was second nature. At the moment, the pod's cockpit wrapped around him. It was a cocoon of holographic displays. Through the canopy, the simulated Rocky Mountains stretched toward a crimson sunset. Their peaks were brushed with snow. Lieutenant Commander Ezra Richardson stood on the observation deck above.

"He's watching us again," Love said from the copilot seat.

Hastings glanced up. Richardson's presence was impossible to ignore. "Maybe he's got nothing better to do."

"Or maybe he's got a special interest." She eyed Hastings. "You related to him or something? He's watched you several times. Not me. You. I've noticed when you're with another pilot, he's got his attention on you."

Hastings kept himself busy with the preflight checks. "Related? Not that I'm aware of."

"Funny. He sure looks like he's rooting for you. What's the story there?"

"No story." Hastings flicked a switch. The console lights shifted to green. "Probably just making sure we don't crash his expensive simulators."

"Uh-huh." Love didn't sound convinced. "Well, whatever it is, he's got his eyes glued to you."

"Let's just focus on the mission."

Love tilted her head, as if calculating whether to push the issue further. "Fine by me," she replied, tapping her console. "Board is green, ready for takeoff."

"Initiating takeoff sequence."

The Osprey's virtual engines came to life, the sound system mimicking the deep thrum of turbines. The simulation enveloped them—a rugged landscape stretching out with jagged peaks and narrow valleys.

"Today's objective," Skyles said over the comms, "is a troop insertion at LZ Bravo. Minimal enemy presence. Terrain hazards expected due to inclement weather."

"Weather's always rotten in these sims," Love said.

"Adds to the fun," Hastings replied, pulling back on the controls.

They lifted off, ascending into a sky thick with dark clouds. Rain streaked across the cockpit window. The wipers engaged.

"Visibility at forty percent," Love said. "Wind shear increasing at higher altitudes."

"Adjusting ascent." Hastings compensated, feeling the resistance in the yoke. The Osprey responded with a sluggish delay—a programmed challenge, no doubt.

"Digitized troops are secure in the bay," she said. "All vitals normal."

He nodded while scanning the displays. "Setting course. ETA fifteen minutes."

They sped forward, the terrain below turning into indistinct shapes of rocky outcrops and sparse vegetation. The weather intensified. Lightning flashed while turbulence rocked the craft.

"Sensors are scrambled. Reading multiple ghost signals." Love frowned at her console. "Instruments are glitching."

"Switch to manual overrides where you can." Hastings manipulated the controls. "We'll have to rely on visual cues."

"Great. Flying blind in a storm with a full passenger load."

He smiled. "Just another day at the Academy."

They approached a mountain range, peaks piercing the low-hanging clouds.

"Flight path takes us through that pass," Love pointed out. "Looks tight."

"We'll manage." He angled the Osprey toward the gap.

The Osprey's sensors showed a holographic rendering of the pass in green lines across their displays. Warning indicators flashed as the craft's computer calculated wind vectors and proximity alerts. All those hours memorizing emergency procedures were about to pay off.

"Proximity alert!" Love punched in commands on a screen. "Wind shear at three o'clock, category four!"

The Osprey bucked hard to port. Warning klaxons screamed through the cockpit as Lee fought the controls.

"Losing stability control," Love said. "Compensators at maximum."

"Switching to manual flight control. Diverting power from nonessential systems."

"That'll kill our safety buffers."

A memory hit Hastings like a magtrain—something dark from his past that he preferred to keep hidden. The image was so vivid, so unexpected and overwhelming, that Hastings's hands jerked on the controls. The Osprey dipped. It lost fifty meters of altitude before he could push down the memory and steady the craft.

"You OK?" Love asked.

"Fine," Hastings said. "Just some turbulence." The stick fought him like a living thing, trying to tear itself from his grip.

"We won't clear the pass at this rate," Love said.

"Diverting around the peak." He banked left, the craft groaning, only to face a sheer cliff face.

"Pull up!" she yelled.

The Osprey's engines shrieked as Hastings yanked back on the stick. Warning lights bloomed across the dashboard—they were pushing the craft beyond its rated tolerances. Through the canopy, the cliff face filled their view, close enough to count the rocky outcrops.

He pulled back harder. The nose tipped up, and they skimmed over the cliff edge with half a meter to spare.

Love let out a breath. "You're insane."

"Maybe." His heart pounded. Why had that memory hit him out of the blue?

"Approaching LZ Bravo." Love moved through the terrain-mapping display. "LZ's a mess. Showing multiple obstacles, uneven ground. Slope gradient at twenty-eight degrees—that's way outside normal parameters."

"Options?"

"By the book? We abort. Find another LZ."

Hastings studied the tactical display. Those troops were counting on them, simulation or not. "Book's about to get a rewrite."

The Osprey's landing lights pushed through the simulated storm, illuminating difficult terrain below. Boulders jutted from the ground, and sheets of rain reduced visibility.

"Coming in hot." Love looked between instruments. "Ground speed one-three-zero knots. Wind gusting to fifty."

"Deploying air brakes. Compensating for crosswinds."

The craft shuddered as another microburst slammed into them. Warning indicators flashed as they descended below the recommended approach ceiling.

"Thirty seconds to touchdown," Love said. "Boulder field dead ahead. We're running out of real estate fast."

"Switching to VTOL mode." Hastings grappled with the control interface as the Osprey moved where he needed it to move. "Rerouting power to vertical thrusters."

A heavy gust caught them broadside. The Osprey lurched, nearly clipping a rock formation.

"Five seconds!" Love's knuckles were white on her harness. "Four… three…"

Hastings fired the landing thrusters and used the crosswind to pivot them into position. The Osprey's wheels slammed onto the ground, bouncing once, twice. Rock fragments sprayed against the hull as they skidded to a stop a meter from a sheer drop.

"We're down," Love said.

"Troops ready for deployment."

"Simulation complete," the AI announced. "Objective achieved."

Love looked over at him. "I don't know how you pulled that off."

"Just did what needed doing."

Hastings had to admit, flying was growing on him.

"Well, color me impressed. You've improved. You've been practicing?"

"Whenever I can," Hastings said.

The simulation faded. The pod's canopy lifted. As they climbed out, Lieutenant Commander Richardson walked in their direction.

"That landing," Richardson said, voice low enough that only Hastings could hear, "reminded me of that infamous battle my squadron got into with the pirates in the asteroid belt. Sometimes the worst conditions bring out the best in a pilot. Keep it up, Cadet."

Hastings watched him go.

"Told you," Love whispered. "He's got a soft spot for you."

"Maybe he's just acknowledging a job well done."

"Don't be modest. That was some damn fine flying."

Commander Skyles's voice boomed through the simulator bay. "Cadet Hastings!"

Oh, great! Hastings thought.

Hastings turned around as Skyles strode toward him. "Commander."

Skyles stopped centimeters from Hastings's nose. "What was that, Cadet? Because I know I didn't just witness a second-year forget basic military courtesy."

Hastings stiffened. "No excuse, Commander!" He went to attention.

"Oh, now you remember." Skyles's voice dropped. "Drop. Now. You forgot that with Lieutenant Commander Richardson too. And since you need a lesson in remembering protocol, you can give me a hundred."

"Yes, Commander!" Hastings moved into position.

"Count them out, Cadet! And if I see one incomplete push-up, we start over!"

"One! Two! Three!" Hastings called out each number, doing his best to keep proper form. By thirty-one, his arms were trembling. At forty-two, they gave out, and he collapsed to the deck.

"Did I say you could stop, Cadet?" Skyles circled him. "On your feet! Start over!"

Love stood nearby, her face a mask of neutrality. Other cadets hurried past, no doubt grateful they weren't the target of Skyles's attention.

Hastings started again. "One! Two! Three!" This time he made it to fifty-eight before his muscles failed. Sweat dripped onto the floor.

"Pathetic!" Skyles said. "Is this the best the Republic Navy can expect from you? Again!"

The third attempt was pure torture. Hastings's arms shook. He reached thirty-six before falling to the floor, chest heaving.

"Get up, Cadet. You don't quit in my Navy. You finish what you start. Now move!"

Hastings forced himself back into position. His whole body trembled, but something in Skyles's words ignited a spark. He wouldn't quit.

"One! Two! Three!"

This time, he pushed through the pain, through the burning in his muscles, through the voice screaming in his head to stop. When he finally reached one hundred, his arms felt like rubber.

"That's good, Cadet! You've impressed me! Now, attention on deck!" Skyles commanded.

Hastings somehow found the strength to spring to his feet, though his legs wanted to give out on him.

"Let this be a lesson to all of you," Skyles addressed the room. "In this Navy, protocol isn't a suggestion. It's the difference between life and death. Between mission success and failure. Between coming home or not coming home at all." He turned back to Hastings. "Do I make myself clear, Cadet?"

"Crystal clear, Commander!"

"Dismissed."

As Skyles marched away, Love stepped closer. "You OK?"

Hastings's entire body shook with exhaustion. He tried to wipe the sweat from his face, but his arms barely responded. "Ask me tomorrow. When I can feel my arms again."

"Come on. Let's get you to the mess hall. You're going to need protein after that. Hell, that was rough, even for Skyles." Love glanced toward where the Commander had disappeared. "But, hey, that landing? You threaded that Osprey through weather that would ground most pilots. Real talent there."

"Just got lucky."

"Luck?" Love shook her head. "I've flown with half the second-years. Nobody handles turbulence like that. Nobody. I mean, you've improved leaps and bounds."

The compliment made Hastings uncomfortable—he wasn't used to praise. "We should hit the mess."

"Right." Love fell into step beside him. "But one of these days, Hastings, you're going to have to accept that you belong here. Just like the rest of us."

"What do you mean?"

"There's something about you. It's like you're here, but part of you feels like you don't belong. You know, your mind is elsewhere. Not that you don't want to be here—that's not what I mean. It's more like you think you're not good enough to be here. But the truth is, you are.

I've been watching the other cadets, and I haven't seen anyone improve as much as you have in such a short time."

As they walked away from the simulator bay, Hastings eyed his reflection in a nearby window. For a moment, he saw himself as others might—as a cadet in the Republic Navy. Maybe Richardson had seen something in him that he hadn't yet seen in himself.

Chapter 7
Under the Oak Tree

Year 2087
The Academy
Colorado Springs, Colorado
Earth

Naomi Love sat beneath an oak tree. Its leaves sent a shadow over her while she looked over the pages of *Aeronautics and Spacecraft Systems*. The book, one of those ancient hefty textbooks filled with diagrams, equations, and detailed explanations, had become her constant friend since she'd begun her studies at the Republic Naval Academy.

The Academy grounds sprawled out before her—lush green lawns divided by concrete sidewalks. Buildings towered all around.

A formation of first-year cadets marched across the quad. Above, a Republic Navy shuttle flew through the clouds. Fourth-year cadets were probably inside the cockpit, running real-life training exercises. Holographic notices blinked along the building walls. They displayed daily schedules and security clearance zones.

Love's attention drifted from the pages to the sound of laughter heading her way. Across the greenery, two young men strolled along a pathway. They were engrossed in conversation. The taller of the two— an individual with chiseled features and a confident walk—threw his head back in amusement at something his companion said.

For an instant, the handsome stranger eyed Love. Time slowed. Her insides tingled. A jolt of electricity flashed through her. His strong jawline, the way his sandy-blond hair caught the sunlight, and the glimmer of happiness in his eyes. It lit a cascade of fireworks in her, sweeping out from her heart to her head. It left her breathless.

She rested her fingertips on her chest. *What's come over me?*

The shorter man, observably oblivious to the eye contact his friend and Love had just shared, gestured and continued to laugh.

Is the small one Troy Alden?

Indeed, it was.

But who's that tall guy?

The tall man nodded, his attention back on the conversation. However, Love caught a brief glimpse of interest in the guy's eyes before he looked away. Or did she?

With a rush of self-consciousness, Love tore her gaze away from the two men and refocused on the book in her lap. She chastised herself for allowing the distraction. A memory of her mom's words crept into her mind: "Getting attention from guys can be an ego boost, but it doesn't compare to the real power that comes from education and knowledge. Stay dedicated to your studies, dear."

Love's dream was to become a pilot in the Republic Navy. Not just any pilot—she had her sights set on the AT-70 Osprey Assault Transport. The obsession had started many years ago when she'd stumbled across old combat footage from the Great War. The grainy vid showed a troop transport similar to an Osprey flying through heavy fire and diving into a hot zone.

She'd watched, mesmerized, as the pilot flew the ship between crumbling buildings, evacuating trapped civilians from some city whose name was lost to history. The troop transport had taken hit after hit but kept flying. Something about the moment of rescue had lodged in her heart that day and never left. Now, every time she saw an Osprey in the Colorado skies, that same thrill rushed through her veins. The Academy had a dozen of them stationed here for advanced training—she just had to prove she was good enough to fly one.

So, she couldn't afford to let anything, especially a moment of attraction, derail her focus. It'd been a year and a half here, and all had been going great. To let it all crash down because of an interest in a guy would border on stupid and lean more toward silly.

Pay attention to your studies, Naomi, she told herself.

Love delved back into the pages and continued reading about spacecraft design and the principles of atmospheric flight. The laughter died into the background as she lost herself in the world of aeronautics.

She looked around. The good-looking fellow had disappeared somewhere. Perhaps he was now in some lobby inside a campus building. Probably talking to a girl much prettier than her. Nonetheless, she wished he had stopped by and maybe said a nice hello.

Why would he talk to me? she thought. He was incredibly handsome, and she was just... herself. Not exactly Miss Attractive, to say the least. *Get your mind out of the gutter, Naomi!*

Lost in her thoughts, Love almost missed the sound of branches snapping behind her. She turned, startled to see the cute stranger peering around the tree she sat under. Her heart skipped a beat when he smiled.

"Hi there," he said.

"Oh, hi. I… I didn't expect to see you there."

He chuckled. "My apologies. Didn't mean to scare you."

"That's quite all right."

He eyed the book in her lap. *"Aeronautics and Spacecraft Systems."*

"Yes, it's my core studies these days."

"Why don't you download it on your data pad?" he asked. "Looks heavy."

"I like to hold a physical copy. Helps keep me in shape."

He laughed. "You lookin' to be a pilot?"

"That's the plan. I've already logged dozens of hours in the simulators."

His eyebrows rose. "You ever done the asteroid belt navigation program?"

"Yeah," she replied.

"Wow. That's advanced stuff."

"Made it through the Kuiper Belt run last week," she said, trying not to sound too proud.

"Now I'm really impressed. Most third-years can't even handle those gravitational calculations. What are you, second-year?"

"I am."

"Me too." He continued to stare into her eyes. "Mind if I sit down?"

"Sure. Have a seat." She patted the ground next to her.

After the man sat, he extended his hand. "I'm Jack Hannigan. Pleased to meet you."

"I'm Naomi Love." She took his hand. The warmth of his grip remained with her for some time even after they let go.

Chapter 8
Trial by Gunfire

Year 2089
The Academy
Colorado Springs, Colorado
Earth

Ripley Willis Lee sat nervously as he waited for the test to begin. Today was a big day—if not *the* big day. He and his classmates would finally put years of classroom instruction and simulator practice to the test. It was the culmination of the two previous years' worth of work.

Lee settled into his seat at the weapon officer's station and surveyed the rest of the simulated bridge. Instructor Harley Chambers sat in the captain's chair, projecting a natural-born confidence. Cadet Lucy Burton was ready at the communications station, and Cadet Isaac Short was nervously fidgeting at the Helm position.

They had all trained for months on the various positions of the ship, but now before they went into advanced, more specialized training, Lee and his counterparts were going to be put through the gauntlet to test their abilities.

Chambers checked in with each of them to make sure that they were ready. Once they had acknowledged him, he sat up as straight as possible before declaring, "Begin simulation."

A voice recording played over the public address system, "You are approaching an asteroid belt under Republic control. Republic intelligence has informed you that the Asian Alliance is attacking a mining facility under our protection, and you have been dispatched to stop them."

All the monitors and workstations populated with images and data consistent with the proposed scenario. As the ship approached the asteroid belt where the mining facility was supposed to be located, Chambers issued orders to Cadet Burton. "Comms, make contact with the station and get us a status update on their situation."

"Aye, Captain," Burton acknowledged.

The instructor turned to Cadet Short. "Helm, accelerate the MPD thrusters to one-third power and take us further into the asteroid belt," he ordered. "We need to get to that mining facility."

"Yes, sir," said Short.

"Weps," Chambers said, directing his next comments to Lee, "have the magrail turrets made ready to fire and activate the targeting systems for the anti-ship missiles."

"On it," Lee replied, busily inputting commands on his workstation.

"Sir," Burton blurted out, "we're receiving a message from the mining station."

A muddled recording played on the PA system, completely unintelligible.

"What's happening?" Chambers barked.

"I, I don't know, sir," Burton stammered. "Let me see what I can do to clean it up."

"Sir," said Short, "two Asian Alliance corvettes have emerged from the other side of a large asteroid near us."

"They're trying to send us a message, but I can't understand it," Burton added, still frantically trying different options at her workstation.

"What's going on?" Chambers demanded. "What's happening at the mining facility? And what is the Asian Alliance trying to say?"

Burton didn't have any answers. "I'm still trying to figure it out, sir."

Chambers was clearly a bit frustrated at this point. "Helm, increase MPD thruster to fifty percent, and head toward the pair of corvettes," he ordered.

"Yes, sir," Short replied, changing their speed and trajectory.

Chambers turned to Lee. "Weps, ready the guns and begin acquiring missile lock on the ships."

"Aye, Captain," Lee acknowledged.

As he was following Chambers's orders, Lee realized that the enemy ships had started jamming his efforts to obtain a lock and were firing on them. "Sir, we're being jammed, and the corvettes have opened fire on us with their magrails," he announced.

"Helm, take evasive maneuvers and increase thrusters to seventy-five percent!" Chambers shouted.

Lee could feel the adrenaline pumping through his body and his increased pulse rate. For a simulation, this was feeling very real.

"Comms, give me an update on the station!" Chambers yelled.

Cadet Burton had one hand over a headset that she was pushing into her ear. Her eyes were closed. "Sir, I'm having a hard time understanding the message from the station with all the jamming," she explained.

"Weps, return fire with the main guns and take those corvettes out," Chambers ordered.

Lee set up the magrails to fire. Each time the guns prepared to shoot, they could hear a slight windup before the bridge vibrated slightly. Unlike standard kinetic weapons on Earth, there was no bang or boom that accompanied the launching of the projectiles; they just felt it as a small tremor under their feet.

Bam!

"We're taking hits, sir!" Lee announced as he grabbed the edges of his station.

The bridge shook. Sparks flew. Smoke began to cloud the bridge. Alarms blared.

Lee's pulse was really beating rapidly now. He kept trying to get a missile lock, but with the enemy jamming, it was proving almost impossible. He was having a hard enough time keeping a solid lock with the guns.

It's almost like it's not supposed to work, Lee thought to himself.

"Weps, get a missile lock and start firing those missiles! You need to get the enemy reacting to us and not the other way around," Chambers yelled hotly. "Helm, evade Pattern Alpha now!" he continued. "Comms, find a way through the jamming. Get a status update sent to the Fleet and a request for additional help. I'm still waiting on that station update!"

As Chambers rode Burton, an idea sparked in Lee's mind. Acting quickly, he routed energy from the rear magrail turrets he wasn't using to the targeting radars he needed in order to acquire a missile lock on the enemy ships.

With the boost of extra power, Lee surprisingly finally got a lock on the enemy corvettes. He began firing the ASMs at the Asian

Alliance ships, while keeping the main turrets going now that he had a steadier lock.

His first couple of shots with the main guns went wide, and Lee's stomach sank. He brushed it off and recalibrated the next shots, watching the next pair score direct hits against the ship's armor. As if perfectly timed, the missiles he'd fired earlier started to impact the corvettes one after the other. One ship blew up in spectacular fashion, and the other maneuvered for another angle of attack, but not before taking multiple hits, sustaining heavy damage.

"Helm, watch out for those asteroids!" Chambers shouted. "You're about to ram one!"

Then, seemingly out of nowhere, the ship slammed into an asteroid, shaking the bridge violently. All of the smoke and alarms suddenly stopped, and the lighting on the simulated bridge went back to normal.

"Simulation ended," announced a female computerized voice. "Your ship was blown up."

Lee looked down and realized that he was practically drenched in sweat. He took a deep breath and let it out slowly, trying to speed up the release of adrenaline from his body.

Part of him was beyond thrilled—he'd scored a kill and blown up an enemy corvette. However, at the end of the day, his team had still lost the simulation because the helmsman had failed to keep track of everything happening around them while the ship was still in battle.
****

After a bio break, the instructor called Lee and his fellow students to review what went right and what went wrong. "The goal of this after-action review is to figure out what you could do better for the future," Chambers explained. "A great way to do that is to learn from each other's mistakes, which is what we're going to do now."

"Lee, how did you overcome the jamming and get a missile lock?" Chambers asked, singling Lee out first.

"I rerouted power from the rear magrail guns to the forward targeting system to get the extra power I needed to burn through the jamming," Lee explained.

"OK. Let's dig deeper. Why did you take the rear guns offline in the middle of a battle like that?" Chambers pressed.

"Sir, the rear gun turrets weren't involved in the battle, so we didn't need them," Lee quickly countered. "However, we *did* need the power they were using. Once I rerouted the power, I was able to break through the jamming and get the lock I needed for those ASMs and my guns. That's how we were able to take out that corvette."

Chambers nodded and smiled approvingly. Lee could tell that he was impressed.

The instructor turned to Cadet Burton. "Did you ever figure out how to clean up the message traffic from the mining outpost?" he asked.

Burton shook her head, looking down at the floor.

"If you would have found a way to clear up the comms, we would have received a warning from the outpost about the enemy corvettes hiding behind the giant asteroid," Chambers explained. He leaned forward. "Did you consider deploying the towed comms array?" he asked.

A towed comms array was a wire net that would eventually extend a few kilometers behind the ship, away from enemy jamming directed at the ship's external communications arrays.

"No, sir," Burton replied. "A towed comms array is normally used for deep listening and reconnaissance missions."

Chambers nodded. "That's true—we wouldn't usually deploy one in a combat scenario," he acknowledged. "But what we are trying to get you to do is to figure out *how else* you might be able to solve a problem. What other resources are available to you? Lee found a workaround to get our weapons back in the fight. Your job was to find us another way to get those comms reestablished."

They discussed the scenario some more. Like a lot of the training simulations the Academy ran them through, it had proven to be a potent learning lesson for all of them.

"Get a good night's sleep," Chambers said, concluding their after-action review. "Tomorrow, everyone switches roles and you'll be tested against a new scenario."

****

Later that Week

It had been a long week of tests, but Lee was ready to chill out with his friends after hours and hit up a fun game of poker.

When he plopped down into his seat, exhausted, his roommate, Jack Hannigan, laughed. "You should have followed me, Naomi, and Alden here on the pilot track, bud," he teased.

Naomi Love also laughed. She handed Lee an open beer. "I didn't drink out of it yet," she said. "Looks like you could use it more than me."

Lee took a swig of the beer and smiled. "Well, I wanted to see the stars, explore new worlds, conquer new planets," he explained.

"Eh, nothing is better than being a pilot," Hannigan countered.

Lee's smile curled up mischievously. "I was meant to be more than an interstellar Uber driver," he joked. "But hey, someone needs to be a battle taxi for those Army grunts."

"Shots fired!" said Alden, chuckling. "But maybe we should settle this dispute with a good old-fashioned game of cards."

Love dealt out the first hand. Hannigan turned pensive. "You know, all joking aside, I'm starting to enjoy working with some of the regular Fleeters. There's Chief Brian Ford, one of the crew chiefs with my Osprey training squadron, and I'd say he's more than all right. Now we're starting flight training with the real deal—no more simulators."

"Maybe you should invite him to the next poker game," Lee goaded.

"You know, it might be considered a bit inappropriate for you to take an NCOs money," Love countered, laughing.

"Who says he'd lose?" asked Lee. "Maybe he'd get a morale boost by taking some of mine."

"Less talking, more cards," Hannigan insisted.

"Not sure you should rush with card shark Lee at the table," said Alden.

They each checked on the first round of betting. Three cards were turned over, two kings and an ace.

"All right, you've convinced me," said Lee. "I'm walking down to Chambers's office tomorrow and telling him I want to switch to being a pilot."

"Are you serious?" asked Love, going all in.

A moment of silence hung in the air as Hannigan and Alden both folded and Lee met her bet. All the cards were turned over to reveal that Love had three aces and two jacks, but Lee had four kings.

"No," said Lee. "Of course not. But I *am* going to have a great time taking your money."

Alden punched his friend lightly in the arm and Hannigan tried to comfort Love as she stung from a bad beat so early in the game.

Love got up and grabbed another beer. "I guess I could have used mine more than you after all," she said, downing a swig before doing a cheers motion in the air toward Lee.

He returned the gesture. "Here's to us," Lee replied.

"Here's to us," they all agreed.

Chapter 9
When You Know

Year 2089
The Academy
Colorado Springs, Colorado
Earth

Love settled against the wide trunk of an old maple. The forest was their refuge—a place where the rules and routines of the Academy were distant, almost absent. She glanced at Hannigan. He lounged beside her on the picnic blanket he'd spread out earlier.

"You went all out," she said. She eyed the assortment of snacks and the nicely folded cloth napkins. "Trying to impress me?"

He flashed that silly grin she'd come to adore, where one side of his lips drifted higher than the other side. "Is it working?"

"Maybe." She tilted her head with a teasing glint in her eyes. "But you know you don't have to bribe me with food."

"Consider it a bonus, then." He leaned back, propping himself up on his elbows. "Besides, it's not every day we get a moment to ourselves."

"True. I was thinking about the Osprey program. I really feel like it's where I'm supposed to be."

"Yeah?"

"There's just something about piloting a transport. You know, being responsible for getting everyone safely where they need to go, and all that jazz. It... I don't know... feels like knowing that every successful mission means families reunited, a Delta mission gone well, supplies delivered to those who need them the most. It feels... right."

He nodded. "I'm happy when you're happy."

Love's heart fell. *An easy reply. Come on, you're smarter than that, Jack.* "Be serious. What do you want to do after we graduate? Last week in Basic Fighter Maneuvers, Commander Peterson said your intercept patterns were the best she'd seen in years."

He shrugged, picking at the edge of the blanket. "Honestly? I was thinking of following your lead in terms of assignments."

Love sat straighter. His response shocked her to no end. "Really? No, no... no. You can't just mold your career path because of me. I've watched you in the simulators, Jack. You handle those split-second decisions like a genius, and I see how naturally combat flying comes to you. You're a wizard with those drones. It's hard to believe you'd be happy just sticking with the Osprey program long-term."

"But, why not? I'd hope we'd be in the same units, the same assignments. Sounds perfect to me." He edged closer to her. "They're already talking about splitting up top performers across different bases after graduation. I'm…"

"Are you holding back?"

"A little. I mean, at least this way…"

She shook her head. "Don't. Please. Just… don't, Jack. You need to pursue what you're passionate about, not just tag along with me. We'll figure out the rest."

"Who says I'm not passionate about it?" He reached out and brushed a stray strand of hair from her face. "Besides, being near you is a definite perk. You know how hard it is for married officers to get stationed together. We gotta stay together. I mean it. I don't know what I'd do without you. It's nuts to think that way, I know, but—"

"Jack," she said. "I—"

"Naomi." He winked at her, cutting her off, then leaned forward and gave her a kiss on her cheek. "I know what I want, Cadet Love. Don't take that from me. You asked what I was passionate about, and it's you. Not these fancy ships, Naomi. It's you."

"I am, am I?" She searched his eyes, thinking of all the times she'd watched him emerge from the fighter sims, his face flushed with excitement after nailing a difficult maneuver. "Just promise me you'll think about it. Really think about it. You gotta go for what you like, not what I want. So… think hard, all right?"

"Deal." He pulled her close, wrapping his arms around her. She relaxed into his embrace. The rise and fall of his chest calmed her.

"You know," he said, "I could stay like this forever."

She smiled. "Until we get caught, you mean."

"Adds to the excitement, don't you think?"

"You're incorrigible." She turned her head slightly, their faces mere centimeters apart.

"And you love it." He closed the gap, their lips meeting in a tender kiss.

When they parted, he gazed at her. "I want to marry you someday."

Her heart skipped a beat. "Is that so?"

"Absolutely." He traced circles on the back of her hand. "In fact… we should get you sized for a ring."

She chuckled. "Are you serious?"

"When you know, you know."

She gave him a skeptical look. "Sounds like something you'd say to get your way."

He feigned offense. "You wound me. I'm being sincere here."

"Uh-huh." She smiled. "It would be nice, though."

"See? We're on the same page."

Before she could respond, a faint rustling reached her ears. Love stiffened. "Did you hear that?"

Hannigan listened. Voices carried through the trees, growing closer.

"Someone's coming," she whispered, her heart hammering. If they were caught, it wouldn't just be about being in a restricted area. Fraternization between same-year cadets wasn't strictly forbidden, but relationships were heavily scrutinized. One wrong move could affect their future assignments. Heck, their entire careers. "We need to hide."

They scrambled to gather their belongings, leaving the picnic basket but grabbing the most incriminating items. After they darted behind a dense thicket more than ten meters away, they crouched low. Love's muscles burned as she tried to stay perfectly still. A branch dug into her back. She didn't dare move. Hannigan's breath was warm against her neck as they pressed together, trying to make themselves as small as possible.

Two instructors entered the clearing.

"I'm certain I saw cadets heading this way," one said, scanning the area.

"This section's off-limits," the other replied. "If they're out here, they'll face disciplinary action. I hope you were just seeing things. Last thing we need is another scandal like last year's couple's incident."

"I wasn't imagining it."

Love held her breath. Her hand found Hannigan's. His fingers interlaced with hers, squeezing. A beetle crawled across her boot. She remained frozen. The instructors' eyes swept over the area but missed the edge of the blanket peeking out from behind a bush. The blanket's green fabric helped things, blending with the forest.

An instructor took a step closer to their hiding spot. Love's throat tightened. One more step and he'd see them. Her career flashed before her eyes—the possibility of reassignment, separation from Jack, the disappointment on her mom's face…

"Maybe they doubled back," the first one suggested before turning away from their hiding spot.

"Perhaps. We should notify campus security, just in case. After that incident with the seniors last year, the commanders made it clear—no tolerance for rule-breakers."

The instructors stayed a moment longer before retreating the way they'd come. Their footsteps faded. Love and Hannigan kept still, listening for any sign of return.

Love leaned her head against Hannigan's shoulder. "That was too close."

"Guess our secret spot isn't so secret," he whispered. "They mentioned last year. You heard about that, right? Two senior cadets got caught, both got kicked out."

They waited another five minutes to make sure the coast was clear. Finally emerging with caution, they walked to their picnic setup to pack up the remaining items.

"Think we should avoid this place for a while," Love said as she folded the blanket. "I can't risk a mark on my record."

"Agreed. Though it's a shame. I like it out here."

A figure stepped into the clearing, startling Love. There Lieutenant Commander Ezra Richardson stood, his posture relaxed. "Cadets," he said, a bit of surprise in his voice.

"Sir," they both responded, snapping to attention. Love's heart sank—Richardson was a decorated officer in the Navy. He'd know exactly what this could mean for their careers.

The commander's gaze fell to the half-packed basket and the blanket in Love's hands. Something sparkled in his eyes—recognition, perhaps memory. He glanced at a worn silver ring on his finger before looking back at them. "Enjoying the scenery?"

"Yes, sir," Hannigan said.

"Cadets, you're aware this area is off-limits?" His tone was gentler than expected.

"We are now, sir," Love replied.

He regarded them for a moment, then pulled out his tablet. Love's breath caught. This was it, he was logging the violation. Instead, he turned toward them to show exactly what he was doing—scrolling through personnel files, scanning over their records. "Love… you broke the Academy's canyon run record in the simulator last month, didn't you? And, Hannigan, that autonomous swarm coordination during last week's multidrone exercise—not many third-years have that kind of spatial awareness."

"Yes, sir," they said at the same time.

He tucked the tablet away. "I recommend you finish up and return to campus. And perhaps stick to approved areas in the future. The Academy's policy on relationships… it's complicated."

"Aye, sir," they said.

Richardson turned to leave before pausing. "And, Cadets?"

"Sir?"

"Be cautious. Not everyone is as understanding." He tapped his ring. "My wife and I… well, let's just say I know something about navigating Academy relationships. But these days, with every branch fighting over the best candidates and postings so competitive…" He shook his head. "They're watching you all more closely than ever. One slipup in the personnel file…" He let the warning float in the air. "Also," he said as he walked into the trees, disappearing from view, "do me a favor and don't walk to campus carrying a blanket and basket. Ditch them. I'll clean up after you."

"Yes, sir," Love said, waiting a few moments before glancing at Hannigan. "We got lucky."

"Very lucky. Did you see his ring? And how he talked about his wife…"

"Yeah. Must have met her here at the Academy." Love fell into step beside him, lowering her voice. "But he's right. I heard they're being even stricter with placement. Something about maximizing operational efficiency."

They retraced their steps, the near miss and Richardson's warning like a barrier between them. After a few minutes of silence, Hannigan spoke up.

"You know, he didn't have to let us off the hook. Could have reported us, separated us into… well, I don't know, but somehow separated us."

She nodded, thinking about the couples who hadn't been so fortunate. "Maybe he remembers what it's like to be young and in…" She trailed off, catching herself.

"In what?" he asked, stepping closer even though they were exposed on the path.

"Don't get so… close." She bit her lip. "Anyway, nothing."

He stopped walking and turned to face her. "In love?"

"Maybe." The word came out barely above a whisper.

Hannigan gave that sideways grin she liked so much it made her hate it at this moment. "Well, that's good to hear."

"You're impossible."

"And you're avoiding the topic." He took her hand, his thumb brushing over her knuckles. "I meant what I said earlier. About the ring."

"Jack…"

"No, really. I'm going to get you that ring. Just wait and see."

"You're serious, aren't you?"

"Completely."

A warmth spread through her chest. "Well, then. I guess I'll have to hold you to that."

"You can count on it."

They resumed walking, the Academy's buildings coming into view through the thinning trees. The sun cast a golden hue over the campus as students milled about in the distance.

"You know," she said, "despite nearly getting caught, today was… perfect."

"I couldn't agree more."

As they approached the main grounds, Love sighed. "Back to reality."

"At least reality includes me."

"And I'm glad it does."

He gave a mock bow. "Glad to be of service."

She nudged him. "OK, OK, funny man."

"But you love it."

"Maybe I do." She paused at the edge of the pathway. "See you at dinner?"

"Wouldn't miss it." He lifted her hand to his lips, pressing a quick kiss before anyone could notice. "Until then."

She watched him walk away, a mix of emotions swirling within her. The promise of a ring, the future they might share—it all was both thrilling and uncertain.

Turning toward her dormitory, she withheld a grin. *Just wait and see*, she thought. *Maybe he really means it.*

Chapter 10
The Last Normal Night

Year 2090
Colorado Springs, Colorado
Earth

Lee strolled into Rocky Mountain Tavern. Inside, he adjusted his Academy uniform collar. The smell of hops filled the pub, along with the smoky scent of the flames crackling in the stone fireplace in the corner. This place was a cozy refuge from the crisp mountain air outside. The wooden tables and benches were packed with patrons.

Lee's wrist comm buzzed with a notification. He glanced at the holographic display hovering above his wrist, dismissing the reminder about a scheduled eye exam next week.

He sat at a round table in the middle of the joint. The smart-surface of the table displayed the evening's specials. He smiled and clinked his glass against those of his friends—Love, Alden, and Hannigan. It was their last hoorah before graduation. Soon, they'd be leaving to separate advanced training schools and going down different paths.

"To surviving the Academy," Lee said over the noise. "May our future careers be as challenging as these past four years have been."

"Challenging?" Hannigan took a sip of beer and raised his glass a second time. "May our careers be easy and rewarded with a beautiful woman."

Love pinched his arm. "Hey!"

"I, my dear, have the most gorgeous woman already. Our friends here clearly do not, and I'm making that fact known far and wide," Jack said.

Love smiled. "Much better. But, as usual, keep it on the down-low."

The group cheered and drank deeply. As they set their mugs down, Alden asked, "So, where's everyone hoping to get stationed after graduation?"

Love grinned. "Jack and I are both thinking the RNS *Bishop*. We're hoping for a joint assignment."

"The *Bishop*?" Alden whistled. "You two would hit the jackpot if you get it. What about you, Ripley?"

"Where I wanna be stationed? Hmm. I don't know, actually."

Love put down her beer after a sip. "How's your family doing, Lee? Thinking about it, you never really talk about them."

A pang ripped through Lee's chest. "No. Haven't heard from them in a while." He wanted to change the subject.

"So, when are you going to put a ring on it, Hannigan?" Lee probed.

Hannigan feigned offense. "So direct, Lee." He laughed good-naturedly. Actually, we're headed over to Vegas as soon as graduation is over, if you must know."

"And you didn't invite me?" asked Alden, seeming genuinely hurt. "I did introduce you two, after all."

"Aw, that's sweet, Alden. You want to be the flower girl?" asked Naomi.

Alden snorted. "OK, no. Not really. But I could dress up like Elvis if you like."

"Don't take this the wrong way," said Naomi. "But well, you all know my mom is my only family and that she wouldn't be the best person to be at the wedding. So Jack and I talked it over, and we just want it to be the two of us."

"All right, I get it. No drunken best man speeches for me," teased Alden.

Lee was feeling especially sentimental at this point. "This is really it. We're really moving on with our lives...separate from the Academy and each other."

"Well, what did you think was going to happen?" asked Hannigan.

"I don't know," Lee answered. "I just focused on the next step this whole time and I guess it didn't really kick in."

"We've all worked really hard," said Naomi. "And I'm going to miss you two sidekicks, but it's time, Lee. We made it! Enjoy the good times. The best is yet to come, right?"

Lee took a swig of his drink. "Yeah, I guess you're right, Love. Congratulations to you and Hannigan, by the way."

Alden sat up straight, realizing he'd breached the friend protocol. "Yeah, congratulations, you two."

Love and Hannigan smiled, and Hannigan lifted his beer. "Here's to the future!"

"Here's to the future," Alden and Lee replied.

Chapter 11
When Tomorrow Came

A Long While Back…

Year 2079
Baltimore, Maryland
Earth

Snow drifted just beyond the window. Each flake was a tiny hope of something pretty in Love's filthy world. The couch's threadbare fabric scratched her fingers where stuffing poked through. Stains showed years of neglect across its surface. At twelve years old, she'd never had a proper Thanksgiving, and it was a few days away. It wasn't that she'd ever wished for one, but she'd heard at school that family usually got together and had meals. Big meals. Meals that made you stuffed for days. Apparently, when she was younger and her dad was alive, they'd had plenty of those get-togethers. After he'd died when she was four years old—which she had a scant memory of—extended family members stopped coming by, and any gatherings, whether it be for meals or simply to visit, had ceased long ago.

Outside the window, a man wearing three layers of ripped coats shuffled through the snow. His fingerless gloves clutched a shopping cart filled with aluminum cans. The plastic bags wrapped around his boots left wet footprints in the fresh powder. Through the paper-thin walls of their Baltimore apartment, the neighbors' screaming match reached a new level—something about money, always about money.

Why's money so important? Love thought—especially if it caused all these problems for those people. She figured if she was them, she'd just ditch the money and live a happier life. Maybe the screaming between them would stop. Why was money so mean to them? Her neighbors' fights had hurt her ears when she was younger, but now she'd become numb to it all.

A dog she called Honey raced across the empty street. She stood to let him inside, knowing the homeless dog wasn't allowed in here. But as her mom snored, passed out on the lounger—a puke-green relic with cigarette burns and dark stains—she thought it wouldn't hurt to let the dog inside, just for a little… would it?

I love you, Honey. I'm coming. Don't worry!

Maybe she could give him some of the toast she'd made for herself for breakfast. Love's stomach growled as she tried to rub her hunger pangs away while she walked across the carpet to the entryway. She bent over to pick up a fuzzy piece of what might have once been some type of food. As she did so, she almost stepped on a used needle. Her heart skipped a beat. Her mother's rules were clear—never touch needles, especially ones left in the house. She'd watched her mother insert liquid gold into her arms daily, but it was only for her mom. That much was clear.

After opening the closet, the moldy food still in hand, she grabbed a jacket and placed it over the needle so she wouldn't accidentally step on the sharp object. Eventually, she'd tell her mom, and her mother would toss the needle in with the others. As Love reached for the door, the holovision caught her attention. The device's projector hung from the ceiling like a metal spider. Its light created holographic images in the air near one of the walls. The History Channel had been her companion all day—her only friend besides hunger. She wished she had real friends to play with, but Mom wouldn't let anyone see their place.

The holovision flashed with footage from the Great War. Combat drones filled the sky while soldiers evacuated civilians from advancing synthetic humanoids terrorizing a neighborhood. The Synths' metallic faces showed no emotion as they gunned down a family. The real humans, the soldiers… those were the true heroes. They saved people. They made a difference.

"Turn that damn thing off!" Her mother's slurred words burst through her daydream. "Too loud… too… loud…" Her mom's voice faded back into snores.

In her mind, Love was one of those soldiers, conducting a rescue mission to save one cold, hungry refugee. Yet she realized she'd already failed—she still hadn't let Honey in the apartment.

She opened the door and tossed the moldy food outside. Honey's tail wagged as he bounded inside, covering her face with kisses.

"I love you, Honey. Oh, yes, I do. I love you so, so much."

On that day, watching soldiers save lives while holding a shivering stray, Love made a promise to herself. Someday, she'd wear a uniform to help others and, most importantly, to help the person most dear in her life—her mom. Someday, she'd make a difference for everyone. Someday, she'd put lots of food on that table and invite everyone she could over, and fill her stomach, and her mom's, up with as much yummy food as possible.

****

Year 2091
Republic Navy Advanced Flight School
Huntsville, Alabama

Hannigan jabbed Love playfully. "Are you OK?" he asked. "Where did you go?"

Love snapped out of her daydream. "Yeah, sorry. I just got lost in some memories, that's all."

"Well, whatever this is, I think it's going to be big, so you might want to join us back in the present," Hannigan replied.

"No, you're right," Love admitted.

All training for the day had been cancelled, and everyone had been told to wait in the auditorium for whatever the announcement was. They'd been waiting for more than half an hour at this point, though, which is why Love had drifted off to another time.

Whatever was going on, it was clear the higher-ranked officers and enlisted were nervous. Love saw the facial expressions of a few senior people, and it made the hair stand up on the back of her neck.

Finally, the base commander, a Navy captain, stepped up to the podium. "All of you remember the expedition that was sent to the Rhea Ab system," he began. "Well, their return has brought with it some startling information. Humanity has long wondered if we are alone in the universe. Well, we now have verifiable evidence that we are not the only known lifeforms."

The room buzzed with startled whispers.

The base commander signaled for everyone to quiet down. "Not only are we not alone—we were attacked in an unprovoked ambush by a vicious alien race we now know as the Zodarks."

The whispers turned to murmurs. The base commander signaled once again for silence. "I have been authorized to show you some raw, unfiltered footage from our recent expedition to New Eden. Steel yourselves."

Blue aliens, nearly three meters tall, with four functioning arms and a third eye in the center of their face, slashed at the Republic Navy exploration team with their long, sharp nails. One pulled out an ensign's heart and howled like a wolf before devouring it. The Zodarks used their multiple appendages to slash with swords and fire blasters at the same time. They were savage.

The room went completely silent.

"Now that you see what we are up against, this next announcement will make so much more sense," the base commander said. "We are officially at war. We don't have time to mess around. Humanity's survival depends on all of us here in this room spinning up as quickly as possible. As such, you are each being promoted a rank. You will be getting new assignments, and many of you will be leaving the advanced training courses early. You're going to need to fill in the gaps through on-the-job training.

"More information about the intelligence we've received thus far, and your future assignments will be transmitted to your data pads. But we needed to show you this footage together here, so you could know that it is true. Unfortunately, this is not a post-production edit. It is very real.

"Get your affairs in order and get prepared to ship out. Dismissed."

Love sat stunned for a moment before she turned to her husband. "Well, we knew it was going to be big, but I guess I didn't have this one on my bingo card," she said.

Hannigan nodded. "I mean, it was always a possibility, being in the military, that we would face combat at some point, but this certainly has upped the stakes."

"Yeah, this isn't just protecting Republic ships from some pirates in the Belt...we're talking about the survival of our species."

"I hope we will live up to the task," Hannigan replied.

Chapter 12
The Bridge

Year 2091
RNS _Trenton_
Earth Orbit

Ensign Ripley Lee stepped off the shuttle onto the starship's hangar deck. Memories of his last interactions with loved ones back on Earth came to mind: Hannigan, Love, and Alden.

Yet even more surprising was the message that had pinged his comm device just that morning before he'd left Colorado Springs. He'd stared at the voice note notification in disbelief. It was from his mother. She hadn't reached out to him in a long while—not since Lee's decision to join the Academy.

Her voice had trembled as she spoke. "Ripley, it's Mom. I heard through the grapevine you're leaving for your ship today. I know we haven't spoken, but... I had to call. Your father and I, the whole community really, we're against violence. You know that. But, son, I still love you. I want you to be safe out there. God will be looking over you, and I'll pray for you every day. Please, just... come back to us. Someday. I'll be waiting."

The message had hit Lee hard. He'd immediately called back, again and again, desperate to hear her voice in real time. Once, the line had connected for a short moment before hanging up. No words, just silence. Now, as he stepped onto the RNS _Trenton_, that silence filled his mind. He missed them. All of them. Mom. Dad. Sisters. And leaving Earth made it that much harder.

Through a holowindow in the hangar, Earth hung suspended in space—a blue-and-white jewel against the dark expanse. Lee knew it was an exterior video feed and not a real window, but it looked so real— he drank in the sight of home, maybe for the last time.

A voice snapped him back to the present. "Ensign Lee?"

He turned to face a young lieutenant. "Yes, that's me."

"Welcome aboard the _Trenton_. I'm Lieutenant Nagumo, I'll show you to your quarters first, so you can drop your gear. There's a tactical officers' briefing in four hours with Commander Morris, your senior TAO, followed by a bridge orientation and a tour of the ship, so you can learn your way around. Oh, and the Skipper, Captain Oldendorf, wants all new personnel fully processed before reporting for duty.”

Lee kept his expression neutral despite the excitement of finally boarding a real warship. “Thank you, Lieutenant,” he replied. “It’s a lot to take in. I guess I’ll follow you to where we need to go next.”

They walked through *Trenton*’s corridors, the lieutenant making small talk. “First time on a warship?”

“That obvious, huh?”

“Most of us get a little wide-eyed at first,” Nagumo said with a grin. “She’s a beauty, though.”

“How long have you been aboard?” Lee asked.

“Four months, like most of the crew,” Nagumo explained. “She’s fresh out of the yard after a few upgrades to her propulsion and power plant. There’s always something new to learn aboard a ship this size.”

“Yeah, I suppose there is,” Lee agreed. “Any advice for a newcomer?”

“Watch your head in the lower decks. And don’t skip the gym. Artificial gravity’s no joke.”

“Noted. How’s the food?” Lee chuckled.

“Beats field rations, but I wouldn’t write home about it.”

They reached a check-in station where Lee received his quarters assignment and his personnel file was added to the ship’s log. With the inprocessing completed, the lieutenant led him through more narrow passages until they reached the berthing section of the ship and a cramped tiny cabin that would become Lee’s quarters.

“And here we are—home sweet home. I’ll leave you here to settle in. You should receive a message shortly, letting you know when and where to head next. You’ll probably meet with the Skipper, along with the other officers who arrived today. With the Fleet preparing to conduct some exercises before we ship out for the Rhea system, there has been a lot of crew reshuffling. Shoot, there’s even been quite a few promotions to fill all the vacations with the new ships joining the Fleet. At this rate, I wouldn’t be surprised if we’re *all* promoted a grade or two.”

Lee smiled. He knew the ranks of the military were beginning to swell, but he hadn’t thought about how many new officers a massive expansion like this would need. “Well, I just graduated the Academy. I suppose if they start promoting us ensigns a couple of grades, things with whatever this war is must be worse than they’re telling us.”

Lieutenant Nagumo shrugged. "My grandfather served. He told me if something is important, the Navy will tell you. Don't take too long to unpack. That meeting with the Skipper is likely to start soon. I'll see you later, Ensign."

Alone in his quarters, Lee took stock of the tight space. The room wasn't exactly a cylindrical tube, but it wasn't far off. A thin bunk, small desk, and storage locker beneath the bed were all that fit. He set his duffel bag down, and ran his hand along the cool metal bulkhead. He didn't have much to unpack, which was good because space was limited. He attached a picture of his family to the ceiling above his bunk—it was the first and last image he'd see each day. Next, he placed his worn, leather-bound Bible on the desk, a gift from his grandfather when he'd turned thirteen. For better or worse, this metal compartment would be his home for the foreseeable future.

A light blinked on the terminal's display, alerting Lee to a new message notification. He tapped the screen and the ship's artificial intelligence spoke. "Ensign Lee, welcome aboard the RNS *Trenton*. You're instructed to report to the main briefing room on Deck 7 in thirty minutes to meet with Captain James Oldendorf. Please do not be late."

Lee closed the message and stowed the remainder of his personal belongings in the locker. He didn't want to be late to meet the Captain on his very first day aboard. Getting lost in the mazelike corridors of a starship was the last thing he needed.

As he stepped out of his quarters, the passageway was abuzz with activity. Crew members hurried about. Lee scanned the directional signs, locating the path to Deck 7.

After making his way down the passages, he came upon the briefing room's doors. Lee took a deep breath, squaring his shoulders before entering. The room had filled with officers and staff, far more than he had expected to find. Looking for an empty seat near the middle, he squeezed past a few others who looked as bewildered as he felt.

"Attention on deck!" Lee heard someone shout from behind him.

He jumped to his feet with the others. Conversations were cut short as the room's main doors parted and Captain James Oldendorf strode in. Lee felt a surge of admiration as the captain moved to the podium, activating a large star chart. He had heard a lot about Captain Oldendorf at the Academy, but when Lee had learned he'd be stationed aboard Oldendorf's ship, he'd read up on his soon-to-be-Skipper. In

Lee's opinion, Oldendorf was one of the more visionary captains in the fleet, having developed many of the current offensive tactics being used. Lee felt there was a lot to learn from a skipper like him and was thrilled to finally meet him.

"Take your seats," Oldendorf announced, his voice calm but firm. "We have some news from the Fleet Commander, Admiral Chester Bailey that needs to be disseminated."

Everyone obliged, sitting down.

"First order of business, I want to welcome our new arrivals," Oldendorf began. "In the coming weeks, I plan to spend a little time with each of you, as I've done with many of my crews. The most valuable asset the Fleet has is its people, and I believe each of you brings a unique value to this crew.

"Listen, I don't mince words, so when I say we are in for a hell of a fight ahead of us, I mean it. Our mission against the Zodark forces will be lengthy and fraught with danger. But make no mistake, we will prevail.

"The Fleet Admiral announced a tripling of the Navy in size, and that'll likely increase again in years to come. With any massive increase in the size of the military like this, there will be challenges, namely, finding enough officers and enlisted to lead this force and the ships being built. To that end, Admiral Bailey has given commanders broad authority to promote and elevate officers and enlisted to higher positions if a need arises."

Oldendorf paused a moment before continuing. "This next part is going to hurt, but it's necessary if we're going to build the navy we will need to win this war. A few hours ago, I received word that one third of my officers and NCOs will be transferred to other commanders, effective immediately. Those being transferred should receive your new orders within the hour. I also want to congratulate each of you on being promoted two full grades from your current rank. You will form the backbone of the new Republic Navy that Admiral Bailey is building while the rest of us continue on with the mission to recapture the Rhea system.

"Those of you who arrived the past few days as ensigns and junior enlisted—congrats, everyone is being a promoted a grade. You will fill in for those who are being transferred and staying behind," Oldendorf announced.

There was a slight rustling in the room as everyone processed that they'd all just been promoted. In one fell swoop, Lee had jumped from ensign to lieutenant, and he'd only been here a day.

"War has a strange way of maturing people," said Oldendorf. "It stretches you and pushes you beyond what you thought you could do. That's what these promotions are going to do—they're going to push you into a leadership role with greater authority and responsibility. It's going to stretch you. It's going to require you to dig deep and push beyond your comfort zone. And you *will* do it—because your country is counting you, your ship is counting on you, and I am counting on you."

The room was completely silent now, to the point of hearing a pin drop. Lee had already felt the war was real, but this sudden news seemed to add a whole new level to the gravity of the situation.

"Now that the ships returning to the Rhea Ab system have finished their upgrades in the shipyards, we are going to spend the next couple of weeks running through a series of drills and exercises to test ourselves and the upgrades the ship received," Oldendorf explained. "In four weeks' time, we'll be jumping to Rhea with a small fleet. Our goal: to capture New Eden from Zodark control. The RNS *Rook*, under Captain Miles Hunt, will lead this force. Those blue aliens killed a lot of our people, and without provocation. We won't stand for that, and we'll meet their response in kind.

"Intelligence is still light on what we know about the Zodarks and New Eden. But here is a little bit of what we know so far." Holographic images came to life, showing Zodark troop deployments across New Eden. Oldendorf continued, "We'll be traversing the treacherous Tauros Rift via FTL jump. It's a risky maneuver, but it will significantly reduce our travel time."

He raised a finger and stepped to the side of the podium. "We stand at a pivotal moment in human history. For many, the idea of encountering an alien race was an expectation. But did we anticipate all-out war? The honest answer for some of us is yes. However, personally, I never imagined we would face such an enemy as this.

"We're confronting the Zodarks, a species with a thirst for domination over all other beings across the stars. So we've concluded after a lot of… research. On New Eden and other planets, we've learned through vital intel that they've subjected entire civilizations to slavery and imprisonment. Intel suggests they have inflicted this atrocity upon multiple species throughout the galaxy. Yes, there are other alien beings out there, but you don't need to worry about that right now. We don't know them. They don't know us. So, what you need to worry about now is this—additional intel from those who survived our last encounter with the Zodarks suggests they are eager to find our planet, Earth. And should the Zodarks find our home, we believe they will try subjugating us without hesitation."

A knot formed in Lee's stomach. The stakes kept getting higher.

"Our mission is not only to defend humanity from death, imprisonment, and enslavement, but to eradicate this blight from the galaxy. We'll strip the Zodarks of their ability to perpetrate such heinous acts of enslavement, forever and for the good of all. We'll ensure that this abhorrent practice ends here and now, and if it ever resurfaces, we will crush it with unwavering resolve. We have a duty to protect and serve our own, and from that, we'll keep their ugly hands off our world.

"Furthermore, we've identified New Eden as a Goldilocks planet, as you've probably heard from numerous media outlets. It's a pristine world, ripe for human habitation and technological advancement. We'll secure this untainted paradise, expanding our reach and paving the way for future generations to expand beyond our planet. Manifest Destiny, ladies and gentlemen. So, make no mistake, my brave crew, our bold actions will be etched into the annals of history. You'll be remembered as the pioneers who forged a path for our species to thrive *safely* among the stars. We'll write a chapter that'll resonate through the ages, showing the truth of our determination to protect our way of life."

He hesitated for a moment and walked back behind the podium. His expression became more stern as he turned on holographic images of the Zodarks themselves. "Now, let's discuss our enemy. Zodarks stand roughly three meters in height, with a physique built for battle. They possess four functional arms and two legs, giving them a significant advantage in close-quarters combat."

Lee studied the holographic representation, noting the Zodarks' intimidating features—their sharp teeth, the third eye positioned between and slightly above the other two, and the long, braided black hair.

"Make no mistake," Oldendorf said. "Zodarks are ruthless. You'll probably never encounter one, but if you do, shoot to kill. They won't hesitate to do the same to you. Our mission is clear—we eliminate the threat to our planet and our people. Keep that in mind at all times."

The hologram changed, displaying Zodark vessels. "Again, our intel is light, but this is what we have been able to put together from a few of those we've liberated from the Zodarks. They call this a Vulture— it's a starfighter and their primary attack craft. Twenty-one meters in length, single-pilot, armed with four blasters and plasma torpedoes. They're launched from cruisers, battleships, or planetside bases."

Next came an image of a Zodark cruiser. Its bow resembled the head of a cobra, ready to strike. "This is what our enlisted spacers have dubbed 'the Cobra.' It's one thousand, two hundred and ninety-three meters long, armed with six lasers and eight plasma torpedo launchers. Each cruiser carries thirty-two Vulture starfighters, twelve Glaive fighter-bombers, ten troop landers, and eighty Zodark warriors."

Finally, the hologram displayed a massive Zodark battleship. Its snakelike head with an open mouth appeared ready to devour everything in its path. "This is their heavy hitter. Detailed specs are still being gathered, but we know it's a formidable opponent. So, study these often. Memorize every detail and spec we have on these vessels, including all data on every weakness and strength we've found on these ships. And remember—each of you represents the best humanity has to offer. We face a ruthless enemy, but our strength lies in our unity. This is key in the Republic military, and especially on my ship. Understood?"

"Aye, sir," came the chorus of responses.

"Outstanding! Dismissed!"

The captain's words resonated deeply with Lee—not just what he'd said, but how he'd said it. Strangely, for the first time in Lee's life, he wanted to be like someone else. Like that man, Captain James Oldendorf. Every syllable was delivered with confidence and strength, the words affecting everyone in the room as if the guy was a motivational speaker. As the room cleared, Lee was rooted to the spot. A newfound spark burned within him.

"That's a lot to take in, isn't," came the voice of Lieutenant Nagumo, who had walked up next to him.

"Yeah, that's understatement. I guess we'd better pin on our new ranks," Lee hesitated.

Smiling, Nagumo motioned for Lee to follow him. "Come on, I'll show you where the quartermaster is, and then we can get some dinner and figure out what's happening next."
****

Three Days Later

Lee grabbed his breakfast tray at the ship's mess hall and sat down at the end of a mostly empty table. As he dug into his omelet with hydroponically grown veggies, he ruminated on the whirlwind that had been the past few days since arriving on the ship. So far, he'd in-processed at the med bay, had a full tour of the ship and learned the fastest ways to get to the bridge from any of the main places the crew would visit or hang out. Then he'd had a tour of the bridge itself and learned the names of the people he'd be working with. It was a lot to take in.

As he shoved another forkful of food in his mouth, someone Lee didn't recognize walked up with his own tray. "Mind if I sit here?" the stranger asked.

Lee, his mouth still stuffed, motioned for him to sit down and tried to speed up his chewing so he could be conversational.

"Hi, I'm Chief Brian Ford," the newcomer said, cheerfully extending his hand to shake Lee's. "How are you liking your assignment so far?"

"Is it that obvious?" Lee asked sheepishly.

Ford laughed. "It's always easy to spot people who have never been to space before," he replied. They have that wanderlust look of awe on their faces for a little while until the mundaneness of the daily grind wears them out."

"So, how long have you been on the ship?" asked Lee.

Ford grinned. "I arrived the same day you did, just like half the crew."

"OK, so where are you coming from then?" Lee pressed. *This can't be his first assignment.*

"I just transferred from a training squadron supporting the Academy's basic flight training and the advanced flight training at Huntsville, where I was a crew chief and maintenance support," Ford explained.

"You know, I had a few friends at the Academy that went that route—being flyers."

"Oh yeah?" asked Ford. "What were their names? Maybe I ran across them."

"Love, Hannigan, and Alden."

Ford whistled and shook his head. "Yeah, I ran across them. Love seems like she's a gifted flyer, a natural-born pilot. Same with Hannigan."

Before they could talk further, Lee received an alert.

"I'm sorry. I'm needed on the bridge, ASAP. I have to dash."

"No worries. Nice to meet you," said Ford. "I'm sure we'll see each other around."

****

As soon as he arrived on the bridge, Commander Morris barked at Lee, "Get to your station!" He started the battle drill immediately. "Let's see if the Academy taught you anything useful."

Lee walked around the tiers of consoles to reach his position at the weapons control station. It was situated to the right of Commander Morris's platform. From this point, he had a clear view of the main viewscreen and could easily communicate with both Morris and the other tactical officers. How close he was to Morris, who stood in the middle, and Captain Oldendorf, who occupied the captain's chair, made Lee aware of the scrutiny he was under.

Lee activated his console. The interface sprang to life—an array of holographic controls and readouts. His station was the nerve center for the ship's weapons systems. In his Academy training, weapons theory had been one of his strongest subjects—the calculations, trajectories, and firing solutions coming to him as naturally as breathing. Still, he couldn't help but wish he'd had the full rest of the school year to master these systems.

He started by bringing the primary offensive systems online. He manipulated the controls as he powered up the two twelve-inch twin-barrel ship-to-ship magrail gun turrets. These weapons, located along the dorsal side of the ship, were capable of accelerating massive projectiles to relativistic speeds using electromagnetic rails. Manned by teams of ten personnel each, along with eight synthetic AI units for targeting, the magrail turrets were the *Trenton*'s heavy hitters. And Lee knew all about them, having studied them in class.

Next, Lee activated the eighteen 30mm quad-barrel point-defense guns (PDGs) strategically placed around the ship's hull. Each fired high-velocity projectiles equipped with high-explosive fragmentation warheads. The proximity fuses would detonate when within effective range of incoming threats, creating shrapnel fields to intercept missiles and fighters. These turrets were operated by crews of three to four personnel, aided by Synths to manage tracking and firing solutions.

He then brought the Vertical Launch Systems (VLSs) online. The *Trenton* boasted four VLS units loaded with forty-two Havoc-II armored-tip antiship missiles each. These missiles were designed to pierce enemy hulls before delivering their explosive payloads. Additionally, the VLS contained electronic warfare decoy missiles and a limited number of Trident-V variable-yield nuclear warheads for extreme situations.

Another four VLS units held seventy-two missile interceptors each. It formed the *Trenton*'s primary defense against enemy missile attacks. Lee made sure that all missile systems reported ready, with munitions counts verified and targeting systems calibrated.

"Lieutenant Lee!" Morris's tone was thick. "Status of your section?"

"All weapons systems online and at full readiness, sir," Lee replied. "Magrail turrets charged and tracking, point-defense guns calibrated, missile systems primed and ready. Defensive screens are powering up."

Morris moved to stand directly behind him. "This is a full combat-readiness assessment," he announced to the bridge. "I want all weapons systems hot, defensive screens up, and targeting solutions prepared. We're already fifteen seconds behind optimal response time. Move it, people!"

Sweat droplets formed on Lee's brow, but he maintained his composure. His eyes flicked across the tactical displays as simulated enemy contacts began to appear—a standard part of the drill designed to test their response under pressure.

"Scenario initiating," Morris declared. "Multiple hostile contacts approaching from bearing zero-four-two, mark eleven. Show me how you'd handle it, Lieutenant."

The tactical display lit up with red markers representing enemy vessels at the edge of sensor range. Lee assessed the simulated threats— a formation of enemy frigates escorting a destroyer.

He input commands, prioritizing targets. "Designating destroyer as primary threat," he said. "Assigning magrail turrets for long-range engagement. Setting firing solutions to compensate for enemy evasive maneuvers."

"Standard procedure," Morris commented. "What if they deploy countermeasures?"

"We increase power to the targeting systems to burn through it, and we launch our electronic warfare decoy missiles to try and overwhelm their own jamming efforts," replied Lee without missing a beat.

"That's right. Maybe you did learn something at the Academy." Morris seemed impressed. "Now back to the situation—counteract their jamming and prepare to fight."

"Affirmative. Preparing to launch electronic warfare decoy missiles." Lee adjusted the VLS settings, preparing a couple of EW missiles. His fingers danced across the controls. "Activating point-defense guns to automatic tracking for incoming fighters and missiles. EW missiles prepared to fire."

"Commander, multiple new contacts detected!" called out the sensor officer. "Bearing one-seven-nine, mark four! Sir, I count three, scratch that—two additional frigates and a second destroyer."

Morris leaned closer. "What do you do now, Lieutenant? The standard protocol the Academy taught you is compromised. Adapt—what do you do next?"

Lee's mind ticked faster. The enemy was attempting a pincer movement that was going to place half his main guns out of position to fire on the enemy. Thinking quickly, he began to realign the ship's weapons to adjust for the changing trajectory of the enemy ships. "I'm redistributing the number of missile interceptors to cover the gap in point-defense coverage," he explained, his fingers moving across his station. "Next, I'm adjusting the point-defense coverage sectors to account for the additional frigates and destroyers and the added weapons the targeting systems will have to account for. Lastly, I'm reassigning magrail turret beta to engage the second destroyer."

"Missile launch detected from both enemy destroyers." The warning came from multiple stations as new alarms sounded.

"Countermeasures?" Morris asked.

"Engaging rolling defensive screens," Lee responded. "Launching interceptor missiles now. Point-defense guns are tracking the incoming threats and will engage any missiles that penetrate our outer defenses."

Lee manipulated the interface to fine-tune the engagement parameters. He adjusted the firing arcs of the magrail turrets, aligning them for optimal impact on the enemy cruisers, and monitored the status of the Havoc-II missiles. They were locked onto their targets and ready to fire.

"Commander Morris, the enemy frigates are breaking formation and accelerating toward us," reported the helmsman as the new trajectory showed the frigates would pass dangerously close to the *Trenton*.

Lee connected through to the point-defense teams along the starboard side. "This is the bridge. Frigates approaching the starboard side of the ship. Prepare PDGs for close-in defense—switch to penetrators. Focus on the lead vessel, and initiate staggered PDG firing to maintain a continuous barrage."

Captain Oldendorf stepped beside Morris. "Lieutenant Lee," he said, "what's your strategy to deal with the frigates while still engaging the cruisers?"

"Sir," Lee replied, "by switching PDG ammo from proximity to penetrators, I can now delegate the point-defense guns to engage the frigates closing in on us, relying on automated targeting protocols enhanced by Synth assistance to cut those frigates apart. This allows us to maintain focus on the cruisers with our primary weapons. I'm also going to deploy our electronic warfare decoys to further disrupt enemy targeting and communication."

Oldendorf nodded, appearing impressed by the new Academy grad. "Ballsy, Lieutenant, but I'll bite. Let's see how this works. Proceed."

The simulated battle intensified. Lee continuously adjusted the defensive screens' modulation to counter the enemy missile frequencies. He monitored the capacitor levels for the magrail turrets, making sure they remained within operational limits despite the rapid firing rates.

"Engineering reports power fluctuations due to high weapons output," came the operations officer.

"Lieutenant, how do we handle the increase demand without degrading our ability to fight?" Morris quizzed.

Lee thought for a moment, then acted. "We compensate by rerouting nonessential power to weapons systems." He slid the dial up on the power distribution interface.

"Enemy destroyers are attempting to flank us," Morris said. "Options?"

Lee thought quickly. "Suggest performing a lateral thrust maneuver and bringing all forward weapons to bear on both destroyers simultaneously."

Oldendorf glanced at Morris, then back at Lee. "Helm, execute Lieutenant Lee's maneuver."

"Aye, sir," the helmsman acknowledged.

The bridge swayed slightly as the *Trenton* adjusted course. Lee capitalized on the new positioning, assigning additional Havoc-II missiles to each destroyer and adjusting firing solutions for the magrail turrets.

"Missiles away," Lee said. "Magrail turrets firing at maximum effective range."

"Enemy destroyers attempting evasive maneuvers," the sensor officer reported.

"Adjusting target lead times." Lee input new calculations. "Predictive algorithms updated."

The simulated weapons found their marks. Explosions blossomed on the tactical display as enemy vessels were hit but not out for the count.

Morris shared a glance with Oldendorf, then straightened as he addressed the bridge. "End simulation."

The tactical display cleared, returning to normal status. Lee felt relieved the sim was over, and judging by the looks of the others around him, he wasn't the only one.

Morris cleared his throat as addressed the crew. "Four minutes, twenty-six seconds. Not awful, but not great. Tactical response was..." His gaze settled on Lee. "Adequate. Lieutenant Lee, it's your first week on the job, so I'll cut you some slack. Your initial response was textbook—perhaps too textbook. However, your adaptability showed promise, and we can hone that further. Your quick thinking to turn the PDGs into an offensive weapon, swapping out the proximity warheads with penetrators was a novel idea—albeit of limited effectiveness, but it'll work in a pinch. The quick thinking to redirect power immediately to the guns when it was needed most was particularly well executed."

As the rest of the bridge crew powered down their consoles, Morris said, "All stations, review your performance logs. I want full analysis reports by 1700 tonight. Dismissed."

Captain Oldendorf remained near his chair, clearly observing. His eyes met Lee's for a brief moment. There was a hint of approval in his gaze.

As the crew filed out, Morris called after Lee, "Lieutenant Lee, a moment."

Lee stood at attention. "Sir?"

"That lateral thrust maneuver and power redistribution—not standard Academy training. Where did you pick that up?"

"Advanced Tactical Operations, sir. Professor Chambers's extended curriculum. He emphasized thinking beyond standard responses and adapting to dynamic situations."

A slight nod from Morris. "Chambers is a good instructor. But remember, Lieutenant, real combat isn't like the simulations. When we reach Rhea Ab, there won't be any reset buttons. Keep that in mind during your next shift—I'm going to place you on nights for a little while so we can drill you more before moving you back to day shift."

"Yes, sir. Thank you, sir."

As Lee turned to leave, he felt a presence by his side. He looked up to see Captain Oldendorf.

"Lieutenant," Oldendorf said. "Not a bad performance for your first battle drill. But there's room for improvement."

"I understand, sir."

"Good. Pay attention to Commander Morris's guidance. He knows what he's doing. Dismissed."

"Yes, sir."

As Lee left the bridge, he knew he hadn't excelled. He hadn't failed either. At least that was good. Real combat might be an FTL trip away, but these drills would come again and again during the voyage to New Eden. They'd sharpen his skills. When they finally encountered the Zodarks, he intended to be ready.

Chapter 13
Point of No Return

Year 2091
RNS *Trenton*
Earth Orbit

Lee sat in the chair opposite Captain Oldendorf's desk. Framed commendations and medals lined the walls in the captain's office. A model of the RNS *Trenton* rested on a mahogany shelf. Behind Oldendorf, the holowindow displayed space. There, Earth's curvature was visible against the black.

Oldendorf's folded hands rested atop a leather-bound logbook. "Lieutenant Lee. We're set to make the FTL jump today. I trust you're ready."

"Aye, sir," Lee replied.

"We've obviously had a lot of change the past few weeks as we get ready to head back to New Eden. A lot of people have had to step into new roles and leadership positions they weren't ready for, but that's the thing about war. It stretches you—forces you to have to make tough decisions and learn to live with them," Oldendorf explained. "This is why I've been meeting with the ship's officers to ensure we're all on the same page. What we're about to face is unlike anything we've encountered. This is the first time humans will battle in space. Out here, we're confined to this ship. There's no running from a fight, only confronting it head-on."

Lee nodded. "Understood."

"The enemy we'll face, the Zodarks—they're... deadly. I guess *formidable* is a more appropriate word. But I have confidence in this crew. Confidence in you. When things get intense—and they will—you stick to your training. Trust in your team. No one is ever truly ready for war, but preparedness and grit will carry us through. I'll continue to remind you and the crew throughout our FTL travel." Oldendorf leaned back slightly. "Do you have any questions?"

"Yes, sir," Lee said. "Can I speak freely?"

"You may."

"Why did you choose me for the *Trenton*? There are others with more experience, especially for a war."

"Experience isn't just about time served, Lieutenant. It's about character. I read something about you in your personnel file from your time prior to you attending the Academy. Commander Jones highlighted a couple of skills he saw in you back in Mexico—resourcefulness and tenacity. Those are qualities we need for officers serving aboard warships. What you have is not something that can be readily taught. Plus, you've shown remarkable growth while attending the Academy."

"Thank you, sir."

"Your tactical instincts are exceptional, and you have a natural gift for understanding weapons systems and how best to employ them. But more than that, I see leadership potential in you. Raw, untested, but it's there."

"Leadership, sir?"

"You're among the most promising officers I've seen. You're not ready to command yet—that takes time and experience—but I intend to accelerate your development faster than any captain in the fleet. It's another reason I chose you. The Republic needs more officers with your capabilities, but they're rare. Very rare."

In truth, Lee didn't understand what Oldendorf saw in him, so it was hard to believe. Nonetheless, he wouldn't question his superior. "Thank you, sir. What's your take on the mission ahead? Beyond the official briefings."

Oldendorf gazed out the holoport for a moment. "The mission is critical. New Eden is a beacon for humanity's future, and the Zodarks threaten that. Our role is to protect that future. When I say future, I don't just mean our advancement as a species. I mean our freedom as a race too. As it turns out, the more intel I receive, the more I learn that the Zodarks are a species devoted to enslaving and subjugating all races they come in contact with. It was no accident they engaged our forces during their first meeting with the Republic.

"It seems they look at all races as a threat… perhaps. Nonetheless, our species wouldn't be an exception to their slaughter, to their enslavement. And throughout our history, we've dealt with slavery. This time, we meet it fist to face to cut the head off before it starts chewing, if you know what I mean. It won't be easy. There'll be long days of training ahead. But every drill, every simulation prepares us."

"Understood, sir."

Oldendorf stood. "Good. The fleet will be leaving soon. Head to the bridge and take your station. I'll join shortly."

"Aye, sir." Lee rose, giving a salute.

Exiting the office, Lee made his way down the corridor. As he rounded a corner, he nearly collided with Brian Ford.

"Whoa!" Ford's toolkit clanked as he adjusted it on his shoulder. Machine oil and plasma coolant wafted from his maintenance uniform. "Easy there, sir. In a hurry?"

"Just came from a meeting with Captain Oldendorf," Lee replied. "Heading to the bridge. What about you?"

"Off to the hangar bay. Got some systems to check before the jump."

They fell into step together. In the distance, the muffled sound of pressurized doors opening and closing marked the movement of other crew members through the ship's arteries.

"Hey, have you heard anything about Love and Hannigan?" Ford asked. "I haven't received any messages."

Lee raised an eyebrow. "You didn't get the news?"

"No. What's up?"

"They got married." Lee grinned.

"You're not pulling my leg?"

"Nope. Quick ceremony at a courthouse in Vegas."

"Married? Seriously?"

"Yeah. And they're stationed at Peterson Space Force Base in Colorado Springs. Assigned to Earth-based operations with the Republic's Transportation Command."

"Guess that means they'll be safe. Sticking to local routes. Good."

"Makes sense," Lee said. "Novice pilots usually start with the Earth-orbital runs before heading into deep space. Plus, with the wartime supply lines, they need reliable pilots back home."

"One less thing to worry about," Ford said.

"Exactly. We'll have enough on our plates soon enough."

The corridor opened into a four-way junction. Yellow safety stripes were painted on the deck and emergency lighting panels were set into the corners. The different atmospheric pressures from connecting passages created a soft cross-breeze. Warning signs glowed on the bulkheads. Their paths diverged at this intersection. Ford headed toward the hangar deck, while Lee's route led to the bridge access corridor.

"Take care, Ford," Lee said.

"You too."

As Ford hurried toward the hangar, Lee continued to the bridge. Upon reaching the doors, he straightened his uniform and pressed the access panel. The bridge's Type-7 blast doors, reinforced with triple-layered titanium and designed to maintain atmospheric integrity even under direct fire, slid open.

"Permission to enter the bridge?" Lee stood at attention.

Commander Morris glanced up from his station. "Granted. Take your post, Lieutenant."

"Yes, sir." Lee stepped onto the bridge, moving to his tactical station beside Morris. His console came to life, displaying *Trenton*'s arsenal—fore and aft magrail batteries capable of accelerating projectiles to .15c, or fifteen percent of the speed of light, point-defense laser arrays with microsecond targeting capabilities, and the newly installed defense grid that could track up to one thousand incoming threats at the same time.

Around him, officers and crew members finalized preparations for the jump. The soft chirping of system alerts mixed with the rapid-fire clicking of fingers on haptic interfaces. Screens displayed an abundance of data—navigation charts spinning in rotations, cascading systems diagnostics in emerald text, and communication logs scrolling forever. The coffee station in the corner released the fresh brew's aroma.

The main viewscreen curved across the forward bulkhead. Its high-resolution display created a window-like effect. The Republic's docking yard filled most of the view, its skeletal framework of metal and plastics sprawled out like a massive stadium. Maintenance drones moved among the station's support struts. Beyond, Earth hung against the black, resembling a blue marble wrapped in swirling white clouds. The sight made Lee's shoulders tighten—it would be the last time he'd see home for a long while.

Moments later, the doors opened again. "Captain on the bridge," announced the communications officer.

"Carry on," Oldendorf replied, striding to his chair.

Morris turned to him. "All stations report ready, Captain."

Oldendorf nodded. "Open a channel to the fleet."

"Channel open to the RNS *Rook* and accompanying ships," the communications officer confirmed.

The viewscreen morphed to display Captain Miles Hunt of the RNS *Rook*. Hunt's face filled the screen, his own bridge behind him.

"All ships report ready for departure, Captain Hunt," Oldendorf said. "We're set to proceed on your mark."

"Understood, Captain Oldendorf," Hunt replied. "The *Rook* is ready. We'll take point formation."

"Affirmative. See you on the other side. *Trenton* out."

The screen returned to the external view. Oldendorf glanced around the bridge. "Helm, initiate undocking procedures."

"Aye, sir. Releasing docking clamps. Engaging thrusters."

A subtle shift shook the bridge as the ship disengaged from the station. The docking arms retracted, and the *Trenton* eased away from the structure.

"Set course for FTL jump point beta," Oldendorf said.

"Course laid in," the navigator confirmed.

The main viewscreen changed to show their destination. Jump point beta blinked like a distant beacon. The RNS *Rook*, flagship of the fleet, dominated the foreground. The battlecruiser's hull stretched far and wide, its reinforced armor plates gleaming under Earth's reflected light. Behind it, the RNS *Voyager*'s profile was unmistakable—the orbital assault ship's broad landing bays and giant troop deployment sections exhibited her unique role in the fleet. A protective screen of destroyers maintained their escort positions, while the smaller frigates patrolled the formation's perimeter.

"All stations, begin final prejump checks." A cascade of new sounds filled the command center—the rapid-fire clicking of controls, the soft chimes of system confirmations, and the low murmur of crew members running through their checklists. The environmental systems kicked up a notch, pushing cooler air through the vents to compensate for the heat generated by the increased system activity.

"Lieutenant Lee," Morris said. "Everything squared away?"

"Yes, sir. Tactical systems are green across the board."

"Good." Morris gave a rare, slight nod.

"Captain," the helmsman reported, "we're approaching jump point beta."

The main viewscreen automatically adjusted its display parameters, compensating for the spatial distortions preceding FTL flight. Tiny fluctuations in the artificial gravity field created a subtle sensation of movement, like standing on the deck of a ship just before a large wave hits.

"Very well," Oldendorf said. "Initiate jump sequence on my mark. Communications, signal the fleet we're synchronizing jump sequence."

"Fleet acknowledges," the communications officer replied.

Oldendorf stood, his gaze on the viewscreen. The vastness of space lay before them, stars shining like stabilized flashlights.

"All hands," Oldendorf announced over the ship-wide intercom, "prepare for FTL jump in ten seconds."

Lee's mouth went dry as he braced himself. He gripped the edges of his console. His palms were slick against the metal surface. The tactical display before him showed their fleet in formation—six ships arranged as blue icons in a geometric pattern. Lee had experienced simulated jumps during training, but this would be his first real one. Nerves belted his insides.

"Ten… nine… eight…" The countdown echoed through the bridge.

Each number resounded in Lee's mind like a farewell. Ten seconds until he left everything he knew behind. Nine seconds until he truly became a space warfare officer. Eight seconds until he faced an enemy humanity had just recently encountered. His training told him he was ready, but a voice deep inside whispered doubts he couldn't silence at the moment.

"Seven… six… five…"

Lee's heartbeat matched the rhythm of the count.

"Four… three… two… one… engage."

The deck plates beneath Lee's feet vibrated as the massive FTL drives spooled up. A deep thrum resonated through *Trenton*'s hull, starting as a low-frequency rumble and building into a penetrating hum. Lee's very bones rattled. The air itself was charged with static electricity, making the fine hairs on his arms stand.

A high-pitched whine built throughout the bridge as the stars on the viewscreen elongated into streaks of light. The view distorted like a digital painting being stretched, colors bleeding into one another at impossible angles. An odd sensation came over Lee—as if every atom in his body was being gently pulled apart and reassembled. His stomach lurched, and for an instant, time seemed to lose all meaning.

The ship surged forward, and the starfield transformed into a swirling tunnel of light. Colors he had no names for blossomed at the edges of his vision. Stars burst into fractals of illumination, then collapsed back into pinpoints, only to explode again in new configurations. Earth, home, everything he knew, fell away behind them at impossible speeds.

Through the disorientation, Lee maintained his focus on his tactical display. The readings seemed to swim before his eyes. He heard Morris's steady breathing beside him, felt the movement of the deck beneath his feet, anchoring him to reality as they crossed the threshold between normal space and the realm of faster-than-light travel.

"FTL transition complete," the helmsman announced, his voice seeming to come from very far away. "All systems nominal. Currently in FTL space."

"Status of the fleet?" Oldendorf asked.

"All ships present and accounted for," Communications reported. "The *Rook* confirms successful transition into FTL space."

Lee released his grip on his console. His first FTL jump had left him tingling all over. They were truly leaving Earth behind now and heading into the unknown. Whatever waited for them at New Eden, there was no turning back.

Chapter 14
Champagne and Combat

2 Years of War Later

Year 2093
Blue Horizon Meridian Transport Vessel
Rhea System, New Eden Stargate

Lieutenant Naomi Love sipped her Taittinger Comtes de Champagne. The bubbles fizzed on her tongue. The taste hinted that it came from the vineyards of France, but with a twist. To Love, it was out-of-this-world good.

Love and her husband, Jack Hannigan, sat nestled together on a bench seat in the observation deck of a civilian vessel. It was a cozy space decorated with comfortable seating.

Before them, a small holoport displayed a view of the FTL jump's twirling colors just outside. The chromas cast a glow and colored the room in shifting hues. Next to them, an older couple kept each other company. The rest of the seats in the room remained empty, and all the better. Crowds gave Love the jitters.

After they clinked their glasses in a toast, Love and Jack watched the FTL spectacle. It was beautiful. This was Love's first opportunity to use faster-than-light travel—and there was nothing like it in the known universe.

Love relaxed deeper in the seat. She couldn't remember the last time she'd been on a civilian transport, let alone on one with Jack. It felt good to be close to him, to have some private time for a change. With assistance from an Academy friend now in naval logistics at Fleet Headquarters, they'd secured a waiver to travel on a luxurious commercial transport, avoiding the standard military vessels to which junior officers and enlisted personnel were typically assigned.

Jack crossed one leg over the other and draped an arm around Love. He pointed at the window. "You see, this isn't ordinary glass. It's a composite of transparent aluminum and synthetic sapphire, able to withstand the stresses of FTL travel. The tech behind it is quite fascinating, actually."

Love rolled her eyes. "You say the most romantic things."

"Hey, that's one of the perks of marrying a pilot with an engineering degree." Jack grinned.

"Touché." Love winked and leaned in for a kiss. Their lips touched for longer than she expected.

"Are you two excited?" a woman asked, the one sitting on the other couch with her own travel companion. Her curly red hair cascaded down to her shoulders. With her pearly white teeth and good skin, she looked to be in her mid to late sixties

Love, still in an embrace, looked at the lady. "Excited for what, ma'am?"

"You're newlyweds, correct? Moving to New Eden?"

This woman is a bit nosy. "Not newlyweds. Married for three years."

The woman's hazel eyes twinkled with amusement. "Do you have children?"

"We've discussed it. I'm thinking in a few years?"

Jack shrugged. "Who knows? Maybe we start trying tonight."

Love jabbed him in the side with her elbow. "Yeah, you wish."

The older woman thumbed to the guy sitting next to her. "Ort and I have been together for forty-eight years. We've got five children and fourteen grandchildren. When you have kids, it'll change life for the better. Trust me. It's instant unconditional love."

Forty-eight years?

Love lifted her glass to the couple. "Congratulations."

Hannigan stood. "Well, if you'll excuse me, I gotta find myself a restroom. I'll return shortly, darlin'."

His fake Tennessee drawl always made Love's heart flutter. Sometimes he spoke in accents when around other people he didn't know, not because he was shy, but because he was Jack Hannigan. Not a weirdo, but he had an interesting sense of humor that not many got. Luckily for Love, she was one of the few who understood, and it rubbed her the right way.

She bade him farewell and turned to the curious lady. "So, what's your secret to a long marriage?"

"Compromise," she said without hesitation. "Most people like to say love, but that goes without saying. You can love anyone, but if you don't compromise, you don't last."

"Interesting." Love leaned closer. "Got any tips on how to compromise effectively?"

"Sure. First, listen more than you speak. Understanding your partner's perspective is the foundation of compromise. Second, prioritize the relationship over your ego; sometimes being right isn't as important as being happy together. And third, always seek a solution that benefits both sides. It's not about one person winning and the other losing. It's about finding a balance where both feel respected and valued."

Surprised by the woman's quick and insightful response, Love said, "You sound like you're a counselor."

She laughed. "Good catch. I've been a marriage and relationship counselor most of my life." She threw a dismissive hand. "Anyway, I'm boring. Enough about me. Now, I thought for sure you two were models on an upcoming photo shoot at the New Eden beaches. Where'd you both meet?"

"At the Naval Academy in Colorado Springs. Took him years to ask me to marry him, but I was overjoyed when he did."

"You're in the military?"

"We're both Osprey pilots for the Republic Navy. We've been reassigned to an Osprey squadron set to be stationed on New Eden. We'll be supporting operations there, helping to secure the planet from the remaining Zodark holdouts."

Around a year and a half ago, the Republic had launched a major offensive to seize control of the planet New Eden. After an aerial bombardment and intense ground battles, the Earthers had emerged victorious. They'd driven out the Zodarks' main military forces from the planet's surface and secured orbital dominance.

However, a faction of the defeated Zodarks refused to surrender. Instead, they transitioned into an unconventional guerrilla insurgency where they employed hit-and-run tactics by exploiting the planet's rugged terrain. It worked well and had since persisted. It was an ongoing threat to the Republic's efforts to build cities, infrastructures, and population centers without worry.

In the aftermath of the invasion, the Republic's mission to liberate the indigenous population—previously enslaved and exploited as forced labor by the Zodark regime—was successful. These liberated natives, the "Sumerians," had since regained their autonomy. They'd been granted protected status under the Republic's administration, something Love couldn't be happier about.

Ort lowered the book he was reading, acknowledging their service with a respectful nod before getting back to the words.

"So, you two are joining the new colonies at New Eden?" Love asked.

"Yes, we are. Ort is a civil engineer, his company is involved with the new government on the planet. There is a lot of new construction happening as you have probably heard. This is our first time off Earth, and first time doing something adventurous like this. We may be getting up there in age, but what an opportunity to start a new life, right?" The woman beamed with excitement.

"Yeah, it sure is. That's neat you guys are part of building something new on New Eden. I've seen holovids of the planet. It's gorgeous."

A lurch hit Love's stomach as the civilian transport exited FTL jump. Streaks of light twirled across the holo-viewport until they came together into a star-studded display of actual space. She gasped from the physiological reaction to reentering normal space without warning and also from the unnerving vista unfolding before her.

She leaned forward. *What is that?*

Far away, orange and white flashes burst in the void and around the stars. Lights streaked. Colors exploded.

She stood and moved closer. *No, it can't be.*

As she squinted, a sickening feeling told her something was wrong. They were supposed to exit FTL near New Eden, not the stargate. Then it dawned on her what she was looking at, and she knew they were in trouble.

I'm watching a damn fleet battle.

Battle at the Stargate

Year 2093
RNS *Kentucky*
Rhea System, New Eden Stargate

Explosions bloomed and lit up space like vengeful angels descending upon the battle. On the main viewscreen, bursts peppered a large vessel's hull in the distance. Its armor was shredded apart by massive secondary eruptions before it practically disintegrated under the onslaught. What was left floated dead in the dark expanse.

"Sir, we lost the *Monroe*," TAO Lee said, his words drowned out by tremors shaking the vessel. A second direct hit by the enemy sent another set of vibrations through the floor of the bridge. Its deck plates groaned.

Lee perched at his tactical station on the *Kentucky*, a Republic Navy *Ryan*-class battleship. Captain James Oldendorf sat to his right in the captain's chair. Fear passed over Oldendorf's expression, something Lee had never witnessed. In the next instant, Oldendorf's face turned stern, confident.

For the last two years, Lee had worked under his mentor, Captain James Oldendorf, learning the ins and outs of captaining, the ups and downs of battle, and how to navigate through it all without showing any doubt. Oldendorf had taught him to cast more confidence outward than he felt, as this was necessary to maintain the crew's morale and trust.

Since that time, they'd gone from the RNS *Trenton* to the RNS *Kentucky*, upgrading to a more advanced ship. The *Kentucky* could take more devastating hits and return fire with even greater force.

Through it all, Oldendorf kept Lee by his side, battle after battle, sharing both the difficult lessons of warfare and the sweet nectar of victory. Each engagement left its bruises, some visible, some not, but all of them making Lee a stronger officer.

Lee's first combat engagement had occurred in 2091, when the fleet had arrived in the New Eden system. Fresh out of faster-than-light travel, the fleet had engaged the Zodarks in a nasty fight for control of the system. When victory came, it came hard and fast, and with a cost. The RNS *Trenton* and her sister ships paid for it with heavy damage, and the number of casualties had almost burned a hole in Lee's heart.

From that time forward, he'd learned to protect his heart, to protect his sanity. There are some things you remember, and other things you force yourself to forget, whether you shove it under a rug and walk around it no matter how many times you see it, or you keep it in front of you like a mirror, haunted by it every day.

Lee preferred keeping it out of sight and, when it came to mind, to amble around it like it wasn't there.

Oldendorf turned to his XO. "Garcia, damage report."

"Captain, we've sustained significant damage to our aft section," Garcia said. "Our offensive capabilities are severely compromised at half capacity."

Lee swallowed the turmoil clawing inside of him. The close combat ignited a deep fear along with a surge of nervous adrenaline. The two clashed within him, and he told himself to calm his emotions. Thing was, it never worked, even when he was resting in his berth between battles.

"Lieutenant Lee, reroute secondary power to our weapons array," the captain said.

"Aye, sir." Lee tapped on the holo hovering above his console. A picture of the RNS *Kentucky* appeared as he redirected power. On his interface, it showed hull breaches in sectors seven through nine. Armor integrity across critical sections averaged twenty-three percent. Some areas were heavily compromised. Primary weapons systems were dropping under half capacity.

Lee leveled his shoulders. His gaze locked onto the screen, ready to steer the fate of the *Kentucky* with his willpower alone. Around him, the bridge was bedlam. Officers and crew members sat at their stations, working at a frantic pace. They read data, analyzed incoming reports, and coordinated responses like a well-oiled machine. Each station served as a node in the neural network of the battleship. All personnel, from navigation to engineering to weapons control, worked together, communication near perfect and in sync.

Captain Oldendorf sat in his command chair. "Reynolds, fire up the secondary maneuvering engines, starboard, now. Bearing two-seven-one, azimuth minus sixteen degrees."

"Aye, Captain," the navigator said.

The main display changed as the *Kentucky* swung toward the starboard forward quarter. The colossal New Eden stargate came into view 8,612 kilometers away. Like the few other stargates humanity had discovered scattered across known space, it remained an enigma—a remnant of some long-vanished civilization that had mastered faster-than-light travel. Massive interlocking rings of a silver alloy shaped the gate and bore patterns of an advanced technology that even humanity's best scientists couldn't decipher. A pulsating blue light radiated from its core. It sent an ethereal glow in all directions. Arcs of electricity sparked across the stargate's surface.

These stargates had become one of humanity's highways among the stars. They catapulted ships across long distances in the blink of an eye and connected a growing network of sectors the Republic was still exploring. Who had built them, and why they'd abandoned them, remained one of the greatest mysteries.

At 1545 yesterday, intelligence had tipped off the Republic Navy about several enemy ships preparing to jump through this gate. In response, the RNS *George Washington*, the Earthers' largest warship, led a swift assembly of forces to mount an ambush. The Republic Navy hastily built stationary weapon platforms near the stargate to create a dangerous perimeter. These defenses bristled with missiles and magrail turrets. It was all designed to catch the Zodarks off guard when those blue giants, and their warships, emerged from the gate.

On *Kentucky*'s main viewscreen, it showed fiery trails of projectiles speeding through space and toward a Republic Navy ship 6,236 kilometers to the *Kentucky*'s fore. When they hit, blasts enveloped a Republic flak frigate. Unable to evade the assault, it was destroyed, internal explosions tearing through it and cracking it apart.

"We just lost the *Defiant*, sir!" The words left Lee, sounding distant and numb.

Everywhere, enemy vessels scattered across space. The Republic Navy had reduced some ships to mere clouds of debris. Masses of metallic carcasses drifted in silence. These once-mighty vessels now resembled nothing more than dead wood caught in the current of a dark, uncaring sea.

Lee's console flashed brighter as an enemy ship slid behind them at 4,900 kilometers off their aft port quadrant. His station's interface identified it as an enemy battleship, a Zodark behemoth of war stretching 2,130 meters from stern to bow, armed with twelve lasers and six plasma torpedo launchers. Its lasers lanced out and carved massive holes through the armor of the RNS *Iowa* 5,500 kilometers off *Kentucky*'s starboard. The giant battleship was engaged in a struggle for survival. The hostiles' assault blasted through the Republic ship's armor. Charred metal peeled away from the vessel.

The *Iowa* retaliated, its twenty-four-inch magrail guns lashing out and striking the foe's scalelike green hull. The shells, set to detonate with a delay, burrowed through the armor before unleashing their fury.

As the exchange of fire intensified, the *Iowa* let loose a volley from its quad-barrel magrail guns. The projectiles hurtled through the blackness all around. Several found their targets and rattled the Zodark ship with detonations, busting open its port side. The breach exposed a critical vulnerability beneath the Zodark ship's tough exterior.

Lee's eyes narrowed as his console's targeting system highlighted a perfect opportunity. The calculations pinpointed a direct path to the Zodarks' main power core. A well-placed magrail round from the *Kentucky*'s own arsenal could disable the enemy vessel altogether.

Captain Oldendorf faced Lee. "Lee, give me a firing solution."

"Captain, I've locked in targeting coordinates on the Zodarks' main power core," Lee said. "A precision strike with our magrail could incapacitate the battleship. Recommend we align for an optimal shot. Distance three thousand, six hundred and fifty-nine kilometers."

It was close range, where the Republic Navy's powerful kinetic weapons had the advantage. It was how the Republic usually won naval engagements—up close and personal.

"Reynolds, set course to vector two-four-five port, pitch minus five degrees," Oldendorf ordered. "Steady as she goes." Without missing a beat, the captain turned to the tactical station. "Lee, confirm magrails are charged. Be ready to fire on my command."

"Aye, sir," Lee said. "Confirmed."

While the *Kentucky* veered toward port, Lee focused on his interface. The weapons targeting system locked onto the glaring fault in the Zodark battleship's armor.

"Fire!" Captain Oldendorf yelled.

The bridge trembled as the magrail guns fired their high-density projectiles. Rounds streaked across space similar to meteors on a destructive path. The Zodark craft adjusted her bearing to port and moved along a dorsal vector. The maneuver caused each magrail tungsten round to veer off course—some missing by slim margins, others kissing the reinforced armor encasing the battleship's critical breach, doing little damage.

The captain ran calculations on his interface. "Recalibrate targeting, adjust point three degrees, pitch ventral point two degrees."

"Adjusting, sir!" Lee said. A moment took eons as he manipulated the coordinates on his holo. "Recalibrated and locked. Ready to engage on your command, Captain!"

Oldendorf raised his chin. "Fire!"

Rounds blazed toward the adversary. They missed, the rounds' fleeting luminescence dwindling into nothingness as the emptiness of space swallowed them whole.

Oldendorf made a fist. "Adjust fire control, recalibrate targeting systems, and engage again!"

"Aye, Captain." Lee input fresh targeting data, but as they fired, the Zodark vessel executed an evasive maneuver. Another volley went astray and struck scattered debris from destroyed ships.

Across from Lee, the XO's console lit up Garcia's face. The XO glanced at Oldendorf. "Hostile ship maneuvering into position on our stern starboard side."

"They're aligning too close to our flank," said Lieutenant Lucia Rodriguez at the communications console.

Lee punched in targeting coordinates. "The incoming hostiles are bearing vector one-six-eight by zero-two-four, with a negative pitch relative to our plane and locking on."

"Redirect reserve power to the stern auxiliary thrusters at maximum intensity. Launch countermeasures," Oldendorf said. Seemingly fine with the new threat, he kept his eyes on the Zodark battleship they'd been attacking. "Maintain fire on current target. Brace for impact."

The *Kentucky* rocked from a hit. Klaxons blared. Lights blinked off and on. Lee's restraining belt pulled him tighter into his seat. He held his gaze on the vessel blasting at them. "Two more incoming torpedoes!"

"Brace!" Oldendorf yelled.

Lee's systems illuminated to show critical issues emerging throughout their ship.

Another shot struck the *Kentucky*, and the bridge quaked. A hiss pierced the air. Lights powered off and died. Metal groaned against metal. An object struck Lee across the face, sparking a shower of stars at the edge of his vision.

When the lights blinked back on, Lee touched his temple, feeling blood. A small beam lay next to him. The emergency lights filled the area in red. Lee's gaze went to the captain's chair, and he froze. "Captain!"

A thick beam had impaled Oldendorf's abdomen, his hands gripping it tightly, his face contorted in agony.

Nearby, blood covered the XO's face. The man dangled lifelessly from his straps, head bowed, eyes open and vacant—dead. Several lieutenants seemed just as lifeless, propped upright only by their restraints. Crimson liquid covered them, and large beams lay beside them, leaving dents in the floor. Smoke billowed from the ceiling, clouding the bridge.

Lee keyed into the comm. "Medical, we need a team here immediately!"

"Affirmative, sir," came the reply.

Lee patched into Chief Engineer Boyd MacGregor. "We have a fire on Deck 7, above the bridge. Immediate response required, over."

MacGregor's reply came fast. "Acknowledged, sending fire suppression teams to Deck 7. Propulsion systems compromised, situation critical. We're on top of the repairs."

Lee and Oldendorf's eyes met as Lee unstrapped himself and made his way toward the captain. The ship lurched, forcing Lee to grasp the edge of a station to stay upright. The communications officer, Rodriguez, watched him, eyes wide. They were both fully aware of the captain's horrendous predicament.

Lee offered a terse nod to Rodriguez as he continued toward his mentor, the man who'd taught him so much.

When Lee reached Oldendorf, he struggled to find the right words. Years of mentorship, of shared victories and losses, of growing from an uncertain junior officer to a confident tactical officer under this man's guidance—all of it seemed to collapse into this moment. "Captain, I..."

Oldendorf coughed, wincing. His eyelids drooped. Blood oozed from his wounds onto the chair. "Tell the XO to take the helm."

"He's dead, sir."

Oldendorf grimaced, swallowing hard. "I'm not long for this world. You're next in line, Lieutenant."

Lee's pulse raced. "Captain, medical is on their way."

Oldendorf's head sagged before he jerked it back up. "They can't fix this. Sorry, Lee. I failed—"

"Sir—"

Oldendorf cut him off. "We're in a crisis. No time for sadness. Get to work, Lieutenant Lee. Save the ship. Save the crew. I order you to assume command, now. It's—" He grimaced, struggling for breath, then let out a long wheeze as the life faded from his eyes, leaving the captain's irises glazed and empty.

For a moment, panic consumed Lee. Images flashed through his mind—his first real combat in the war, when Oldendorf had found him hyperventilating in the tactical room, talking him through the panic until his breathing steadied. Over the years, those episodes had become less frequent, thanks to his mentor's guidance. The countless late-night strategy sessions in the captain's quarters had done more than teach tactics. They'd helped Lee process the trauma, turn the nightmares into manageable memories when he was brave enough to face a few. That horrendous engagement during the battle for New Eden where they'd lost half their fleet but somehow survived... Oldendorf had been there through it all, showing Lee how to carry command without breaking under it. This battle dwarfed them all in intensity. Nothing in his years of combat experience had prepared him for this level of destruction, and now, his captain's death.

Lee's breathing quickened and became shallow. The world accelerated around him. He forced himself to focus and slammed his fist against his thigh, grounding himself in the present. His breaths evened out as he returned to his station, where he addressed the crew. "Captain Oldendorf has fallen. I'm assuming command as acting captain. All stations, report status immediately."

Klaxons blared as a laser blasted into their port.

"Breach on Deck 2, Section 3!" an officer's voice boomed at the damage control station.

Lee checked his console for the damage report and pressed the comm. "Engineering, sensors detect a breach on Deck 2, Section 3. Auto seals have failed. Initiate emergency manual seal procedures on the affected section immediately."

The engineering crew needed to manage the rupture to prevent atmospheric loss, and now. In the unforgiving vacuum of space, a breach in a spaceship's hull was nothing short of a death sentence. Without immediate sealing, the breach would suck out the life-giving atmosphere and turn the interior into a cold, airless void. Crew members near the breach risked ejecting into the expanse. The ship would suffer as well. Its vital systems and structural integrity would become jeopardized.

"Aye, sir," MacGregor responded. "We're already on it."

Lee checked the weapons array and ammunition. So far, all was good. He targeted the weakened hull of the Zodark ship they'd been attacking. "Firing now."

The floor under Lee's boots quivered as more magrails were expelled with lightning quickness. In the next moment, the *Kentucky*'s barrage on the Zodark battleship found its mark. The rounds burrowed into the enemy vessel's exposed flesh and struck the heart of its power core. An eruption illuminated the surrounding space in blinding colors— a temporary sun born from the ship's total annihilation. This fierce blaze of glory was extinguished by space's vacuum as abruptly as it had ignited.

Lee realized he must delegate the tactical operations to focus on his responsibilities as acting captain. He'd learned this lesson the hard way years ago, when the senior tactical officer had been killed during the battles at New Eden. Back then, as a junior officer suddenly thrust into the senior TAO position, he'd tried to do everything himself, and it had nearly cost them the ship. Oldendorf had pulled him aside afterward, explaining that effective leadership wasn't about doing everything yourself but making sure everything got done. "Trust your crew," he'd said, "like I trust you."

"Lieutenant Varik, assume command of the tactical station."

"Affirmative, Captain," Lieutenant Varik said. The young man moved quickly to the tactical console to oversee the ship's weapons and defense systems.

Extraction of Captain Oldendorf from the command chair seemed impossible as the beam impaling his abdomen anchored him to the seat itself. To the captain's left sat Executive Officer Garcia's lifeless body, suspended by his restraint harness. With due respect, Lee released

Garcia's restraints and laid the fallen officer on the deck. Lee assumed the position in the XO's chair.

"Sir," a lieutenant said. "We're being locked on, and they're firing."

Lee's tone cut through the bridge as he stared at Reynolds, the navigator. "Evasive maneuvers!"

"Aye, sir!" Reynolds said.

As the *Kentucky* heaved into action, the ship's main holo lit up with new data. Lasers lanced out from the attacking ship. Each shot struck. *Kentucky*'s systems blinked out on the large screen one by one.

A knot formed in Lee's throat as the bridge's holoscreen displayed several alerts—direct hits to propulsion and life-support systems; main engine's cooling system at twelve percent capacity and continuing to fall. All this threatened to overheat the engines, causing irreversible damage to the propulsion system.

Lee patched back into Engineering. "Keep engine core stability above critical threshold, no matter what it takes. Get personnel to start emergency repair protocols on the O_2 generators and scrubbers now. We need full restoration of atmospheric controls and pressure stabilization. Confirm when life support is back to operational status."

No one replied.

"Engineering, do you copy?"

There was no response.

On the other side of the bridge, an ensign sat frozen, his eyes wide. Flashing alarms reflected off his face.

Lee caught the lapse. "Harris, snap to and manage those damage control teams!"

"Aye, sir!" Harris complied and returned to action, punching in commands across his console's holo.

The *Kentucky* whined under one more hit, its structure shuddering as the crew fought to keep her on course. The bridge's lights oscillated. The consoles died for half a second before jumping back online. Another blast, double the force. The lights went out, plunging the bridge into darkness. Emergency illumination flared to life, bathing everyone and everything.

In the dim, Lee's eyes darted between his main display screen and the crew, assessing, calculating.

"Engineering, report," he said into the comms.

He was met with silence.

"Engineering! Report!"

Nothing but dead air came through the comm.

The engine reserves continued to drain.

Outside, space teemed with war. A dozen Republic Navy and half a dozen Zodark vessels exchanged fire. The *Kentucky*'s armor groaned. They wouldn't get out of this alive without a miracle.

Grim doesn't even begin to cover it, Lee thought. *This is beyond dire. It's bordering on hopeless.*

As the *Kentucky* turned, the attacking Zodark battleship came into view.

"There she is." Lee glanced at the main holo. He clenched his jaw as he read the streaming data. His stomach fell. Half of his ship was nonoperational, especially with weapons. Secondary SM-97 Starbursts were online. Those were ready-to-launch missiles that would detonate in flares to blind sensors and cripple their targeting systems momentarily. But primary weapon systems were off-line.

We won't survive this fight, but neither will you.

Lee made a fist, much like his commanding officer, James Oldendorf, usually did. "Let's punch them with all we have. Reynolds, position us for weapons engagement."

"Yes, sir!"

The main holographic interface showed the visage of the Zodark ship, its dragon-like jaws seeming to open wider.

"Fire!" Lee ordered.

When the *Kentucky*'s magrails fired, each tungsten round struck with the force of thunder and blasted chunks of armor from the enemy's battleship.

The Zodarks retaliated with a barrage of lasers in a full onslaught. A storm of light and energy engulfed the *Kentucky*. The ship convulsed under the impact, a fierce quake coursing through its frame.

The *Kentucky*'s emergency lights died, only to send the bridge into darkness. A suffocating silence fell over the crew.

I tried and failed. Lee's gut plunged into his boots, his insides a hollow pit. *I'm sorry, Oldendorf. I made a bad decision and failed you.*

Chapter 16
Against the Clock

Year 2093
RNS *Kentucky*
Rhea System, New Eden Stargate

As death loomed, time lost its meaning. The threat of dying slowed the world around Lee. It stretched thin like a thread about to break. Darkness surrounded him. *Why am I still alive? Why hasn't the Zodark ship destroyed the* Kentucky? *Are the Zodarks deliberately prolonging their attack to torture us?*

All unanswered questions that seemed to go on for eons in Lee's mind.

Snap to it, Lee, he told himself.

Lee found the comm switch on the XO chair's armrest. "All hands, we've lost primary illumination, but remain at your stations. Take it upon yourselves and fix what you can. Engineering, report status on the emergency power, ASAP."

Once more, no reply came from Engineering.

Are all the engineers dead, or have the communication lines in the engineering section failed?

"Reynolds," Lee said to the navigator, "what's our heading?"

"Unknown, sir. Navigation is nonoperational. We're in a free drift."

Reynolds's tone suggested he shared Lee's confusion. Why was the *Kentucky* still intact?

In such grave circumstances, panic, horror, and dread would be expected responses for a person shoved into the captain's position for the first time. However, Lee experienced an unexpected calmness that made little sense to him. He went with it anyway.

"Is anything online?" Lee asked.

"Life support, antigrav, and communications, sir," an ensign said.

"Communications, establish a ship-wide PA system. Keep the crew informed and calm."

"Aye, Captain."

Captain Oldendorf personified what it meant to be a true captain. To be addressed by that title himself felt unfamiliar. Almost foreign.

"We're going to die..." a voice said. It was low and no doubt belonged to an ensign. Lee could make out who it was: Ensign Harris.

When the man whispered it a second time, Lee couldn't stop himself. He spoke words only his best teacher from Basin Mennonite School could force Lee to remember. One of the best Shakespeare lines he knew. "Fear not, for 'Cowards die many times before their deaths; The valiant never taste of death but once.'" He turned in Harris's direction. "We stand in the face of danger because we've made a promise to risk our lives for humanity. We do this because we're born protectors. You are some of the greatest men and women ever created, so embody that right here, right now. Hooyah!"

"Hooyah!" replied the rest of the crew.

The Shakespearean verse and Lee's own words appeared to motivate those around him. Somehow, it also calmed the energy on the bridge.

A buzz sounded. The bridge lights powered to life. The main viewscreen streamed data: internal comms restored, hull breaches sealed, and engineering teams actively repairing life-support systems.

Although in a critical condition, this ship continued to tick. It was why the *Kentucky*'s engineering was among the top in all the Republic Navy.

On the holo and ahead of the *Kentucky*, remnants of early countermeasure deployments floated. SW (sand-water) missiles had previously exploded and released clouds of water and sand into space. This mixture was designed to form a barrier, scattering and weakening the energy of enemy laser fire.

Lee opened a channel to Engineering. "Do you copy?"

MacGregor replied, "Aye, Captain."

"When can I get outside communications and maneuvering engines restored?"

"Time unknown. We're rerouting and working on it. We're practically sweatin' our hair off down here, sir."

"Understood."

A continued battle unfolded around them. The *Iowa*, which they had defended, now joined by the *George Washington*, launched an assault on the Zodark battleship previously attacking the *Kentucky*.

Around the *George Washington*, military drones zipped through space, scanning for threats and relaying real-time data back to the *George Washington*.

Volleys flew back and forth between the Zodark battleship and the two Republic Navy warships until the enemy vessel landed a devastating hit on the *Iowa*'s starboard side. The impact tore through the hull. Debris and bodies were ejected into space.

Kentucky's main screen zoomed in on the *Iowa*. Countermeasures filled the space around her, with chaff clouds released to confuse sensor arrays and divert incoming enemy torpedoes. The chaff fluttered like swarms of metallic insects, each piece glittering as it reflected the distant starlight before fading into the darkness.

"Sir, we're getting a transmission from the *Iowa*."

External video and audio communications were out, but the *Kentucky* was able to receive text-based transmissions. It was better than nothing.

On the main holo, *Iowa*'s commander, Captain Jonathan Moon, sent a dire message to both the *George Washington* and the *Kentucky*. The *Iowa* had sustained severe damage on their starboard flank. Casualties were high and mounting. They needed immediate assistance. Their ejection pod system was out of commission.

"Inform them we're in a critical state and unable to render aid," Lee said.

"Aye, sir." Rodriguez hesitated as she read *Iowa*'s response. "Captain, Moon's transmitting that life support's failing. Their engineering department took a direct hit. All dead. They're requesting shuttle transfer of any able engineers available from the *Kentucky* and the *George Washington*."

Problem was, *Kentucky*'s engineering was in a heap of trouble as well. According to the casualty icons on the bridge's interface, not many of *Kentucky*'s engineers had survived this battle.

"Much as I'd love to help the *Iowa*, we just can't transfer anyone right now," Lee directed. "Hopefully the *GW* can spare some personnel."

"Aye, sir. I'll let them know."

Up on the vid screen, the *George Washington* engaged. Magrail rounds collided with the Zodark vessel. Havoc missiles cut through its defenses. Laser cannons tore it apart as the enemy ship began to fall apart. It spewed debris into space as its structural integrity failed.

The Republic Navy firepower overwhelmed the alien vessel as it suffered catastrophic internal explosions. Red-and-orange blasts flared, the eruptions severing the ship in two. The fore section drifted in one direction as its momentum carried it away, while the aft segment floated listlessly in the opposite.

"Reynolds," Lee said, "flood the mains, all ahead full."

"Aye, sir." Reynolds pressed several buttons on his holo. "Navigation systems are failing to respond, Captain."

Lee glanced at the viewscreen, confirming Reynolds's report. The display was a sea of red indicators: the main driving engines were nonfunctional, the fusion reactors showed critical damage, and auxiliary engines were inoperative. The readout confirmed the worst. All propulsion systems, from the primary fusion drive down to the smallest maneuvering jet, were beyond repair. A devastating hit to their operational capabilities.

Lee opened the engineering channel. "MacGregor, what's the status on engine repairs?"

"We lack the capacity to repair most of them, sir. With the amount of damage sustained, repairs require us to dock at a shipyard. Hell, at the best and most equipped shipyard we can find. But we believe we can get engines two and five online in a few minutes."

Outside, charred parts of Zodark ships floated around the stargate. The Republic Navy had cut the Zodark forces down to three ships, and now the Republic Navy outnumbered them four to one. Instead of regrouping or trying to hold their position, the Zodark warships dispersed. They separated from each other and moved away from the stargate with Republic Navy ships in hot pursuit. The Zodarks tactical decision seemed counterintuitive and made little sense.

Why aren't they attempting to escape through the stargate? To extricate themselves from these losing battle conditions? Lee wondered.

The stargate's intensity magnified as its core emitted a blinding light. Electric-blue streaks of lightning shot from its center and branched out in jagged lines. Orbs of energy flew erratically and illuminated the surrounding space with bursts of colors. From deep violets to radiant reds.

Through this luminous maelstrom, a fleet of Zodark cruisers and troop transports burst forward on a course toward New Eden.

The viewscreen then showed an extra blip eighty-three thousand kilometers away. Could it be a Republic naval ship moving to provide support and intercept the incoming Zodark vessels?

As the data streamed on Lee's interface, he withheld a gasp. *What are civilians doing here? Talk about the wrong place at the wrong time. Their FTL drive must've malfunctioned.*

"Sir, sensors indicate that's a civilian vessel on a course for New Eden. They came out of FTL jump too late. The Zodark ships are headed right for them, Captain," a lieutenant said.

Lee needed the *Kentucky* to fire upon those cruisers now if they were to have a chance of saving that civilian vessel. He opened the channel to Engineering. "MacGregor, what's the ETA on getting our weapons back online?"

"Sir, two-zero minutes to bring the weapons systems online."

"Twenty minutes isn't good enough. Get them online faster or we're going to lose that civilian ship."

"Captain, there's a serious risk involved when we skip certain protocols," MacGregor said. "Accelerating the process could cause our power relays to burn out, leading to a complete shutdown of what's left of the ship's propulsion system."

The recently emerged Zodark cruisers and troop transports continued their advance, gaining distance on the *Kentucky* and closing on the civilian craft. Republic ships were ordered to abandon their current fights and rush to stop the Zodark vessels from reaching the civilian transport.

The distance between the new Zodark fleet and the civilian vessel closed quickly. It became clear the enemy would reach them well before the Republic's forces could intervene. It was possible the Zodarks would pass the civilian ship, ignoring it as they continued their sprint for New Eden. But after battling with Zodarks for as long as he had, everything in Lee told him otherwise.

They'd shoot down that ship just for fun, or out of irritation, whatever came first.

"MacGregor," Lee said. "Risks be damned. Fix the weapons immediately or else that ship is done for."

Chapter 17
From Passenger to Pilot

Year 2093
Blue Horizon Meridian Transport Vessel
Rhea System, New Eden Stargate

At the moment, and to her surprise, Love had a front-row seat to a scene of distant combat playing out against the black expanse. Flashes. Explosions. Bright lights.

Ort and his wife quieted for a moment before his voice broke the stillness. "What's going on out there?"

Love continued to watch. She picked up as much detail as she could. Beyond the fight was a gigantic structure—the New Eden stargate. Then, a realization dawned on her. "Oh, that's not good. We must've overshot the FTL exit and come out by the gate and not at New Eden."

She stared at the stargate. It looked like a giant ring suspended in space. It pulsed. The middle surface shimmered with azure energy. She'd only seen such structures in simulations and briefings, never in person.

My word, it's funky looking. So far away, though. Looks like a toy.

The older woman stood and walked toward the window. "Is that… a battle happening near it?" She faced her husband. "They told us we needn't worry about a war, Ort. How is one supposed to not worry? It's right there. Everyone can see it! Oh my… Ort. They've taken us into a war zone. What's—"

"Donna… Donna…" Ort strode toward his wife and shuffled her back to their seat. "Dear… don't worry. The pilot knows what he's doing. Everything will be fine."

"Looks like we've arrived smack-dab in the middle of something, that's for sure," Love said.

Donna gasped. "Something bad?" She fidgeted with her sleeve, squeezing the fabric hard.

The pilot's voice came over the intercom. "Ladies and gentlemen, this is your captain speaking. I want to inform you we exited our FTL jump a few seconds later than scheduled, which caused us to overshoot the New Eden jump point. Instead, we've exited near the stargate due to a malfunction with our drive system. Uh… I believe everyone may have noticed there appears to be a battle taking place near the gate. I urge everyone to remain calm and not panic. I've already notified the Republic Navy, and they're dispatching an escort to ensure our safety. We're in a secure position and there's no immediate danger to our vessel. Please stay seated and follow the instructions of our crew. We'll keep you updated with any further developments. Thank you for your cooperation."

Love eyed a powered-down digital display panel beside the window. She activated it. A map of their immediate sector materialized. It pinpointed their location relative to New Eden. They'd been promised a five-minute final approach to the planet's surface, but they'd deviated way off course. They were thirty-eight minutes out.

"Are we safe here?" Ort asked.

Love hesitated. Her instincts as a military pilot wrestled with the uncertainty of their situation. In battle, or even near it, you were never safe. Ever. So, she did the only thing she could think of… and lied. "We're moving away from the conflict. So, we should be safe. No worries at all. Unless…" Her voice trailed off. *Why did I say unless?* From the look on their faces, Love had spooked them.

"Unless what?" Donna asked, mouth agape.

Love continued to chide herself. She should've kept her mouth shut. Why hadn't she kept her mouth shut?

Space warfare was unpredictable. A laser could bridge the distance to their civilian craft faster than a thought. The chances of being targeted were slim, of course, but in the theater of combat, even slim odds were too much.

Love's gaze drifted back to the digital display. *What's taking Jack so long?* The screen showed the conflict 83,450 kilometers away from the civilian transport's location. For most, it would seem far. In a Navy mindset, it was too close. Way too close.

Love manually zoomed in and moved the image around until she came upon ships. She magnified the display. Her breath caught. Those were Zodark ships. And, worse yet, they were approaching at breakneck speeds. She tensed. A bright bluish-silver glow from the stargate gleamed off the crafts.

Oh no…

She swallowed hard. If any nightmare could come from this, it would be Zodark vessels heading in their direction. And around a dozen in total were on their way, four of them massive. They sped toward them like sharks ready to kill.

Love's face drained of color. Anxiety poured through her. Civilian ships lacked the firepower to even put a dent into a Zodark ship. This craft she was on was a Meridian CIT-890, made to transport eight hundred people. The pilot would have access to a civilian point-defense system used for small rocks or debris in space. It was useless in any confrontation, especially against the Zodarks. If the enemy maintained their course, they might treat this civilian vessel like a nuisance, knocking it out simply for being in the way, or even near their path. It seemed unlikely, but with these warlike aliens, who could say for sure?

Love tapped in commands on the digital display. She marked the oncoming enemy to find their time of arrival. At the civilian transport's pace, the attackers would be on top of them in twenty-three minutes.

The civilian ship executed a sharp turn, no doubt to speed away from the Zodarks' course. Good move. She wanted to give the pilot a pat on the back, because any way out of here and farther from the enemy was the only way to safety.

She turned from the window and moved quickly down the corridor. Emergency equipment lined the walls and holographic signage blinked with status updates. The vessel's life-support system hummed. She passed a line of doors before arriving at a section inlaid with symbols for the restrooms.

Love knocked on the first bathroom door. "Jack? You in there?"

"Yeah."

"Zodark ships are inbound, vectoring directly toward us."

Hannigan flushed the toilet. "Heard it over the intercom. I think we're safe. Or did things change?"

"I think we're OK, but with the Zodarks, who knows?"

The Zodarks treated humans as slaves. Well, they treated everyone as lower than them and either killed them or enslaved them. Whatever they desired in the moment, they did. It was never for the benefit of any species other than their own.

A sudden thought invaded her mind: *What if the enemy dispatched a ship to abduct us and the passengers, forcing us into servitude in one of their mining operations?*

She shook her head, sighing. *Don't think like that.*

Jack stepped out into the corridor. "The pilot is taking us out of the Zodarks' path."

"Yes, he is."

They walked toward the viewing room.

"Then we're probably fine," Jack said.

When they entered the viewing chamber, Ort and Donna were no longer there. Jack peered out the holowindow. "Well, can't say we're not exposed and an easy target. That much is true."

The ship changed course a second time and veered to port.

Jack squinted at the display. "Did you see that?" He motioned toward the magnified image of the lead Zodark cruiser.

"I did."

Both Jack and Love, seasoned Republic Navy pilots, recognized the brief flare of light—a Zodark cannon firing a laser. It lasted only a split second. If the cruiser indeed aimed its laser at this civilian transport and achieved a direct hit, the impact would have struck in less than a second. Given their continued safety and the transport's intact condition, it was clear the enemy vessel had either missed or aimed at a different object. Possibly space debris or small asteroids obstructing the Zodarks' course.

The civilian transport ship continued to veer and went into a dorsal vector.

"He's getting us out of their trajectory," Jack said. "We can watch through the window here or go to our suite."

"I vote for our room." Although she doubted the Zodarks would shoot this ship down or take them prisoner, still, jitters ran through her. Something didn't feel right.

As they turned the corner down a corridor, two flight attendants, one a large man and the other a petite woman, held back a young man whose long brown hair whipped across his face as he tried to push through. "Let me see the pilot. This is urgent."

The male flight attendant blocked his path. "Access to the cockpit is restricted for security reasons and to ensure the pilot's ability to focus on navigating the ship safely. Especially in a critical situation like this."

The woman flight attendant stood beside her colleague. "If you don't calm down, I'll have to call security."

The young man spat at her. "Let me through! I know the Zodarks. I studied them, and they'll go after us no matter what. We need to get farther away, change our trajectory, and the pilot's not taking us far enough. Look, we have—"

The male flight attendant shoved the young man against the wall. "Go back to your suite now, or you'll be facing jail time as soon as we land on New Eden."

Love suspected the young man must be someone influential. Perhaps a politician's son or royalty from Earth. If not, the flight attendants would've called security by now.

The lady gestured at Love and Jack. "Move along, please."

As they began to leave, the woman talked into her shoulder comm. "Request security to sector three immediately."

The young man protested. "I'm a pilot, and I can navigate this ship better than anyone here! You're all going to kill us if I don't get into that cockpit!"

What's that kid's deal? Love thought. *The pilot's doing what he can.*

Hannigan and Love continued down the corridor until they reached their suite. Inside, the room was modest but comfortable—a bed, a holodisplay mounted on the wall, and a door to a cramped bathroom.

Love sat on the edge of the bed. She leaned forward, elbows on her thighs.

Hannigan lay down beside her. "You look worried."

"I am."

"We'll be fine."

"I know, but I've got this weird feeling. Remember Operation Pacific Glide? The training mission where my avionics malfunctioned midflight, forcing me to eject over the Pacific? I had the exact same feeling even before that mission."

"I recall." Hannigan exhaled. "Did you have that feeling before we boarded this ship?"

"No. Just now. It's probably nothing."

A knock at the door interrupted them. Love opened it. A flight attendant stood there with a data pad. She looked frantic, her breathing a bit labored. "Are you Jack Hannigan and Naomi Love, Republic Navy pilots?"

Love nodded. "Yes."

Words poured out of the flight attendant's mouth at a hundred kilometers per hour. "You two are the only qualified pilots on board. We need you to put on EVA suits immediately to access the cockpit safely, as there's no oxygen in that section now. We need your expertise to navigate and ensure everyone's safety."

Love stepped back. "Whoa. Hold on. Slow down. Why do you need us to do all that?"

Hannigan sat up. "What's going on?"

With each passing second, the flight attendant looked increasingly likely to faint. She placed her fingers over her chest. She was visibly shaken. "In light of an unfortunate accident, our pilot is dead."

Chapter 18
Darlin'

Year 2093
Blue Horizon Meridian Transport Vessel CIT-890
Rhea System, New Eden Stargate

In a small chamber, Love stood in the momentary quiet, surrounded by the lifeless forms of EVA suits hanging from the walls. Metal racks lined the bulkheads. Each held a suit. Tubes meandered across the floor and connected to various ports and panels.

"How did the pilot die?" Love asked.

The flight attendant slid into her EVA suit beside Love. "Laser fire." Her voice shook, no doubt fear coursing through her veins.

"Really? Wow, I guess we got lucky it didn't hit something that could have caused an explosion or damaged the airlock to the flight deck." Hannigan pushed his arms into the sleeves of his own suit. "Did we take any other hits to the ship?"

The bulky EVA suits were designed for extravehicular activity but were also made to protect personnel within the ship in emergencies like this. Their thick, layered fabric resisted punctures and tears. They were well made, some of the best protective clothing. A reflective outer layer guarded against radiation and extreme temperatures. Inside the ship, EVAs also provided a mobile safety shell in case of sudden decompression or fire.

A male flight attendant in a white-and-gray EVA suit turned from securing a locker. "Negative, at least not yet. Near as we can tell, it was dumb luck they hit the captain. From what we can see on the camera feeds of the flight deck, we think most of the controls are still operational."

"Most?" Love adjusted the helmet over her head. The visor snapped down with a click. The HUD display came alive and displayed a simple layout of the ship's status: green and red dots showed functional and nonfunctional systems.

"The damage report says we may have lost some of the secondary navigation controls," the attendant said. "But the readout also says this isn't a critical problem, and we can fly without them."

"I see," Love replied.

At any minute, they could succumb to the same fate as the pilot. Still, Love remained calm and collected. Throughout her years in the military, she'd received training for the worst of the worst situations. All of it had rendered part of Love numb, her constant exposure to danger dulling her emotional responses. Over time, this numbing extended to a specific region of her brain, the amygdala. This area processed fear and anxiety. That part of her brain had phased out the incessant worry about death, allowing her to operate in life-threatening situations with a detachment necessary for survival—so said medical and scientific tests, confirming this condition in her.

It held her back in some ways, but for the military—for her—it was perfect.

Guided by the attendants, Love and Hannigan exited the chamber. At a hurried pace, they stepped into a corridor leading to the airlock that separated the flight deck from the rest of the ship. After a long minute, they reached their destination. The door to the airlock leading to the flight deck stood closed, its surface a metallic barrier. Piping ran along the walls around them and intersected with sealed hatches. Upon entering the airlock, the doorway they had just passed through closed with a hiss, sealing them inside.

As the room pressure matched the flight deck, they unsealed the door, making their way in to join a pair of emergency medical technicians tending to the body of the now dead pilot. The laser had vaporized the pilot's head—there was no saving him. A faint tug from the antigrav systems pulled from under their feet, their boots keeping them anchored to the deck.

Despite Love's low susceptibility to the fear of death, the sight of something so gruesome still triggered a reaction. She felt bile rising in her throat before she regained control of herself and swallowed it back down. Hannigan averted his gaze, getting to work assessing the situation.

After the techs carried the dead pilot out of the cockpit, the flight attendant motioned for Love and Jack to take over. As they moved forward, she turned to Love and spoke through the helmet comm. "Our fate is in your hands now."

Love grimaced, nodding as she tried to look strong. "We'll do our best. You can count on that."

As Love looked around the flight controls, she spotted the hole in the floor where the laser had hit. Looking to the ceiling and back to the floor, she still couldn't believe the luck involved in this shot not hitting something flammable. An explosion would have ripped the ship apart. A meter to the left of the hole on the floor, Love spotted an oxygen line—that certainly would have done it.

A meter to the left, and we all would have been dead, she realized. Hell, if the flight deck hadn't been sealed from the rest of the ship, the sudden decompression could have ripped it apart.

Love's throat constricted as she took in the full extent of the death. At least the pilot had passed on quickly. He likely never knew what happened—best way to go.

Hannigan stood beside her and scanned the flight controls. He took in every detail.

Love moved closer to the control panel. "We got it from here."

The flight attendants nodded and exited, the door to the airlock closing behind them.

Love's predicament—the ship's predicament—was complicated, with no clear escape. Love and her husband needed to save as many individuals aboard the ship as possible before it was hit by laser fire again. If they'd shot at this craft once, they'd do it again.

On the other hand, she could wish for dumb luck, with Love steering the transport as far from the enemy's course as possible in the hope the Zodarks would disregard the civilian vessel as a mere nuisance and leave them alone.

The holographic dashboard before them flashed with new alerts. Love viewed the display. "Enemy bearing two-eight-nine at thirteen thousand, one hundred and twenty-four kilometers, approaching rapidly. The Republic Navy is in pursuit, but they're over sixty thousand kilometers out from our pursuers."

Republic forces fired continuously, but their shots streaked through the void, missing their marks. The enemy's ships maneuvered in complex, erratic patterns, making it nearly impossible for tactical officers to predict their movements at those distances, and every missile the Republic let loose wound up disintegrated by the Zodarks' point laser defenses.

"Why are they coming our way?" Hannigan asked as he sat in the copilot's seat beside Love. "Why do the Zodarks care about a small craft like this one?"

"They don't care. We're just in the way," Love replied. "What the hell happened to cause us to overshoot our jump point? We shouldn't even be here."

An icy shiver of horror traced Love's spine as the tactical display left no room for illusions about their fate. There was nowhere to hide and nothing to shield themselves from the predator on its way toward them.

The engines were running at max power, but this was a civilian passenger ship; it struggled to gain speed, making any attempt to outrun the enemy futile. Despite the potential for evasive maneuvers, open space offered no refuge and no place to hide in an unarmored transport. The inevitability of their situation came at them even harder now.

If we don't figure a way out of this, we're done for.

Love gripped the controls and veered, trying to make them harder to track and hit. "If we can buy more time—let our ships get closer—maybe we'll have a chance."

Hannigan cursed in frustration. "If the Zodarks slow down any, they risk our ships hammering them. We have to abandon ship. We can try to buy time to get everyone off, but we can't outrun this, and if we don't act—everyone's dead."

Love turned to her husband. "I hate it when you're right. Best make the call. Inform the crew and passengers that we're initiating emergency evacuation protocol."

Hannigan opened the intercom system. "Ladies and gentlemen, this is Lieutenant Hannigan from the Republic Navy. We are being pursued by several enemy warships we cannot outrun. I am ordering the evacuation of the ship immediately and have alerted Republic Forces of our location for recovery. I need you to proceed to your nearest ejection pods calmly and quickly. This is not a drill. I repeat, this is not a drill. The ship's crew will help you into the life pods, so do not panic. Follow the attendants' commands at all times. If you do so, you'll be safe. Like I said, ladies and gentlemen, leave your suites and follow the attendants to your designated life pods. Thank you for flying with Blue Horizon." Hannigan pressed an alarm button. Klaxons screamed throughout the vessel.

Love shook her head. "Thank you for flying Blue Horizon? Really?"

He shrugged. "I'm sorry. I don't know why I said that."

The Zodarks weren't stupid. They no doubt realized if they slowed to take out every pod the attackers could find, the Republic Navy would be on top of them soon enough and eat them alive.

The ship continued to turn every few minutes. "I'm maintaining an erratic course until all pods are filled. We have to get out of here ourselves," Love said, watching the video feed of people filling into the different life pods nearest their seats.

"With dozens of civilian transport ships to choose from, the Republic had to send us on this one?" Hannigan chided.

"Ironic, isn't it?" Love retorted.

"I hate that word."

"Me too." She laughed.

Ten minutes later, when the interface displayed an indication that all passengers had made it into their specified ejection pods, Love gave her husband a look.

Hannigan's face went grim. "It's a miracle we're still alive."

She blew Hannigan a kiss. "I love you."

"I love you back."

With a twist, Love steered the ship dorsal and maneuvered toward port. The holoscreen zoomed in on the oncoming enemies and magnified the attackers. In spite of their distance, the detail was clear: predatory designs with hulls mirroring snakeskins.

Love plunged the ship into a ventral dive. "Enemy at nine thousand and five kilometers and closing. Republic forces are tracking at fifty-six thousand, four hundred and forty-four kilometers to the hostiles' position." She pressed the ejection pod release buttons. On the display, the pods loaded with passengers detached. They shot out and away, into the void—each trajectory a desperate bid for life. "Evac pods, away!"

The ship shook violently this time. Alarms blared and red lights flashed.

Hannigan scanned the display with a worried look. "Zodarks hit us again."

"Engine two is dead. I'm showing depressurization in the cargohold." Love pushed down her fury and anxiety. This wasn't the way she'd imagined her life flaming out. In fact, she'd fantasized about living a hundred years or more with the man beside her.

Hannigan stood. "Come on. We've done all we can do. We are living on borrowed time, darlin'." He yanked Love from her seat as they entered the airlock, sealing themselves in before hitting the emergency pressurization button. This pressurized the chambers in seconds, allowing them to enter the rest of the ship and race for one of the few remaining life pods waiting for them.

They rushed past empty seats and the viewing room, where they had first seen the distant battle that now consumed them. Once they reached the ejection pod chamber closest to them, they encountered a moment of calm amid the turmoil. Rows of empty launch bays stretched out, littered by absent life pods—all gone and propelled into the cosmos, except one. It remained docked, its hatch open like a beckoning gateway.

"Let's go," Love said to Hannigan.

They were climbing in when a woman's voice cried out. "Help! Is anyone still out there?"

Love stopped mid-stride, and pivoted. A figure in an EVA suit stood at the launch bay entrance. As the woman approached Love, she could see the matted red curls at the woman's forehead and knew immediately who it was—Donna from the viewing room.

The woman pointed behind her. "Ort. He's... I don't know," Donna choked out. "He's not responding, and I can't carry him."

Hannigan surged forward. "Where is he?"

"In my suite, room 14," the woman said through tears. "Get him. Please. I can't move him. I'm just not strong enough—"

"Jack will get him. Just get in, ma'am." Love motioned her toward the last remaining evac capsule.

Donna's face contorted in distress. "Not without my Ort."

Seconds later, Hannigan appeared. He heaved an unconscious man down the corridor toward them. "I've got him. We're coming!"

BOOM!

An explosion erupted, throwing everyone to the deck. Anything that wasn't fastened down was being sucked out a giant hole where the rear of the ship had just been. Love saw Donna screech in terror as she was sucked out into space. Love grabbed desperately for anything she could, until her magnetic boots grabbed the floor with a force she didn't know was possible. She desperately looked for Jack, hoping he had somehow found something, anything to hold onto.

Love spotted Jack gripping the railing along the side of the corridor, a deeply pained look on his face. The vacuum was gone now—the ship's internal atmosphere had already blown into the void. Through the EVA's comm unit, Love called out, "Jack, are you OK? Can you hear me?"

"Yeah, I'm still here—Ort...I couldn't hold onto him," Hannigan's voice trailed off.

"Don't worry about that. We have to get the pod. It's our only escape," she pleaded with him.

She watched him move toward her, one step at a time. But that pained look on his face never left.

"What's wrong, Jack?"

"I'm hit. Something pierced my suit—it speared me in the back. I can feel some sort of metal. It hurts bad," he stammered through gritted teeth.

"Come on, Jack. You can do it. You're almost to the pod. Once we're sealed up, I can take a look at it and we can patch you up," Love tried to encourage him despite the tears that were beginning to stream down her face.

Love lunged forward and grabbed Jack's hands. Once she hauled him into the ejection pod, she closed the door, sealing them in. Love kept her gaze on Hannigan as she dropped to the floor beside him. Her husband gasped for air inside his helmet, his face turning pale.

"Stay with me, Jack. You don't leave me!" she shouted.

She hit the launch button that shot the ejection pod away from the doomed ship. She then turned her attention to the life pod's life support system and activated it. The cabin began to pressurize as oxygen levels rose until it was safe to take her helmet off.

She kneeled beside her husband. Hannigan's grip on Love's hand tightened in response as she removed his helmet.

Hannigan smiled at her, a tear running down the side of his face as he struggled to say, "I love you."

Love's shoulders drooped at the words. "No. You're not going anywhere." She pulled him closer as an explosion erupted outside, the flash of the civilian transport illuminating the blackness of space for the briefest of moments.

"Jack," she whispered. "Breathe for me. Breathe."

Hannigan's grip loosened, his eyes beginning close.

"No, Jack. I love you too. Just… open your eyes."

He opened his eyes, and a faint smile graced his face, and then his body went limp.

Chapter 19
Oldendorf's Legacy

Year 2093
RNS *Kentucky*
Rhea System, New Eden Stargate

The medical team zipped the white body bag over Captain James Oldendorf's still form and lifted the bag onto a gurney. The captain was the last of the dead to be moved from *Kentucky*'s bridge. It was yet another death at the hands of the Zodarks. In a galaxy full of planets, humans had happened to stumble upon a species of warriors. Three years had passed since the initial conflict between the Earthers and the Zodarks, and it'd been one hell of a bloody brawl.

Lee stared at the body bag. He swallowed the nausea coming up his throat, forcing calm into his churning insides. As he watched his mentor being wheeled away, he whispered a silent prayer for the man. The guy meant everything to him. Lee did everything he could to hold back his emotions.

Outside, the battle had subsided. It left a dark truth on the bridge of the RNS *Kentucky*—combat kills more than just the casualties. Warfare, violent conflicts, military campaigns—all of it was a stake in the heart of those who survived, painful memories to be pushed away and dealt with later.

In front of Lee, the bridge's main viewscreen displayed the lifeless hulks of enemy ships all around. Along with his dead captain, the defenseless civilian ship out in the open expanse gnawed at Lee.

Did the transport survive? "Do we have a status on the civilian transport?" Lee asked.

Lieutenant Varik at the tactical station brought up sensor reports on his console. "An explosion was detected at coordinates Alpha-Nine-Three-Tango in the direction of New Eden. Ejection pods were deployed. Uncertain on survival count post Zodark flyby, but our forces are actively pursuing the Zodarks. RNS *New York* is en route for ejection pod retrieval and survivor assistance."

So, there were survivors. For a moment, Lee relaxed.

A data feed streamed across the screen from the captain of the RNS *George Washington*. The holo displayed the battle status and requested a sitrep from the *Kentucky*. With it came a priority query: Could the *Kentucky* deploy to New Eden for intercept and engagement against the advancing Zodarks?

"Rodriguez," Lee said, "patch us through to the *George Washington*. Inform them we're assessing our status and will provide an update shortly. Let them know we're working on fixing external audio and vid comms as well."

"Aye, Captain," Rodriguez said. She worked on her console. "Link established with the *George Washington* and information sent."

Lee patched into Engineering. "MacGregor, report on the status of external comms and propulsion."

"Sir, external comms are patchy, but we should have them fully operational within five minutes. As for propulsion, we've got one engine marginally functional. It's not much, but it'll move us. The rest are shot, beyond repair at this juncture. Need some coffee down here, Captain. Loads of it."

Lee glared at the stars shining on the main holoscreen. "Understood. Keep me updated on any progress."

"Aye, sir."

Lee turned to the navigation station. "Reynolds, calculate our ETA to New Eden with current propulsion capability."

After a moment of hurried tapping on his interface, Reynolds looked up. "Captain, at this rate, it'll take us three days and twenty-two hours to reach New Eden."

Lee nodded. "Rodriguez, relay our status and ETA to the *George Washington*. Inform them we're unable to assist with the New Eden operation."

"Aye, Captain."

Lee stood amidst the ruins. The bridge showed scars from the intense battle. Sparks hissed from exposed panels. The smell of burnt electronics wafted in the air.

Was this the result of Lee's command decisions? A doubt clawed at him, calling into question the soundness of his leadership. Had he hesitated when he shouldn't have? Had he fired at the wrong times, in the wrong locations—and hell, had he just simply given the wrong orders? What course would Captain James Oldendorf have charted during the conflict? And what would he think of Lee's performance?

Were my actions as acting captain up to par?

MacGregor's voice crackled through the bridge's comm system. "Captain, good news. Bandwidth is stabilized, encryption protocols are in place, and signal integrity is secure for all outbound transmissions."

"Excellent. I appreciate your hard work."

"Captain," Rodriguez said, "the fleet is advancing to New Eden. Command has decided to allocate a smaller escort for our protection. Specifically, two flak frigates: the RNS *Resolve* and the *Intrepid*."

"Give them my regards." Lee faced Reynolds. "Set course to New Eden. We'll limp along, but we'll get there."

Four hours had passed since the battle. Lee kept *Kentucky*'s sensors trained on the stargate, alert to the potential threat of another enemy fleet jumping through the vortex of blue energy. The *Kentucky* advanced toward New Eden. Flanking her were the RNS *Resolve* on the port side and the RNS *Intrepid* on the starboard. Both vessels were positioned in a way to cover the *Kentucky*'s vulnerable points in a standard V-formation. It ensured a 360-degree defensive perimeter.

Reynolds's voice boomed through the bridge. "Captain, we're picking up a distress signal from an ejection pod."

"Any survivors inside?" Lee asked.

"Thermal sensors detect two occupants, sir."

"Any more pods out there?"

Reynolds shook his head. "None that our sensors are picking up. Seems the *New York* missed this one."

"Bring it up on the screen."

On the main viewscreen, the evacuation pod appeared. Its design was like that of an egg. Elongated, with sharp, angular sides, it tapered to a point at both ends. A matte black material specialized to absorb rather than reflect light covered the capsule's surface, rendering the pod nearly invisible in deep space.

Charred damage on one side dotted the exterior. The metal skin was blistered and warped. Two port windows, one at the stern and one at the bow, showed the only visible break in the pod's exterior. These windows were crafted from a dark translucent material. They blended with the capsule's hull to ensure its low visibility profile.

Lee keyed into the ship's intercom to the hangar deck. "Prep a shuttle for ejection capsule retrieval."

"Acknowledged, Captain," the Ops officer said. "We'll brief the shuttle crew and prep the pilot. Launch sequence initiated, T-minus zero five mikes."

"Sir," an ensign said, his voice a little frantic, "anomaly detected at the stargate."

On cue, another window on the main holo opened. It showed the stargate pulsating, its swirling vortex signaling imminent transit activity—meaning a ship would be coming through any minute.

Lee contacted the RNS *Intrepid*. Captain Abel Johnson appeared on the screen, his uniform decorated with medals and insignia denoting his rank and achievements.

"Captain Johnson, we're observing unusual activity at the stargate. Can your ship confirm readiness status for potential hostiles?"

Abel stood tall, hands clasped behind his back. "The *Intrepid* is battle-ready. Our railguns are fully operational. We, alongside the RNS *Resolve*, are prepared to engage any threat emerging from that stargate."

"Understood, Captain. Stay alert and stand by for further orders."

"Will do. *Intrepid* out."

It felt odd to be the decision-maker at the top in this situation, but Lee shrugged off the feeling. After this ordeal, he expected to be demoted to a more practical role, one where he'd contribute to making final decisions rather than bearing sole responsibility for them.

A deck officer's tone rattled through the comm. "Shuttle is away, ETA to evac pod thirty seconds."

The shuttle displayed on the viewscreen. It was a small vessel with thrusters blazing, propelling the ship through space toward the evac pod. When it reached the capsule, mechanical arms extended from the shuttle and secured the pod with a series of locks and clamps before conducting a controlled tow back to the *Kentucky*.

Meanwhile, the stargate's activity increased. Its energy readings spiked. Something was about to fly through. Lee prepared himself for another big fight.

"Captain, sensors are registering escalating quantum fluctuations at the stargate, exceeding five terajoules and climbing," an ensign said from the sensor station.

Lee activated the comm link to both frigate captains. "Prepare for hostile engagement. Stargate activity suggests imminent enemy incursion."

"Sir, evac pod is secured in the bay," reported a maintenance officer from the *Kentucky*'s hangar bay. "The hatch is fused. We're prepping hydraulic cutters for extraction."

"Keep me updated." Lee kept his eyes on the stargate.

"Something big is coming through, sir!" a lieutenant said.

The stargate's core blazed with a sudden flare. Its energy spiked in a flash of luminescent tendrils lashing out into space.

Chapter 20
Old Friends

Year 2093
RNS *Kentucky*
Rhea System, New Eden Stargate

"The stargate's boiling! Zodark ships could burst through any second," shouted spacer Ian Murray, a young crewman, his blue uniform slick with perspiration. Chief Brian Ford watched him rush across the bay. With no time to lose, Murray grabbed the hydraulic cutters from a toolkit pressed against a nearby shuttle. He sprinted across the deck toward Ford.

Ford, known to his team as Chief, kept his focus on the holoscreen plastered against the shuttle bay's far wall. The stargate loomed on the display—a massive ring, built by an unknown ancient race, that floated in the abyss of the dark void like the mouth of a volcano ready to erupt. Blues and oranges flared outward at the stargate's center. The colors swirled and lashed out. At any moment, what little safety they had could shatter when hostile ships burst through the gate.

Murray reached Ford and thrust the hydraulic cutters into his hands. "Chief, the cutters."

Ford nodded and grabbed the heavy metallic device, its jaws able to slice through steel like nothing. He turned and strode toward the escape pod, the one recently hauled in from space. The evac capsule, a massive egg-shaped pod with its exterior frosted over, showed the scars of its short time adrift in the cold vacuum. Ice crystals clung to its surface. Thick ice obscured both stern and bow windows, leaving the occupants inside invisible and trapped.

Several deckhands positioned themselves around the pod. Ford's eyes met those of a tall figure standing a few meters away. "Petty Officer Kravitz," Ford said. "Keep your eyes glued to that screen. Holler the second anything pops through that gate."

"You got it, Chief," Kravitz replied.

Mechanical whirs pierced the air. Massive cargo haulers, starfighters, and bombers lined the hangar. Behind Ford, a crew of technicians and dockworkers scurried about. Protective visors covered their faces as they tended to the machinery. Gantries towered overhead, their robotic arms extending, spinning, and retracting as they moved heavy containers and gear to create space for more life pods.

Turning his attention to the pod, Ford positioned the cutters at the door's seams and activated the tool. The hydraulic jaws came to life with a low thrum, biting into the alloy. Metal against metal pierced the area.

"Shimizu, Murray, get ready to pull the door once I give the nod," Ford said. The two deckhands nodded, taking their places on either side of the door.

"Bazzo, I want medical on standby the instant we pop this hatch," Ford ordered. He adjusted the cutters to get a better grip. "These folks might need it pronto."

"Yes, Chief!" Bazzo tapped his comm device to relay the order.

The cutter's jaws adjusted and clenched down harder. The cutting device bit through another chunk of the door's edge. Ford wrinkled his brow in concentration. Beads of sweat dotted along his forehead as he worked the tool. For a fraction of a second, he glanced at the stargate on the hangar's giant holodisplay. Blue colors blasted outward like tongues licking at black death, but still, nothing came through.

"Everyone sharp! The moment that door opens, we move fast and clear." Ford's voice carried across the shuttle bay. He glanced at Kravitz, who remained fixated on the stargate.

With a twist, the door groaned, breaking apart. "Now!" Ford said.

Shimizu and Murray lunged forward, pulling at the metal with all their might. With a screech of tortured alloy, the door gave way. It clattered to the deck with a heavy thud.

Ice-cold air hissed out from the opening. Ford peered inside, looking into the pod for survivors. In the corner, a woman in an EVA suit with her helmet off cradled a man in her lap. The guy's suit was covered by a dark, dried crust of blood around his midsection, where a piece of metal was protruding. A fatal wound, no doubt. If they'd been in the pod and out in the void for long, the guy would have had no chance of surviving. The woman's gaze lifted, her eyes wet.

Ford stepped into the pod. "Ma'am, we need to get you to safety."

"No," she said quietly.

Ford bent down next to her and checked the man's pulse. There was none. He reached out to the deceased individual. "I'm going to have to take him." He glanced at the pod's port window to take a look at the growing disturbance on the stargate but saw only melting ice crystals on the glass instead.

"He's dead." Her tone came out a mere whisper.

"Please, ma'am. I know how hard this is, but my priority is to help you now and to give your friend here a proper burial."

He almost choked on his words. Ford wanted to sound kind, but it had come out stern. *Was that the right thing to say?* he thought. Probably not. Most likely the worst thing at the moment.

The woman's head dropped. She tightened her grip on her dead friend.

"He's gone, but you're still here, and we need to get you out of this pod," Ford said.

"Leave us be…" Her pitch was laced with agony.

Ford crouched closer. At the same time, he wondered if a Zodark fleet had poured out from the stargate or if the threat had been delayed. His knees hit the pod's floor.

"I did everything to help Jack, but Jack…" The lady couldn't finish, her words caught in her throat.

Looking at the man, Ford thought he looked familiar. *No, no. It can't be.* He squinted, and even in the dim light, Ford could see the face of someone he'd trained with during his days with a training squadron at the Academy.

"Lieutenant Jack Hannigan?" The name slipped out before Ford could stop himself. He pushed down the sudden lump of emotion trying to rise into his throat.

The woman looked up. "Brian?"

"Yeah, it's me." Ford hesitated. "Naomi?"

"Yes. It's been a while."

Wow I haven't seen them in a couple of years. What are they doing here? he wondered. *Why were they on a civilian transport, of all things?* "Well, you're safe now. Let me take care of Jack and get you out of here."

She nodded, her face tightening as she released her hold on her husband. Ford lifted Hannigan from her lap, cradling his friend in his arms.

He swallowed down an emotional response—a crack in his voice, a falling tear. Now wasn't the time… if ever.

As Ford left the pod while carrying Hannigan, Petty Officer Kravitz approached. "Looks like the stargate's calming down, whatever that means."

"Good. We're still in rough shape," Ford grunted. He shifted Hannigan's weight as he stepped out of the pod. "Let medical through."

The medical team surrounded Hannigan, their equipment clicking as they confirmed what Ford already knew.

His friend was dead.

Hannigan's wife, Lieutenant Naomi Love, followed Ford with unsteady legs. Her gaze fell on Hannigan's still body lying on the gurney, and her knees buckled. Ford lunged forward and caught her just as she collapsed.

"Hold on, Naomi." Ford lowered her to the ground, his back against a nearby forklift. She breathed in heavy, wheezing spurts. In a span of seconds, she began to hyperventilate.

While cradling her in his lap, Ford calmly directed, "Just breathe. Nice and slow, like this." He demonstrated, his own breaths exaggerated but calm.

She gasped for air, her chest rising and falling rapidly. With wide eyes, she trembled. Ford rested her head in his hands.

"Easy, Lieutenant, easy," he said. "Look at me. Focus on my breathing." He took deep breaths, exaggerating the motion of his chest and abdomen. "In through your nose, out through your mouth. Let's do it together."

She struggled to match his rhythm. Her breaths came in short bursts. Ford rubbed her forehead with his thumb, brushing away beads of perspiration.

"That's it, Naomi. Slow and steady. You're safe now." He rested his hand on her chest, feeling the beating of her heart. "Breathe with me. In… and out. In… and out."

In a short time, her breathing synced with Ford's easing pattern. As the minutes ticked by, her hyperventilating vanished, replaced by deep, controlled breaths.

"Good, that's good," Ford said. "Keep going. You're doing great."

Love nodded. Ford continued to reassure her she was safe. Whatever had happened before was over. As the medical team walked their way, ready to move her, Lieutenant Love's fingers squeezed around Ford's arm. Her eyes pleaded with him not to leave her.

Ford smiled softly. "It's all right. They're going to help you better than I can. I'll see you as soon as I can, OK?"

"Over my dead body," she said. "Those Zodarks will pay for what they did." A second later, her strength gave out, and her eyes fluttered shut.

"Medic, get here faster," Ford yelled. As the medics hurried and took her, Ford looked at the gurney on which Lieutenant Jack Hannigan, his friend… was being pushed out. He'd lost too many friends since the start of this war. Too many of the cadets he'd watched turn into great pilots were dead. It was the cost of war, becoming harder to bear as it dragged on.

"Chief, looks like that was the last life pod. We're ready to resume regular operations," a voice behind him mentioned.

Ford stood, wiping a lone tear as he clenched his jaw.

We'll get our revenge…

He turned to Murray. "Gather the dock crew and start unloading those supply crates from the *Daedalus*. We need to empty before we dock at New Eden. It's time to get back to work."

Chapter 21
Coop's Game

Year 2093
Firebase Nova
Tempas Mountain Range, Manta River Highlands
New Eden

In the shadow-draped barracks, Lieutenant Blake "Coop" Cooper sat like a seasoned ace—cool and defiant. Or, rather, the way he expected an ace to present himself at all times. He scanned the makeshift poker table where a game of Texas Hold'em unfolded.

Two dozen drone pilots watched, all spectators in this battle of wits and luck. Twelve players had started, but now only two remained in the game: Blake Cooper—call sign Coop—and a rival, Lieutenant Lance Danning—call sign Strike.

Scattered chips and worn cards lay on the table. In the middle, a king, an ace, a two, and a five. All different suits. Coop held in his hands a pair of kings, which gave him three of a kind. It would be difficult to beat, but not impossible.

"You got something good?" Coop asked Strike.

Strike glared at him, his face like a rock. "You talk a lot when you get nervous."

"Nervous? Buddy, the only time I sweat is when the AC's busted in the cockpit," Coop said. "But you? You're like a rookie hitting Mach 1 for the first time. Shaky and way too easy to read."

Strike clenched his jaw. Coop could tell the guy didn't like the insult. Coop would do anything to wear this man down and get Strike to make a stupid move or give a strong tell.

Instead, Strike relaxed. "Like I said, you talk too much."

"I'm dealing the last card." Time moved like molasses as the dealer, a fellow pilot, dealt the river card—the fifth and final community card on the table.

Coop's heart thumped rapidly. The card hit the felt and the air thickened with anticipation. Everyone held their breath. The king of hearts showed. Coop masked his face with an expression as impenetrable as the night sky. Too bad for Strike, Coop held four of a kind, an unbeatable hand at this point in the game.

Across the table, his opponent tried to mask his reaction, but Coop saw through him. The guy didn't get what he wanted. Still, Coop would make it seem like Strike had the best cards.

"You got a king or an ace in your hand, don't you?" Coop said. "At least one. Wait, you have two aces in your hand?" Coop shook his head. "Nah, impossible. But you're holding one of the aces. I can see it in your eyes. Dang, you got some luck on your side, man."

Strike shook his head. "Me? Luck? No. Skill, Cooper. Skill. You should look into it sometime. You see, luck might get you a good hand once in a while, Coop, but up there, it can't fix your flying."

The crowd laughed. Someone in the audience yelled out, "Get 'em, Strike!"

Coop lowered his head and grasped his hair, playing like he didn't know what to do next. When he stood, he paced back and forth in front of his seat. While doing so, he fidgeted with his pants. Anything to make Strike think Coop didn't have the hand he wanted.

For an instant, Strike's shoulders and jaw muscles relaxed a bit. Coop's opponent took the bait. In fact, Coop guaranteed Strike thought he had the better hand about now.

Strike leaned back. "Your bet, Coop."

Coop sat and let out an exaggerated exhale. *Does Strike have anything at all? Did he bluff this far into the hand?* Coop hoped Strike held an ace. It'd give Strike confidence, and Coop would still come out on top.

Coop sat, staring at Strike. The guy raised his index finger and scratched the bridge of his nose. It was a tell. Strike had done it several times in the past when he'd held an ace.

Good, Coop thought. *Strike's got a great hand.*

"Well…" Coop hesitated for a moment, dragging out his feigned doubt. "I don't think you have the ace. So…" He paused for a good second longer. "I'm going all in."

"All in?" Without hesitation, Strike pushed his chips forward, the sound loud in the quiet room. "I call." Strike stood so fast, it pushed his chair over, and it crashed to the floor. "Guess what, Coop? I got the ace." He threw his cards down, face up. The five of diamonds and indeed the ace of clubs. It gave Strike two pairs.

A fantastic hand. A few people in the crowd patted Strike's back. Most cheered.

"Sure, luck plays its part, but masking a powerhouse hand with a bluff? That's strategic mastery on my part." Coop flipped over his hand, his smirk widening. "Two kings. Looking at the community cards, I think that gives me a four of a kind."

Strike flexed his fist and dipped his head at Coop before walking away. The room's atmosphere shifted as the other pilots groaned, their expressions full of disappointment.

The harsh static of the intercom pierced the air as a voice sliced through the barracks. "Immediate briefing in the operations room. Aviators, move out. Condition Yellow."

In an instant, everyone forgot the game. Cards scattered as the dealer rose. Pilots' faces transformed from relaxed to focused. Coop stood and managed to swagger even in the swift way he collected himself.

Coop strode down Firebase Nova's corridor. The gray reinforced walls echoed the muted footsteps of the two dozen pilots of the 117th Tactical Fighter Wing, comprising the Eagle and Falcon squadrons. Each squadron maintained twelve pilots. Down several passageways, dozens of other pilots streamed into sight.

The corridor, usually lit with strong white lights, now glowed with amber that signaled Condition Yellow—an alert status of heightened readiness, though not an immediate threat.

They filed into the operations room, where rows of foldable metal chairs faced a raised platform. Most pilots remained on their feet. Coop sat in the front.

Before Coop, and in front of holographic displays, stood Colonel Marcus Vale. Screens lined the walls and tactical readouts streamed incoming data. One of the holos behind Colonel Vale lit the room with a projection of New Eden's orbital space. Icons representing Republic Navy vessels chasing Zodark crafts 21,600 kilometers from New Eden appeared on the interface. Additional Republic Navy ships orbiting the planet headed toward the oncoming enemy.

"Listen up!" Vale's tone was rough like sandpaper. It commanded immediate silence. "A Zodark fleet is inbound, ETA fourteen minutes—four Zodark heavy cruisers escorting troop transports. Our battleships and frigates will engage, but we need to prep for ground incursion. Our primary objective is to neutralize this invasion before it gains ground."

Coop clenched his teeth at the mention of the Zodarks. Memories of his friend, killed in a nighttime blitz on a small New Eden military installation almost a year ago by these same foes, fueled a fire within him.

Coop's hands itched for the controls of his F-97 Orion RPC (Remotely Piloted Craft) simulator pod. He yearned to show these aliens what an Earther pilot incited by vengeance could do. *Time to make the skies nasty for them.*

Vale continued and motioned to the holodisplay, where the icons of the Zodark cruisers and transports were marked in red. "Eagle Squadron, you're tasked with air-to-air assault operations. Your mission is to engage and destroy the Zodark troop transports if they penetrate our atmospheric defenses and hit lower orbit. We need those skies clear of enemy ships to maintain air superiority. I expect you to employ your F-97 Orions to their maximum capabilities, utilizing your full missile complement to disrupt their landing operations and to help eliminate ground forces before they can even think of fortifying. Several New Eden bases have responded and will send drone bomber and starfighter strike groups. There'll be hundreds of you in the sky. Communication is a must."

The colonel turned to address another group. "Falcon Squadron, you'll be piloting B-99 Raiders today. Your targets are the Zodark troops and their transports if they land. These ships are heavily armored and will require precision and skill to take down. Coordinate with our orbital defense platforms to take 'em out before they can deploy their ground forces. And for any Zodark ground forces that make it to the surface, we've got AS-90 Reapers ready and waiting for them.

"Furthermore," Vale said, "should any of those Zodark forces manage to land, Eagle and Falcon Squadrons will transition to close-air support, providing ground troops with aerial firepower to repel the invaders. This will be a dynamic combat environment. So, stay alert to changing orders based on real-time battle developments. And for sectors requiring heavy ordnance or where enemy fortifications are identified, our AS-90 Reapers will be deployed. Pilots rated for the Reapers, be prepared for rapid deployment and target saturation. Remember, if those Zodark scum breach our atmosphere, it'll be up to Eagle Squadron to ensure they find no sanctuary in the skies. We'll meet the Zodark threat with unbelievable force and protect our sovereignty. Got it? Good! Now, get to your sim pods! Dismissed!"

Coop and the other pilots dashed out of the operations room and down the corridor. They reached a large metal door marked "Simulation Room: Delta Sector."

Inside, an array of seventy-two simulators filled the large space. These sim pods were designed to mimic the exact feel of flying. They rested slightly elevated above the ground, which allowed for a range of motion mimicking real aerial maneuvers.

Coop approached his designated simulator, a unit labeled "Eagle 05." He slid into the comfortable seat. It adjusted to fit his form, lifting slightly to create the sensation of floating. Before him, VR goggles and a headset rested on a polished console. They were thin and lightweight, crafted with a glossy black exterior. Coop placed them over his head and fit them on properly before pressing the On button. In an instant, he was immersed in the virtual cockpit of his F-97 Orion and, like always, he let out a gasp as a surge of exhilaration hit him the moment the RPC pod activated. Adrenaline pushed through his veins. His toes and fingers tingled. The hair on the back of his neck rose.

The virtual environment synced with Coop's F-97 Orion fighter drone's systems, creating a sensation akin to the rush of a high-speed takeoff. The digital plunge into another reality blurred the boundaries between the physical and virtual worlds. The experience immersed the pilot so deeply that those unaccustomed to piloting a drone might believe they were actually inside the fighter itself. Only, unlike a manned aircraft, these drone fighters could do maneuvers that would never have been possible with a human being inside. Coop didn't have to worry about pesky g-forces and the limits of his physical body.

On the panoramic display in front of Coop, strategic icons and a countdown timer mirrored the situation in the operations room. "Zodarks three minutes out," the display flashed, maintaining a constant update on the enemy's approach.

Can't wait to down some of these Zodark bastards, Coop thought.

A visual of the first Zodark he'd ever seen on the holo channels while at the Academy filled his mind.

It was but a short time ago that humanity had made two shocking discoveries—a Goldilocks world called New Eden in the Rhea Ab system and the existence of an alien race known as the Zodarks on said planet. This was the first time in recorded history that humans had encountered an intelligent extraterrestrial species. During first contact, the Zodarks had responded with hostility, and the situation quickly escalated into a full-scale war.

Shortly after, Earthers had discovered prisoners that looked like humans—Zodark captives—on New Eden. These human-like extraterrestrials, called Sumerians, hailed from another planet, called Sumer. A world still suffering under Zodark occupation.

This war intensified in 2091 with the first real battle against Zodark ships. The conflict gave Republic forces a victory, and they gained control of the Rhea system from the Zodarks.

The outbreak of the interstellar war was a pivotal moment in Coop's life. Before then, he had been just skating by at the Academy, barely passing his classes, and getting into a little too much trouble. As news of the conflict spread, Coop consumed holovids showing the fresh battles and naval combat stories from officers and pilots. Each story planted a seed deep within his mind—a growing realization that he could no longer sit by while the fate of humanity stood in jeopardy. While Coop had watched the footage of brave men and women fighting to protect humanity from an alien threat, he began to see a way out of his own predicament. It was a chance to escape his father's grip and make a real difference in the world and in a sector of space far from his dad. By the time he graduated, Coop's instructors had recognized him as the "most improved" student.

Colonel Vale's voice boomed over the comms. "Pilots, we launch at my mark. Stay alert, and be prepared to engage the moment those transports breach our atmosphere."

Strike, the leader of Coop's squadron, came on the line. His voice always carried an undertone that grated on Coop's nerves. "Eagle Squadron, check your systems and sync your auxiliaries. We're the first line of defense. Let's keep those Zodarks out of our skies."

Displaying on Coop's screen, the Republic Navy defensive forces engaged in a fierce orbital conflict against the four Zodark heavy cruisers. The cruisers, marked in red, unleashed volleys of laser fire and torpedoes. The Republic countered with a barrage of magrail and missile fire, their positions now just above the planet's orbit. Amid this engagement, icons representing the Zodark troop transports flew through the fray. A moment later, one of the transport icons flickered and disappeared from the screen, signaling its obliteration. The remaining vessels pressed on, breaching the upper layers of New Eden's atmosphere. Their descent was shown by trailing fire on Coop's display. Coop narrowed his eyes, his fingers over the controls. The troop transports plunged into the planet's defensive ring.

Coop calibrated the drone's weapons systems. *Time to end these aliens and end them good.*

The colonel's voice filled Coop's sim cockpit. "Eagle and Falcon squadrons, this is it. Launch your drones. Let's show these Zodarks that New Eden is ours."

With a swift motion, Coop initiated the launch sequence. His sim pod vibrated as the drone, mirroring his movements, lifted off its own platform in the real world. Outside, the engines roared to life, and his F-97 Orion, along with its sister drones, soared into the twilight sky of New Eden.

I'm gonna end this invasion before it begins. Hooyah!

One Year Ago

Year 2092
Schriever Space Force Base
Colorado Springs, Colorado
Earth

The squadron office was quiet. Heavy snow fell outside the windows of Schriever Space Force Base. Love sat at her desk, data pad in hand. She'd been reviewing the requests from logistics of what cargo needed to be moved for the last hour; however, the numbers had started to blur together as she tried to ignore the holiday music that was being played throughout the building.

The last of their friends had left in the morning, rushing off to catch flights home with cheerful "Merry Christmas!" wishes. It made Love's heart ache. Like always, she hid it well. She'd said goodbye while maintaining the lie that staying here at the base was her choice, that her family could wait until next year.

Thing was, her mom had died shortly after the war with the Zodarks had begun. They'd found her charred remains in a house fire. No one knew how it had started. Love figured her mom had burned it down to end her miserable life. With her daughter off and starting her own career, her mom had nothing other than her suicidal thoughts and whiskey.

But who knew?

Still, Love stayed home, pretending any extended family had to wait until another time. In truth, she didn't even know where those people were and had no desire to look them up after how they'd abandoned her mom long ago.

To her, this lie was better than admitting that, besides Jack Hannigan, she had no one. In the distant past, her mother's Christmases had consisted of empty bottles and white lies. So, what was Christmas anyway? Holidays made her feel uncomfortable, so who cared?

Love jerked back at the sound of her office door. "Jack?"

Hannigan's head poked around the doorframe. "I brought you something."

"Oh?"

"Bring it in, boys," Hannigan said, stepping aside.

Three of Hannigan's friends walked in. One set down a short, artificial Christmas tree that had been decorated with makeshift ornaments crafted from spare parts. Another brought in strands of Christmas lights that he plugged in and immediately started draping across the office. A third brought out two covered plates of food and took the metal cloches off with a flourish, revealing a traditional Christmas dinner.

"How did you…?"

"Found the lights in storage," Hannigan explained. "The tree's from the commandant's office—don't worry, I asked first. And dinner…well, I had to call in some favors with the kitchen staff, but they left us something special."

Love was so confused. "I thought you left to go spend Christmas with your parents," she said.

"Oh, that." Hannigan smiled. "I stayed at Chuck's place last night, setting up the surprise," he explained, patting his friend on the back. "Thanks, guys, I think we've got it from here."

"No problem, Jack."

"See you later, man."

"Merry Christmas, love birds."

Jack waited for his friends to file out of the office, then reached into the box he'd brought in and pulled out some silverware and cloth napkins he'd managed to procure, as well as some cups and a bottle of sparkling grape juice.

"I couldn't get the real thing, obviously, since you're still on duty," he apologized.

"I'm still getting over the fact that you're here," Naomi said. "Didn't you want to spend the time with your family?"

"You are my family, Naomi."

A lump formed in Love's throat and she decided it would be best to concentrate on the food before she started crying. She took a deep breath, smelling the aroma of her dinner. "That's real turkey, Jack—not the 3-D printed stuff."

"Yep," he agreed, smiling. "You should dig in, while it's still warm."

She obliged and took a bite. "Is that real cranberry sauce too?"

"Mom sent it," Hannigan replied. "She always makes extra."

"I never…I mean, my mother didn't…"

"I know." Hannigan's hand found hers across the desk. "Consider this your first real Christmas, Naomi. I know you said you wanted to stay here to take someone else's place that had a family, but no one should be alone on Christmas."

"Thank you," said Naomi, barely getting the words out.

He squeezed her hand. "Merry Christmas, Naomi. I can't say it enough, but I love you."

"I love you too." She looked around at the twinkling lights, the falling snow outside, the steaming plates of food. For the first time in her life, she understood what Christmas was supposed to feel like. "Merry Christmas, Jack."

That night, they spent hours talking, laughing, and sharing stories. He taught her how to make paper snowflakes from old mission briefings, and she taught him how to fold them into origami stars. When the kitchen's ancient sound system crackled to life with century-old carols, he pulled her up to dance, neither of them caring that they didn't know the steps.

****

Year 2093
RNS *Kentucky*
Rhea System, New Eden Stargate

Love could hear what sounded like unmitigated chaos surrounding her before her eyes fluttered open. The sharp lights of the room attacked her vision. She winced. Her head throbbed and each heartbeat sent a fresh wave of pain radiating through her skull.

"Where… where am I?" she croaked out, her voice hoarse.

No one responded to her right away. Maybe they couldn't hear her over the sounds of crying and groans of pain. She looked around and realized that she was in a very crowded med bay. Exam table after exam table was filled with people, being treated for electrical burns, shrapnel wounds, you name it. Love saw a medic place a robotic arm over someone's wounded leg; they were sutured up faster than any human could have ever performed that function. Another medic set someone's arm before a robotic arm added a cast.

A doctor in a lab coat walked over to Love, apparently alerted to her change in vital signs. "Where am I?" Love repeated.

"You're in RNS *Kentucky*'s med bay," the woman explained, checking over the data pad that was attached to the bed where Love now sat.

"*Kentucky*?" Confusion crossed Love's face. She struggled to sit up as her muscles protested the movement.

"Yes," the doctor confirmed. "Do you remember anything?"

Love closed her eyes, trying to piece together the fragmented memories swirling in her mind. "A little, maybe?" Her brow scrunched in concentration.

A heaviness pressed down on Love's chest. Something had occurred and it was something bad. Call it a woman's intuition, call it whatever, but she could feel it, and deeper than the darkest pit on Earth. "What happened?" She dreaded the answer the moment she asked.

"You were on a civilian transport en route to New Eden, when your ship was attacked by Zodarks," the doctor explained.

Panic set in. "Where's Jack?" Naomi pressed. "Where's my husband."

The doctor was kind but matter-of-fact. "He didn't make it, Lieutenant. He's…gone."

The words hit Love like a knee to her gut, stealing the air from her lungs. She froze, her eyes wide. "No." She shook her head. "Can't be."

"I'm so sorry to be the one to tell you this, but it is true, ma'am," the doctor replied.

Love's heart shattered. The pieces scattered like shards of glass. Tremors rippled through her body. Her hands shook as her mind replayed the images of her husband, dying in her arms as they drifted alone in a life pod.

She remembered. Everything.

Around her, the sounds of medical equipment amplified her anguish. She clutched the hospital blanket as she fought to regain control of her emotions.

"I'm sorry," the doctor repeated. There was a kindness in her eyes, but also the professional detachment one would have to have to thrive as a doctor on a large ship like this.

Love's mind flashed with memories of Hannigan. His infectious laughter, the way his eyes crinkled when he smiled, the gentle touch of his hand on her cheek. Without him, what kind of future would she have? Hannigan had always helped her through the darkest of times, made life easier, more fun. Surprises after surprises always made her love him more.

"I remember it all now," Love explained. She sighed. "Could you please leave me alone for a bit?" she asked the doctor. "I need some time."

The doctor, apparently satisfied that Love's condition was sufficiently stable, nodded and pointed to the buzzer attached to her bed. "If you need something, just give us a ring." Then she rushed off to attend to other patients.

As the doctor walked away, Love curled up on the bed and cupped her head in her palms. Something tugged at her arm. When she lifted her hands away to look, the quick motion ripped an IV tube out of her arm. On cue, a nurse hurried to her side.

"Lieutenant Love, we need to keep the IV in," the nurse said. "You've lost a lot of electrolytes, and your body needs the fluids to recover."

"I'm sorry. I didn't mean—"

"I'll help you put that back in, miss."

"I need time to myself."

"Yes, yes. But let me put that IV tube back in, OK?"

Love closed her eyes. "I need to be alone."

The nurse took Love's hand. "Yes. Just be a little more careful next time, OK?"

Love looked at the nurse and swallowed hard. She nodded, allowing the nurse to put a clean line into her arm and reinsert the IV. "All right."

Love squeezed her eyes shut, thinking of Hannigan. Immediately, a memory of their wedding day hit her. They'd interlocked fingers, and she'd looked into Hannigan's eyes as they'd exchanged the "I dos" before sharing their first kiss as a married couple.

"Jack," Love said. "Come back. Please come back."

Chapter 23
Second Chances

Year 2093
RNS *Kentucky*
Rhea System

Chief Brian Ford stood outside Lee's quarters. The stress of the previous day's events sat like an Osprey's engine upon his shoulders. Although the crew he worked with had survived the battle—a cause for celebration—the loss of Jack Hannigan, who he'd come to regard as his good friend during his stint at the Academy, made him feel as though a shadow blanketed him.

Ford had only a few close friends. When he let someone in, he dealt with the fear of losing them by pretending they were somehow immortal. Sounded strange, he knew. To him, it was easier than facing reality. He hadn't had much growing up, let alone family, so on the streets, loss had come plenty. In this way, it created a barrier in front of him, shielding him from unwanted emotions.

Other than Carl, who'd practically saved his life, Ford kept most people at arm's length. He stayed distant. Always. Because by doing this, he pushed away a sense of responsibility, relieving him of the hell that came from loss, something he was experiencing now.

Throughout his life, people had found his behavior puzzling. And for good reason. He had a pattern of forming connections, good ones. Then, when it felt too close, he'd vanish without explanation. He'd leave no trace—no phone call, no message, no hint of his whereabouts or reasons for departing. He hadn't done that with Carl. Still, Ford despised this aspect of his own personality. Countless times, he'd vowed to change this destructive habit. He'd promised himself, time and again, he'd stop running away from relationships.

He rapped his knuckles against the metal door. A muffled "Come" sounded from within. The door slid to the side.

Ford stepped into the chamber. He straightened his posture as he stood before his superior officer.

Lee, seated at his desk, looked up from a data pad and gestured for Ford to take a seat. "At ease, Chief."

Ford asked, "May I speak freely, sir?"

"You may. Take a seat."

As Ford sat his rump in the chair opposite Lee, he studied his face. The two had been through thick and thin together since their days on the *Trenton*. Hence, Ford knew the guy well. Despite Lee's attempt to maintain a stoic expression, pain was etched in the lines around his old friend's eyes. Oldendorf's death had hit them all hard, but Lee, who'd been under the commander's tutelage, seemed more affected.

"How you holding up?"

Lee waved a dismissive hand. "I'm fine, Chief. Part of the job. We all knew the risks when we signed up." The weariness on his face told a different story. Oldendorf's death haunted Lee. Ford could tell. After a moment, Lee leaned forward, clasping his hands on the desk. "What's on your mind, Ford? What can I do for you?"

Ford hesitated, unsure of how to broach the subject. "Sir, it's about Jack."

"Hannigan? Haven't seen him in years. Married Naomi Love and… anyway… why do you bring Hannigan up?"

Ford's throat tightened. "That's actually why I'm here. We found Hannigan and Love in the escape pod from the civilian transport."

Lee wrinkled his face, no doubt confused. "What were they doing on a civilian ship?"

"They were being reassigned to an Osprey squadron on New Eden. From what I've read, the Fleet was moving a lot of military people with civilian transports to surge more soldiers and spacers to New Eden." Ford stopped for a moment to gather himself for the next part. "Hannigan didn't make it. Found him dead in the escape pod."

Lee remained stoic, though the side of his mouth twitched. "I see." He went to speak but halted. After gathering himself and clearing his throat, he asked, "And Love? Is she…?"

"Alive, sir. Shaken up. Grieving. But physically unharmed." The image of Love's anguished face flashed in Ford's mind.

Lee ran a hand over his face and his shoulders slumped. "I'm glad she's safe. To lose Jack…" He shook his head. "I know it's gotta be hard. We'll need to notify their squadron and let them know what happened. I'm sure if Naomi needs some leave, they'll give it to her. It's good you came here to let me know. I can get her off the ship as soon as we dock."

Lee stood and sighed. "Unfortunately, we still have a lot to take care of with our ship, Ford. For now, let's focus on what we can do to get ourselves ready to fight again, should we have to. You're dismissed."

Ford left Lee's office and walked through the *Kentucky*'s corridors. While he rounded a corner, a voice called out to him. "Good job back there, Chief. We got those people free all right."

Back where?

Ford turned. Deck Hand Ian Murray, one of the many who'd assisted with the escape capsule's rescue efforts at the landing bay, strode toward him. Ford gave a tired smile. "Same to you."

Murray beamed at the praise as Ford continued on his way, stepping into a lift. He pressed the button for Deck 3, taking him to the mess hall. The doors slid shut, and he rested against the wall, closing his eyes for a brief moment.

I need a nap.

When the elevator doors opened, Ford stepped out into the busy mess hall. Long tables and benches engulfed the open space. Dispensers lined the walls. They provided a variety of hot and cold meals, snacks, and beverages.

Ford joined the line and waited as the people ahead of him made their selections. He grabbed a tray and moved along the dispensers, choosing a simple meal of a fruit pack and a cup of strong black coffee.

Ford scanned the room for an empty seat. He spotted one at the end of a table and made his way over, settling down like a heavy log on the bench. As he began to eat, someone walked in his direction.

Ford glanced up. His eyes narrowed as he recognized the officer—Petty Officer Kravitz. The man, sensing Ford's displeasure, gave an apologetic smile. "Sorry, Chief. I didn't mean to intrude." Kravitz set his tray down beside Ford's.

Without a word, Ford gave him a pointed stare.

Kravitz got the hint and gathered his tray. "I'll just… find another seat."

"Good man."

As Kravitz hurried off, Ford returned to his meal. His mind drifted back to a time long before he had joined the Republic Navy. He remembered the cold, lonely days spent in a beat-up car parked on the side of the road, where he'd struggled to stay warm as he tinkered with the engine, using whatever spare parts he could scavenge.

One particularly frigid afternoon, a knock on the car window startled him. Ford glanced up to see a man in a navy-blue one-piece mechanic's outfit. The guy motioned for Ford to roll down the window.

Ford complied. "Yeah?"

"I'm Carl." Misty clouds of breath billowed from his mouth, mixing with the chill in the air.

Ford stared.

Carl blew hot breath into his balled-up hands. "Did you build the engine in this thing?" He peered at the hood with an impressed look.

Ford nodded. "Yeah, I did. What's it to you?"

Carl's eyes crinkled at the corners. "I've seen you drive this thing around and park here the past few months. Saw you working on it, too, using spare parts from just the streets. How'd you manage that?"

Ford shrugged, his gaze on the steering wheel. "Grew up a son of a mechanic. I can fix old cars and new cars, doesn't matter."

"You want a better life?"

Ford snorted. "Are you a Republic military recruiter or something?"

"Nope."

"Police?"

"No."

"OK. Then be on your way." Ford went to close the window.

"Wait." Carl put his finger through the gap. "I can help you. You've got talent. You just need some more tools, some teaching, and you'd shine."

"Shine?" Ford made a face. "What are you talking about? Besides, I've got a good life. Just hit a rough patch this past year. I'll be back up and at 'em soon enough."

"Sooner rather than later?" Carl asked.

"Do you need something?"

Carl motioned for Ford to get out of his car to follow him. "You know damn well why you parked next to my business. And you got your way, so I'm giving you the chance you hoped for. Yes, I've been watching you, and I'm beyond impressed with what you can do. But I'll only ask you this once, and that's for you to come with me. I've got something I want to show you, something that'll change your life forever."

Year 2093
Firebase Nova
Tempas Mountain Range, Manta River Highlands
New Eden

The Orion's remotely piloted cockpit's gauges, switches, and displays illuminated on the dash before Coop. He scanned the array. The fuel level displayed full. The engine status indicators brightened to a steady green. The weapons readouts appeared optimal—laser cannons primed, their charge levels at maximum capacity. The missile bays showed fully stocked, each projectile armed and ready to blast into the Zodark forces.

After each take off with his F-97 Orion, Coop had always made it a habit to perform multiple checklist verifications.

Coop flipped a toggle switch to engage the inertial dampeners to make sure the intense acceleration and maneuvers wouldn't crush the Orion's equipment. Next, he adjusted the throttle quadrant and set the desired thrust levels for the maneuvering engines.

"Eagle Squadron, this is Strike," the lead pilot's voice blasted over the comm. "Four Zodark Beadles incoming. They're loaded to the brim with enemy soldiers. We're taking them down. Coop, you're with Raven. Talon, you're with Banshee. The rest of you, get with your assigned partner and engage at will."

Coop's jaw clenched as he maneuvered his Orion into position beside Raven's fighter. *Sure, the jerk calls my name out over the comms, but wingman duty? I mean, come on! Next time I'll let Strike win a poker round. That spiteful piece of...*

"Raven, this is Coop," he said. "I'm on your six. Let's light them up."

Raven's acknowledgment came through the comm, and together they flew their drones forward.

The sim pod's cockpit whirred with energy as Coop pushed the Orion. Through the holovid screen, dark, twisted trees stretched out into a forest. Gnarled branches reached toward the cloudless night sky.

Above, the stars twinkled, and the three moons brightened the landscape below.

Coop activated the targeting computer by tapping on the control panel. This allowed him to acquire and track potential threats. He fine-tuned the sensor array's sensitivity by turning a dial. With a few flicks of a series of holographic switches, he powered up the weapons systems, arming the 20mm magrail guns and JATMs—Joint Advanced Tactical Missiles. He adjusted the weapon targeting parameters using an adjacent dial. There, he raised the level for the Lead Compensator Guidance to account for the speeds and distances involved in dogfighting. Lastly, he initiated the tactical display.

Beyond his HUD, a holographic screen inside his sim pod projected a holo of the battlefield. Using a third dial, he zoomed in and out to analyze friendly and enemy forces and their positions.

It's time to kill some ugly blue guys, Coop thought.

Coop's face hardened while he sat in the sim pod's cockpit. In front of him, a flock of odd bat-like creatures flitted through the air. Their leathery wings silhouetted against the darkness as he flew past them. He couldn't make out the details of their exact appearance, but their weird, erratic movements sent a shiver down his spine.

Their skin glistens like Zodark scum.

"Strike, this is Raven," Coop's wingman's tone filled the squadron-wide channel. "I've got eyes on multiple troop transports, bearing two-seven-zero, altitude nine hundred kilometers, low orbit."

As Coop continued to ascend his drone fighter, multiple groups of Orion fighters appeared on his HUD—ten more squadrons. They equaled over 240 Republic pilots. Above and in higher orbit, a major battle took place between Zodark heavy cruisers and the Republic's naval forces. Bright explosions lit up Coop's holodisplay.

"Copy that, Raven," Strike said. "All units, be advised. We have confirmed enemy troop transports inbound. Lock targets on the Beadle at grid coordinates Alpha-Niner-Four-Three. That's our primary target. All pilots, concentrate fire on that Beadle transport. I repeat, Alpha-Niner-Four-Three is the primary target. Engage at will. Execute maneuver Delta-Five. Ascend to nine hundred and two kilometers and prepare to engage on my mark."

Coop's grip tightened on the controls. Maneuver Delta-Five, known as the "Hawk's Dive" among the pilots, was a tried-and-true tactic for dealing with heavily armored targets like troop transports.

He glanced at his radar and watched the positions of his squadmates as they moved to comply with Strike's orders. The altimeter climbed as he guided his starfighter upward.

As he leveled out at the designated altitude, Coop scanned the darkened lower orbit horizon and spotted the approaching transports.

"This is Strike. Commence attack run on my mark. Do not impede Republic forces. Out."

"Aye, sir," came the pilots' replies.

Coop's finger hovered over the trigger. On his HUD, a series of segmented circles appeared and contracted around the hostile craft until they snapped into a solid reticle. It indicated a successful target lock. Numerical data streamed across the bottom of the display to provide real-time updates on the target's speed, distance, and projected time to intercept. A warning icon flashed in the top-right corner. It alerted Coop to the target's active countermeasures and the potential need for evasive maneuvers.

"Three, two, one, mark!"

At Strike's command, Coop pushed the Orion into a steep dive. The fighter cut through space like a tomahawk. The enemy troop transports, also called Beadles, grew larger in his sights, their hulking forms ripened for the taking. They were a menacing sight with their black bodies, octopus-like heads, and yellow markings dotting their exterior. Each transport stretched an impressive 1,529 meters in length and dwarfed the Orions. These giants of the sky carried a large amount of troops and ships within their holds.

The Beadles engaged. Bright flashes erupted from their exteriors as laser fire lashed outward. Torpedoes launched, the fiery objects heading for incoming Republic fighters.

Strike spoke over the comm. "Deploy chaff and SW countermeasures now!"

Coop pressed on the controls. Chaff clouds burst forth. The SW missiles detonated, and a barrier of sand and water scattered in hopes of weakening the laser fire.

Intelligence reports claimed every Beadle could carry up to thirty-five hundred Zodark warriors. Furthermore, they could hold and launch sixteen Vulture starfighters, forty medium cargo transports, ten large cargo transports, and fifty troop landers. Those would launch any minute now.

As the chaff and SW clouds filled the space around them, the Beadles began to let loose their cargo. Vulture starfighters poured out, darting through the debris-filled battlefield. Rectangular medium and large cargo transports followed suit. They carried supplies, along with equipment to support the Zodark ground insurgency below. Troop landers brought up the rear, their bulbous bodies looking like giant snake eyes. Each one ferried hundreds of Zodark warriors toward the planet's surface as they blasted in that direction.

Amidst the turmoil, Coop's sensors found a torpedo hurtling toward his Orion. The plasma warhead glowed. With fast reflexes, Coop jerked the controls and released countermeasures. He threw his craft into a spiral, his wingman maneuvering in the opposite direction. The torpedo shot past them and slammed into some of the chaff's metallic particles. A small, fiery cloud burst behind Coop's F-97.

"I've got another one on me, Coop!" Raven said.

Coop veered his Orion around toward Vultures and Republic starfighters in a tangled fight all around and located the torpedo bearing down on Raven's craft. "I'm on it!"

Coop lined up the shot, centering the sim cockpit's reticle on the incoming projectile. Through the heads-up display, the torpedo's heat signature and trajectory data were overlaid on the crosshairs, allowing Coop to anticipate the projectile's movements. He squeezed the trigger and the magrail guns thrummed with power, sending high-density tungsten rounds streaking at the incoming torpedo.

The rounds found their mark. Blinding flashes of light filled the screen for a moment. Coop's heart skipped a beat as he watched the explosion. The shock wave rippled through the planet's lower orbit. Raven's Orion emerged from the blast, its armor covered with dying embers.

Dang, I'm good, Coop thought.

Raven's voice crackled over the comm. "Thanks for the save!"

"Not a problem."

Coop would make certain Strike wouldn't put him in a wingman roll again. Heck, once this was finished, he'd tell the guy to his face. He tallied one torpedo down by his own hands, a difficult trick even Strike would have a tough time performing. When this was over, it would be fine to compare flight performance and, again, shove the results in Strike's face.

Hopefully, command will see the discrepancy between him and me.

"Raven, status?" Coop asked.

"Starboard armor at seventy-eight percent. No biggie. This Orion's still in the fight."

Coop nodded. "Roger that. Take up my wing. We'll take these bastards down."

"Negative, Coop. You're on my wing per orders."

Coop grimaced. "Aye, moving to your six."

As they whirled back into the fray, Coop studied the frenzy unfolding around them. To his port, a Vulture starfighter erupted in a ball of flames. Its wreckage careened into the path of another Zodark fighter. The two crafts collided, burning into a flash of warped alloy and charred engine parts.

All around, ships flew erratically. Burst of red-and-orange eruptions surrounded Coop's holo.

"Ninja, watch your nine!" Ghost Dog's tone boomed through the communication link. "You've got a bogey incoming!"

To Coop's starboard, Ninja's F-97 engaged in a dogfight with a Vulture. Ninja banked hard, his craft's twin engines flaring as it took a tight turn. The Vulture mirrored the maneuver and closed the distance between them with incredible speed.

"I could use some help here!" Ninja called out.

Plasma torpedoes streaked past Ninja's canopy as the Vulture opened fire. As the enemy craft spat lasers, Ninja sent the F-97 into barrel rolls while ejecting chaff.

Without hesitation, Coop rolled his Orion and dove toward Ninja's position. "I'm breaking formation. Hold on, Ninja. I'm on my way."

"Negative, Coop!" Raven's voice burst into the comms. "Maintain your position on my wing. I repeat, maintain your position!"

Coop ignored the order. He focused on reaching Ninja before it was too late.

"What the hell are you doing?" Ghost Dog shouted. "Coop, you're in my line of fire! I can't get a clear shot at the Vulture!"

Coop was too close now to break off his vector. He moved his Orion into position behind the Vulture and grinned. "No one will remember you, buddy," he said under his breath to the enemy pilot.

Just as Coop went to fire his magrails, Ninja cut the throttle and slammed the air brakes. The Vulture overshot. Its pilot struggled to compensate for the unexpected move. Seizing the opportunity, Ninja unleashed a hail of magrail rounds.

The Vulture corkscrewed through the tungsten round spread and evaded the metal projectiles with mere meters to spare.

"Disengage, Ninja. I'm on this guy," Coop said.

Ninja veered away as Coop pursued, matching the Vulture's movements—the two fighters now locked in a spiral heading toward New Eden's surface.

Coop clutched the pod's controls with a firm grip. His knuckles whitened. Both fighters flew through the atmosphere and banked into a cloud. The Vulture closed in on his sights. In seconds, the gray haze disappeared as he followed the enemy's dive. The altimeter rapidly counted down—10,542 meters, 9,389 meters, 8,476 meters. The ground rushed up to meet them, a dark landscape of forest and jagged boulders lit up by the flashes of explosions above.

The enemy Vulture pitched, trying to evade Coop's chase. Coop held his breath as the altimeter ticked down to 5,400 meters. The Orion's magrail guns locked onto the Vulture. The crosshairs brightened red in the simulator cockpit. Coop pressed the trigger. High-density rounds screamed toward the enemy starfighter.

In seconds, the projectiles slammed into the Vulture's rear thrusters. The impact tore through its armor. The Zodark craft shuddered. Its engines erupted in arcs of electric-blue lightning. Flames engulfed its fuselage. With a final explosion, the Vulture disintegrated. Its debris rained down upon the dark countryside below.

"Coop, get back to your wingman. That's an order!" Strike's voice resounded through Coop's helmet.

That's one Vulture kill and one dead torpedo. What do you got, Strike?

"Roger!" Coop pulled back on the controls. His Orion climbed away from New Eden's surface. When he caught sight of a swarm of Zodark troop landers and cargo transports heading toward the surface, he leveled out to meet them.

"Negative, Strike. Request immediate air support, six thousand, three hundred meters, Kilo-Lima-Eight-Seven. Tally enemy landers and cargo units in visual range. Engaging targets to prevent hostile deployment on the ground. Over."

"Allied Orions are inbound to your position, Coop. B-99 bombers are currently engaging hostiles near the LZs. All units, weapons tight. Form up on your respective wingmen, and that includes you, Coop. Over."

Coop refused to let these Zodarks in front of him land, even if allied fighters were heading in his direction to deal with them. "This is Coop. Request clearance for autonomous engagement. Over." The landers and cargo transports grew larger on his HUD as he steered his F-97 closer.

Strike replied, "Negative, Coop. Rejoin Raven. Out."

On Coop's HUD, Orion F-97s closed in. They'd arrive too late, or rather, later than Coop wanted. He had to end these ships, and now. It'd pad his stats too.

He armed his missiles as he neared the targets, five landers and four cargo ships. The sound of the target lock filled the cockpit as he sighted a lander. Coop punched a sequence of commands into the weapons computer, designating the JATMs as the active ordnance. With a tap, he enabled the seeker heads so the missiles could acquire and track their intended targets.

On the tactical display, the targeting reticles zeroed in on the enemy positions. Several more targets locked on as the JATMs armed, ready to unleash their devastating thunder.

Coop squinted in concentration. Once those missiles launched, there would be no turning back from Strike's anger after this mission ended.

He smiled. *Good.*

With a determined growl, Coop released a volley of missiles. The projectiles slammed into two troop landers. Balls of fire lit up the night sky. The rest of the enemy ships sent a barrage of laser fire in response—Coop banked hard and released SW missiles. Once the SW missiles detonated, covering a massive radius with sand and water, he swiftly moved out of their targeting range.

His HUD lit up with enemy icon indicators, and his heart sank. "There's a lot more of them!" Over a dozen new Zodark landers and cargo transports came into view, heading toward a mountain range in the distance. "Lead, requesting additional air support to my current position, grid reference zero-three-four-seven-eight-five, angels six. What ally fighters are being sent won't be enough. Encountered numerous enemy ships, require three dozen additional flights of F-97s for engagement, over."

"More on their way," Strike said. "Get up here, Coop! Now!"

Coop's HUD acquired a lock-on tone, indicating an inbound threat. He ripple-fired a salvo of countermeasures. They bloomed across the sky in rapid succession. As he executed a hard turn, laser fire sank into his craft's nose from a pair of hostile Vultures. When Coop rolled his Orion in the opposite direction, more Vulture weapons fire went wide, impacting the terrain below and turning clumps of trees into fiery messes. Smoke wafted upward toward his Orion.

The proximity alert blared and pierced the pod. Hostile contacts flooded Coop's screen—enemy starfighters and a horde of troop landers. Stars twinkled in the background. Moons hung low on the horizon.

A direct hit breached his port hull. Coop fought for control, the damage causing error messages to appear across his pod's HUD. His Orion entered a flat spin. The landscape below whirled as he tumbled through the atmosphere.

Warning lights flashed. Through the holo, sparks showered from ruptured conduits inside the F-97's cockpit. As Coop tried to straighten his fighter, his craft dipped toward hills covered in trees as far as the eye could see.

"Mayday, mayday, this is Coop. I've taken a hit and lost control authority. She's departing controlled flight."

As Coop turned inside his sim's cockpit, out of the corner of his eye, he saw a Vulture headed in his direction with laser fire shooting from its wings.

Chapter 25
A Hundred and Fifty Million

Year 2093
Firebase Nova
Tempas Mountain Range, Manta River Highlands
New Eden

The fact that Coop controlled a remotely operated drone sometimes made him a little too daring with his tactics. Piloting from a secure location, detached from the physical risks, allowed him to push the envelope and execute maneuvers as daring as in a video game.

Coop reduced his stress quite a bit by not worrying about the astronomical costs or the potential loss of his own life. However, his accurate split-second decisions had always kept his Orion F-97 alive, even when he flew it into the worst kinds of danger.

If a pilot lost one of these starfighters in combat, the man in charge would blow an FTL coil, metaphorically speaking. It'd be like the superior's own child had died. Still, along with the habits Coop had perchance acquired from his father, keeping his equipment intact became second nature to him. And, regardless of the circumstances.

Today, things changed.

Coop fought to regain control of his damaged craft. A Vulture's laser fire had ripped through the starboard hull and sent Coop's Orion into a spin. Klaxons blared inside Coop's sim pod. Red warning lights flashed across the instrument panel.

With every ounce of skill, Coop wrestled with the controls, trying to stabilize the Orion. His fighter shuddered, pitched, and shifted into a dive. Even from within the pod and through his helmet, the groaning of the F-97 cockpit's actual frame under immense stress reached Coop's ears.

He glared at his dash's flashing displays. His mind sought to find a solution. In mere seconds, the Orion fighter would break apart. On Coop's HUD, it showed the Vulture close in for the kill.

In a last-ditch effort, Coop fired off a volley of countermeasures. The flares streaked through the night sky and, for an instant, confused the Vulture's targeting systems.

The enemy swung around and shot a barrage of laser fire. The beams sliced through the Orion's hull. The drone's wings were sheared off, sending it spinning away into the darkness. The fuselage buckled like clay under pressure, its internal components exploding in an array of sparks and shrapnel.

Inside the Orion's cockpit, the world disintegrated. The canopy shattered. The rush of decompression tore at the control panels and dashboard. Debris pelted the camera feed, and Coop jerked back as a piece of metal slammed into the lens and covered the pod's holoscreen for a brief second. The F-97's instruments burst into flames. Readouts warped. Static filled his sim pod's HUD until…

A bright light. Then the Orion erupted into an explosion. The eruption consumed the drone, and everything went black. The holodisplay in Coop's pod powered off and it plunged him into darkness. Besides the sudden silence, all he could hear now was the ragged sounds of his own breathing.

Coop sat motionless. Sweat trickled down his temples, the salty droplets stinging his eyes. He grimaced. He couldn't believe it. He'd never tell his father what had happened today and hoped his dad wouldn't weasel his way into the Republic command logs, after-action reports, or classified repositories. The man had done it before. A mouthful from his old man always ended in shouting matches.

He dropped his head into his palms. *I'm better than this! I'm the best pilot in this squadron.* He grunted.

As Coop stared at the blank holoscreen, a transparent window showing a glimpse into the black expanse of the simulation room's piloting facility replaced the holographic simulation.

Through the window lay rows upon rows of sim pods, housing pilots engaged in their own fight against the Zodarks. Arranged on multiple decks, pods cascaded down from the highest level to the lowest platform. Coop's drone pod, number five, sat on the topmost deck in the rear, giving him a bird's-eye view of the entire complex. All around, holographic displays lined the walls. Streams of data and tactical information flowed across their interfaces.

Coop took a deep breath, doing his best to calm the growing anger welling up inside of him. "Stupid move, Coop. Just… stupid!"

Coop wouldn't let this setback define him. No, not for a second. He set his jaw and activated the comm system. "Command, this is

Lieutenant Blake Cooper of Eagle Squadron, call sign Coop. Requesting permission to reengage with a new F-97 Orion. Over."

After a brief silence, static crackled over the link. "Lieutenant Cooper, this is Command. Your request for reengagement is granted. Proceed. Available Orion F-97 drone fighter in Hangar Bay Gamma and ready for immediate deployment. Acknowledge. Over."

"Command, I acknowledge. Proceeding to link up with Hangar Bay Gamma for immediate deployment. Out."

The world around Coop fell away, and for the second time today, the virtual cockpit of an Orion F-97 took its place. The displays blinked to life, and the holographic screens illuminated him in a soft blue glow. Through the helmet's audio feed, the growl of the craft's engines grew in strength as the F-97 sat ready to take off on the hangar deck.

"Initiating link," a voice intoned. "Synchronization in progress."

A disorienting sensation came over Coop as his sim pod merged with the Orion's systems.

He shook it off and glanced around the hangar bay, taking in the bustling activity of the ground crews. Technicians scurried about as they made final adjustments to the starfighter.

"All systems nominal," a voice said. "Orion F-97 ready for deployment."

Coop nodded. "Requesting clearance for immediate takeoff."

"Lieutenant Cooper, you are cleared for takeoff. Good hunting out there, over."

"Roger that, Command. Coop out."

He engaged the thrusters and the Orion lifted off the hangar deck. The craft shot forward. The hangar walls blurred past as the F-97 gathered speed. The ship pushed through the night sky, the stars stretching out before him as he ascended higher.

After a few minutes, Coop leveled off in low orbit as his comm system boomed to life. "All units, be advised," a voice said. "Troop landers have breached the perimeter. B-99 Raiders are engaging with payload delivery on designated coordinates. Maintain air superiority and neutralize any remaining enemy craft."

Coop acknowledged the transmission with a "Roger that." The Raiders were the heavy hitters, their devastating payloads capable of turning a city block into rubble. The Raiders were vulnerable as well, and they relied on the Orions to keep the skies clear of Vultures.

Communications erupted with Eagle Squadron chatter. Pilots called out targets, requested support, and relayed their combat status.

"I'm hit!" a voice cried out. "Port engine's gone!"

"Vulture on my tail!" another pilot shouted.

Coop scanned the tactical display. Enemy and ally signatures crisscrossed in low orbit. On the screen, he spotted Raven, whose icon flashed red, pursued by a Vulture.

"Hang on, Raven," Coop said. "I'm coming. Bank to port on my mark."

Coop punched the throttle. The Orion surged forward. The Vulture grew larger in his sights. Cargo ships and troop landers pocked lower orbit on his HUD as they launched from a Beadle cresting the horizon.

"Mark!" Coop ordered.

Raven banked his Orion. The sudden maneuver exposed the Vulture's flank as it followed Raven. Coop squeezed off a volley of magrail rounds. The projectiles tore through the enemy, and the ship ballooned into a flash of bunging metal. Its shattered remains spun away toward the thicker atmosphere below.

Raven's tone punched through Coop's audio. "Don't leave my wing again, Coop! Stick to the formation."

Coop bit back a retort. "Roger."

As Coop fell back into formation behind Raven, Vultures swarmed. Orions wove, their magrails spitting streams of red-hot rounds.

In front of them, the last Zodark Beadle floated like a wounded beast. Half of its fuselage had been broken away by allied fire. It listed and fell toward New Eden. Its edges burned with the heat of reentry.

Strike's voice burst over the comms. "Converge on the remaining Beadle. Take it down with everything you've got. JATMs, magrails, the works. Fire at will."

Orions concentrated around the Beadle. Missiles streaked through the black. Magrail guns chattered. Lasers flashed.

Coop released a slew of JATMs, the missiles homing in on the Beadle. They rocketed away, fire breathing out of their sterns. When they impacted the Beadle, a series of eruptions rippled across the transport's surface.

The Beadle shuddered. Hull plating peeled away.

"Going in for a second run," Coop said as he poured fire into the dying ship. "Missiles outbound." The enemy troop transport shook with the force of each impact. Small explosions burst across its exterior.

The Beadle lumbered on, its engines flaring. Vultures gathered around it, their lasers lashing out in an attempt to ward off the Orions' assault.

Strike sent orders to the squadron. "Eagle Two, Eagle Six, concentrate fire on the port engine. Eagle Three, Eagle Four, target the starboard side. Eagle Eleven, Eagle Twelve, hit its maneuvering engines. Follow your wingman. Let's finish this!"

Orions swooped in with their magrail guns roaring. The rounds slammed into the Beadle's engine housing. Blasts erupted, and the engine's flare burned out.

Across the Beadle's hull, other Orions released their payloads. Missiles impacted. The Beadle listed more to starboard. An open gape in its side belched smoke. The few remaining point-defense turrets fired sporadically.

Coop followed Raven as they veered around. "Lining up another shot," Coop said.

"Hold. Wait until I'm locked on," Raven replied.

It's right there. I have a perfect angle. "Holding."

The Beadle's hull filled Coop's targeting grid, the crosshairs settling over a critical area in its flank. He exhaled.

They closed in as Vultures headed in their direction, both Raven and Coop covering the void in front of them with countermeasures as they evaded and looped around yet again.

For the second time, the perfect shot presented itself. Coop cursed under his breath. "I have the shot. Let me take it."

"Negative, Coop," Raven said.

"I have the perfect—"

"Negative!"

This could end the Beadle in a hurry, if only Coop fired. "I have a firing solution. I'm going in for the shot."

Raven's voice erupted into Coop's sim pod, but Coop ignored him. After Coop fired off a salvo, each one hit, and hit dead-on. The Beadle imploded. Its decks blasted fire in all directions, the shock wave buffeting the Orions like leaves in a hurricane. Most importantly, this would look good on Coop's résumé.

The remaining Vultures scattered, their formations breaking apart.

Strike spoke. "All units, regroup and prepare for landing. Command reports that some of the Zodark troop landers have reached the surface but are taking heavy fire from ground forces and bombers."

"Command, any word on Zodark troop numbers?" Coop asked.

"Negative, Eagle Five. Initial reports are unclear. If any Zodarks survived the landing, it won't be a significant force. Ground teams are mopping up now.

"All right, Eagles," Strike continued. "Let's get back to base. Rearm, refuel, and be ready for anything. The Zodarks may be down, but they're relentless."

Coop turned his Orion toward the planet's surface. The craft sliced through the atmosphere. Ahead, the expanse of the Republic base sprawled outward, nestled in a valley and tucked against a mountain. High walls with reinforced concrete encircled the perimeter. It all bristled with gun emplacements along with sensor arrays. The landing maw gaped open, ready to swallow the returning Orions.

Coop guided his craft through the opening. The Orion's thrusters fumed as Coop settled his craft onto the landing pad. His pod blinked off, and light poured in.

Once Coop climbed out of the Orion's pod, a figure strode across the simulation room. It was Colonel Vale, his face in a scowl.

Vale came to a stop before Coop, his jaw set. "Lieutenant Blake Cooper," he said. "Come with me."

Coop swallowed hard. His mind twisted in circles as he fell into step behind Vale, the two of them walking out of the drone pod room and into the many corridors making up the base's interior.

The hallways stretched like tunnels for what seemed like kilometers, branching off into countless rooms and chambers. Soldiers and technicians hurried past as Coop and Vale strode in silence. They passed through the command center, a large room filled with displays and the chatter of comm traffic. Officers leaned over consoles while streams of information flowed across their screens.

Coop caught snippets of conversation as they walked, talk of airstrike plans and artillery positions. When they reached Colonel Vale's office, the colonel palmed the door controls. The heavy metal door slid open.

Vale stepped into his office, motioning for Coop to follow. Inside, bare walls, save for a few framed commendations and a large display screen, surrounded him. A desk with its surface cluttered with data pads dominated the center.

Vale moved around to the other side of the desk and clasped his hands behind his back. "Lieutenant Cooper. We need to talk."

Coop's heart thumped hard against his chest. "Yes, sir?"

Vale's lips contorted into a sneer. "You seem to think you're above the chain of command. That you can disobey orders and do as you please, consequences be damned."

Coop's anger swelled at the accusation, but he stayed calm. "With all due respect, sir, I was doing what I thought was necessary to protect my squadron and complete the mission."

"And who gave you the authority to make that call? I'd love to know this. Because if I can get *that* answer, I might just expel that person from the squadron. It would save me a hell of a lot of hassle with you." Vale quieted and straightened his fatigues. "You're a damn cog in a machine, Cooper. Your job is to follow orders, not to question them and go by your own luck. You cost me a hundred and fifty million dollars today. I understand if it happens during combat, but if you're not following orders, then you're killing more of my starfighters! It's simple, Coop! Simple!"

Coop's lips tightened into a straight line. "I understand, sir. It won't happen again."

"You bet your ass it won't." He rounded his desk and stood nose to nose with Coop. "Listen to me, young man. I've kept you here as a favor to your father. Your father and I both see your talent, your fast reflexes, and your eye for detail. You could be the force's best. Instead, you let your ego do the flying and throw away every chance you have to climb the ladder."

I am the best, hands down! Coop thought. "Understood. I'll make sure I don't do that again, sir."

Vale stared at him for a long moment, no doubt searching Coop's face for any sign of deceit. With a final nod, Vale's expression softened. "See that it doesn't. Learn to work within the system. Otherwise, you're no good to me. Now, get out of my face. Dismissed!"

Chapter 26
Lunch Stains

Two Years Later

Year 2095
RNS *Pershing*
Mars-Jupiter Transit Zone
Asteroid Belt, Sector Theia-459

The RNS Pershing, Lee thought. *What a career I'm having, huh?*

He didn't like sarcasm, yet he found himself thinking in a sarcastic tone these past many months. Heck, years, probably. Out the viewport, EVA-suited miners worked the asteroid field.

The transfer from the *Kentucky* still stung, even if command had dressed it up as a promotion. It'd been two years, and yet it bit at him day in, day out.

At the moment, he sat in his office. The desk held his personal console and a data pad with numerous patrol reports. Behind him, his Academy diploma hung next to his service record—a steady climb from ensign to lieutenant to lieutenant commander. Combat medals sat on a shelf beside him. They each told a story of valor that seemed to belong to someone else these days.

The RNS *Pershing*, named after General John J. Pershing, who'd led American forces to victory in World War I, was a Neptune-class corvette. Instead of facing down Zodark battle fleets with this small warship, Lee coordinated with two other corvettes to protect mining operations, merchant vessels, and civilian transports from pirates who preyed on the Belt's shipping lanes.

He watched maintenance drones buzz past his viewport. Their red warning lights blinked as they inspected the hull. He felt like shooing them away back to where they were supposed to be working—with the miners.

Out here, not all tech worked as intended. Drones would sometimes go rogue or shut down for no apparent reason, usually due to lack of maintenance. Sometimes they'd drift out of their assigned sector, only to be discovered months later during routine patrols—machines floating through space, waiting to collide with a meteor or other debris.

Lee took a bite of food, his lunch break just beginning. To put it simply, he'd never had better food on a ship. Somehow, he'd lucked out with the best chef in the entire Republic fleet, or so he liked to believe.

He turned to the holographic display of the ship's armament on the wall. It was a diagram he found himself studying far too often. It was well known that weapons were his passion. He pored over their specifications with the same intensity with which a microbiologist might examine specimens under a microscope. At the moment, it showed the ship's twin-barrel magrail guns before it shifted to the missiles it held, images of each type fading in just as others would fade out. The *Pershing*'s advanced ECM suite came into focus as the missile systems vanished on the screen, only to disappear as defensive systems appeared, something he'd barely tested in the two years he'd commanded this vessel.

Taking another bite, he chewed while facing the viewport again. Out in the void, a massive excavator carved into an asteroid's surface. It kicked up clouds of rocky debris.

Mining was essential to the Republic's war effort. The refined metals and rare elements fueled their shipyards and weapons factories. Yet after commanding the *Kentucky* in a fleet engagement against the Zodarks at the New Eden stargate, watching over mining operations felt like a demotion wrapped in a promotion's clothing.

Lee touched the edge of his desk as he recalled the *Kentucky*'s final battle under his command—a command forced on him rather than earned. They'd saved the ship and most of the crew through unconventional tactics. Apparently, Central Command had wanted something different from him. Now he captained his own vessel near Earth, closer to Mars—far from where humanity needed its best officers.

Tactical displays hovering above his desk showed the positions of his small flotilla—the *Pershing*, flanked by the corvettes *Kingston* and *Winnipeg*. They maintained a protective screen around the mining facility. They'd spent days preparing for a pirate attack that had never come. But out here, that didn't mean they were safe. Sometimes an attack would occur, but most times, they never presented themselves. Rumors, mostly. Almost always rumors.

For the last two years, Lee'd been running regular patrols. Yes, occasionally, they'd tangle with pirates or smugglers. But it was nothing like the intense combat he'd seen at New Eden.

A framed photo on his desk showed the *Kentucky*'s crew. Next to it sat Captain Oldendorf's picture along with all the accolades of the man's amazing career, a career cut short. Oldendorf had led Lee to a promising path in the Navy, and now his absence had somehow led him here, watching rocks spin in the dark expanse while the real war raged on without him.

Lee checked the patrol schedules for the umpteenth time. He'd never let his crew see his frustration—they deserved a captain fully committed to their mission, even if it felt beneath him. The miners below were counting on them, as were the freighter crews and colonists who passed through these lanes.

In quiet moments like this, watching EVA teams harvest resources instead of coordinating fleet maneuvers against humanity's greatest threat, Lee wondered if he'd somehow failed. RNS *Pershing* was a fine ship with a capable crew, but they could be doing so much more than chasing pirates—though mostly ghosts—through the belt.

A status report from the *Yorktown*'s captain flashed on his console. Another routine check-in, another quiet watch. The woman's visage appeared on the holo.

"Lieutenant Whitney." Lee nodded at the woman. "Good to see you enjoying your lunch break as well."

"And you, Commander Lee." She lifted her fork in a mock salute. "Another thrilling day watching rocks."

They shared a knowing laugh. "Remember that 'pirate raid' last month? Three ore shuttles with faulty transponders?"

She chuckled. "Don't remind me. I had the whole crew at battle stations."

"The most excitement we've seen out here for a year." Lee shuffled his food around the plate. "Sometimes I wonder if this is what my career's come to—you know, chasing sensor ghosts through the belt."

"It can get that way, for sure, Commander."

"Two years," Lee said. "Don't get me wrong, the *Pershing*'s a fine ship, but…"

"But you feel sidelined." Lieutenant Whitney set down her fork. "That's not what this assignment is, you know. You understand that, right?"

"I think… well, what are you getting at?"

"Look, these belt patrols… monitoring claim jumpers, checking mining beacons, watching for pirates slipping between the rocks… they're to prepare us."

Lee frowned. "Yes. I understand."

"I apologize for being blunt, but during our last private transmission, I caught something I hadn't noticed before. The first time you really showed your hand to me."

"Don't follow you," Lee replied.

"You're having a harder time than most officers assigned to deep-belt duty. Constant navigation through the debris fields, mining colony inspections, endless drone maintenance, yada, yada…"

Lee nodded. "Perhaps. I assure you my commitment to the service is absolute."

"I know it is," Whitney said. "Understand that this is what Command does with promising officers. They give them vessels to lead, sometimes a small armada, and put them out here between Mars and Jupiter, test how they handle independent operations. When the time comes for fleet engagements, promotions, transfers, you name it, they know exactly who can command under pressure."

She smiled. "It's not in any Fleet directive, just how the brass operates. Hell, they've been monitoring my performance too. I'm hoping we both get called to the front soon. You know, where we can make a real difference, not just chase annoying flies between the rocks, if you know what I mean."

"That would have been nice to know two years ago." Lee shook his head. "Could've saved me some—"

Alert klaxons cut through both ships' corridors. Lee fumbled with his lunch, the food tumbling into his lap as he jerked upright. Red markers bloomed across the screen—a dozen ships, heavily armed, burning hard toward their position.

"Lieutenant Whitney," Lee said, "are you seeing this?"

"I am. This time, no false alarm. Count twelve vessels, light corvette-class and gunboats."

Three corvettes against a pirate fleet this size. The odds weren't the greatest.

"Lieutenant Whitney, form up on my position. We'll coordinate defense of the mining facilities. *Pershing* will take point." He stood, brushing at the food stains on his uniform. "Good hunting."

"Understood, sir. *Yorktown* moving to support." The transmission powered off.

Lee strode toward the bridge. These miners needed him, and his crew waited.

Chapter 27
An Indirect Goodbye

Year 2095
New Eden

Lieutenant Naomi Love finished up another supply run. There were less soldiers she was transporting these days, and more equipment that the military was using to fortify their colony on New Eden.

Love had spent two years with an Osprey squadron, stationed on New Eden. Without Jack, the time had been rather lonely. But Love was used to being alone, even from her days as a child. She had poured herself into her mission, heart and soul. Her inner drive had kept her company as she strove to do her part in eliminating the pockets of Zodark resistance on New Eden.

Lately, though, vengeance felt like an empty motivator. It was getting harder to push down her grief and just keep going. Different people mourn the loss of someone close to them in a variety of ways: Love's go-to method had been ignoring the sadness and focusing on her work. But the "one foot in front of the other" approach was wearing thin. She longed for something else to give her a reason to get up in the morning.

As she entered the squadron office, Lieutenant Nadaeu approached. "Getting a little bored of moving equipment yet?" he asked.

"Mission first," she replied.

"You always say what you're supposed to," Nadaeu said with a laugh. "But I have some good news for you. You really need to check your messages from the squadron commander."

"Really?" asked Love. "Don't want to give me a hint?"

"Nope. I'd rather see your face when you read it," Nadeau teased.

She walked over to her terminal and logged into her secure messaging system. There it was—a set of new orders. "Operation Swift Response, assigned to the RNS *Gallipoli*," Love read aloud with a smile. "You headed there too?"

"Yep. And unlike you, I am perfectly willing to admit that I, for one, am thrilled for something more exciting than 'construction assistant.'"

Love lifted her left eyebrow. "Exciting…sometimes adventure isn't all it's cracked up to be…" her voice trailed off.

Nadeau went quiet. "I'm sorry, Naomi," he finally said. "It's just been quiet around here, and I guess I want to feel like I'm making more of a difference."

"It's all right, Nadeau," Love replied. "I guess I miss that too."

Nadeau perked up. "So our transport shuttle leaves in thirty-six hours," he said. "On the other side of New Eden, apparently, they've encountered the last death throes of this Zodark insurgency. A FOB fell six days ago. Lost fifteen Ospreys and their crews during a night raid. A Sumerian hospital was hit three days ago—over two hundred casualties. It looks like, when they can, the Zodarks are targeting the infrastructure. Took out a bridge yesterday, killing many construction workers and a few civilians. Three more human transport crews lost during medical evacuations a few days back, as well." Nadeau handed her a tactical tablet. "They're running coordinated attacks, Lieutenant. It appears to be ramping up.

Love studied the tactical overlay. "Current pilot status?"

"Twenty-eight combat-qualified pilots lost this month alone. Delta teams are ready for insertion, but we're critically short on experienced transport pilots."

"Understood." She squared her shoulders. "I'll need immediate access to the mission briefings and crew manifests."

"Already loaded on your data pad."

"Then I guess I'll see you on the *Gallipoli*," Love replied.

Part of her ached to stay in this safe, predictable routine. A deeper part thrilled at returning to the action—to purpose and action instead of memories.

The truth was, she needed this. It was time to face the fight. For the first time since Jack died, she felt right with the world.

Chapter 28
Rock Hammer

Year 2095
RNS *Pershing*
Mars-Jupiter Transit Zone
Asteroid Belt, Sector Theia-459

Compared to the RNS *Kentucky*, the *Pershing*'s bridge was small. Not too compact, but headroom sometimes became an issue, and Lee's height caused some headaches every so often—literally.

After knocking the crown of his head on a lower portion of the bridge's ceiling, Lee eyed the tactical display. Twelve red dots moved toward his small fleet in a wedge formation. These pirates, just a bit over forty-eight thousand kilometers out, were looking for an easy score.

"Sir, we're being hailed," the communications officer said.

"On screen."

A scarred face appeared on the main display. "Republic vessels, this is Captain Rush. That facility is operating in our territory, which means those resources belong to us. Clearly, you and this mining outfit can't take a hint, so we're going to remind you who runs this place. If you're not going to leave, we're going to make you leave."

Lee kept his face relaxed. "This is Lieutenant Commander Lee, Republic Navy, captain of the *Pershing*. This dispute has already been settled. This territory belongs to the ABE Corporation, Asteroid Belt Excavation, along with its workers." He studied the man's face. "Which organization are you with, Captain Rush?"

"Who I work for isn't your concern, Republic. What matters is we've got twelve ships to your three. You really want to die protecting some corporate rocks? Protecting money and assets, protecting the rich while the poor suffer? Is that what you've dedicated your life to?"

"If you proceed, you'll find out exactly what I've dedicated my life to." Lee nodded to his communications officer. "End transmission."

The pirate's face vanished from the screen. Although only three Republic ships patrolled this area compared to a dozen pirate ships heading his way, Lee knew the pirates had picked the wrong mining operation to raid.

"Communications, get me the mining facility," Lee said.

"Channel open, sir."

"Mining Control, this is Lieutenant Commander Lee. Recall all EVA personnel immediately. Emergency protocol one-one-two."

The response crackled through. "Understood, Commander. Beginning recall now."

Lee calculated possibilities. The pirates had numbers, but he had position and preparation, not to mention combat experience, trained staff and crew, and newer weapons. "Navigation, plot us a course to asteroid cluster Beta-Six. Tactical, coordinate with mining control. This will put us directly between the pirates and the mine. I want those excavators and drones repositioned to these coordinates."

Lee tapped on the command console, marking specific asteroids. Tactical officer Lieutenant Barasa Omondi acknowledged and began relaying the orders.

"Lieutenant Whitney, Lieutenant Navani," Lee opened frequencies to the other corvettes. "Form up on my position. Triangle defense pattern, using the larger rocks for cover."

The *Kingston* and *Winnipeg* moved into position. The pirate ships grew closer in a loose formation.

Overconfidence, Lee thought. *Good.* He opened a wide comm channel.

"Mining Control. I'm sending coordinates for your robotic excavators and mining drones. We're going to use the excavators and drone demolition charges to our advantage. When I give the signal, we'll detonate specific asteroids in sequence, creating a debris field right in the pirates' path. Send them to the coordinates I've given… now."

"Sending now," came the reply. "Should be complete in exactly eleven minutes, give or take a minute or two depending on distance and speed differentials."

Lee transmitted the tactical display to all ships and to the mining facility. "The fragmentation will force them to break formation or risk heavy damage. That's when our corvettes will engage. All we need is to strip away their numerical advantage. Then they'll flee or surrender. We've dealt with this kind of thing before. Let's make this quick and painless."

"Commander… those charges aren't meant for combat. Just giving you an FYI," came a new voice from Mining Control.

"No, but they'll serve. We don't need to pulverize the asteroids. Just break them up enough to create disarray in their ranks. Position your equipment as marked and stand by for my signal."

"Understood, sir," Mining Control replied.

"Clever," Lieutenant Whitney said. "We'll be ready on your mark."

The pirates continued to draw closer. Twenty-eight thousand kilometers.

Twenty-five thousand.

Twenty-one thousand.

Everything was falling into place.

"Sir, all EVA crews secured," the communications officer, Lieutenant Ana Batista, said.

"Mining drones and excavators in position," Lieutenant Omondi added.

Lee nodded. The pirates were almost in decent firing range, no doubt expecting three corvettes to be easy prey. Sixteen thousand kilometers and coming in fast. Speed was always an advantage with smaller craft like the pirates had, but superior technology and firepower frequently trumped even speed, and these Republic vessels outmatched any pirate when it came to weapons.

"Stand by on my mark." Lee studied the inbound enemy formation. "Tactical, target solutions on their lead vessels. Comms, battle channels only from here out."

The bridge crew worked fast, readying weapons. On the viewscreen, the pirate ships—a collection of converted freighters, old gunboats, and outdated light corvettes—bristled with cannons.

"Sir, they're entering optimal range," Omondi reported.

"Execute mining charges," Lee said. "All ships, prepare to engage."

Multiple explosions rippled through the asteroid field as several mining charges went off all at once. Massive chunks of rock burst outward. It created a field of debris between the pirates and their target. Two smaller ships took hits right away, their armor shredding as rocks smashed against them.

The pirate formation broke up as vessels scattered in different directions, trying to avoid the unexpected asteroid storm. Lee withheld a smile.

"Three distinct groups breaking off," Omondi reported. "Four ships heading port, five starboard, three trying to punch through the center."

"Whitney, take the port group," Lee said. "Navani, starboard is yours. We'll handle the center. Focus fire on their command ships. Look for the ones giving orders."

The three Republic corvettes surged forward, each targeting their assigned group.

"Sir, center group is attempting to reform," Omondi said.

"Target their flagship," Lee ordered. "All forward batteries, fire!"

The *Pershing*'s magrail guns thundered. Magnetic accelerators hurled thick projectiles at the central pirate vessel. At eleven thousand kilometers, the shots connected, ripping into the larger ship's hull.

"Direct hits," Omondi reported. "Their bow plating is compromised."

Lee keyed his command console. "Mining Control, detonate charges in sector four."

Another series of explosions sent asteroid fragments careening through space. Two pirate gunboats collided while attempting to dodge the debris field. Their hulls crumpled together.

"Sir, *Kingston* reports heavy damage to two targets in their sector," Lieutenant Batista said.

The pirates' wedge formation had dissolved. Individual ships now darted between floating rocks, trying to regroup. Lee had anticipated this. He tapped his console again, asking for Mining Control to trigger a third wave of mining charges. New debris bloomed across their escape vectors.

"They're breaking formation entirely," Omondi explained. "Three ships disabled, two more showing critical damage."

A pirate corvette emerged from behind an asteroid. Its guns blazed. The impacts sent tremors through the *Pershing*, rattling bulkheads. The deck shuddered. The bridge crew braced themselves as the ship bucked, inertial dampeners whining. Lee maintained his grip on the command chair but didn't flinch. Through the hull came the deep, resonant sound of multiple hits finding their mark.

"Helm, bring us about. Show them our broadside."

The *Pershing* pivoted, presenting her full array of weapons. It was almost as if Lee had predicted the pirate ship's maneuver. He had, and as the enemy vessel tried to move away, he grinned. The pirates couldn't have positioned themselves better if Lee had given them direct orders. "Fire all port batteries."

Multiple magrail rounds struck true and shredded through the corvette's engine section. Explosions burst along its hull.

"Sir, remaining hostile vessels are attempting to withdraw," Omondi reported. "They're making for the outer system."

Their retreat vector materialized on the screen. "Not today. Lieutenant Whitney, move to heading three-five-three. Cut off their escape route."

The *Kingston* blasted ahead, its engines flaring as chunks of space rock drifted past. The pirates were boxed in, Republic ships on three sides and a dense debris field behind them.

"Two more trying to break through the asteroid field," said Omondi. "Heavy damage to both vessels from collision with debris."

"Fire!"

The *Pershing*'s guns spoke again, shots disabling engines and weapons systems without destroying the ships outright. Republic protocol was clear on this—complete destruction wasn't an option when pirates might have innocent lives aboard, whether stolen cargo, abducted civilians, or coerced crew.

While in the asteroid belt, Lee had made sure his squadron was ready for scenarios like this, running countless simulations during their quiet patrols. Captain Oldendorf's voice still resounded in his mind: "In combat, most don't rise to the occasion… they fall to their level of training. So, it's good to understand that battle-readiness is training-made." And those endless drills had been worth every minute.

"Sir, we're receiving surrender signals from three vessels," Batista said. "The others are still trying to run."

"Navani, target those runners. Disable only. We want prisoners for questioning." Lee faced Lieutenant Omondi. "Status report?"

"Six ships disabled or surrendered. Four floating aimlessly from debris or collision. Two still attempting escape."

The remaining pirates didn't last long. Caught between Republic fire and the asteroid field, they soon joined their companions in defeat. Lee surveyed the tactical display. Not a single Republic casualty, and minimal damage to his own ships.

"All hostile vessels neutralized or surrendered," Omondi confirmed. "No further threats detected."

Lee opened a channel to all Republic ships. "Well done, everyone. Begin recovery operations. I want Ranger boarding teams ready in five minutes. These pirates might have useful intelligence about others operating in the sector."

He turned to Lieutenant Batista. "Get me a priority channel to Republic Command. We'll need reinforcement vessels for prisoner transport and recovery operations. With this many disabled ships, we're looking at a multiday operation at minimum. Alert nearby sectors we may need additional detention facilities and processing support. Authentication code Sierra-Six-Five. Mark it urgent."

****

A week had gone by since the pirate encounter had ended in a decisive clash that left no illusion to who controlled this area of the Belt. Lee enjoyed a rare moment of solitude in his quarters. He stared at the holoport, watching as ships continued to arrive to assist with the aftermath of what some were calling the largest pirate skirmish the Belt had seen in years.

This posting was supposed to be a quiet one, he thought.

During this recent engagement, his trio of outdated corvettes had taken a number of prisoners from the disabled pirate ships. Each ship taken out of action, each crew that could no longer harass the mining operations was a victory worth celebrating.

At the outset of the engagement, Lee had no idea that it had turned into such a skirmish that it had attracted the attention of civilian news outlets that monitored activity in the Belt. However, the local space around the mining facility and the site of the battle had become a crowded mess as more vessels arrived to render aid and begin salvage operations of the vessels Lee's task force had disabled and destroyed in the melee. A whole host of interplanetary tugs had arrived to assist in towing many of the wrecks back to Earth and the breakyards that disassembled destroyed ships.

Lee heard a knock on the door, interrupting his quiet reflection.

"Enter," he commanded.

Lieutenant Barasa Omondi pushed past the door as he brought a pair of coffee mugs into Lee's room that also doubled as his office. "I figured you could use a fresh cup with all the reports you've had to file," he offered as he handed Lee the hot liquid.

"Oh, man, you have no idea how much I needed this," Lee replied excitedly.

"Hey, out of curiosity, have you heard anything more about this new alien race the RNS *Franklin* encountered?" Omondi asked as he leaned against the wall. "It's been four or five months since it happened, and all we've been told is something great has come of it, but nothing more."

Lee grunted at the question, then placed his mug down. "What makes you think I know any more than you?"

"Cause you're the skipper, and the skipper always knows," responded Omondi jovially.

Lee chuckled to himself. "You know, I once thought the same thing about the captain of a ship. When I was on the *Kentucky*, I once asked Captain Oldendorf how that worked—if there was a secret captain's chat channel we didn't know about, and that was how skippers always seemed to stay a step ahead. You know what he told me?"

"What?"

Lee leaned forward and motioned for Omondi to come close. "He told me there is no secret. He said it all comes down to projecting confidence and conviction in whatever it is you decide to say. He told me that half the time he was guessing what happening beyond our ship. His job was to focus on our ship, our crew, and the ships immediately around us." Lee waved his arm about. "Whatever else is happening, it doesn't concern us until it does. Control what you can control, and let go of what you can't."

Omondi leaned back against the wall, quiet for a moment as he pondered what Lee had said. "It sounds like your skipper was a wise man."

Lee nodded. "He was. I learned a lot from him. But in answer to your question, no. I don't know any more about this new alien species the *Franklin* encountered than you. The few tidbits of news Space Command has shared with me, I've passed along to the rest of you. If what they're saying is true, I think we might just stand a chance at defeating those blue bastards."

Just then, Lee's comms unit chimed. He tapped a button. "Yes?"

"Sir, priority communication from Fleet Headquarters," his communications officer said.

"Huh. OK, put it through," Lee responded, motioning for Omondi to give him some privacy.

Rear Admiral White's hologram materialized as the message decrypted and began to play. "Lieutenant Commander Lee, I want to commend you on a job well done this past week in protecting the ABE mining facility. You have done a good job of safeguarding the steady supply of materials needed for the shipyards. Attached with this message is a new set of orders for the *Pershing* and for yourself. Your ship is to return to the John Glenn immediately for reassignment. Upon arrival, you will relinquish command of the *Pershing* to your executive officer, who will assume command of the ship.

"You are hereby ordered to report to Admiral Halsey, Commander of Second Fleet, New Eden, immediately. The Republic transport, *Doris Grey*, will transport you to New Eden. I don't have any further details to share with you, Lee, other than to say, 'Well done, and thank you for your service within my command.' Out," the image of Admiral White disappeared.

For a moment, Lee sat there, stunned by the sudden turn of events. He knew from the half dozen trips he'd made to the various Republic shipyards escorting supplies and materials that the Navy had been busy building warships like they were going out of style. He knew something big must've been in the works but had no idea that a whole new fleet had been formed in New Eden. It had been years since he'd last seen the Rhea system.

Well, I guess I best get going and see what new adventure the Navy has for me next, he thought. He smiled as he read the orders that would promote Omondi to Lieutenant Commander and replace him as the new skipper of the *Pershing*. He couldn't think of a better, more qualified person to relieve him than his own XO. He was thrilled to be the one to give him the news.

Chapter 29
Death by PowerPoint?

RNS *Doris Grey*
En-route to New Eden

Lieutenant Commander Lee walked into a giant cargo hold along with more than a hundred other officers that were either the same rank as him or one above. The entire cargo hold had been transformed into what looked like a giant SCIF or Sensitive Compartmented Information Facility. The vast space was filled with rows of chairs seated in front of what looked like half a dozen giant monitors facing the chairs and tables toward the rear of the room. Along the far side was a pair of tables with multiple pots of coffee, and coolers with assorted drinks and snacks.

"Wow, would you look at this place," someone said to the left of Lee. "They must be getting ready to bore us to death with PowerPoint if they're starting the briefing with coffee at three in the afternoon."

Lee laughed at the comment along with a few others. "I'm Ripley Lee," he introduced himself, extending his hand.

The tall broad-shouldered mountain of man shook his hand with one of those vice grips that made Lee wonder if he might need to stop by sickbay to check on his hand.

"Nice to meet you, Lee. I'm John Cotton, and this is Ludwig Brenner. His German accent's a little thick, but you'll get used to it," the man introduced himself and the officer with him from the Tri-Parti Alliance.

"You know, John. It's not a contest to make a person say, 'uncle' the first time you meet them," the German chided his friend as Lee opened and closed his hand to make sure he hadn't broken it.

Cotton laughed as he shrugged the comment off, walking toward the refreshments.

"It's nice to meet you, Lee. Here, let's grab ourselves a seat at the table over there," Brenner pointed as he and Lee moved to claim the table before others got the same idea.

"Attention everyone! Good afternoon," a tall, slender figure at the front of the room announced. "If everyone can please take your seats, we'll go ahead and get this going."

The seats quickly filled, especially the ones with a table. Conversations began to die down. A few minutes later, a couple of soldiers entered the room and took positions near the exits, closing the doors.

Cotton sat next to Lee, passing him and Brenner each a coffee.

"You'll thank me later," Cotton said as he downed his own coffee, practically in a few gulps.

"Good, everyone's seated. We can begin. Major Lenski, have your soldiers seal us in and make sure the doors stay sealed until we're finished," the mystery man in the front said. The Republic Army soldiers obliged by locking the doors into the cargo hold.

"I want to welcome all one hundred and sixty-two of you aboard the *Doris Grey*. My name is Colonel Alfred Bates, and I'm from Republic Intelligence. Whether you know this or not, each of you has been handpicked and selected by Admiral Halsey, the Director of Fleet Operations, to receive the information you are about to receive. As most of you are aware, there has been a raft of changes happening across the Republic—most notably our discovery of a yet another alien race. Fortunately for us, it would seem we humans appear to have caught break. This new race of highly intelligent aliens is also at war with the Zodarks, which as fate would have it, means we share a common enemy.

"Let's just say, our chances of surviving this war with the Zodarks just went up considerably. The short version is that they have offered us assistance in defeating the Zodarks, and the leaders above us have accepted it," Colonel Bates explained.

Monitors behind Bates now displayed images of this new alien race: shorter than humans, pale skin, light on the hair on their heads, with eyes that seemed to be all pupils, and additional fingers on their hands. "These aliens call themselves Altairians, and no, I have no idea if they have visited Earth before, or if these are the little grey men who kidnapped your crazy uncle Joe," this comment elicited some laughs which helped break the tension and surprise of this newly revealed information.

"All kidding aside, my job for the next couple of weeks as we slow boat our way to New Eden is to share a host of classified information with you about the terms of this new alliance. As our civilian-led government steadily reveals more and more of this information to the public, I have been asked to share with you the more pertinent military information you will need to know for your new assignments once we arrive in New Eden."

Excited whispers grew louder. Bates held his hands up to quiet them. "Listen, I get it. This is all new and exciting, and you want to talk about it. There will be plenty of time for that on our trip. For now, I have a lot of information I need to share before I dismiss you for dinner and the rest of the evening."

For the next couple of hours, Lee listened with rapt attention as more details of this alien race was shared. The alliance they now found themselves a part of apparently had a host of other intelligent alien beings as well. One species, the Primords, looked as if elves and Vulcans had manifested in the real universe and had babies—they had pointy ears, and long, angular noses. The more Lee heard, the more his head began to swim.

After learning about the different species that were a part of the Republic's new alliance with the Altairians, Bates regaled them of tales of the Zodarks' allies. Apparently, they were aligned with a cyborg species called the Orbots, which had four metallic, spider-like legs on the bottom, and a biological upper half that could resemble any of the other aliens the Zodarks and the Orbots had conquered at some point. There was even another race called the Pharaonis, an ant-like race with freakish demonic faces. They were told this particular enemy wasn't one the Republic would likely have to deal with, which was a relief to Lee and the others. They were the one race that gave him the heebie-jeebies.

How is any of this possible? Lee wondered. *Not just one intelligent alien species, but half a dozen?*

As dinner approached, Bates had each of them sign for a tablet which contained a series of briefing notes and slide decks containing more information and details they had yet to discuss. He encouraged each of them to spend the evening reviewing the files on the encrypted tablets they had been given and be ready to resume the information download after breakfast.

****

Three Days Later

Lee sat at the table with a fresh cup of coffee as he closed his eyes for a moment. His head was swimming with the amount of data being thrown at him. It was like drinking from a fire hose, but it also helped to explain a lot of what had been happening across the Republic the past six months. It didn't help that his last assignment had kept him largely isolated from the daily happenings of the Republic and the Navy writ large. News and regular updates were far and few between for those living and working in the asteroid belts of Sol. Months could go by before his ship and crew received a news dump of what was happening beyond the Belt.

He took a sip of his coffee and sighed. He found himself rubbing his temples, trying to keep a headache that was trying to form at bay.

The past three days had been a blur as Lee and the others had sat and listened to Colonel Bates. Bates had done his best to break it down Barney Style for them, but it was a lot to take in. Not only did they find out who the Altairians were, but they'd all learned about the alliance the Altairians represented, the Galactic Empire, and been enlightened as to how the Republic fit into this alliance.

Lee hadn't been so out of the loop in the Belt that he didn't know about the factions of Earth consolidating into one government, but he had figured it was because the leaders of the world had sorted out that this was their best chance of surviving against the Zodarks. Instead, Lee learned that the reason for this newfound unity was because the Altairians had insisted that they would only work with one ruling government.

In theory, it made sense to have one government ruling Earth. *Shoot, I'd always thought humanity would reach this point some day,* Lee thought. He just hadn't necessarily thought it would come about so quickly. *I certainly didn't think it would happen because of the coercion of some foreign, alien power.*

"Regardless of how this new unified government came into being, you need to know that it is done," Colonel Bates had insisted. "No one has asked for your opinions on this matter. Your job as officers is to salute and carry out the orders of the Fleet Admiral, who takes his orders from the newly appointed Republic Chancellor. The *only* purpose in sharing this information is for you to have an understanding of the facts."

By the end of the second day of their journey, they had learned the alliance the Altairians led consisted of several additional space faring races. There was the Tully, a race that reminded Lee of old movie reruns he'd seen with Wookiees in them, except that they had shorter, more matted hair. They were apparently very intelligent and had a very muscular physique underneath their hairy exteriors. The Altairians regarded them as brawlers—great fighters. However, despite having colonies on seven planets spread across four different star systems, the Tully were few in number.

Then there was the Primords again, a race Lee could only describe as what would happen if Vulcans had a baby with the elves of Santa's workshop. Their hair was thick and long, and their eyes were quite striking with piercing blue, green or purplish irises. The Altairians spoke highly of the Primords, praising them for their industrious nature and their fierce fighting capabilities in battle. They were also among the second largest species in the alliance with more than thirty populated planets and moons across seven distinct star systems. Lee had to do a double take when he saw they had a population of more than twenty-eight billion people.

How can a society of space faring people this large be under threat by an adversary like the Zodarks? he wondered.

"Make it stop, Lee," pleaded Lieutenant Commander Ludwig Brenner, before starting their briefing on the third day. "My God, I'd heard of the term 'death by PowerPoint'—I never thought I would experience it."

Lee stifled a laugh as he finished the last of his coffee. He was about to get up for a refill when Commander John Cotton walked up to their table with a fresh pot in hand.

"Stow it, Lee," said Cotton. "I'm past the stage of getting up for refills. I figured I'd just save us the trouble and bring the pot with me."

"Top me off, big guy, before you sit." Brenner extended his arm, holding his half-empty cup.

"I feel like this is finals week before graduation at the Academy," mused Cotton as he placed his tablet down on the table. "I heard today we're supposed to learn about some new sort of warships designs the Altairians are going to share with us."

"Really? I'll bet they have some super crazy advanced warships and weapons," replied Lee excitedly.

A voice boomed over the PA system before they could talk further, announcing the start of the day's brief. Instead of Colonel Bates leading the discussion, a Navy captain walked to the lectern as the monitors behind him came to life.

"I'm Captain Willie Rosentreter. I was the Captain of the *Texas* during the first battle we fought with our new Altairian allies in the neighboring system next to Rhea. I have seen firsthand the power and capability of these Altairian warships, and it is incredible. I was there when we lost the *New York,* and the *Maine* in that final battle, and I can tell you this—if our ships had had the armor and weapons the Altairians do, we wouldn't have lost those battleships."

"I lost a good friend of mine from the Academy on the *Maine,*" hissed Cotton angrily.

Lee had learned about that battle nearly a month after it was over. He'd been stunned to hear that the Republic had lost more than twenty-one hundred spacers from two ships.

"In the aftermath of that battle and to give us a fighting chance in the future, our Altairian allies have collaborated with our engineers and a few ship captains' to devise a new class of warship," Rosentreter explained. "These vessels will be a hybrid of the best human and Altairian capabilities that'll be melded together to create a new class of warships. While it will take some time before our shipyards can begin to mass produce these new vessels, the Altairians have already devised a way to get some of these ships into our hands,"

Schematics of a warship appeared on the monitors behind Rosentreter. He pointed to the visuals as he continued. "This vessel you see here is going to be called the Type-002A, or *Kraken*-class heavy cruiser. There are plans to create a total of three variations of this ship, each with a specific function. We intend for the *Kraken*-class heavy cruiser to become the workhorse of the Navy. As you can see from the schematics, this vessel is going to pack a punch and hit well above its weight class."

Lee let out a soft whistle before he realized he was doing it.

"Whoa, that ship is a beaut," commented Cotton. "It's bristling with more weapons than a *Ryan*-class battleship."

"This next schematic is for the Type-001 Decator-class escort frigate," Rosentreter announced, briefly flashing an image of a heavily armored warship before switching back to the heavy cruiser. "Like the cruiser, there will be three variants, but we'll cover those later."

A voice from the far side of the room cut in. "How big is this cruiser? Crew size?"

"Good questions, Commander," Rosentreter replied without hesitation. "The heavy cruiser is just over a thousand meters long. There's a battlecruiser variant in the works—thirty percent larger, with more gun turrets. As for crew size, these ships are heavily automated, so we only need about six hundred and fifty spacers, give or take. That may change as we retrofit them for human crews—the Altairians designed these originally, and we've got different requirements."

He gestured to the schematic again. "The Altairians are mass-producing these ships. Dozens are under construction at any given time. Once we settled on what tech and weapon systems to integrate, they paused production to modify the hulls and weapon configurations for human use. That means faster deployment for our forces."

Rosentreter zoomed in on the ship's primary weapon systems. "Now, let's talk firepower. This cruiser carries six turrets, each packing dual twenty-four-inch magnetic railguns. These kinetic weapons aren't widely used by most spacefaring navies, but they're devastating against Zodark warships. Their armor is designed to absorb high-energy weapons like lasers, but kinetic penetrators? That's their Achilles' heel." He smirked. "So much for 'advanced' warships."

He brought up a cutaway of the magrail turrets. "With Altairian help, we've enhanced our depleted uranium slugs—advanced materials in the tips allow them to punch through at least a meter of enemy armor before detonating inside. That either guts the ship outright or weakens the plating for follow-up shots to rip through. The Altairians also improved turret automation and the magazine system. This cut down the crew needed to operate them and increased the rate of fire by seventy percent—that's game changing, gentlemen."

Rosentreter let the schematic linger on-screen for a moment before turning back to the room. "This ship is built for war. And soon, we'll have them in the fight."

"And what about lasers? Will these hybrid ships still use the same energy weapons as the Altairians?" a lieutenant commander on the far side of the room asked.

Rosentreter nodded, pulling up another cutaway schematic. "Yes, Lieutenant Commander Perry. These hybrid warships incorporate the best of both our technologies. While the cruiser has six twin-barreled magrail turrets, it also carries twelve triple-barreled ship-to-ship turbolasers. These weapons are on par with anything the Zodarks deploy—even on their battleships. In fact, they're more powerful than anything humanity has built to date."

He zoomed in on the ship's power systems. "Driving these weapons are four Altairian Gen-II Arkanorian Reactors. I'm no engineer, but I'm told each one generates sixteen hundred megawatts. That's an obscene amount of power." He let the statement hang in the air, allowing the officers to grasp the sheer scale of the ship's energy output.

Rosentreter continued, shifting the schematic to propulsion. "These reactors also power the ship's two Cyclone MPD thrusters for interplanetary travel and two Ark-Fold FTL drives for interstellar jumps. As you all recall, Ark-Fold drives cut FTL travel times from two light-years per month to one light-year per day. That means the old six-month haul from Earth to New Eden is now just six days." He glanced around the room, noting a few raised eyebrows. "Obviously, that's a game-changer."

After going over details for a few more hours, Rosentreter let out a deep breath, apparently sensing the information overload. "All right, I can see I've overwhelmed you all. Let's break for lunch. You've got three hours to eat, ask questions, and clear your heads before we dive into your crew training programs. Dismissed."

As the group filed out, Lieutenant Lee turned to Commander Cotton, whose eyes were glassy despite downing four cups of coffee. Lee snapped his fingers in front of his face.

"Wake up, Cotton. You survived the PowerPoint death match."

Cotton blinked, rubbing his temples. "Barely."

"Come on," Lee said, clapping him on the shoulder. "Let's get lunch and hit the gym. That was brutal."

****

"I don't know about you, but that whole session on the Mass Field Replicator—no one's going to eat that crap," commented Lieutenant Commander Ludwig Brenner as he dug into his beef stroganoff and green beans.

"You forgot to mention it's a fifth-generation MFR," joked Commander John Cotton, who had nearly finished his own stroganoff before Lee and Brenner had even sat down.

"Dude, Cotton. Do you even taste your food, or just inhale it?" Lieutenant Commander Ripley Lee jested, watching in amazement at how fast the man could devour a meal.

"Hey, laugh all you want. But when your parents are poor and you're the fifth out of six boys and two girls at the dinner table, you learn to eat quick—or one of your siblings might eat your portion," Cotton retorted before gulping down half his glass of water and returning to savage the remains of his dinner.

"Good Lord, your parents had eight kids?" Brenner asked in shock.

"Sure did. I grew up in rural Nebraska on a farm. After the AI War of the 2040s, farming was big business. People needed food, and our family grew it," Cotton explained.

Brenner furrowed his brow. "If farming was big business, why was your family poor? And how could they afford to have so many kids—so many mouths to feed?"

Cotton just shrugged. "I don't know much about my granddad other than he fought in the war and was never really the same afterwards. When he came back to the family farm, he didn't run it well—never had a head for business. My Pa was seventeen when Granddad offed himself. Figured he was worth more dead than alive. Had a life insurance policy that got the creditors off our backs, kept the farm in the family."

Lee and Brenner exchanged glances, but neither said anything.

"But it meant my Pa had to take over. We were too poor to afford one of those fancy Walburg synthetic humanoid workers like the big ag farms. My Ma and Pa cranked out farm workers the old-fashioned way—they had kids, lots of them. Growing up, we just didn't have much, so you ate when food was available," Cotton explained.

Lee remembered how hard it had been for his parents and grandparents following the AI War of the 2040s. A lot of families had gone hungry after the collapse of the United States and dozens of other nations. That war had reshaped the world—leading to the rise of the Republic, the Greater European Union, and the Asian Alliance. It had also led to the creation of the Space Exploration Treaty (SET), the very thing that had set humanity on its path to the stars.

"I'm sorry about your grandfather. It sounds like you had it rough growing up," Lee said.

Cotton waved it off. "I survived, didn't I?"

Brenner exhaled, rubbing his forehead. "Still, you really think people are going to accept using this kind of technology, though? Food replicators? It's kind of out of a sci-fi novel, isn't it?"

Cotton snorted at the comment. "Of course, it's sci-fi. You think a highly advanced spacefaring race like the Altairians or others wouldn't have come up with something similar to this by now? Do you know how difficult it is to supply a *Ryan*-class battleship with food while underway? Or the *George Washington* for that matter? The amount of hydroponic food that needs to be cultivated and grown is huge. Even augmenting this with dehydrated food, it takes up enormous amounts of space and energy. Hell, why do you think the Navy has entire hydroponic ships that travel with the fleet? Food is hands down one of the toughest logistical challenges for any space navy to overcome."

"You seem to know a lot about this, Cotton. I don't think I asked what your previous position was. What *was* your job exactly?" Lee asked, genuinely curious. He knew a little about the topic of keeping a ship supplied with food and consumables from his time commanding the *Pershing*. It was the first time he had had to worry about that kind of stuff since becoming an officer.

"Logistics, or at least that's what I've been doing my last couple of assignments," Cotton replied. Taking a sip of his coffee, his expression turned serious. "Listen, not everything we hear is always going to make sense. Sometimes, it might sound downright crazy. But here's the thing—these Altairians? I've been devouring anything and everything that's been made available to us about them. We seriously lucked out being discovered by them. The advancements in every field…it's incredible. If our dues or membership to be a part of their alliance means fighting alongside them—helping to liberate enslaved planets while protecting our own people, growing our footprint among the stars—sign me up. "I'm not sure what kind of ship class you two are being eyed for. Last night, Captain Rosentreter shared that I'll probably be assigned to some new, crazy massive ship they're calling a *Saturn*-class fleet sustainment vessel. It's like a floating factory, packed with massive 3D printers and advanced manufacturing to support an entire fleet with whatever logistical needs they have while deployed." He set his coffee down and leaned in. "And that's where these food replicators come into play."

Lee raised an eyebrow. "All right, break it down for me. How does it actually work?"

Cotton smirked. "All right. Imagine a highly advanced 3D printer, but instead of making engine parts or armor plating, it's printing food. It's called the MFR-5 Mass Field Replicator, and it doesn't just print food—it constructs it at the molecular level. It's a mix of bioprinting and molecular assembly, meaning it takes organic base compounds—proteins, fats, carbs, vitamins—and restructures them into whatever meal you order."

Brenner looked skeptical. "So, it's lab-grown meat and algae paste, just with a fancy new coat of paint?"

"No, it's a hell of a lot more than that." Cotton shook his head. "Unlike those old protein bricks and dehydrated sludge packs, this thing can recreate nearly any meal with the right texture, taste, and nutritional value. It doesn't just extrude paste like some glorified MRE maker. It bioprints muscle fibers for steak, layers carbohydrates for pasta, and even simulates cooking reactions like browning and caramelization."

Lee crossed his arms. "And how fast does this thing work? Because I've seen chow lines on a fully crewed ship—there's no way something this fancy could keep up."

"That's the best part," Cotton said with a grin. "Each MFR-5 can print and assemble a full meal in about 10 to 15 seconds. It's completely automated—a crew member walks up, picks from three to five meal options on a holo-display, and boom—hot meal, ready to go.

Multiply that across hundreds of replicator stations on a battleship or carrier, and suddenly, you're feeding an entire crew in record time."

Brenner was still processing the idea. "So… what's stopping us from just setting one of these up planetside and wiping out food scarcity?"

"Power and supply." Cotton tapped the table for emphasis. "An MFR-5 still needs organic base compounds to function—lab-grown protein cultures, hydroponic vegetables, synthesized fats, and yeast starches. Ships will still have hydroponics and microbial bioreactors to keep the supply flowing, but this system eliminates the need for massive food storage rooms, freezers, and resupply convoys. That means more room for weapons, armor, and spare parts. More endurance in the field. Naval warfare is about sustainability, and this is a logistical game-changer."

Lee let out a low whistle. "So instead of wasting space hauling pallets of rations and frozen meat, we just keep a supply of organic base compounds, plug it into the replicator, and print whatever we need?"

"Exactly." Cotton nodded. "It means we can operate longer, go deeper into enemy space without needing a resupply, and keep our personnel well-fed without sacrificing quality. Plus, in a worst-case scenario, we could even recycle food waste back into base compounds—nothing goes to waste."

Brenner leaned back in his chair, rubbing his chin. "Damn. If this thing works the way you say, I get it now. We're not just talking about making meals more convenient—we're talking about strategic independence."

Cotton smirked. "Now you're catching on. That's why these Altairian advancements are a big deal. We're not just upgrading weapons and ships—we're upgrading the way we fight wars."

Chapter 30
Climbing the Ladder

Doris Grey
New Eden Orbit

"Lee, come on in," Captain Rosentreter motioned for him to enter.

Lee stepped in, snapping to attention in front of the captain's desk as he saluted. "Lieutenant Commander Ripley Lee, reporting as ordered, sir."

"At ease, take a seat," Rosentreter said, gesturing toward one of the chairs. As Lee sat, the captain leaned forward. "We'll be arriving in New Eden soon, and you'll be receiving your new assignment. Once we settle into orbit, the shuttles will begin ferrying personnel to the surface. You and the others will report to Headquarters, Second Fleet—located at the Victory Base Complex, just outside Emerald City, the planet's capital."

Rosentreter studied Lee for a moment before continuing. "Now, let me ask you something. We've thrown a lot of information at you these past few weeks. I know it's a lot to take in. What's your honest opinion about the Altairians and this new interstellar alliance we've joined?"

Lee hesitated, but the captain's last sentence put him at ease. "You can speak freely," Rosentreter added. "No repercussions. No career suicide."

Lee exhaled slightly. He wasn't the type to challenge orders, but this was... a lot. The sheer shock of discovering multiple space-faring species was still sinking in.

"Well, sir," Lee said, "like you said, it's a lot to take in. But the other day, I was having lunch with a couple of officers I met when we first arrived. One of them, Commander John Cotton, put it this way—'If the price of admission into this Altairian alliance is fighting alongside them, helping to liberate enslaved worlds, protecting our own people, and expanding humanity's reach into the stars, then sign me up.'"

Lee paused, then added, "At first, I wasn't sure what to think about the Altairians. I mean, it wasn't that long ago that we first encountered the Zodarks."

The memory of the Battle of the Gate still haunted him—Captain Oldendorf's death, the raw fear of watching their fleet struggle against an enemy they barely understood. Before boarding the *Doris Grey*, Lee had begun to doubt if they had any real chance of winning this war, especially after the loss of the *New York* and the *Maine*.

Rosentreter nodded, eyes locked on him. "And what do you think now?"

Lee started to answer but stopped himself. He took a moment, considering his words carefully. "I think John's right. Our discovery by the Altairians—it's our best chance at surviving this war. Look at the hybrid warships you briefed us on. Before the Altairians intervened, we were barely holding the line against the Zodarks. Hell, we were losing. But now? These advancements—they change everything. We're not just upgrading weapons and ships, sir, we're upgrading our entire navy—our entire way of fighting wars."

Lee leaned forward slightly. "And it's not just the military, either. The civilian applications alone move humanity forward by a hundred years or more."

Rosentreter smiled, leaning back in his chair. "Captain Oldendorf was right about you."

Lee frowned slightly. "Sir?"

"One of his last comments before his death—he noted in your file that you had a good head on your shoulders. That you see the big picture when others don't." Rosentreter tapped a few commands on his desk console, bringing up a file. "Two weeks ago, when the *Doris Grey* departed for New Eden, we selected one hundred and sixty-two officers for a series of evaluations throughout the journey."

Lee suddenly felt his blood run cold. Had he unknowingly failed some kind of test?

Rosentreter chuckled. "Relax, Lee. You passed."

Lee exhaled, feeling his shoulders relax.

"If you recall from one of my earlier briefings," the captain continued, "I mentioned the Altairians temporarily pausing their shipbuilding to modify some of their warships for human use—

combining the best of their technology with ours to create Altairian-human hybrid vessels."

Lee nodded.

"As we pull into orbit, you should see some of them in formation around the *George Washington*. In fact…" Rosentreter pointed at his computer monitor, where a sleek warship was displayed. "This ship, right here—the RNS *Poseidon*—is yours."

Lee blinked. "Wait… what?"

Rosentreter opened a drawer and pulled out a small black box, sliding it across the desk. "Go ahead. Open it."

Lee hesitated, then flipped the box open. Inside, resting neatly in the center, was a Commander's rank insignia.

His breath caught in his throat. "I… I don't understand," Lee stammered. "I'm not eligible for promotion for another few years. And I've never commanded anything larger than an outdated corvette."

Rosentreter gave a knowing smile. "We're a nation at war, Lee. The Navy is expanding at an astronomical rate. The Altairians have provided us with a dozen of these hybrid heavy cruisers, a couple of battlecruisers, and two dozen escort frigates. More are being built as we speak."

He leaned forward. "Of the one hundred and sixty-two officers on this voyage, thirty-eight were chosen for command. Others will serve as executive officers or senior staff. But you? I chose you for *Poseidon*."

Lee swallowed. "I appreciate that, sir. I really do. But… why me?"

Rosentreter smirked. "Why you? Why not?"

Lee shifted in his chair, processing everything. Finally, he spoke. "Captain Oldendorf once told me a story about how fast officers were promoted in the U.S. Navy during World War II. He said sometimes, the easiest answer for why someone got promoted was because everyone ahead of them was dead."

Rosentreter didn't say anything.

Lee exhaled. "I don't think that's entirely the case here, but I suspect it played a role. That said… you mentioned Oldendorf believed I had a knack for seeing the bigger picture. If I had to guess why you selected me, I'd say it's because of that."

Rosentreter nodded approvingly. "And the Padawan becomes the master."

Lee smirked slightly.

"It wasn't just me," Rosentreter continued. "Admiral Halsey had final say. After reading my report and recommendation, she agreed—you're the right man for *Poseidon*."

The captain's expression turned serious. "Now, let me give you a word of warning," said Rosentreter. "We're gearing up for a major operation with the Altairians. If you recall, the Primords—they have a planet called Intus. It's occupied by the Zodarks."

Lee straightened.

"It's a major world for them, and it's been under occupation for years. I don't have all the details yet, but what I do know is that you won't have much time to get your crew and ship ready to fight. The personnel assigned to these hybrid vessels have already undergone months of training. They'll know the systems. But you're the skipper. The buck stops with you."

Lee gave a sharp nod. "Understood, sir."

Rosentreter held his gaze. "I don't have an exact timeline for the operation yet. But trust me, it's coming fast. Get yourself ready."

They exchanged a few more words before Rosentreter dismissed him. As Lee left the office, his mind raced.

In eight hours, he'd be on the surface, meeting with Admiral Halsey. And then… he'd be stepping onto the bridge of the *Poseidon*.

Chapter 31
Expansion

Mid 2096
Victory Base Complex
Emerald City, New Eden

The shuttle pitched slightly forward, angling into its final descent toward Emerald City, the capital of New Eden. From his seat by the window, Commander Ripley Lee took in the stunning transformation of the planet's surface.

It had been six years since the first human boots had stepped onto New Eden, and four years since they had liberated it from the Zodarks. Back then, in the early days of its discovery, the city was barely more than a frontier outpost struggling to keep a foothold on a foreign world. Now, it was a burgeoning metropolis, its skyline punctuated by sleek, angular high-rises stretching toward the sky. Emerald City sprawled along the white sandy coastline, the turquoise ocean glittering beneath the late morning sun. Even the sky around this new capital buzzed with activity; transport ships, passenger shuttles, and atmospheric craft zipped across the sky in coordinated lanes. Lee could see the progress being made with the hyperloop system as it snaked outward from the city in perfectly symmetrical arcs, connecting it to future planned settlements near and far along the continent.

As they passed over Emerald City, the scenery shifted, revealing a vast military complex—the Victory Base Complex (VBC), the Republic's primary military installation on New Eden. It had initially been constructed during the battle to liberate the planet from the Zodarks, but it had been dramatically expanded upon it following their defeat. The VBC now stood as an armored fortress-city, hardened against orbital assault. It was also a launchpad for future Republic operations against the Zodarks. Its sprawling spaceport would serve as a hub for military transports, supply freighters, and fighter squadrons.

Lee spotted the massive space elevator at the edge of the spaceport, its terminal glistening like polished steel. Even from this altitude, he could make out the titanic support structures anchoring the orbital tether. Hundreds of shuttle-sized cargo pods rode the elevator's track, ferrying supplies, personnel, and munitions up and down between the planet and its growing network of orbital shipyards.

"Wow, look at this place."

Commander John Cotton whistled as he gestured toward the view.

"Tell me about it," Lee replied, his eyes scanning the ever-expanding infrastructure. "That spaceport we're heading to wasn't even here the last time I was on New Eden."

He wasn't exaggerating. The last time he'd set foot here, VBC had been little more than prefab shelters and field tents. Now, the entire area was a hardened military installation, complete with reinforced hangars, supply depots, and defensive batteries.

His gaze drifted upward, back toward the dozens—maybe hundreds—of warships in orbit above the planet. They weren't just Republic vessels, either. Among the Republic's growing fleet, he could see Altairian warships, their distinct sleek, hull designs contrasting sharply against the blocky, utilitarian look of human-made ships. There was also a growing number of Primord vessels joining the fleet as well.

And then there were dozens of transport vessels—massive planetary assault carriers, troopships, and supply freighters.

"It looks like an armada assembling up there." Lee felt an unsettling weight against his chest.

Something big is coming.

"Agreed," Cotton replied. "This is exactly what Captain Rosentreter was talking about—the fleet's massing for something huge."

"But why?" Lee questioned. "Whatever it is, it looks like it's going to happen soon."

Cotton sighed, shaking his head. "Wish I was going with you guys. The *Mimas* won't be finished in time to join whatever operation this is."

Lee smirked, trying to lift his friend's mood. "Ah, don't worry about it, John. Something tells me this war isn't ending anytime soon."

Lee turned serious for a moment. "It's still hard to wrap my head around the fact that the Altairians and the Zodarks have been fighting each other for hundreds of years. And now, we're caught in the middle of that war." He paused before adding, "By the way—congrats on your selection for captain. When do you get to pin it on?"

Cotton brightened slightly at the change in topic. "In a month. Just before I take command of the *Mimas*. I still can't believe how massive that thing is."

"What did you expect? It's a mobile factory, following the fleet." Lee shook his head. "It's a hell of a ship."

A chime sounded through the cabin as the pilot's voice came over the speakers. "Attention passengers, this is the flight deck. Please remain seated as we prepare to land. Upon landing, retrieve your carry-on bags and proceed to the transport buses. They will take you to base lodging, where you will receive your next set of instructions."

Someone a few rows ahead snorted. "Whoever said military life is tough clearly never served in it. The Navy tells you where to go, when to be there, and even picks your wardrobe. How much easier can life get?"

Laughter rippled through the cabin.

As the shuttle touched down, Cotton turned to Lee. "See you in the auditorium at 1500. Save me a seat if you get there before me."

Lee nodded as he reached for his bag, but Cotton was already moving down the aisle before he could reply.

****

Three Hours Later
Second Fleet Headquarters
Base Auditorium

Lee walked toward the base auditorium, along with hundreds of officers and senior enlisted personnel already filing inside, their uniforms crisp and spotless. There was an unspoken tension in the air since his arrival hours earlier. This was the first time he had seen so many commanders, captains, and admirals in one place, as if everyone knew something big was about to be revealed.

Lee glanced at his watch—1447 hours. Thirteen minutes until whatever was in the works was revealed, and Lee could begin to prepare himself and the crew of his new ship he still had yet to see. As he entered the auditorium, he looked for his two friends, Commander Cotton and Lieutenant Commander Brenner. It took only a moment to find Cotton. His six-foot five stature made it easy to find him in a crowd. Lee walked briskly toward them and the empty seat they had saved for him.

"Cutting it a little tight, Lee. Did you doze off after checking in to your room or what?" Brenner joked good naturedly.

"Attention everyone." A voice boomed over the room's speakers before Lee could reply to Brenner. "The briefing is about to begin. Please find an empty seat, or you can stand in the back if you would like. However, this may be a long brief, so I suggest finding a spot to sit."

"Oh great, another death by PowerPoint meeting about a meeting," Cotton bemoaned. His voice was just loud enough for Lee and Brenner to hear—they had to stifle their laughter so as to not make a scene.

A few moments later, someone near the rear of the auditorium shouted, "Room, Atten-shun!"

Lee and the entire room jumped to their feet as an entourage of military brass entered the room and headed toward the stage. As he stood rigidly at attention, watching the procession move down the center aisle, Lee saw the Fleet Commander, Admiral Chester Bailey leading the group, followed closely behind by Admiral Abigail Halsey, Second Fleet Commander, and newly promoted Admiral Miles Hunt, a former mentor of Lee's first commander, Captain Oldendorf. To Lee's surprise, walking alongside Admiral Hunt appeared to be one of the Altairians and what must have been a Primord officer, given the uniform he wore.

Oh wow, this must be something big if our new allies are involved in the briefing, Lee thought. This was the first time he had seen any of their new alien allies in person and not just a video or picture of them.

As the group reached the front of the auditorium, they took their seats along the front row. Admiral Bailey walked onto the stage and cleared his throat.

"At Ease!" Bailey exclaimed. "Take your seats!" His voice boomed with the authority and confidence of a man who knew his role and felt complete confidence in it. "As some of you may have gathered, two of our new allies have joined us for this briefing. From the Altairians, we have with us one of their fleet commanders, who will also be accompanying us in the operation you are about to be briefed on. His name is Admiral Pandolly." The Altairian briefly stood, surveying the room before taking his seat.

"This is Admiral Bjork Stavanger, the Primord Fleet Commander our forces will be working with for this operation." Bailey motioned to the Primord, who briefly stood. Like the Altairian before him, he too surveyed the room before returning to his seat.

Lee watched the giant wall monitor behind Admiral Bailey come to life as it projected a three-dimensional star map unlike anything he'd seen before. He saw the Rhea system, Sol, and a host of stargates, some named, others numbered. He also saw regions lightly colored in blue, others in light shades of red, and the three systems the humans held in light green. It was a visual map of allies and enemies, encompassing most of the Milky Way.

"Gentlemen, Ladies, the alliance has planned to invade a Primord system by the name of Intus," Bailey began. "It's named after the planet Intus, a former Primord core world the Zodarks captured, and we have been asked to assist them in retaking it." Next to the Intus star system, which was highlighted, a blue line illuminated, connecting it to the Rhea system through several stargates.

"This will be the first time we humans will fight with our Primord allies," Bailey continued. "We will show them why we are the toughest, meanest, soldiers in the galaxy. In the coming weeks, you will be given more details about this coming invasion and what role each of your ships and commands will have in it."

"I will give you the gist of the plan now, so you can better focus the training of your crews for this coming battle. When we attack, it will happen in phases, to allow us to overwhelm the enemy at various points in the battle. The first armored fist of our attack will come as Admiral Halsey leads the first wave of our ships into the Intus system. As her force engages the enemy near the gate, Admiral Hunt will lead a strike force with a contingent of our Deltas in a daring orbital HALO assault. Our augmented super soldiers will insert from low orbit to destroy a series of planetary defensive weapons around this area of Intus.

"When these Ion cannons are destroyed, it'll create a gap in the planet's defenses our ships will exploit, allowing us to deploy further soldiers to the surface. This is when the Republic First Army will land and expand our beachhead on the surface. While this fight is underway, those of you in command of the hybrid ships—these ships will form the core of the second wave of Republic ships that will jump into the system, our trump card if you will. This is also the force that will accompany the bulk of our Republic Army ground force.

"The Altairian and Primord fleets will be integrated with ours. We will endeavor to fight as one cohesive force but understand some of that may be challenging as we figure out how best to communicate during a battle," Bailey explained. He paused to survey the room. "Look, this is going to be a tough fight. We are going to take a lot of casualties, and we are going to lose a lot of ships. But this is the first step in defeating this Zodark scourge. After you leave today, your sole focus is to prepare your ships and crews for this operation. In the coming weeks, you will receive your orders and timeline of events. Until then, drill your crews hard and remember this—we fight as we train, and we train like we fight. Dismissed!"

A low murmur spread across the room as everyone processed what they'd just been told.

Brenner smiled. "Well, we may have died by PowerPoint, but I feel their conclusion has brought me back to life," he commented. "They let us 'out with a bang' as I believe I've heard you North Americans say."

Lee grinned. "I'm going to miss your dry German humor," he replied.

"Let's just hope we all survive to tell the tales of Intus," said Cotton.

"If we do, I'll buy you fellows a beer—a real, German one, of course," Brenner offered with a wink.

"Deal," said Lee, sticking out his hand to shake Brenner's.

Cotton stuck out his hand as well, but Brenner laughed. "Fool me once, shame on you, fool me twice, shame on me—isn't that how your expression goes?"

Chapter 32
Like Father, Unlike Son

Year 2086
Charleston, South Carolina
Earth

Coop's breath caught in his throat. He couldn't believe it. No matter how much his mind told him not to, his body went on automatic pilot, and he walked into his father's office. There, he stood at attention. "Permission to speak, sir."

Coop's father stopped typing on a tablet and looked up. "Granted."

Since Coop was a child, his father had spent most of his time in here, a nook big enough for three rooms. His father's oak desk sat in the center on a burgundy-and-black rug costing more than most hover vehicles. Around him, shelves were stacked with books of all types, mostly military. Two massive windows allowed the sunshine to filter through partially opened curtains. Above, a domed ceiling displayed a painting of the Battle of Waterloo, spread out wide.

Coop was seventeen, and in two hours, a girl he'd crushed on the entire year was holding an end-of-the-school-year party, and she'd personally invited him during the last period of school today.

"Request permission to attend a social gathering tonight, sir."

"That's not how we address a superior officer, Blake," Coop's dad said. "Try again."

Coop swallowed hard. "Sir, I respectfully request permission to attend a social gathering this evening at nineteen hundred hours, sir." He extended his hand, offering a note.

His dad opened the note and read. His lips pursed as he looked into Coop's eyes. "Once again, you've failed to properly prepare your request form. Where's the operational brief? I need the host's full name, parents' names, occupations, exact address and duration of the party, complete list of attendees, detailed timeline of events, transportation plan with backup options, and emergency protocols with contact numbers. And where's the adult supervision confirmation? I don't see it, Blake. Where is it?"

"I'm sorry, sir."

"Sorry?" His father's voice rose. "Sorry is not in a soldier's vocabulary, Blake. Sorry is what weak men say when they've failed to prepare. Are you weak, son?"

"Negative, sir."

"Do you think I'll let you go to this party?"

Coop didn't know but hoped. Deep down, he figured it was a no. His father rarely let him do anything. Still, he nodded. "Yes, sir."

"Have you completed all your chores for today?" his dad asked.

"I have, sir."

"I don't see a map of the area with exit strategies—unless you sent it over via hololink?" Coop's father paused. "Did you, Blake?"

"Negative, sir."

"See that you do that, and return. I'll have my decision then. Dismissed."

After Coop complied and returned with the map in hand, exit strategies penned on the hand-drawn diagram, his father asked him to complete a hundred push-ups within a half hour. When Coop completed the exercise, his dad still looked unconvinced. He stood in the hallway, arms crossed, while Coop waited with a bag in hand, ready to leave. "Son, you won't go tonight."

Coop's heart nearly stopped. "Sir? But I—"

"Are you questioning a direct order, Blake?"

Coop's shoulders drooped. "Dad... I—"

"Go to your room and sit. I want the homework you have that's due on Monday done before dinner. Do you understand?"

Coop bit back what he wanted to say, all the anger burning in his heart, the years spent bored in his room, writing out detailed reports on things that didn't matter in his life but instead mattered to his dad. "Yes, sir. Understood."

He spent the early evening finishing homework, ate in silence along with his mother and father, and made a choice that night. He'd never do this to his own kids, if he ever had any. Also, he'd show his dad that he could do anything, at any time, no matter what it was, and he'd do it well. That he didn't need permission from his dad to do a damn thing after he graduated high school. He'd show his dad the world wasn't as restricted as his father wanted, wasn't as harsh as his father claimed. Coop could make his own fireworks, could do his own thing, whenever he wanted, no matter the job. And he'd do it better than anyone else, without the strict protocols and perfect structure to do so.

That night while lying in his bed, Coop stared at his ceiling. Usually, at these times, almost nightly, his father's voice reverberated in his head. Tonight, something was different. The anger normally burning hot had cooled into something else—determination.

He sat up, grabbed his data pad, and started typing his own plans. Real plans. The best damn plans ever created. If his father wanted perfection, Coop would show him perfection. If he wanted excellence, he'd get excellence. Yet it would be Coop's way.

He wrote until his eyes burned:

Get into the Academy.

Excel without the constant oversight.

Lead through talent, not fear.

Succeed on my own terms.

His father's footsteps passed his door. The man was probably doing his nightly inspection rounds. Coop didn't flinch this time. Instead, he kept typing, creating his future. He'd show his pops that success didn't need to come wrapped in rigid protocols, or control, for that matter. Freedom could bring better results than micromanagement ever could.

One day, he thought, *I'll show him that strength isn't about stupid rules. I'll show him I can do it my way, and it'll be just as good as his way, if not better.*

He saved the file, naming it "Mission Parameters," and smiled. His father had taught him discipline, attention to detail, and adherence to military guidelines. Coop told himself he'd take those lessons and reshape them into something better, something more… fun.

The party he'd missed tonight? Just one small battle. The war for his future? Now that was something he intended to win. He'd break free from these shackles and live his life on his own merits.

Coop switched off his tablet and lay back down. Tomorrow would be another day of "sir, yes, sir," but he'd just created a secret weapon—a purpose for himself, a giant goal.

Graduation was over a year away, but "Mission Parameters" would keep Coop going, would keep him sane until he broke out of this prison—a prison called home.

****

Year 2096
Firebase Nova
Tempas Mountain Range, Manta River Highlands
New Eden

Coop yanked off his sweat-soaked flight gloves, tossing them into his locker with more force than necessary. Another mission, another success. Three years after Coop had lost his Orion near New Eden, though, Vale still wouldn't let up on him. No matter how well he did, no matter that he continued to lead his squadron—and, heck, all the drone pilots on New Eden—in kill count… if it wasn't one thing, then it was another. Coop did his best to push down his anger after yet another talking-to from Vale after a drone outing.

How many more years of this can I take? he wondered.

Steam from the showers filled the ready room, along with the smell of sweat that seemed permanent in these spaces.

Raven watched him from the bench, still in his flight suit, brown hair plastered to his forehead. The set of Raven's jaw told Coop everything he needed to know about what was coming.

"I apparently went NORDO," Coop said as he peeled off his flight suit. "My bad."

Ghost Dog's movements at the end of the bench caught his attention—he stopped untying his boots. The man's hazel eyes locked onto Coop like a weapons system acquiring a target.

Coop pulled his white PT shirt over his head. The silence in the room pressed against him like g-forces in a tight turn.

Ninja's arrival broke the tension. The blond pilot bit into an energy bar, towel wrapped around his waist, apparently oblivious to the brewing storm. "Why's everyone so dang quiet? If memory serves, I'm pretty sure we just splashed the Zodark bandits again. Shall I sing it out loud? 'Again, and again, and again, like the story of our lives, these sick Zodark bastards can't handle us… again, and again.'"

"Lousy song, Ninja," Ghost Dog said. "You make that up?"

"Yep, and it'd hit the top of the charts if I damn well put it out there."

After throwing on pants, Coop headed for the exit, hoping he didn't have to hear Ninja's terrible singing voice ever again. Before he could reach the door, Raven's finger jabbed into his chest, driving him back against the lockers. The impact rattled through his already keyed-up body, making him flinch.

Coop balled his fists, his pulse thundering in his ears. "What's your problem?"

"You." Raven's nostrils flared, and the man was close enough that Coop could see the whites of his eyes. "After years of this, I've had enough."

The dozen or so aviators froze midactivity. A shower shut off. Sweat trickled down Coop's back, his PT shirt sticking to his skin.

"Then say what's on your mind, Raven." Coop curled his upper lip.

Raven jabbed his finger again, each word punctuated with a sharp poke. "You went rogue on me up there… again. Just like Ninja's song. Again and again. I'd tell you to knock it off, but those words died on you years back. You broke formation and I'm getting sick of it. Every time we go pilot those drones, I'm nervous. Not about the Zodarks, but about what you'll do. You screw things up for the rest of us, just so you can showboat and get that kill count high."

Coop knocked Raven's hand away and shoved his locker closed with a bang. "There were threats that—"

"Threats?" Raven snatched a towel from a nearby bench and whipped it against the lockers just centimeters from Coop's head. "You're the threat, Cooper. Not as much the Zodarks. You!"

Coop's hand shot out, catching the next towel snap midair. He yanked it, pulling Raven off-balance for a moment. They stood there, both gripping the towel between them.

"When you're up there," Raven continued, "we never know. Like I said, we ask ourselves, 'Is he going to try to impress the upper brass this time around or is he going to see if he can score the most kills?' We, your team, all of us, are simply afterthoughts to you."

The tension in the towel increased as Coop stepped forward. "I save your butt up there… again and again!"

"I wouldn't need saving if you were there in formation as my wingman!" Raven released the towel, sending Coop stumbling back a step. "That's the thing you don't understand. We work as a team. We move and communicate together. All of us do but you, Coop." He kicked an empty water bottle. It skittered across the floor. "This question begs an answer, one I've been wanting to ask you ever since I saw your sorry mug. Why are you here? To fulfill your old man's ambitions? What? Tell me, Coop? What?"

Coop's jaw clenched so hard his teeth hurt. He grabbed his own water bottle and crushed it. Water sprayed across the floor between them. "What do you want from me?"

"What you can't give."

Footsteps reverberated in the room. "Knock it off." Strike's voice sliced through the tension like a laser through hull plating. He faced Coop, his blue eyes aflame. "What's going on?"

"Nothing, sir." Coop dropped the mangled water bottle into a recycling bin. Water dripped from his hands. "Just a miscommunication."

"Yes." Raven's glare could have melted durasteel. "A… large… miscommunication."

"All right," Strike said. "Coop, come with me."

Great! Berated by the colonel, then Raven, and now Strike. This ought to be good. Coop's boots squeaked against the wet floor as he followed Strike, feeling the stares of his fellow pilots burning into his back.

Strike's office felt even more cramped than usual, the shelves of miniature craft taking up way too much room. Coop stood at attention as Strike circled his desk. Strike handed Coop a data pad.

Coop's hands were still trembling with leftover adrenaline as he looked down at the device. Transfer orders were in front of him.

"Sir, I don't understand." Coop set the tablet down harder than he meant to. "Why am I being transferred to the *Gallipoli*?"

And at 0500 hours? he wondered. *Is the orbital assault ship in high orbit above us right now?* If so, it was news to Coop.

"Because that's where you're needed, Lieutenant."

"Did you put in for this transfer, sir?" Coop shifted in his stance.

"Negative." Strike walked around his desk and closed the door. The latch clicked and Strike strode back, leaning forward with his hands planted on the desk's surface. A model Orion drone—exactly like the one Coop had just flown—teetered near the desk's edge.

"Lieutenant, I'm disappointed in you. Seems to be a pattern for me… constantly being disappointed in you. Why do I have to keep telling you it's time for you to start taking your responsibilities seriously?

You have an incredible talent as a drone fighter and pilot, and you're wasting it with your reckless behavior."

Coop's fingers twitched. He wanted to steady the model from wobbling. He opened his mouth to protest, but Strike held up a hand, silencing him.

"The Coopers are known for producing war heroes. Your squadron counts on you to have their backs."

"Yes, sir." The words tasted like ash in his mouth.

"We're in this fight together. When you step into that Orion drone pod, you're expected to follow your training."

Coop held his breath, watching the model drone rock with each gesture from Strike. "Sir, if I'm put in the right place, I'll show you what I can do."

"You'll earn your spot like the rest of us."

You've purposely held me back! The thought burned in his gut, but he forced his expression to remain neutral. "Understood, sir."

"Remember that when you board the *Gallipoli*. You have potential, Cooper. Don't waste it. I'll see you on the *Gallipoli*. Dismissed."

He'll see me on the Gallipoli? *Was he transferred as well?* Coop snapped to attention. The movement caused the model drone to tip over. He caught it, setting it upright before saluting and turning on his heel.

The door clicked shut behind him with the finality of a coffin lid.

Chapter 33
Renaming Genesis

Year 2096
RNS *Gallipoli*
New Eden Orbit

Stop thinking about Jack. Just stop! It's been three freakin' years!

The memory of just about every good experience Love had had with her husband ran through her mind on autopilot. She thought there was something wrong with her. *Shouldn't a widow get over her dead husband by now?* She couldn't turn off the memories no matter what she tried to do.

That was until she stepped onto the flight deck of the RNS *Gallipoli*, an orbital assault ship.

As she made her way through the corridors, a numbness settled over Love. Her mind ceased racing over Jack; perhaps the familiarity of going back to work on a ship was doing the trick. *Maybe I can finally think straight.*

Until recently, numbness had constantly nagged at her since her husband's death three years ago. Ice had seeped into her innards, but on the transport ride to *Gallipoli*, somehow it had disappeared into a haunted hell of every wonderful memory of Jack.

Love reached the squadron's administrative office, personnel staff moving about. She walked to the nearest desk. "Lieutenant Naomi Love, reporting for duty."

"Ah, yes. Lieutenant Naomi Love," said the woman behind the desk. "We've been expecting you. Please have a seat while I gather your datawork."

Love sat in a chair while the woman behind the desk tapped away at her tablet. After a few moments, she handed Love a thin black device.

"This is your designated data pad," she explained. "All necessary documentation and briefings have been transferred to it. Please review them at your earliest convenience."

"Yes, ma'am."

"Lieutenant Love?" a voice called from across the room.

A tall man with graying hair strode toward her. The squadron commander insignia was stitched onto his uniform.

"I'm Commander Rhett Granger," he said. "Welcome to the *Gallipoli* and to the FMT-466 'Wolfpack.'"

"Thank you, sir. I'm glad to be here."

Granger motioned for her to follow him. "Come with me, Lieutenant. I'll give you a quick tour of the hangar bay and introduce you to your crew chief."

As they walked, Granger spoke in a matter-of-fact manner. "So, you're part of Wolfpack now. Keep all classified intel locked down tight here. No leaks. Follow the chain of command to a T. And coordinate closely with our allied forces to make sure our joint ops run smooth as silk. We're counting on you to act like the consummate professional you are and represent the 'Pack' with pride. You're one of us now, and I know you'll fall in line without any issues. I've taken it upon myself to review your past flights. I'm happy to have you aboard."

"Aye, sir."

Granger led her through several corridors and gestured to a row of doors on the left. "Each member of our squadron has their own private bunk, but space is limited, so you'll need to keep your personal belongings to a minimum."

As they continued down the passageway, Granger pointed out the mess hall, the medical bay, and the armory. "You'll be expected to maintain your weapons and gear to the highest standards," he said, halting outside the armory door. "We can't afford any malfunctions in the field."

When they reached the end of the corridor, they stepped through a set of heavy blast doors into the hangar bay. Tools clanged. Engines roared and shut off, the technicians and Synths checking various systems on several starfighters. Ships of all sizes lined the area.

Granger led Love to a corner of the bay where a transport ship was parked, its ramp lowered. The name RNS *Genesis* was stamped on its side in bold white letters.

"This is your bird, Lieutenant. An AT-70A Osprey-class troop transport. She's a beauty."

Love agreed. She'd flown these for years, but a brand-new Osprey always impressed her. Not a ding in sight.

"And this," Granger continued, his attention on a man stepping out from beneath the ship, "is your line supervisor, Chief Brian Ford."

Love squinted. *What's he doing here?* she asked herself.

Last she'd seen him, he'd helped calm her down immediately after Jack's passing. Regardless, seeing his face dropped a load of stress from her shoulders, and she did everything she could to hold back a smile. She could tell Ford held in a grin as well.

Ford nodded. "Lieutenant Love."

"Chief Ford," Love said, returning his nod.

Granger looked between them. "I'll leave you two to get acquainted. Lieutenant, report to meeting room nine at 0800 tomorrow for a briefing."

"Yes, sir." Love gave a salute.

As Granger walked away, Love turned to Ford. "It's good to see you again, Chief."

Ford grunted, but Love could see the hint of a smile in his eyes. "Likewise, Lieutenant. Welcome aboard the *Gallipoli*."

"You knew we'd be working together, didn't you?"

"I plead the Fifth."

"I see how it is, but I'm glad," she said.

"Ditto," Ford replied.

Love turned and glared at the name on the troop transport—*Genesis*. It sat wrong with her. She walked closer to the Osprey and placed a hand on its metal skin.

"What you think, Lieutenant?" Ford asked.

I'm thinking a million things, Chief. "About the *Genesis*? Not much. It's new, no doubt about that. But *Genesis*? An odd name for a troop transport. What's the story behind it?"

"From what I gathered, the brass wants to convey a message of rebirth and new beginnings."

How ironic. "I see. Still, it's a bit presumptuous, don't you think? Calling it *Genesis* before we even know the outcome."

Ford wiped a tool off with a cloth. "I hear you, Lieutenant. You know how they like their symbolism upstairs."

"Well, regardless of the name, we need to make sure she's ready to fly."

"Yes." Ford watched her for a moment without saying a word, silence between the two of them. "For certain."

"Well, how's she looking, Chief?"

"She's in top shape. One of the best transports I've seen." My team has gone over her with a fine-tooth comb. The preflight checks came back clean as a whistle. This ship is healthy and raring to go."

"Good to hear. We'll be carrying a full complement of troops, so I want everything running smoothly."

"You can count on me, Lieutenant. We'll have *Genesis* prepped and ready for whatever any operation throws at her."

"Excellent." While she walked around the Osprey, Love began to talk to it, her voice low. "You and I are going to be together for a long time," she said. "I'm going to keep you safe, and you're going to treat me right. If you treat me right, I'll treat you right. That's something we're going to have to agree upon, all right?"

Out of the corner of her eye, Ford watched her. She didn't care. *Is it a coincidence he's paired up with me?* she wondered.

Granger headed in her direction. "Lieutenant Love, I have information that you need to report to administration to receive your quarters assignment at one-niner-three-zero hours," he said.

"Aye, sir," Love replied.

As Granger left, Love faced Ford. "Chief, can you get me a can of paint?"

"Excuse me, Lieutenant? I'm not sure I heard you correctly. Did you say can of paint?"

"Yes," Love said. "Or a spray can?"

"Aye, ma'am. I'll be Oscar Mike in a hot minute." Ford walked away to fetch the requested item.

When Ford returned with spray paint, Love took it from him with a thanks. She headed over to the Osprey and painted a red line through the name *Genesis*.

Beneath the crossed-out name, Love painted a new one: *Jack*. She stepped back to admire her handiwork, her lips a straight, tight line. "Much better."

Understanding dawned on Ford's face. "The *Jack*," he said, almost like testing the name on his tongue. "I like it. It fits the ship well."

"It does, and I'm glad you approve, Chief," she said. "See you at 0800 tomorrow. We've got a lot of winning to do."

Year 2084
Austin, Texas
Earth

Ford stepped out of his battered car to follow the man in the navy-blue coveralls. He glanced back at his vehicle, parked haphazardly near the mechanic's shop. "Where you want me to go?"

Carl looked over his shoulder at Ford. "My shop."

"Why?"

"Don't play coy."

"I'm not playing coy… and who the heck says that word?"

"I do." Carl picked up his pace, striding across the street.

Ford had managed to cobble together a functional engine for his own car using loose parts scavenged throughout the city. He'd always repaired it in full view of Carl, whenever the shop's main doors remained open. It turned out Carl had been watching Ford for some time now.

As they crossed the road, Carl turned to Ford. "You know, you could have just sent in an application, and I'd have made sure you had an interview."

"I did. Five times. Been turned down each time." He huffed. "I don't need charity, if that's what you're offering."

Carl waved him forward. "It's not charity, kid. It's recognizing talent when I see it."

Ford could feel the small bag of heroin tucked away in his pocket with each step.

"Come on," Carl said, leading the way to his shop. "Aren't you a little young to be homeless?"

"No. There's younger people than me."

Carl shook his head. "My Lord, this world's falling apart. OK, just keep walking."

"Wenthrow Nanotech Refitters" stretched in bold letters on the building's sign. Carl Wenthrow specialized in repairing military shuttles using high-end parts. As Ford knew well, the mechanic shop worked on engines for troop transports and frigates, but nothing larger. The two-story building filled an entire block on the edge of Austin. Barred windows dotted the building on all sides.

As they approached the shop, Carl stepped onto the sidewalk. "I've seen you around. Watching, learning. You've got a knack for this stuff."

"I just like figuring things out."

"And you're damn good at it," Carl said. He stopped at the main entrance—an open garage door. "You coming in or not?"

Ford halted, looking the shop owner up and down. "Really, what do you want?"

"Help."

"With what?"

"A lot of things." Carl motioned for Ford to step inside. "You've walked this far, so come on in."

In truth, Ford had scoped out this building many times, always wanting to see what treasures lay inside. This was a different mechanic's outfit. Cars and motorbikes needing repair went someplace else. Instead, ship engines of many military models were fixed and constructed here. Since he was a kid, Ford had been enamored with military craft. As he'd grown older, the art of rebuilding them, fixing them up, had intrigued him the most.

Ford stepped into the giant warehouse-sized workshop. The air was filled with the whir of machinery, the clang of metal against metal. Mechanics in grease-stained coveralls leaned over engines bigger than buses. They tightened bolts. Soldered wires.

As he walked further, Ford gawked at the engines themselves. The aerodynamic curves of their casings disguised the raw power that thrummed within, the kind of power able to propel a military shuttle through space. Something he'd never thought he'd get the chance to touch, let alone work on.

One mechanic, a burly man with a thick beard, used a plasma cutter to slice through a sheet of titanium alloy. The man's brow furrowed in concentration. Another mechanic, a wiry woman with her hair pulled back and a bandanna covering her head, worked with a hydraulic lift to maneuver a massive turbine into place.

Ford's skin crawled. *I really need a fix.* He could hardly think straight.

"Are you OK?" Carl asked.

"Yeah."

Ford scratched an itch beneath his skin. He shifted uncomfortably, his hand unconsciously drifting toward the pocket where he kept his stash.

Carl introduced him to the other mechanics. They looked up from their work, nodding in acknowledgment as Carl called out their names. They went back to work right away.

As they made their way through the shop, an older woman with curly gray hair passed by, her arms laden with data pads. She bent slightly as she walked, her movements slow. Ford realized the woman was over sixty years old. Her age would have been unthinkable before the advancements that took place after the Great AI War.

"Hello," she said.

"Hey," Ford replied.

Carl led Ford to his office, a small, cluttered space tucked away in the back of the building. He motioned for Ford to take a seat and sat himself, leaning back in his own chair.

This room was little more than a storage closet. The smell of burning plasma filled the space. A single fluorescent tube cast a blue light over the area. Behind Carl, stacks of dog-eared technical manuals tilted unsteadily, grease streaks added to their creased spines and smeared pages. Tangles of patch cables snaked their way across the floor, some curled up in a corner. Scorched thruster casings, distributor coils, bent drive conduits, amongst other components, buried his scarred permacrete desktop. A battered old nano-defabricator sat against one wall. Several trays overflowed with its rematerialized guts. Smoke-stained walls stood plastered with byte-printed pin-up images of Orion starfighters and Republic cargo haulers.

Carl waved a calloused hand in the air. "Sorry about the mess..."

Better than my car. "It's fine."

"If you're going to work here, there are a few things you need to know. First and foremost, I expect miracles from you. I've seen what you can do with that car of yours, and I know you've got the skills to make it here."

Ford shifted in his seat. "What are you talking about?"

"You need a job. I'm giving you one."

"I like what I do, and I don't need a job."

Carl crossed his leg over the other. "You need one."

"I'm happy." Ford's stomach growled.

"You're as happy as a dog chewing on a carburetor."

"What? No, I'm fine."

"There were times in my life, though long ago, when I'd spend three days looking for food. Hell, I've snuck into a person's backyard before and stood in their shed at night while it rained, not daring to fall asleep just in case they found me conked out at six in the morning. I did that three weeks in a row and had to run from the cops when someone spotted me. I've hunted squirrels in the park so I could eat. People have stepped over me when I slept on the sidewalk without an inkling that they should ever help me, or even notice my presence. I've camped outside for months in alleyways, digging through garbage cans for whatever I could find. I've spent a year under the South First Street Bridge, freezing my butt off and using nothing but my ragged clothes and cardboard to keep warm. That's how I know."

Those words hit Ford hard, and he bit his lower lip to keep himself from crying. He kept a stoic expression. "So?"

"How old are you?"

"Seventeen."

Carl cleared his throat. "I also expect you to get clean."

"Clean?"

The mechanic's expression turned more serious. "I know you're struggling with addiction. We'll get you into a drug program right away, get you the support you need to kick the habit."

"I don't do drugs." The lie sounded hollow even to his own ears.

"I've been there."

"Been where? If you're talking drugs, then I'm sorry you were there, but I'm not a user."

Carl raised an eyebrow. "Have you looked in a mirror lately?"

Ford looked down at his pale, clammy hands. "No."

"Well, let me tell you what you'll be doing here. You'll be retrofitting new frigate engines, studying them while you work. All the information you need is on the data tablet I'll provide, and the tools are all in the shop. We have a strict policy against cutting off hands."

Ford's head snapped up. "I haven't even said I'll take the job."

Carl bent forward, his face intense. "I'm offering it." He pointed to the open doorway. "But if you really don't want it, there's the exit."

Ford held his breath. This would change everything. The dream he had nurtured for as long as he could recall—landing a position here—was finally within his reach. He knew he needed this job. Heck, anyone looking at him for even one second knew it as fact.

"Why are you doing this?" Ford asked. No one did anything kind for him. Ever. Why now?

What's the catch?

Carl's face softened. "Because I see potential in you," he said. "I've been in this business for twenty-eight years, and I know talent when I see it. It's up to you whether you want to pursue that potential or not."

What's in it for him? "I don't have much experience. I'll screw up."

Carl's expression hardened. "If you screw up, you're out of here. Plain and simple. But I'm not talking about the work. I'm talking about the drugs. Today, you stop. We'll get you a program, a doctor, a regimen of medication to help you quit. But it's up to you to follow through."

"Again, why are you doing this?"

"Because someone did it for me. Now, there's a shower in the back. Get washed up. Use the towel. Fran will drop off some new mechanic's coveralls for you."

Ford stood, his legs shaking a bit as he made his way toward the door. He paused in the doorway, looking back at Carl.

"So that's it?" Carl asked. "You're leaving? Giving up on me just like that?"

Ford shook his head. "I'm going to look for the showers."

"Good man. Stick with me, and you'll make diamonds out of everything we create and rebuild here. Trust me, I know what I'm talking about."

"OK, sir."

Carl smiled. "What are you waiting for? I can smell you from here. Go. Shower up."

"All right." Ford turned the corner, the idea of fresh water running over his body lessening the load he felt for the first time in a long time.

Chapter 35
The Cooper Name

Year 2096
Tempas Mountain Range, Manta River Highlands
Firebase Nova
New Eden

Lieutenant Cooper's boots crunched on the gravel as he neared the base's major runway. The sun beat down on his shoulders as he carried his gear. He'd been transferred. Sure, he knew he was one of the most unpopular guys at the firebase, but he'd been getting used to it. Also, the fresh air, the wide-open spaces of planetside life—a far cry from the stale recycled atmosphere inside a vessel.

Gotta make the best of it, I guess. He grimaced. *When Dad finds out the reasons they transferred me, it'll be open season on every mistake I've made. Great.*

As he approached the Osprey troop transport, Coop took a deep breath. The scent of jet fuel and hot asphalt carried to his nostrils. Still, better than living on a giant RNS orbital assault ship, the very place he was heading to now. He'd grown fond of this smell. It meant freedom. As he went to board the transport, he knew it was a farewell to everything he'd come to know on this part of New Eden.

Coop stepped into the Osprey's cabin. His heart sank as he took in the faces of the other pilots already seated: Raven, Ghost Dog, Ninja, and Strike. All there, along with pilots from different squadrons. Coop and Raven looked at one another for a moment before Raven turned away, saying nothing.

Coop found the only empty seat, next to Ninja. He settled in and stowed his gear beneath him.

The captain's voice came over the comm. "We're about to depart from the firebase for the RNS *Gallipoli*. Make sure you're strapped in and your gear is secured. It's gonna be a short flight. ETA to the *Gallipoli*, twenty mikes. Sit tight and enjoy the ride."

The Osprey's engines grumbled to life as the aircraft prepared to lift off. Coop stared straight ahead, trying to ignore the crappy feeling in his gut. Why were Strike and Raven here, let alone Ninja and Ghost Dog? He thought he'd left them for good. His bad luck got worse.

Figures, Coop thought.

As the Osprey rose into the air, the holoscreen high on the cabin's wall in front of him showed the firebase falling away below them, the buildings and runways shrinking until they were nothing more than specks on the horizon. The cabin trembled as the transport gained altitude.

Ninja turned to face Coop. "So, what do you think about the transfer?"

Leave me alone, man.

Coop shrugged. "It is what it is."

"I heard the *Gallipoli* is a good ship," Ninja remarked. "Lots of action coming."

Good ship? What's that mean? "I see. Interesting."

"You think you're ready for it?" Ninja probed.

"Of course." *What a stupid question.*

"We gotta get another poker tournament going," Ninja continued, oblivious to how much he was annoying Coop. "You think the fellas up there on the *Gallipoli* will want to play?"

What is this guy, five years old? "Uh… maybe? I don't know."

"I rarely see you lose in poker."

"That's right," Coop replied.

"How are you so good?"

I've studied it forever. "I'm lucky."

Ninja snorted. "That's not it. Seriously, did you play while growing up or something?"

"Something like that."

In truth, his mom had taught him. Growing up, he would accompany her out to a research lab where she worked. There, she studied game theory and decision-making processes for the government. Amongst many types of games, she'd used poker as a means of conducting experiments and collecting data. She'd taught Coop the game along the way.

Coop's mom had trained him to notice the subtle tells players often showed. She'd taught him to watch for things like eye movements, facial tics, changes in breathing patterns, and other pertinent gestures—all usual giveaways, revealing important information about an opponent's strategy. She also drilled into him the value of controlling his own tells. Through countless hours of practice, she helped Coop develop a poker face rivaling the professionals'. He learned to maintain a steady breathing rhythm, to keep his body language natural, and to avoid any habitual motions or mannerisms. Unless—and this was all too important—unless he wanted his opponents to think a certain way.

The most common tells, his mom had explained, were fidgeting, excessive blinking, touching the face or neck, and changes in posture or betting patterns—all telltale signs even experienced players sometimes struggled to hide. Coop had been trained from a young age to both recognize them in others and eliminate them from his own behavior. She once told him if it wasn't for his father, she'd have urged him toward a professional poker career.

"Someday," Ninja said, "you gotta tell me your poker secrets."

"Nope."

"Well, I guess that's that."

"I guess so."

Ninja fell silent as Coop watched the display. The Osprey climbed higher into the sky until clouds enveloped them in a white haze. Coop leaned back in his seat. As the Osprey ascended through the atmosphere, g-forces pressed him harder into his backrest. The transport's inertial dampeners kept the worst of the acceleration at bay, but he still felt the stress of the climb in his chest and a slight disorientation as the aircraft turned.

The blue sky outside darkened, fading to black. Stars appeared as distant pinpricks of light against the void. Once the curvature of the planet fell away, the vastness of space beyond took its place. In the cabin, the holodisplay showed their progress. The Osprey's icon moved toward the RNS *Gallipoli*. As the minutes ticked by, the estimated arrival time counted down from twenty minutes to fifteen to ten.

Raven and Ghost Dog sat a few seats down from Coop, engaged in friendly banter. Raven cracked a joke about the possible food on the *Gallipoli*. Ghost Dog laughed.

As they flew closer to the *Gallipoli*, the sheer size of the vessel impressed Coop. It was one of the largest orbital assault ships in the Republic Navy, a behemoth of metal.

The Osprey veered toward the landing bay. The maw of the ship opened to receive them. The moment the Osprey flew through *Gallipoli*'s opening, it decelerated rapidly. Thrusters fired to counteract their momentum as the bay's artificial gravity took hold. The transport tugged downward as it transitioned from inertial dampening to the *Gallipoli*'s gravitational field.

Ahead, a mighty deck sprawled outward. It swarmed with activity. Armored personnel carriers along with heavy artillery pieces sat in formations, awaiting deployment. Crews of deckhands, technicians, and Synths scurried between the military hardware. Behind them, antigrav lifts stacked containers. In a rear section of the hangar, robotic wrenches the size of a mech's arms repaired shuttles, and officers ordered crew members around.

Once their Osprey settled onto reinforced landing struts, Coop caught glimpses of other arrivals through the holo's interface—dropships practically regurgitating fresh platoons of soldiers. They shouldered rifles and gear. Alongside one wall, synthetic humanoids set crates atop metal shelving. Humans worked across from them, inspecting craft. The Osprey's engines powered down as the rear ramp lowered.

Coop unbuckled his harness. He stood, stretching his legs before he grabbed his gear. He followed Strike and the other pilots out of the transport. They walked across the hangar bay and through sliding doors into the corridor beyond. The group made their way to the administration office, and Coop signed the necessary forms and received his new assignments, including the designation of his F-97 Orion's drone pod.

The next day, they found their way to the simulation room, where pod 7 awaited him. Coop climbed inside, settling into the comfortable chair. The controls were familiar, yet more advanced than what he was used to on the firebase on the planet below.

Coop touched the controls. "This feels good. Dang good." For a minute, he felt at home again. "You and me, buddy. We're going to kick some Zodarks off the face of the galaxy. There ain't no two ways about it."

"All right," Strike announced. "Exit the modules and secure your gear. We're cutting footprints to the ready room for transition briefs at 1930 hours. After that, I want hawks in the nest by 2000. Settle in, get squared away with your racks, and there you'll meet the rest of your squadron, the DFS-103 'Jolly Rogers.' Any wags, bring 'em up with me on the way. Let's go."

As Coop followed Ninja, Ghost Dog, and Raven down the corridor toward his bunk, he still reeled from Raven's taunts in the locker room yesterday. He walked with his head down.

A second later, he collided with someone. The impact jarred him out of his thoughts. Coop stumbled back, his eyes widening as he realized he'd just bumped into a woman. She was slender with blond hair pulled back into a tight bun. Her fatigues bore the name "LOVE" and the rank of lieutenant.

"Excuse me, pilot," the woman said. "Keep your head up and your eyes forward."

Coop opened his mouth to reply. The words died on his lips as he caught sight of her face. She was stunningly beautiful, with high cheekbones and full lips. Surrounding it all, sadness shrouded her features. Her eyes, a deep blue, appeared distant. She carried a heavy burden for some reason or another, and part of Coop wanted to know why.

"I… I'm sorry, Lieutenant." Something about this woman made him want to make amends, and for her to know he meant what he said… because he did.

She turned to walk away, her stride and posture down the passageway… perfect. Everything about her… perfect.

Coop shook his head. *Get your head straight, man!*

Six minutes later, Coop walked into a large, cramped room. The space was already occupied by numerous pilots. Coop counted twenty-four beds in total, each one a narrow bunk stacked three high against the walls. The pilots fit tightly into the chamber, with just enough space to move around without bumping into each other.

The pilots already in the room glanced up. A heavy silence floated in the air. Coop found his assigned bunk, a thin mattress and a single pillow.

Coop began to store his gear in the narrow locker beside it when someone piped up, "Lookee here, it's the FNGs!" The man's voice was full of sarcasm, his eyes bearing down on Raven. "Don't worry, we'll make sailors out of you yet."

The room of pilots crowded around Raven and Ghost Dog while Coop kept his head down. He ignored the verbal jabs, knowing better than to engage. Still, a fire boiled up inside him. These pilots had no idea what he and his team were capable of, and he resented being treated like a green recruit.

Another pilot chimed in. "I see the new crop of biners just rolled in. Don't pee yourselves on the first day now."

Raven bristled at the comment. He dropped his gear on the floor and clenched his fists. "Watch your mouth." He took a step forward, eye to eye with the guy.

The man's nostrils flared, his nose almost touching Raven's. "They finally let you out of the womb, did they? Well, welcome to the real Navy, leech."

Coop had had enough. "You want to say that again, tough guy?"

The man turned toward Coop and stared. Finally, the pilot smiled and started to clap. The rest of the pilots in the room began to laugh.

A ridiculously muscled pilot hopped down from his bunk. "We're just razzin' you. Protocol for us when it comes to new members. Nonetheless, I like your spunk. You'll fit in well. Welcome to the Jolly Rogers. I'm Lieutenant Lincoln Bowmen. You can call me Bear."

Raven nodded. "Glad to meet you. I'm Raven, this here's Ghost Dog and Ninja. That over there's Coop."

Bear eyed Coop. "Heard a lot about you. We're in good company. Now, if you don't mind, I've got some resting to do." He climbed back onto his bunk, and everyone sat. The chatter in the room grew louder.

Interesting way to break the ice, Coop thought. He liked it. Once settled, he hopped onto his bed while the rest of those he'd arrived with on the RNS *Gallipoli* made small talk with their new friends. The mattress squeaked beneath Coop's weight.

Coop reached into his pocket and pulled out his great-great-grandfather's journal. He opened it to a random passage and began to read. The leather cover was worn and faded from years of use, the pages yellowed with age.

Coop was no stranger to the legacy written in the history of combat. As a descendant of Second Lieutenant Presley Paul Cooper, he was part of a lineage as famous as the Earth itself, or so he told himself. His great-great-grandfather, Presley, had carved the skies with "Hazel II," his P-51 Mustang, as a member of the 52nd Fighter Group, 5th Fighter Squadron, during the tough years of World War II. This heritage was Coop's compass, always steering him through the thickness of battle. Yet there, in the Second World War, Presley was able to fly a plane while in the actual cockpit. Somehow, it made Coop feel small. Since Coop flew a drone, the level of personal danger was nil. So, between him and his great-great-grandad, there was a huge difference.

One risked his life while saving his nation; the other only risked his drone.

The call sign "Coop" had traveled down from Presley Paul to his son, then to his grandson and great-grandson, and finally to Blake "Coop" Cooper. It had become a belief, a pledge of bravery, skill, and a diehard commitment to respect the family name and patriotic service to Coop's country. Along with the call sign, generations had passed down Presley's pilot wings from generation to generation. They had reached Coop's hands several years ago, and he now kept them stowed away in his gear bag.

The pages of Presley Paul's personal diary were filled with handwritten stories of combat, glory, and his invincible will. Today, the passage Coop read described a dogfight during World War II, with Presley engaged in an aerial battle. As he read, a quote caught his eye, words of wisdom from his ancestor: "Adversity tests our spirit, not our strength."

Coop was about to turn the page when the sound of heavy boots walking nearby interrupted him. Everyone went quiet. All eyes turned to the tall, broad-shouldered man in the doorway. Strike's gaze swept over the room.

"Listen up, everyone," Strike said. "I'm your new squadron leader. Many of you've been handpicked for this squadron. You're the best of the best. This is an elite unit, and I intend to maintain that level of superiority. Subpar work or half-hearted attempts won't be tolerated. I expect your unwavering commitment to maintaining those high standards. We'll be having a briefing soon, so I suggest you get yourselves ready."

The thought of working under him, taking orders from the man who'd always had it out for him, made Coop's stomach turn over.

When Strike finished, the pilots filed out of the room. Coop tucked his great-great-grandfather's journal into his bag and jumped down from his bunk.

As he turned to follow the others, Raven bumped into his shoulder. He grinned. "Thanks, Coop."

"For what?" Coop asked.

Raven motioned toward the area where the confrontation had occurred between them and the other pilots. "You stood there like a badass, not even flinching, man. Thank you."

Coop looked away. "Yeah. Don't read too much into it."

"Right." Raven shook his head. "All right, Coop. Understood."

While they walked down the corridor, Coop's father came to mind, his voice loud and clear the minute he'd seen Coop off on the first day at the Academy: "You better not screw this up, you hear me? The Cooper name is on the line, and I won't have you tarnishing it. Don't you dare pull any dumb stunts or get yourself splashed. You understand me?"

I understand, Dad. Coop kept walking, anger rising from his belly. *It's always about the name. Always about flying. Maybe you could have played catch with me once, given me a damn pat on the back. That too hard for you, old man?*

Actions spoke louder than words. As Coop turned the corner, he saw Strike leading the way, all the pilots in his squadron behind the man. From this point forward, he'd show Strike the truth, that actions indeed spoke a hell of a lot louder than words, and he'd shove it down Strike's throat if he had to.

Chapter 36
Taking Command

Year 2096
New Eden Orbital Station
New Eden

After greeting the station's commander, Lee had been escorted to the viewing area overlooking the space dock. Lee stood alone with his hands clasped behind his back, observing the star-filled void visible through the station's curved windows. In the distance, several ships underwent repairs within the station's dock. Robotic arms and technicians worked in tandem, mending damaged hull plates. Beside the vessels under repair, a team of synthetic humanoids, otherwise known as Synths, worked on a new ship. On a web of scaffolding, these robotic Synth builders fused joists together using electron beam welding torches.

The Synths moved with incredible skill. Tireless workers capable of enduring the horrible conditions of space, these humanoid machines had slowly become the backbone of space industries, including the military. Without the need for rest and sustenance, Synths could labor for days on end. They could function for a week, depending on the duration of the battery charge. Heavy-duty models lasted up to ten days. Powerful batteries existed to sustain these robotic humans for months, but politics and past circumstances strictly prohibited them from accessing those power cells—a precautionary measure implemented after the devastating Great War of the 2040s.

However, it was the ship to the side that captured Lee's attention… and in truth, his heart—the RNS *Poseidon*, a Type-002A Altairian-Human hybrid warship. It floated in the space dock, its imposing weaponry a declaration of the incredible power it held. The heavy cruiser brought a smile to Lee's lips.

Before arriving at this station, Lee had handpicked some of the finest officers from the RNS *Kentucky* to join him on the *Poseidon*: Lieutenant Lucia Rodriguez, a brilliant communications officer; Lieutenant Connor Rhom, a seasoned tactical expert who'd be instrumental in devising strategies and overseeing the ship's weapons systems; Lieutenant Lewis Reynolds, a navigation expert; and Boyd MacGregor, the *Kentucky*'s chief engineer, now promoted to chief engineer on the *Poseidon*. MacGregor's skills and years of experience in the engine room had made him the natural choice for this all-too-important role on *Poseidon*, where he'd have full authority over the ship's systems.

Lee knew MacGregor well and was confident the man would keep the *Poseidon* running in tip-top shape, though the man tended to find himself in the hot-tempered, cranky department a little too much. Still, MacGregor was one of the best and most knowledgeable engineers in the business.

"She's a beauty, isn't she?"

"She is," Lee said.

His old, dead commander, James Oldendorf, motioned toward the *Poseidon*. "Commanding a ship like that is a great responsibility, Lee. That ship is an extension of yourself. Pour your heart and soul into her. In return, she'll carry you and your crew through the toughest battles, and the most treacherous space. Trust in yourself, trust in your crew, and trust in her. Together, you'll achieve great things. We have a galaxy to save."

Lee turned to respond to his mentor and instead cleared his throat. He shifted on his feet, standing straighter. Because when he looked, no one stood next to him. He thought he'd slept enough. Apparently not. Hearing ghosts or figments of his imagination rattled him a little. After taking a deep exhale, he blinked several times to gather his bearings.

Nerves, he thought. *I'll get back in the rhythm of things when I step aboard my ship.*

Footsteps came in his direction, and he turned. Commander Boyd MacGregor walked in his direction.

MacGregor snapped to attention. His body stiffened as he brought his right hand up in a crisp motion, fingers joined and thumb hugging the side of his hand, before touching his fingers to his brow in a salute. "Commander Lee, it's an honor to be serving under your command on the *Poseidon*. I've heard great things about her, sir." Grease stained his fingers, and despite the grime on his Republic Navy uniform, Lee could tell he wore it with pride.

"As have I." Lee returned the salute. "At ease. The honor is mine. I have no doubt that you'll keep the *Poseidon* running like a well-oiled machine."

MacGregor grinned, his red hair cropped short and his piercing blue eyes seeming to smile too. "Aye, sir. She's a magnificent vessel. My engineering team and I will keep her systems running slicker than a superconductor. Those neutrino injectors for the FTL nacelles? Rerouting the conduits through them will let us sustain a steady cruising speed for a good long time. Speaking of which, did you see the readings from the sweep on the port nacelle? The new baffles they put in during the install work like a dream, Captain. Like a damn dream."

Lee nodded. "I'm very glad you approve of our new ship."

"Like a—"

"Dream?" Lee winked. "I've heard."

"I'm sorry, Captain. I'm just excited."

"Good. Now, bring that excitement on the ship. Spread it wide, along with your work ethic, and we should do well."

"Oh, I will, Cap. I will."

Lee withheld a grin. Being addressed as "Cap" sat well with him.

"Mac," Lee began, shortening MacGregor's name just as MacGregor had called him Cap instead of Captain, "some people at the base last night asked if my Mexico adventure actually happened."

MacGregor let out a hearty laugh. "Aye, Cap, it's about time you stop answering that question. When I met you all those years ago, you were all the buzz. I got used to it, but you were on quite the tall pedestal until we really got to know you. Now who knows how many people you have as fans rather than people you are in command of? They'll look at you differently."

"They'll look at me like a hero, Mac, and that's a good thing. They'll respect me."

MacGregor shook his head. "Can I speak candidly?"

"You may."

"Sir, being a hero is being on a pedestal. It's a tall order. You don't want people liking you as a captain; you want them fearing the ever-living hell out of you."

"I won't be running a ship like that, MacGregor."

The chief engineer pushed out his lower lip, nodding his head slowly. "Aye, sir. I get it."

Lee kept his eyes on the *Poseidon*. Its hull glistened from the planet's glare.

After a moment, Lee's eyes widened. "Hey, do you remember my niece I was telling you about?" He raised a fist and shook it. "She did it—valedictorian of her graduating class."

"Congratulations. What university again?"

"Columbia."

Lee clapped a couple of times. "Impressive. Where'd she get those brains?"

"Not from me, that's for sure." MacGregor hesitated for a second. "Why don't you ever talk about your family?"

Lee's expression stiffened and he gave MacGregor a look telling the chief engineer he'd crossed a line with his superior officer.

MacGregor backpedaled, his palms up in apology. "I'm sorry, Captain."

"Understood."

A tall, beautiful Asian woman walked toward them, her boots loud against the tiles.

"MacGregor," Lee said. "You may go."

"Aye, sir."

When the woman came within a few meters of Lee, she stood at attention, her posture perfect. She saluted. "Commander Lee, I'm Lieutenant Commander Noriko Sato, your new executive officer. I've been transferred from the RNS *Iowa*."

Lee returned the salute while assessing his new XO. He'd expected to meet her the moment he arrived on NEOS, but her shuttle had arrived late due to the new security protocols. "Welcome, Lieutenant Commander Sato. I trust you've familiarized yourself with the ship and its crew?"

"Yes, sir. I've studied the ship's specifications and personnel files extensively." She handed him a data tablet. "I've brought my transfer orders and service record for your review, sir. The records have also been uploaded to your office inside the *Poseidon*."

Lee accepted the data pad and scrolled through the information. As he read, Sato's record impressed him. She'd served on a variety of ships—frigates, flak frigates, and battleships. Experience oozed from her résumé.

On the RNS *Cyclone*, a flak frigate, Sato had served as the chief weapons officer, overseeing a team of fifteen personnel. Her innovative tactics had resulted in a twenty-five percent increase in the ship's point-defense efficiency, earning her a commendation from the ship's captain.

During her tenure on the RNS *New Jersey*, she'd coordinated the ship's fighter squadrons. Under her leadership, the squadrons had achieved a remarkable ninety percent mission success rate, with minimal casualties.

Perhaps most impressive was Sato's service on the RNS *Iowa*. As the tactical officer, she'd been in charge of a department of over fifty officers and enlisted personnel. During the battle at the stargate, Sato's decisive actions had been credited with saving the ship. She'd earned the Republic Navy Cross, one of the highest military decorations.

As Lee read through the performance evaluations from Sato's superior officers, a clear picture emerged—she was an officer who consistently exceeded expectations. Phrases like "unparalleled dedication," "exceptional leadership," and "strategic brilliance" appeared repeatedly. There was no doubt Lee would find her an important asset under his command.

"I see you were aboard the RNS *Iowa* during the battle at the New Eden stargate," Lee said.

"Yes, sir. I served as the tactical officer at the time."

"With me, Sato, you can be more at ease."

"Aye, sir." Her shoulders relaxed a bit.

He handed the tablet back. "Your experience will be invaluable on the *Poseidon*. We've got a lot to learn from her. We'll be training soon after boarding."

"I'm ready to face it head-on, sir," Sato replied. "She's an amazing ship, and I'm eager to put her through her paces."

"I've no doubt that you'll excel in your role as XO, Lieutenant Commander." Lee turned his full attention to Sato. "Walk with me. I'd like to discuss your previous experience."

As they strode along the corridors, the glass windows showing the dock to his left, a myriad of closed doors to his right, Lee listened as Sato described her background, her role on the RNS *Iowa*, and the recent combat. "I've fought the Zodarks for several years now, Commander."

"Call me Lee or Captain."

"Aye, sir."

When Lee first saw Lieutenant Commander Noriko Sato's name on his assignment roster, it had taken him a moment to place it.

But when he reviewed her personnel file, the memory hit like a shockwave.

They had fought in the same battle—two and a half years ago—at the New Eden stargate.

Back then, he'd been a lieutenant, the tactical officer aboard the *Kentucky*. She had held the same rank and the same job aboard the RNS *Iowa*. Both ships had been part of the same battered Republic task force thrown against a larger, more prepared Zodark formation.

When the *Kentucky* had lost power during the engagement and drifted helplessly in the path of a Zodark battleship, Lee had braced for the end. But the killing blow never came. Only later—after the battle— did he learn why.

The *Iowa* had moved between them and the enemy. It had drawn the fire, shielding them just long enough for the *Kentucky* to reboot her reactors to get back into the fight. At the time, Lee had chalked it up to good fortune and great commanding. But reading Sato's after-action report now, he saw the truth.

She'd suggested the maneuver. She'd seen the risk and convinced her captain to act. That move had saved his life—and the lives of everyone aboard his old ship.

Now, two promotions later, she was standing beside him as his newly assigned XO aboard the *Poseidon*. And this time, he was the one in command.

As they walked the corridor overlooking the *Poseidon*'s freshly waxed flight deck, where a maintenance crew was working on one of the shuttle transports, Lee broke the silence.

"I read your AAR from the *Iowa*," he said quietly.

Sato tilted her head slightly, processing his tone. "Sir?"

"The New Eden stargate engagement. The maneuver that put your ship between the *Kentucky* and that Zodark battleship." Lee paused. "That was you. *You* made the recommendation."

"It was Captain Moon's decision," she replied, professional and composed. "I only advised the option."

Lee nodded slowly. "It saved us. I was the tactical officer on the *Kentucky*. If your captain had hesitated… if you hadn't spoken up… we wouldn't be having this conversation."

She looked away for a moment, the barest flicker of emotion crossing her face before it settled back into the same calm resolve.

"I appreciate that, sir. But we all did what we had to that day. That's what training is for."

Lee gave her a long, considering look. "Training's one thing. Courage under fire is another."

She didn't respond to that. She didn't need to.

They walked in silence for a few more steps before Lee continued, "After that battle, they gave me command of a beat-up destroyer and sent me to run patrol routes in the Belt. Other than the occasional pirates, it was boring as hell. But it was a test—to see if I could command. I guess I passed, because now I'm here."

He glanced at her. "And I'm damned glad you're here too."

"Thank you, Captain."

"You're sharp, by-the-book, and clearly know your way around a warship. That said…" Lee offered a thin grin. "We'll need to loosen you up a little."

Her left eyebrow rose. "Loosen me up, sir?"

Lee smirked. "Not everything in war goes the way it's supposed to. Sometimes you have to tear up the rules and improvise on the fly."

"I'll keep that in mind."

Lee chuckled, then added, "Oh, and heads-up—our squadron commander, Captain Roberts. Guy's a real ball-buster. Tough as hell, doesn't sugarcoat anything."

"I've heard of him," Sato said dryly.

Lee nodded. "Then you know. We'll be meeting him soon enough. For now, let's focus on getting the *Poseidon* prepped. The invasion of Intus isn't going to wait."

Chapter 37
Expect the Unexpected

Year 2096
RNS *Poseidon*
New Eden Orbit

Commander Ripley Lee and his chief engineer, Commander Boyd MacGregor, had cooked up an exciting simulation to help challenge the crew in cases of dire emergency. At least, MacGregor certainly seemed to think it was exciting. He'd waltzed into Lee's office with a giant grin on his face, and a cup of coffee in his hands. He looked like a little kid who'd just gotten everything he'd asked Santa Claus for that year.

"Are you ready for the show, Cap?" asked MacGregor jovially.

"I think so," said Lee. "I guess the real question is, are the crew ready?"

"Aye, sir, that it is." He ran his fingers through his hair. "Oh, I can't wait. This'll be fun."

Lee smiled. "You may not have the standard view of fun, MacGregor, but I certainly can appreciate your love for the ship and its inner workings."

MacGregor's eyes twinkled. "Can I do the honors, Cap?" he asked.

Lee chuckled. "Sure, Mac. Be my guest." He flourished with his hand to show his chief engineer what to push to initiate the training protocol.

A female voice that sounded artificially generated spoke over the ship's public address system. "Shipwide training scenario number eleven: the magrail systems have gone offline, and hostiles are inbound. You have fourteen minutes to fix the issue before a potential battle, and Commander Lee is incapacitated. Time starts now."

From their seats in Commander Lee's office, Lee and MacGregor could watch video feed of the pertinent areas of the ship. Commander Sato on the bridge was the first to act.

"Tactical, I'd like you to reboot the fire control software," she ordered. "Let's try the easiest route first while I hail engineering."

"Aye, XO," said Lieutenant Rhom.

Sato attempted to hail MacGregor. He did not respond.

MacGregor rubbed his hands together in delight. "Ooh, this is gettin' good," he said to Lee.

Sato, realizing that the chief engineer was supposedly out of commission in this scenario, hailed the next-in-line, Lieutenant Rosa Diaz. After the two of them confirmed the situation, Diaz sprang into action.

"XO, I'm initiating a diagnostic scan of the power grid to identify any breaks or damaged relays."

"Sounds good, keep me updated," Sato replied before turning to Rhom. "Any luck with that software reboot?" she asked.

"Negative," Rhom replied.

During these training scenarios, the ship entered a sandbox mode. The appropriate damage would display until resolved, but no actual changes were made to the ship. And even though the goal of the simulation was to make the magrails fire, they would only "mock" fire before ending the training scenario. It was all meant to be as real as possible, without causing any irreversible damage.

Half a minute went by, and then Diaz hailed Sato. "XO, I believe I've identified the possible source of the problem. It may have been caused by a power conduit overload. I'll need to send a repair drone into one of the maintenance tunnels to confirm."

"That's a good lass," said MacGregor, smacking his leg in approval.

Seconds ticked tensely by for a moment. Lee and MacGregor could watch the drone Diaz had sent into the tunnels travel toward its destination. When it arrived, an orange light was illuminated next to a particular power conduit. Since they couldn't actually damage the ship just for a training exercise, this signaled that the area that needed "repairs."

"XO, I've got a visual on the issue. I'm going to reroute power from a secondary conduit," said Diaz.

"That's the easiest way to do it," MacGregor told Lee. "Although one time, I had to jury-rig a bypass using power cells."

Lee took a sip of his own coffee and smiled, amused by MacGregor's extreme joy in this situation.

Sato hailed Diaz. "So, I don't want to put a damper on things, but we only have a few minutes until we could really use those magrails, Diaz. Is there any way to speed things up?"

"Doing my best, ma'am. Should have it patched up shortly," Diaz replied. Her voice had a tenseness to it, and from his vantage point in his office, Lee could see her face strain as she concentrated.

"Tactical, I want you to prepare our other weapons systems for use," Sato ordered. "We're going to want to use some of our lasers and other long-range weapons to keep the Zodarks at bay until we can swoop in for the kill with the magrails."

"Aye, XO," said Rhom.

"Once you have a firing solution, fire at will," Sato ordered.

"Yes, ma'am."

There was a momentary pause. "Firing now," Rhom confirmed.

"I've got it, XO!" Diaz exclaimed. "You should have those magrails ready for use now."

"Excellent work, Diaz," said Sato.

"Rhom, let's give 'em hell."

The female artificial voice that had begun the scenario spoke again. "Training scenario eleven passed. Final time, eleven minutes and twelve seconds. Your crew has passed."

MacGregor's face darkened. "Well, that was fun, but I suppose it's time to get back to our regular jobs now," he remarked.

"That was a decent performance," said Lee. "Diaz performed well, and we can keep working on improvements in response time."

"I know you're right, Cap," MacGregor replied. "It's just, I love doing these so much, it's a bit of a letdown when it's over, you know?"

Lee laughed. "Mac, I don't think I've ever met anyone as passionate about their job as you. You and I are going to get along just fine."

"Thank you, sir," said MacGregor. "I think we will as well."

****

Next Day

Ripley Lee leaned back against the bench, cradling a steaming mug of black coffee. He was beginning to enjoy these quiet little moments in the ship's atrium. He really admired how the Altairians had efficiently used every space within a ship—nothing went unused or didn't serve a purpose. This atrium was a prime example of how meticulously planned and engineered the Altairians were. While their ships made use of a food replicator system, the atriums played a critical role in augmenting the base materials the replicators used in the bioprinting and molecular assembling of a meal. The science and engineering that went into creating a system of feeding people aboard a starship was phenomenal.

The Altairians' sustainable technology would allow them to keep a vessel underway almost indefinitely without the need of outside logistical support. They had even found a way to recycle uneaten food back into base compounds for reuse in the entire process. It was such a radical departure from the way Lee had been taught at the Academy about the mechanics involved in space warfare and the necessity of managing logistical support for a vessel while on patrol or part of a larger fleet.

Sitting in the atrium, watching the Synths tending to the aquaponics and hydroponics was somehow very relaxing for Lee. There were no decisions to be made, no orders to be given, no reports or logs to be written—just the freedom to sit and watch the synthetic humanoid workers effortlessly maneuver their way through the narrow floor-to-ceiling pathways of leafy greens, vegetables, and fruits. The plants were continuously being grown, pruned, and harvested before repeating the cycle once again. Above, the latticework of vines and mesh filtered the ship's artificial light, casting crisscrossing shadows over the space. If not for the low whir of *Poseidon*'s FTL drives running through the grass-covered floor, Ripley might have forgotten he was deep in the void.

Across from him, Sato scanned her data pad. She tapped through screens filled with training metrics. Beside her, a stainless-steel bento box sat open. It showed a flattened golden-brown dish drizzled with dark plum-colored sauce. She sipped her tea, squinting as she processed the information on her display.

"What are you eating?" Lee broke the silence, glancing pointedly at her plate.

"Okonomiyaki," Sato replied without looking up, her lips curling faintly. "A Japanese dish."

"Looks like a vegetable pancake. But the sauce… didn't get that from the mess, I'm guessing."

"I made it," Sato said, setting the data pad on the bench. "Before my shift ended. This is left over." She tapped the edge of the neatly cut squares. "Flour batter, grated mountain yam, cabbage. Plum and soy sauces."

"Made it? Wow, you should see if they can program it into the MFR for you. It'll save you a lot of time and you can have it more often if you like."

Sato plucked a piece with her chopsticks. "Yeah, maybe. I kind of like to tinker in the kitchen when I have the time. It's relaxing for me and reminds me of home."

"Ah, so it wasn't something you picked up on the side at the Academy?"

"Haha, that's funny, no, I had no time for anything like that at the Academy." She placed the bite in her mouth, savoring it, before continuing. "It's traditional. I was taught it as a child."

It looked too good to stop talking about it, and the smell? Divine. "Looks delicious. Mouthwatering, actually. Must've had one hell of a teacher."

Sato's chopsticks stilled over the next piece. Something in her gaze hardened a tinge, though her tone remained even. "The first time I tried—when I was younger—everything was wrong. My flour-to-water ratio, the heat under the griddle, even my mixing technique."

She set her chopsticks down, fingers steepling over her plate. "Truthfully, it wasn't the cooking that made it difficult—it was the context. Let's call it… a complicated household." She leaned forward. "My family didn't welcome the Asian Alliance. Not then, not ever."

He tilted his head. "Why not?"

"They remembered," she said. "After the Great War, forgiveness wasn't a generational luxury. My father despised China for what had been done—what he'd seen during the occupation of our cities. The forced takings, cities reduced to ash, centuries-old relics destroyed. When the Alliance formed out of necessity, he saw it as a betrayal. He worked in the Japan Preservation Ministry before it was disbanded during reintegration. After, he turned his anger into sabotage."

"Sabotage?" Lee said.

"Leaked documents, reignited protests, sowed discord during votes for joint operations. To him, the Alliance spat in the face of memory. He wouldn't let it stand."

"Dangerous business, working against your own government."

"To him, it wasn't the government—it was an enemy in all but name." Sato drew her tea closer. "But you're correct. It wasn't sustainable. We were discovered when I was nine."

Her voice lowered as though the atrium had ears. Even the Synths seemed paused midtask. "We were home. My father had just finished showing me how to flip an okonomiyaki without breaking its shape. We served it up on two small plates, and he smiled at me when I proudly drizzled the plum sauce in neat, even lines. I remember him taking the first bite—and that's when they came."

Lee's bench creaked as he leaned deeper into her story. "I'm guessing it wasn't a good thing they came."

"Negative, sir. The Alliance police," she continued, her eyes half-lidded as the memory drew her back. "Not soldiers, but police. Armed. They burst down the door. No warning, no announcement."

Her fingers curled tightly around the cup's edge. "My mother grabbed me and pulled me to the back. My father... he stepped forward—defiant, you know, and unarmed. He shouted at them about history, about his rights, about their atrocities. And then..."

Her voice wavered for the first time, steadying only when she inhaled sharply. "One shot. To the chest. That's all it took. I saw him fall with half his plate still in his hand, the other half shattering on the floor. The okonomiyaki we'd made spilled across the tatami like nothing. Then they dragged his body out. My mother and I hid until a sympathizer got us onto a ship bound for America."

"I'm sorry. That must have been—"

"I make that same recipe now," Sato said, interrupting her captain, "not just to remember him, but to remind myself why I chose this path. My father believed in fighting corruption from the outside. He thought exposing their wrongs would force change. But I learned, and perhaps on that day, that real change comes from within. That's why I'm here—in the Republic, on *Poseidon*. When systems fail, you don't just protest them. You rebuild them, better."

She relaxed her fingers around her cup. "That's why when I swear an oath—to the Republic, to *Poseidon*, to you—I don't take it lightly. The Alliance police who killed my father? They took an oath too, but to them it was just words. Here, in the Republic, we're actually advancing humanity. We have principles, and we stand by them. That matters to me more than you know."

Lee understood her words about the Republic all too well. For her, as for him, it was a calling. And Lee's own family's estrangement, while not as violent, had left its scars on him too. He raised his mug in a gesture of respect. "To surviving—and making it mean something."

"To surviving." She tapped her tea against his coffee.

"All right. Thank you for that, and back to work."

"Aye, Captain."

They fell into the rhythm of reviewing their data pads. Training outcomes during FTL transit lined both their screens—times and error rates from drills, combat-readiness assessments from Navigation, firing solutions from the bridge crew. Sato highlighted a persistent lag in lateral control synchronization during evasive maneuvers. Lee flagged a pattern in a younger officer's hesitation under simulated pressure.

"Hobson's still inconsistent," she pointed out, gesturing to his entry.

"He'll get there," Lee replied. "He'll be ready."

Sato glanced sideways at him. "And the *Poseidon* will be ready."

His brows tightened. "It better be. We don't have any other option. Once we reach the Intus stargate and link up with the rest of the fleet, it's going to be the fight of our lives."

Chapter 38
Unwanted Attention

Year 2096
RNS *Gallipoli*
New Eden Orbit

Lieutenant Naomi Love sat in the mess hall, her tray still full of food. She'd been staring at it for ten minutes, her mind everywhere and nowhere at the same time. Across from her, Chief Brian Ford ate some mashed potatoes. The guy could talk, and he did so in abundance now. She did her best to pay attention.

"You see, Love, the similarities… uncanny," Ford said. "Ancient civilizations on Earth spoke of beings from the stars. The Hopi, for instance, talked about the 'Kachinas' who guided them through great cataclysms."

Love nodded, her gaze drifting to the viewport beyond. Space stretched out, dotted with distant stars.

Ford continued. "And now we're facing the Zodarks. Ever wonder if any ancient Earth cultures spoke about them? Nah, that would imply the Zodarks would have known where Earth was, and they would have enslaved us. Anyway, you heard of the ant people, or Kachinas, or have you heard that the giants of our past might be from another galaxy altogether?"

"Mm-hmm." Love pushed her food around the tray.

Ford forked a piece of meat. "You all right there, Love? Seem a bit… distracted."

Love blinked, forcing herself to focus. "I'm fine, Ford. Just… thinking."

"About?"

Her grip tightened on her utensil. "Don't worry about it."

"OK."

Love swallowed hard, memories flooding her mind. Jack's sarcasm, how many times a day he told her how beautiful she was, the way he held in a laugh at the wrong time. The ache in her chest wanted to overwhelm her. No way she'd let it, so she pushed it down. She figured this would be a normal part of her life now, slamming shut the door to any memory about Jack. It was exhausting.

"It's just… today would've been…" She trailed off.

"I'm sorry. I didn't realize."

Love feigned a smile. "It's fine. Really. I'm fine."

"I—"

A voice cut Ford off. "Mind if I join you?"

Love looked up to see the guy who'd run into her the other day, his name, "COOPER," emblazoned on his Navy uniform. He stood by their table, tray in hand with a funny expression on his face. Eyebrows up, weird smile that seemed forced, and eyes wide.

Why's he doing that? Love wondered.

"Not at all," Ford said. "Have a seat."

Coop sat next to Love, his knee briefly brushing against hers. She shifted away.

"Thanks," he said, still wearing that weird expression. "Been meaning to introduce myself. Lieutenant Blake Cooper, but everyone calls me Coop."

Love nodded. "Lieutenant Naomi Love."

"I know," Coop replied, his smile widening. "Heard a ton about you. Your flying skills are legendary."

Love raised an eyebrow. "Is that so?"

Ford cleared his throat. "Coop here is one of our top drone pilots. He's been making quite a name for himself."

"I didn't know you knew me," Coop commented.

"Ford here knows everyone," Love said. "And eventually, everyone knows him."

Ford shrugged. "Not really. Anyway, Love, meet Coop. He's of the Cooper family."

"Who?" Love asked. "You make them sound famous or something."

"Nah, not famous," Coop said. "Just some heroes in the last few wars. Anyway, what I do is nothing compared to what you do, Love. Just happy to meet you. I mean, flying those Ospreys into hot zones? That takes guts."

Love jabbed the fork at her food. Her appetite was nonexistent. "It's what I'm trained for."

"So, Coop," Ford said, "you think about the theory that the Zodarks might have visited Earth in ancient times?"

"Excuse me?"

Love shook her head. "Just go along. He's excited about this stuff."

"Hey," Ford replied, "I thought you had some interest too."

Love shrugged. "Sometimes. You should write a book, Ford. You got a lot of info in that noggin of yours."

Ford's eyes lit up. "I should." He faced Coop. "You ever heard about the Nazca Lines? Some people think a few were landing strips for alien spacecraft."

As Cooper launched into his own theories, Love found her mind drifting again. She could almost hear Jack's voice teasing her about her "flyboy admirers." The memory brought a slight smile to her lips, quickly replaced by a pang of grief.

"Are you ready for the mission? You've been briefed yet?" Coop asked Love.

Love snapped out of it. "What?"

Coop repeated himself.

"Oh… ready? Yeah. The Intus Campaign. Ford and I were briefed, of course."

Coop massaged his knuckles. "I'm excited to knock some Zodarks out of existence. How about you?"

Who is this guy? "No offense, but I don't fly drones. You're incredible at what you do, all of you drone pilots are, so don't get me wrong. But for me, when I drop off troops to do my job, I know I'm losing some of my men and women down there, so I wouldn't call what I do exciting."

Coop slumped a little. "Yeah, that makes sense."

An uncomfortable silence fell over the table. Love looked at Coop, noting the sheepish expression on his face. She felt a tinge of regret for her response.

"Hey," she said. "I know you pilots have an important and tough-as-hell role. We're all in this fight together, right?"

Coop took a bite of his meal and chewed. "I've got the utmost respect for what you do. In a way, you're a hero to me. I've read a little about you."

"You have?" she asked. "Why? Kinda boring, don't you think?"

"Reading about you? Never."

What the hell? Is this kid trying to hit on me before we go on a mission? The guy lonely or something?

"Well, now that we've got that sorted…" Ford said. "Coop, tell me, what do you like to do for fun back home? Any hobbies or interests?"

"You know, I'm really into outdoor adventures. Rock climbing, hiking, that sort of thing. There's something special about being out in nature, pushing your limits." Coop turned to Love, his gaze warm. "What about you, Love? You have any hobbies you enjoy when you're not flying missions?"

Are you kidding me? We're in a war and this kid looks at me like I'm a princess? Give me a freakin' break. "Uh, well… it's kind of hard to think about those things lately. But I had times enjoying a hike, too. Most people do. I'm normally in front of a TV, watching something funny with…"

"With who?" Coop asked.

"Just… anyway. I enjoy surfing. Was a hobby when I was younger."

"Where'd you grow up?"

Ford spoke for her. "Baltimore. Yeah, lucky gal."

"You can surf over there?" Coop asked.

"No. When I was younger, I was… well… who cares. Just got down to Florida sometimes when I had an old friend who'd drive me, but it was rare. Went to Cocoa Beach. Sometimes Jacksonville."

"I want to surf someday," Coop said.

"Maybe I can teach you?" *Wait! Why did I say that? Plus, I'm not even good!*

"I'll take you up on it. You ever done any rock climbing? Some incredible spots in the Rocky Mountains I could show you."

"I can't say that I have." Love forced a grin.

"Well, we'll have to go sometime when we're Earthside," Coop said. "Would be happy to show you some of the best locales."

How do I get his mind off me? "Ford, you were saying about the aliens?"

Without hesitation, Ford went into his excited mode. "Now, what if the ancient legends about celestial beings descending from the heavens were accounts of extraterrestrial encounters?"

Love tried her best to look interested as Ford launched into an animated explanation.

"Take the Native American stories of the 'star people' for instance. Descriptions of radiant beings arriving in flying vessels, sharing advanced knowledge. Could those have been alien civilizations making contact?"

As the conversation carried on, Love relaxed into it. The weight of her memories of Jack lifted.

Ford, she thought. *You son of a gun. How do you do it, and so well?*

Lately, Ford could get her mind off Jack and help her in ways she couldn't understand. It wasn't that Ford was in love with her, or she'd distance herself in a hot minute. It was something else entirely. She couldn't put a finger on it, but it was almost like he'd been hired to be her psychologist, crew chief, and friend, all in one.

"Gentlemen," she said as she stood. "Got to go. I've had something made."

"What is it?" Ford asked.

"Tomorrow on our first training run, you'll see. I'll see you there, Ford—and, Coop, if I need your back while on an op and you're near, I'll be calling on you."

"Yes, ma'am."

She nodded before walking away, her thoughts centered on the engraved metal plate she'd recently commissioned. With approval from her superiors, she planned to have it installed on the wall at the top of her Osprey's loading ramp. The plate bore a Latin phrase that held special significance for her and Jack. Now, she felt it was time to give those words a new purpose.

Chapter 39
Silent Running

A couple of weeks had passed since Lee had taken command of the RNS *Poseidon*. As on many vessels in the Republic Navy, beneath Lee's command chair, a concealed compartment housed several essential items for emergency situations. Two high-powered blasters were securely holstered in a quick-release mechanism. Alongside these, a compact medkit contained nano-infused bandages, broad-spectrum antibiotics, and a portable tissue regenerator. A small but powerful portable oxygen supply unit was also stored here, capable of providing breathable air for up to an hour in case of sudden depressurization.

Also, since he'd taken over the ship as captain, he'd spent every moment making certain his crew became familiar with their new home. As he sat in the captain's chair on the bridge, watching his crew readying for one of their last training sessions before they took the ship out of space dock, Lee thought about his old mentor from his time on the RNS *Kentucky*. A vivid memory surfaced like it'd happened just yesterday.

"Listen up," Oldendorf's voice resounded through the *Kentucky*'s corridors. "I know you're all itching to jump back into tactical simulations, but with me, we're doing things differently."

Lee, then a fresh-faced lieutenant, exchanged a puzzled glance with a fellow officer as they followed their captain through the ship.

Oldendorf halted at a passageway junction, his hand resting on a bulkhead. "Like myself, most of you are new to this ship. But how many of you took the time to walk through her and *really* understand her? The looks on your faces are telling me none of you. This ship is your lifeline in the void of space. You need to know every nook, every cranny. Feel the pulse of her engines, understand the rhythm of her life-support systems. Only then can you truly command her in battle, and only then can she truly trust you with her life."

Oldendorf touched a seam in the wall, revealing a hidden access panel. "See this? In an emergency, knowing details like this could save your life or the lives of your crew. Inside here are several first aid kits."

He patted the wall. "She's a good ship. She deserves our best, because she's a beauty designed to keep us in one piece, and she'll do everything to protect us. Got it?"

Throughout the day, Oldendorf continued showing Lee and the rest of the staff every detail inside the *Kentucky*. He was getting everyone acquainted with the vessel. Down the line and throughout the years, Oldendorf would personally walk new recruits through the *Kentucky*, no doubt proud of the ship that had carried him through so many battles.

The lesson had stuck with Lee, shaping his approach with his new ship. For over a week, he had heard the rumors and seen the glances from his own crew. They didn't understand why so much focus was placed on familiarizing themselves with the inside of the vessel. To Lee, it was their new home, and doing otherwise would be like buying a new house but only using one room, never exploring the rest of the house.

So, he emphasized the importance of knowing the ship's layout—the lay of the land—to everyone. He assigned several key personnel, like his chief engineer, Boyd MacGregor, and Chief Medical Officer Dr. Stewart Kahn, along with other senior officers, to lead daily walkabouts throughout *Poseidon*. With over five hundred crew members, it took long hours to accomplish this each day. Still, Lee believed it was worth it. He conducted his own walkabouts several times as well.

"Commander," Sato spoke up from her station, "all systems are a go."

"Sato, inform all departments," Lee said. "We're initiating our next tactical war game scenario in fifteen minutes."

Every system on *Poseidon* impressed Lee. It was designed with efficiency along with crew safety in mind. The ship's layout allowed for rapid response to any situation. The integration of synthetic humanoids into the crew complement meant they could operate with a smaller human crew without sacrificing an inch of capability.

"All departments report ready, Commander," Sato said.

"Excellent. Tactical, bring up the scenario parameters," Lee ordered.

"Aye, sir," Rhom confirmed.

"Navigation, prepare for simulated evasive maneuvers."

"Acknowledged," said Reynolds.

"Comms, I want constant updates from all sections during the exercise."

"Yes, sir," answered Rodriguez.

The familiar surge of adrenaline before a challenging simulation hit Lee. Still, a deeper sense of confidence underpinned Lee's state too. Whether in the Olympics, during training as a junior officer, or after taking over a ship, for some reason, Lee kicked into another gear. He rose to the occasion. Over the last several days, everyone had worked well together, and they'd succeeded during more combat sims than they'd lost.

Lee surveyed the bridge as the lighting dimmed red. On the main viewscreen, the tactical situation unfolded before him. The display showed their current position relative to an enemy blockade—a formidable barrier of Zodark warships guarding the only route to their objective. Icons representing battleships and cruisers formed an imposing wall, their positions clearly marked at coordinates 042 by 258, approximately one hundred thousand kilometers from the *Poseidon*'s current location. The instant the combat simulation commenced, Lee's vessel was already on silent running protocols, the *Poseidon*'s covert operations suite. They were in combat-readiness, tactically maneuvering under clandestine conditions.

The main holodisplay streamed data, briefly explaining the scenario. They'd been thrown into a silent running situation that would require them to essentially leverage their passive sensors and towed array to identify targets and the surroundings instead of their active sensors, which would have given away their position the moment they started pinging the system with their various radar and LIDAR signals.

"Status report," Lee said, his voice slightly above a whisper.

"All nonessential systems powered down," Lieutenant Clayton responded from the bridge's engineering station. "We're running on minimal power signature, no active sensors or communications—deploying the towed sensor array. Additionally, we're utilizing our hull's metamaterial coating to absorb and redirect enemy radar waves. Engineering teams have initiated silent running protocols. Commander MacGregor reports all systems nominal and noise discipline is being strictly enforced."

"Emission dampeners at maximum," Rhom said from the tactical console.

"Prepare to launch decoys," Lee said.

On the viewscreen, the vast enemy blockade loomed ahead—a formidable array of ships, sensor buoys, and defensive platforms guarding the only passage to a besieged outpost on the other side. The screen zoomed in, and the Zodark vessels were now more clearly visible. Their predatory shapes seemed to absorb the starlight around them. Lee could make out the distinctive silhouettes of at least three Zodark battleships, their massive forms flanked by a dozen or more cruisers.

Rhom tapped a series of commands. "Decoys away."

A dozen small, stealthy probes streaked away from the *Poseidon*. Their onboard computers were programmed to mimic the ship's energy signatures, active sensors, and flight patterns.

As the decoys scattered, they weaved erratic courses deeper in space and farther from *Poseidon*. Enemy sensors flicked to life, locking onto the false targets.

"They're taking the bait," Lee said. "Helm, take us in nice and slow. Set heading four-one mark two-five-six, one-quarter thrust."

Reynolds acknowledged the order. On the holo, the distance to the blockade decreased.

"Enemy vessels continuing to respond to decoys," Rhom said. "Two cruisers breaking formation at bearing zero-four-four mark two-five-seven."

"Good. Let's hope they chase our ghosts for a while. Tactical, continuous passive scans. I want to know the moment they suspect anything's amiss."

As *Poseidon* crept forward, Lee studied the enemy formation. The Zodark ships were arranged in a loose sphere, their positions carefully calculated to provide overlapping fields of fire and sensor coverage. Still, there was a weakness—a slight gap between two of the outlying ships. If they could approach any other way, they would. However, all enemy ships surrounded the outpost in every direction.

"Helm, adjust course," Lee said. "Bearing four-two mark two-five-eight. Thread us between those two cruisers at extreme range."

Now at fifty-eight thousand kilometers away, the tension on the bridge was palpable as the *Poseidon* edged nearer. The crew's faces were illuminated by the soft glow of their consoles, each officer focused on their tasks.

"Sir," Lieutenant Rodriguez's voice cut through the silence. "Detecting increased comm chatter among enemy vessels. They may be growing suspicious of the decoys."

"Understood. How long until we reach the gap in their formation?"

"At current speed, seven minutes, sir," said Reynolds at the helm.

"Not good enough." Lee weighed his options, knowing that increasing speed would raise their risk of detection. But if they didn't make it through soon, the Zodarks would certainly realize they'd been tricked and that the decoys were indeed fakes.

"Helm, increase engines to one-third power."

"Aye, engines to one-third."

The *Poseidon* surged, eating up the distance to the blockade. The gap between the enemy cruisers grew larger on the viewscreen.

"Emission levels at two percent of normal, sir." Rhom's pitch was hushed.

"Excellent. Status on enemy movements?"

"Our passive sensors and towed array indicate no significant enemy activity. They're still pursuing decoys."

"Reynolds," Lee said, "hold your course and speed."

"Aye, sir."

Sato sat rigid beside Lee. She scanned between the various displays emerging from her chair's armrests. She ran the same calculations as Lee, weighing their odds of slipping through undetected.

"Sir." Rhom's low tone sounded urgent. "Enemy vessels are breaking pursuit of the decoys. They're beginning to sweep the area with active sensors."

Lee's grip tightened on the arms of his chair. "Steady as she goes. Helm, prepare for evasive pattern Gamma on my command. Rhom, I want you to dynamically control our electromagnetic emissions. Keep them at an absolute minimum."

"Aye-aye, sir."

The crew minimized the ship's electromagnetic signature. This crucial step reduced excessive electromagnetic radiation, which could potentially compromise their covert approach and give away their position.

The bridge fell silent as they closed in on the blockade, the distance readout ticking downward at a fast pace.

"Forty-eight thousand kilometers," Reynolds reported, his voice taut.

"Hold course," Lee ordered.

At forty thousand kilometers, the massive Zodark cruisers loomed larger, their sensor sweeps probing the surrounding space.

Thirty-six thousand kilometers.

A bead of sweat trickled down Lee's temple. Any sudden movement could betray their position to the enemy's sensors. Even though this was a simulation, everything about it appeared real.

The *Poseidon* flew onward, the countdown continuing. Twenty-five thousand… twenty thousand… fifteen thousand… ten thousand.

Five thousand, two hundred kilometers.

Reynolds's knuckles were white on the helm controls as they moved ever closer.

Three thousand, eight hundred.

In twenty seconds, they'd pass between the Zodark cruisers.

One thousand, two hundred kilometers.

"Proceed as before, no alteration to course," Lee said.

When those seconds passed, the bridge crew held their collective breath as *Poseidon* slipped between the two Zodark cruisers.

Sato turned to Lee. "I'm picking up steady communication across the Zodark comm lines."

"Aw, crap. We've been spotted. They must have spotted a visual distortion as we passed the light of a known star or something. They've triangulated their active sensors right on us," Rhom said. "Enemy vessels powering weapons."

"Helm, execute evasive vector keel inversion. MacGregor, emergency power to engines."

Rhom's voice cracked with tension. "Incoming plasma torpedoes!"

"Retract the towed array and switch to active sensors and get us some targeting solutions. Helm, begin evasive maneuvers! Deploy countermeasures!" Lee's mind ran through tactical options. "Reynolds, set course zero-nine-eight mark one-eight-one, full thrust. Rhom, ready aft missile pods."

The bridge erupted as officers relayed orders and status reports. From the icons on the tactical display, red dots representing enemy torpedoes closed in on their position.

"Launch chaff clouds. SWs, too. Pattern Theta," Lee said. "Reynolds, on my mark, execute a helical maneuver. Three... two... one... mark!"

The *Poseidon*'s engines roared to life, pushing the ship into a tight, corkscrewing turn. Slow and steady. Chaff and SW exploded outward, creating a brilliant cloud of metallic sand, and water particles in their wake.

Explosions blossomed behind them as enemy plasma torpedoes detonated when they flew into the countermeasures. The bridge shook violently, simulating near misses and glancing blows.

"Damage report," Lee demanded.

"Minimal damage," Rhom said, his eyes on his monitors. "Sensor and targeting coming in. Gun crews are spinning up to fire, sir."

On the large holographic display, the blockade fell away behind them. Ahead was the faint outline of their objective, the besieged outpost, its defensive perimeter a thin line of flashing energy barriers beside scattered defense platforms. It would take a long moment for the enemy ships to turn around to pursue the *Poseidon*.

New contacts appeared on the display. A wave of Zodark Vulture reinforcements headed toward them from multiple vectors.

"Commander," said Sato, her tone tense, "we're vastly outnumbered. That's a full battle group bearing down on us."

"Full retreat," he ordered. "Reynolds, set course one-six-eight mark two-nine-one, maximum thrust. Get us out of here."

As Reynolds input the coordinates, enemy fire peppered their exterior. The *Poseidon* shuddered under the onslaught, klaxons blaring across multiple stations.

"Rhom, return fire. Give me everything we've got in our aft arc. I want a wall of flak between us and those bastards."

The ship's weapon systems came to life, spitting a furious barrage of defensive magrail fire, lasers, and missiles at their pursuers. On the tactical display, the distance began to increase between them and the Zodark forces.

Just as they were about to escape, the main viewscreen turned to static. The scene of space battle faded away, replaced by streaming data across the main interface.

"Simulation terminated," the AI announced. "Mission parameters: failed."

The lights on the bridge returned to normal levels. Lee exhaled and stood to address his crew. "This was a tough scenario," he said. "But we don't give up. We do it again, and again, until we're perfect." He met each officer's gaze. "Reset the sim. We go now. This time, we make it through. If we don't succeed, or even if we do succeed, we continue this scenario all day until it's ingrained in every cell of our body. Sato, begin."

Chapter 40
Touch for Luck

A few days ago in the mess hall, Coop's eyes had lingered a moment too long. His gaze was a combination of admiration and something more. It was a look Naomi Love had seen before, on faces barely old enough to shave, let alone fight in a war. She felt a twinge of sympathy. She knew Coop's crush would fade as quickly as it had formed. Her thoughts drifted briefly to the young guy, acknowledging his good looks with detached appreciation. It was as far as it went. Jack had been her soulmate, her perfect match. No one could ever take his place.

Love stood before her Osprey. She touched the name she'd painted on the hull. "Jack."

The hangar bay bustled with activity around her. No one paid a lick of attention to her, which was good. Mechanics and pilots scurried about, performing their tasks.

She leaned in close, her forehead pressing on the ship's cool metal. "Hey, Jack," she whispered. "I miss you, you know that?"

She patted the ship's exterior as if soothing a living being. "You're my backup now. Watching over me and all those troops we transport. It's a heavy load, I know. Remember how we used to joke about you being my guardian angel? Guess it wasn't really a joke after all."

She stepped back, wiping a stray tear from her cheek. With a determined set to her shoulders, Love strode up the Osprey's ramp and into the cabin.

The interior of the troop transport stood before her. Seats lined the walls, capable of accommodating up to sixty-four soldiers and several crew members. Overhead compartments housed emergency gear and supplies, their latches securely fastened. The floor was reinforced to bear the weight of fully equipped troops.

Just behind the cockpit sat two raised jump seat platforms—one on each side of the troop bay, positioned to give gunners or mechanics a commanding view of the main cabin. Crew chief Brian Ford often perched on a jump seat, starboard side, where he performed last-minute checks. This strategic positions allowed for quick access to both the cockpit and the main cabin to ensure he could respond swiftly to any situation during the flight.

In one corner, a compact medical station stood ready, stocked with essential supplies for in-flight emergencies. Along the bulkhead, weapons racks were securely fastened, their contents locked away until needed.

She faced a metal plaque mounted on the wall near the ramp. Earlier in the morning, a few mechanics had welded it to the wall. Latin words were inscribed on its surface: "Vivere Pugnare Alium Diem."

This meant "live to fight another day." It was her idea for soldiers to touch a plaque like this for luck before their missions—to help them come back alive and intact. Who knew if it would actually work, but to Love, anything to spark some hope in the soldiers was always a good thing.

With eyes forward, she walked into the cockpit. Controls and displays widened out before her. The holodisplay in front of her showed a view of the hangar bay. Two chairs dominated the small space. One for her, and one for her copilot, Lieutenant Caleb Green, who'd arrive soon. She'd flown with him a few times. Love settled into her seat.

She pulled up the ship's diagnostic systems, running through the preflight checks for the upcoming simulation. The engines were online and functioning within normal parameters. She verified the weapons systems next to ensure the sixteen multipurpose smart missiles and sixteen antipersonnel high-explosive fragmentation missiles were armed, ready to deploy when needed.

Next, she checked guns to make sure they were ready. The Osprey had a chin mounted twin barrel gun turret that turned with the pilot's eyes, ready to fire its .50-cal magrail slugs. Finally, she checked the pair of machine guns mounted on either side of the flight deck. These were the guns the crew chief and his flight engineer or loadmaster would use during a mission if necessary.

After the weapons check, Love verified that the ECM/ECCM suite of electronic countermeasures and counter-countermeasures was ready and working, along with the flare and chaff dispensers. With all the defensive equipment checked, she felt confident in the ship's ability to withstand enemy fire during whatever simulated scenario confronted her.

Satisfied with the comprehensive systems check, she rested back in her seat to scan the holo providing a view of the hangar bay. She opened a digital window on the interface to scan the mission parameters.

"Executing a hasty withdrawal under heavy enemy fire," she read aloud. "Starfighters providing covering fire and suppressing enemy pursuit as transports evacuate friendly forces from a compromised location."

Footsteps approached the Osprey. She turned to see Chief Brian Ford entering the cabin. His face was set in its usual mask of concentration, although Ford never did a good job hiding his bright spirit behind the facade.

"Chief," she said before he could take more than a couple of steps. "Touch the plaque."

"You're here early."

"I am. Now, touch the plaque. It's for good luck."

Ford paused. His gaze fell on the new addition to the cabin wall. He read the inscription aloud, and a slight nod of recognition crossed his features. "Live to fight another day."

He reached out and gave it a solid slap. The sound echoed through the cabin. "That's what you want the soldiers to do. Hammer it for luck."

Love shook her head. "It'd fall off if they all kept doing that. Have you seen how big those Deltas are?"

"True enough," Ford said. "Touching it is just fine, then."

"How do you know how to read Latin?"

"My mom."

"Your past is such a mystery, Chief."

Ford shrugged. "It's really not. She taught me Latin as a kid because she believed it would improve my cognitive skills and help me understand scientific terminology better. She was a lab tech, always pushing for intellectual growth."

"Did it work?" Love asked.

"Well, I'm here, aren't I?"

"You never talk about her."

"Yeah. Didn't see her much. I left home when I was young," Ford said.

"Maybe we can chat about it later. Someday, maybe?"

"Perhaps."

"You ready for the sim?"

"Aye, ma'am." Ford glanced around the troop bay. "Thought I'd be the first one here, but looks like you beat me to it. Williams should be arriving shortly." He motioned toward the rear of the transport. "I'm going to run some preflight checks, ensure all systems are green before we lift off. Starting with a comms check and then I'll move on to securing all equipment for transport."

"Roger, Chief. Conduct your checks and report any discrepancies."

"Copy, Lieutenant. I'll give you a SITREP once I've completed the bay inspection."

Minutes later, Lieutenant Caleb Green stepped in, his flight suit freshly pressed, helmet tucked under his arm. Despite his rank, he carried himself with confidence. Like his name, Green, he was still fresh but had proven himself competent in previous simulations with Love.

"Permission to come aboard, Lieutenant?" Green asked with a nod.

"Granted, Lieutenant," Love replied. "Good to have you back in the copilot seat."

"Glad to be here, ma'am. Ready to see if third time's the charm."

"Hopefully, the sim throws us something new today."

As Green strapped himself into the copilot seat, Love turned back to the troop bay to see Petty Officer Third Class Tyrell Williams heading up the ramp.

"Reporting for duty, LT," Williams said.

"Acknowledged. Proceed to your station and stand by for orders. And, Chief, all systems good back there?"

"Magrails primed and ready on starboard side, Lieutenant. Williams has port covered."

"Roger that." She tapped a few commands into her console, bringing up the preflight diagnostics. "That coffee this morning was brutal."

"Tell me about it." Green chuckled as he adjusted his helmet's visor. "Tasted like it was brewed with swamp water."

In the back, Ford chimed in over the intercom. "You think that's bad? I swear I saw something swimming in mine. Probably a new form of life."

Williams snorted. "Could've used it to strip the carbon scoring off these magrails."

Before they could continue their banter, Commander Rhett Granger's voice crackled over their helmet comms. "Attention all Osprey pilots. We've got a squadron of Orions providing support for this extraction op. You all showed impressive skills in the recent training missions. Keep it up. Countdown to sim starts in thirty seconds. Acknowledge."

"Aye, sir," Love said, echoed by the other Osprey pilots preparing for the training session.

"About that coffee," Ford continued, "I think I swallowed a slug and some amoebas."

Love smirked. "I took one sip and ditched it. Couldn't risk compromising the mission."

"The skipper even complained," Williams said.

Green looked over the dash's interface. "Well, if the captain's not happy, you know it's bad."

"Starting in ten… nine…" Granger's voice counted down.

Love inhaled deeply. "All stations, get ready."

"Port magrail standing by," Ford said.

"Starboard magrail locked and loaded," Williams reported.

"Blasters are hot," Green said beside her.

"Four… three… two…" Granger's voice faded as the holodisplay flickered to life.

The hangar bay transformed into a dense jungle environment. Icons representing the other Ospreys appeared on the tactical display, showing their designated landing zones near Love's position.

This is different from the standard op parameters, Love thought, scanning the simulated terrain.

On the holo, Republic Deltas in full battle gear sprinted toward the Ospreys, their movements surprisingly lifelike. Green initiated the virtual ramp sequence. Moments later, the sim indicated troops were boarding.

"Tangos at two o'clock," Ford called out from the port side. "Distance four-nine-eight meters and closing fast. Grid reference thee-six-two-four-one-nine."

"Copy that," Love replied. "Green, bring the blasters to bear. Engage hostiles."

"Roger, engaging now," Green said, manipulating the controls.

The crosshairs on Love's display aligned with the incoming Zodark combatants. She squeezed the trigger. Blaster fire erupted from the chin-mounted turret, illuminating the shadows beneath the canopy. Explosions rocked the simulation as energy bolts found their targets.

"Direct hits," Green said. "Hostiles neutralized in sector Alpha."

Ford's tone lowered. "Shifting fire to sector Charlie. Starboard magrail engaging."

The thunderous boom of Ford's magrail filled the cabin as he unleashed a barrage on enemy positions. From the port side, Williams's magrail joined in, the coordinated fire creating a lethal cross fire.

"Good shooting, both of you," Love said, maintaining her grasp on the controls.

"Ironhorse, this is Love," she transmitted over the comms to a fellow Osprey pilot. "We've got you covered on your nine o'clock. Commence exfil when ready."

"Copy that, Love," came the response. "Initiating dust-off now."

Love watched Ironhorse's icon lift off, its troop complement secure. She kept up a steady stream of suppressing fire, ensuring a safe ascent for her comrade.

"Multiple hostiles, eleven o'clock low," Ford said. "They're setting up heavy weapons. Recommend immediate action."

"Green, prepare missile salvo," Love ordered. "Target grid twenty-two-twenty-three-fifty-six."

"Missiles locked," Green confirmed. "Firing now."

Twin streaks of light soared from the Osprey, homing in on the enemy emplacements. The resulting explosions sent plumes of virtual dirt and debris skyward.

"Target eliminated," Green said.

As they continued to provide cover for the evacuating forces, adrenaline pumped through Love. Even in a simulation, the intensity of combat always quickened her pulse.

"All remaining birds, this is Hawkeye. Prepare for immediate dust-off. Multiple tangos inbound. I say again, multiple tangos inbound. Our position is about to be overrun," the lead Osprey pilot said over the comm.

When the last of the Deltas boarded, Love hovered her fingers over the main thruster controls as she keyed the comm. "All units, this is Love. Troop extraction complete. Preparing for dust-off."

"All friendlies clear," Ford said. "We're the last bird on deck."

Love initiated their own takeoff sequence. "Roger that."

As the Osprey lifted off in formation, Love scanned the holoscreen. Multiple blips appeared on her radar.

"Wolfpack Squadron, we've got incoming bogies. Vultures at three o'clock high," Hawkeye said to all Ospreys.

A familiar voice cut through the chatter. "Wolfpack Actual, this is Strike. Inbound and ready to intercept. Jolly Rogers are here. Providing overwatch."

A squadron of Orion starfighter drone icons appeared on Love's display, closing fast on their position.

"Roger that, Strike. Glad to have you with us," Hawkeye said.

As the Ospreys climbed toward the cloud cover, laser fire from the Vultures lit up the sky around them.

"Hercules taking fire! Jolly Rogers, where are you?" an Osprey pilot's voice called out.

"Hang tight, Hercules. Phantom here. Engaging hostiles now."

Orions flew like bullets past Love's ship, heading toward the enemy fighters. Explosions erupted in the simulated sky as Orions let loose missiles.

"Scratch one Vulture," an Orion drone pilot reported.

"Make that two," another added a moment later.

The last voice sounded like the young lieutenant she'd met yesterday, Coop. From what Ford said, the kid was supposed to be good. He'd acted like a bit of a hotshot, but perhaps he indeed had skills warranting that behavior.

Despite the Orions' efforts, the sheer number of enemy fighters overwhelmed them. One of the Osprey icons on her interface winked out, accompanied by a gut-wrenching detonation just off starboard.

"Strike, this is Love," she said, hailing the lead Orion starfighter pilot. "We're taking heavy fire from those Vultures. Need some help clearing a path."

"Copy that, Love. Coop here. Raven and I are on it. Going gun-camera hot!"

Two Orions blazed around a few enemy Vulture fighters. Red magrail fire traced through the air. Eruptions bloomed as Raven and Coop blasted the enemy.

"Got another Vulture," Raven said.

"Another down," Coop said as another hostile blip disappeared.

As she continued to rise in the sky, an Osprey transport burst into flames.

"Damn it, we just lost Hawkeye!" she said. "Green, I need you on those missiles like yesterday!"

"On it! Locking targets… firing smart missiles!"

Two bright streaks lanced out from Love's Osprey toward a pair of trailing Vultures. One missile found its mark, the Vulture disintegrating in a fireball. The other projectile went wide, sidewinding down in a short arc. It slammed harmlessly into the ground below.

"Lost lock on the second one," Green said. "Deploying kamikaze drones!"

A cloud of small drones swarmed out, homing in on the Vulture fighters. At the same time, the Osprey's twin magrail cannons opened up with an earsplitting roar. Seconds later, the kamikaze drones fell out of the sky, dropping toward the surface.

"What happened?" Love asked.

Green read data on one of the interfaces on the dash. "It looks like we experienced a critical malfunction in the drone swarm's guidance systems. According to the telemetry, the drones initially deployed as intended, but their targeting algorithms failed to properly acquire the Vulture fighters. The data shows a sudden spike in electromagnetic interference just before the drones lost cohesion. Did you do a full weapons check before the simulation?"

"Of course!"

"We've got a bandit on our aft, Love!" Ford said. "It's coming about hard starboard!"

Love grimaced. "I see it." She pulled her transport into an evasive roll just as the Vulture's lasers raked across their tail section. "Hang on, I—"

Her words caught in her throat as a blazing trail of light slammed into the pursuing Vulture from above. The enemy fighter disappeared into a blossom of fiery debris as one of the Orions screamed past.

Love raised her voice in relief. "Nice shot, Coop!"

"Anytime," Coop's voice crackled over the comms. "Let's get you out of here!"

"Blue's down! I repeat, Blue's down!" Ironhorse's voice burst through Love's helmet.

Love barely had time to process the loss before her own Osprey shuddered. A Vulture had broken through the Orions' defensive screen and was now trailing her.

"Love, leech riding your tail," Coop's voice rang out.

Love banked her craft as she tried to shake the pursuing fighter. "Can't shake him!"

Coop swooped in from above. A burst of fire from the Orion drone obliterated the Vulture.

"Bandit down," Coop reported.

Another shudder ran through her ship. Warning lights flashed across her console.

"Port engine's taken a hit," Ford said. "I'm on it."

Love gritted her teeth, fighting to keep the Osprey level as Ford moved to assess the damage. Even in a simulation, the sim techs programmed realistic malfunctions within the ships to test the pilot and crew's abilities.

"Skyburn, this is Love," she said to the new Osprey lead. "We're hit but still in the fight. Trying to limp home."

"Copy that. We'll keep them off you," Skyburn responded.

"Love, this is Coop. I'm providing top cover."

As Love struggled with the controls, blasts continued to light up the sky. Coop's voice provided a steady stream of updates, each downed enemy fighter a small victory in their desperate flight.

"Love, status update?" Skyburn's voice cut through the chatter.

"Still airborne," Love said. "Chief's working on the engine. How long, Ford?"

"Almost there," Ford called back. "Working through an access panel in the cabin. Running redundancy checks now. I'll have to initiate a bypass loop around the failed thrust vector control module and temporarily reroute reactor output through the cooling network. Once that's done, I can restore nominal power distribution to the drive. But it's a delicate process. I'll need a few more minutes to complete the sequential reboot procedures."

Love nodded, focused on keeping the Osprey as steady as possible, aware of the virtual troops in her care and doing her best to hide her ship in the clouds.

"Love, you've got two more incoming at your four o'clock!" Coop's warning came just as Love spotted the enemy fighters on her display.

"I see them, Coop. Can you intercept?"

"Working for a shot," Coop said. His Orion flew in to engage the threats.

Love watched in amazement as Coop's drone executed a series of impossible maneuvers, drawing the Vultures away from her crippled Osprey. In a matter of seconds, both enemy fighters erupted into fiery bursts.

"Threats neutralized," Coop said.

"Nice job, Coop," Love replied.

"Engine back online!" Ford said. "We're not at full power, but it should be enough to get us home."

Love felt the Osprey respond as the repaired engine kicked in. She adjusted her course, heading toward the upper atmosphere.

"Love, heading back into formation," she said over the communication network. She patched into her troop bay. "Williams, any sign of pursuit?"

"Negative, Lieutenant. Skies are clear."

As she began to relax, a notification blinked on her console. The simulation wound down and dissolved, replaced by the metallic sheen of the hangar bay.

"Simulation complete," Commander Granger announced over the comms. "Debrief in thirty mikes. Good work, everyone."

Love unstrapped herself from the harness and stood, stretching her arms above her head. "Gonna walk this one off."

Green joined her in the cabin. "Not bad, Lieutenant."

Ford and Williams stood from their jump seats, heading for Green and Love.

"Damn good work, Lieutenant," Ford said with a grin.

"Your quick fix kept us in the air," Love replied. "Nice job back there."

Williams nodded. "Glad I could contribute. Magrails didn't jam this time."

"Always a plus," Love said with a chuckle.

As they descended the ramp, Love paused. "You guys go on ahead. Need to check something."

Ford gave her a knowing look but said nothing. Green and Williams headed toward the locker rooms.

Once alone, Love returned to the cockpit. Her gaze settled on the worn photograph taped beside her console—Jack's smiling face looking back at her.

"Thanks, Jack. Though it's just a sim, you got us through another one successfully. So far, you're undefeated, you know?" A wistful smile crossed her lips. "Well, yeah, of course you know."

With one last look, Love turned and rejoined Ford, heading down the ramp and into the hangar bay until their next training op—no doubt sooner rather than later.

Chapter 41
Something Human

Year 2096
RNS *Gallipoli*
New Eden Orbit

The simulation pod's hatch opened. Coop yanked off his neural interface helmet and stepped out. The sim room stretched before him. Tiers of white pods arranged in neat rows. Other pilots emerged from their pods. In short order, it was a sea of flight suits in different states of dishevelment—sweat-soaked, wrinkled, one sleeve higher than the other, and a myriad more.

For Coop, perspiration soaked through everything. Well, almost. The outside of his helmet remained dry. The inside? Forget about it. Might just wring it out if he could, give the floor a nice puddle.

At the observation deck, and behind the tinted glass, figures moved about. Brass, probably. Dissecting every maneuver from the safety of their cushy seats. Coop's lip curled. Let 'em watch. They'd seen a master class with him today.

As he strode down the center aisle, Strike stood ten meters away beside Raven's pod. The squadron leader was deep in conversation with Coop's wingman.

He waited for Strike to acknowledge him, to give even the slightest nod of approval. Nothing. The squadron leader took one look at Coop and walked toward the exit.

That guy's got a problem. Ever think of uniting your whole team? Not too big to hold a grudge, eh?

"Yo, Coop!" Raven said, resting his shoulder against his pod. "That was some sick flying, my man."

Coop grunted, keeping the same pace without slowing as he walked by Raven. Yes, a jerk move, but Raven bugged him just as much as Strike… sometimes.

Raven hurried to catch up. "Seriously, you were flying circles around those bogeys. Never seen anyone juke a torp like that. Ice water in your veins, much?"

"Uh-huh," Coop said.

When they entered the passageway, they joined the stream of pilots heading for the barracks.

Raven chuckled. "Hey, if it takes a cute girl to make you fly like that, I'll fly gopher with you anytime."

Coop stopped. "What?"

"That girl—"

"What girl?"

Raven scrunched up his nose. "The one you were...well, it doesn't matter. What I'm saying is—"

"If you'd spent less time gawking, or spying, or whatever it is you do, and more time flying," Coop said while shaking his head, "you wouldn't have been so close to eating dirt on that last run."

"Whoa, easy there," Raven replied. "You jokin', right?"

"Have you ever heard me joke before?" Coop shot back.

"No."

Without another word, Raven quickened his pace, leaving Coop behind. He caught up to Strike. The two of them disappeared around a corner. Ten minutes later, Coop entered the barracks, walking into a room full of chatter. Bear dominated the center of the room. Raven, Ghost Dog, Ninja, Reaper, Phantom, and several others crowded around. Jokes. Laughing. It was enough to call this a middle school party, Coop thought.

Strike lay sprawled on his bunk, a pillow covering his head as he attempted a nap. Smart move. At least someone knew where priorities lay, resting up, but why wasn't he being a leader and telling them to settle down?

"You shoulda seen it," Ghost Dog said, gesturing wildly. "This Vulture was all over me, riding my butt like a tick on a dying hound. I tried yanking and banking, but the bastard stuck to me, man. Only chance was to pull a max g-reversal. I cranked that stick back hard and kicked those rudders. Must've pulled nine g's." His voice lowered to a gritty rasp. "For a split second, I was behind the bandit. Didn't even need to lead, just ripped the trigger and stitched his tail from stern to tip." Ghost Dog mimed the shuddering recoil of the cannon. "Lit up that bogey like the Fourth of July before he even knew what hit him. One moment he was on my tail, the next just a fireball."

Bear let out a booming laugh. "That's nothing, rookie. Try taking on two of 'em at once. There I was, sandwiched tight between the pair of them. They're peppering my armor, alarms blaring like the devil's orchestra. No room to maneuver, no way to break free. Only chance was to pull a pedal turn. I cranked hard opposite rudder and pitched back. I could hear the airframe groan even through the drone's pod, but my Orion cartwheeled around those bandits like nothing. And then, suddenly, I had them both square in my HUD, just for a heartbeat. Didn't need to think, just stomped the missiles off the rails. Flew right between them as the JATMs sparked both targets." He made an explosive gesture with his hands. "They never even saw it coming. One blink they had me cornered, the next they were dusted."

"Aw, come on!" a man called Bobcat protested. "No way that happened."

Another pilot, Hellfire, chimed in, "I dunno, man. Bear's crazy good enough to pull it off."

"Speaking of crazy," Raven cut in, "did you catch Ninja's performance?"

All eyes turned to Ninja, who struck a dramatic pose. "Gather 'round, children, and let me regale you with the epic tale of my glorious demise." He paused for effect. "There I was, three minutes in, feeling invincible. Decide to thread the needle—as they say—between two Zodark fighters. Halfway through, my stabilizers give out. I'm spinning, alarms screaming, and suddenly…" He made a whistling sound, tracing a downward spiral with his hand. "Boom! Splattered across the landscape like a bug on a windshield."

The barracks erupted in laughter. Even Strike stirred slightly in his bunk.

"But hey," Bear said, wiping tears from his eyes, "did any of you catch Coop out there? Now that was some real magic."

Coop, who'd been making his way to his bunk and doing his best to be invisible, froze. Attempting to slip in unnoticed had failed, and now all eyes were on him.

Can't leave me alone for a second, can they?

"Yeah, Lieutenant," Bear continued. "Anything to report? 'Cause if you check that stat column, I'd say you owned this sim."

Coop shrugged. "It's nothing. Just doing my best for the team."

"Bashful, this one," Bear said, turning to the others. He jerked a thumb over his shoulder at Coop. "This guy's a true freakin' flying genius. I'm telling you, some of the best piloting I've ever seen."

Coop climbed up to his top bunk, pulling his great-great-grandfather's journal from his pack. He tried to focus on the worn pages, but the conversation below continued.

"No joke," Raven said. "Was there beside him the entire time. Incredible. No mistakes. And that torp dodge? Never seen anything like it."

"All right, all right," Coop called down. "Let's not get carried away. We all did our part out there."

Bear shook his head. "Always the modest one, eh, Coop?" Everyone laughed, knowing how untrue those words were. "One of these days, you're gonna have to learn to take a compliment."

"Or give one," someone said under their breath before a few people chuckled.

As the conversation drifted to other topics, Coop returned his attention to the journal, grateful for the distraction. The handwriting of his ancestor grounded him, as it always did. It reminded Coop of the legacy he had to carry. He read over a particular passage, one he'd seen countless times before:

"Up there in the wild blue, we're all the same breed. Been doing my part against Hitler's boys since this mess started. Jerry's gotta be stopped, plain and simple. But sometimes, when I'm up there dodging flak, I catch myself thinking about the poor bastards I'm supposed to shoot down.

"They're just doing their job, same as me. Following brass orders, believing whatever line they've been fed. Both sides treating us like we're disposable—just more numbers in the big push.

"Got me thinking about this one time. Standard patrol… if you can call anything standard when Krauts are trying to ventilate your hide. My Mustang took some lead, engine smoking something fierce. Fuel gauge dropping faster than a lead brick, base looking mighty far off. Had just tangled with a bunch of 109s—gave 'em hell too.

"Then I spotted him. A German pilot coming in hot. Figured my number was up right then and there. Turned to face him. Might as well go down swinging.

"But this Kraut, he did something peculiar. Waggled his wings, flew right up beside me. Close enough to see his mug through the canopy. Then he dipped his wing again and peeled off, disappeared like a ghost.

"Makes you think, y'know? Under all that gear and those crosses, we're just fellas caught up in something bigger than us. Brass on both sides, moving us around like pieces on a board while they sit pretty and talk strategy. Can't fault 'em really—war's war. Always has been, always will be.

"Sure messed with my head, though. Made it tough to squeeze the trigger for a spell after that. Funny how one decent act can shake everything you thought you knew about the enemy.

"Had to figure it out, though. We all did. War ain't pretty, but sometimes you catch a glimpse of something human in all this madness."

Coop closed the diary and lay back and shut his eyes. He thought to himself, *Listen, Great-Great-Gramps, I'm gonna make you proud. I know I never could with my dad, but with you... I'll do right by our name, you know? I'm gonna be better out there. Not just in combat, but with my squadron. That's a promise.*

Chapter 42
Too Easy

Year 2096
RNS *Poseidon*
New Eden Orbit

Lee glared at the holographic display before him. The simulation had just begun, and the crew had settled into their stations.

Sato turned to face him. "Sir, the sim gave us twenty ships in our fleet. Yet I've noticed a glitch in the system. Ship designations aren't showing up."

"Very well," Lee said. "Let's designate them ourselves. Frigates will be Tango One through Eight, cruisers Echo One through Eight, and battleships Sierra One through Four. Make it happen."

"Aye, sir."

As the designations appeared on the screen, a massive gas cloud looming ahead also filled the display.

"Tactical, what do we have on that cloud?" Lee asked.

Rhom peered at the readouts on his console. "Sir, the cloud's composition is making it difficult to get clear readings. High concentrations of ionized particles are interfering with our sensors. We can't definitively say if there are any Zodark ships hiding in there."

"Keep your eyes on it, Rhom. I want to know the moment anything changes."

"Aye, Captain."

"Rodriguez, monitor all frequencies. If there are Zodarks in that cloud, they might slip up and transmit something."

"Yes, sir."

As they approached the cloud, a lone ship appeared on their sensors, approximately one hundred thousand kilometers ahead.

Lee studied the image. "What's that?"

The vessel was unlike anything he'd ever encountered. It was massive, easily ten times the size of their largest ship. Its hull was a network of geometric shapes, blended into an organic whole. Glowing lines moved across its surface, pulsing. Although it was all from the simulation AI's mind, it appeared real.

"Reynolds," Lee called out to his navigator, "bring us to bearing zero-four-five mark two, one-quarter thrust. Keep us at fifteen thousand kilometers from that ship."

"Aye, sir. Coming to bearing zero-four-five mark two, one-quarter thrust."

Lee tapped his comm. "Bridge to Engineering. Mac, I want full power to engines. We're approaching an unknown vessel."

"Understood, Cap. Diverting power now."

As they drew closer to the derelict vessel, Lee's face became stern. This was a simulation, but one designed to mimic real-life scenarios. He needed to react as he would in an actual first-contact situation. With prudence and military discipline.

"Sato"—Lee lowered his voice—"assemble an away team. I want our top engineers and xenobiologists geared up and ready to board that alien ship. Full environmental hazard suits and armaments."

Lee turned to his ops officer. "Scan that derelict ship for any sign of active systems, power sources, or potential threats. I don't want any surprises once we're aboard. And keep those sensors reading everything under the sun and more."

"Aye, sir."

He pressed on the fleet-wide comm. "All ships, assume defensive formation Delta-Four until we have a better assessment. Weapons on standby. Let's see what secrets they're hiding."

Digitized captain voices replied with their acknowledgments in return, the sim doing a good job of making them sound human.

As Sato began coordinating the away team, proximity alarms blared across the bridge.

"Multiple contacts!" Rhom shouted. "Fifty-two ships emerging from the gas cloud, bearing Zodark markings!"

The simulation just became very real, Lee thought. "All hands to battle stations! Cancel the away team, Sato."

"On it, sir."

"Tactical, target the lead Zodark ship. Echoes One through Four, form up on our starboard flank. Tangos Five through Eight, port side. Sierras, take up defensive positions around our cruisers. Fire at will when in range."

"Aye, sir," Rhom replied.

The sudden appearance of Zodark ships emerging from the gas cloud transformed their routine simulation into a high-stakes engagement.

Lee grimaced, not liking the change. Through all the trainings, probably hundreds by now in a short span of time, this sort of thing had started to eat at him. Over the last couple of sessions, he'd found himself getting annoyed at any sudden change.

Get yourself together, he told himself. *This is what it's like in real combat. Nothing goes as planned. Nothing.*

Lee's gaze locked on the main viewscreen. Where ranging data should have been displayed, giving them a clear picture of the tactical situation, there were only dashes—a glaring absence of information. Another simulation glitch.

"Simons," Lee said, his voice clipped as he addressed the ops officer, "get those sensor readings back online. I need hard numbers on spatial separations, not just empty placeholders."

"Working on it, sir," said Simons as he typed on his interface, attempting to rectify the faulty readings.

"Sir, my console works fine," Rhom said. "Lead Zodark vessel at four hundred and eighty-seven thousand kilometers and closing. Their fleet is in a tight formation, spanning roughly fifty thousand kilometers from vanguard to rear."

Lee nodded. "Navigation, bring us about to heading three-one-five mark twenty. All ships to assume wide delta formation, maximum dispersion. I want a twenty-thousand-kilometer spread between our vanguard and rear."

"Aye, Captain," Reynolds responded. "Coming to new heading. Transmitting formation orders to the fleet now."

As the fleet maneuvered into position, Lee addressed the bridge. "We're facing a numerically superior force, but we have the advantage of range. We're going to hit them hard and fast before they can close to effective torpedo range. Rhom, blast the screen with SW countermeasures, and prepare a full spread of JATMs. I want them targeted on their lead ships."

"Aye, sir. JATMs armed and ready. Awaiting your command."

Lee watched the tactical display as the distance slowly decreased. When the range hit four hundred and fifty thousand kilometers, he gave the order. "Fire JATMs, full spread!"

"Missiles away. Time to impact: approximately seven minutes, thirty seconds."

"All ships, commence random evasive maneuvers," Lee commanded. "Rodriguez, initiate ECM protocols. Let's make it harder for them to get a lock on us."

As the missiles streaked toward their targets, Lee spoke to his tactical officer. "Rhom, charge magrails. As soon as we're in range, I want concentrated fire on their lead ship. Coordinate with Echo group for maximum effect."

"Aye, Captain. Magrails charging. We'll be in effective range in approximately ninety seconds."

The bridge fell silent as they watched the JATMs close in on the Zodark fleet.

"Simons, I need you to hurry up," Lee said. "I need numbers on the screen."

"Understood, Captain. I've bypassed the external sensor linkups. Drawing coordinates from our internal navicomp. Separations coming through on my screen now, but not on the main holo."

"Fix it."

"Aye, sir."

An instant later, bright flashes erupted on the tactical display. The JATMs had hit their targets.

"Multiple impacts confirmed!" Rhom called out. "Three Zodark vessels showing significant damage. Two more with minor hull breaches."

"Good start," Lee said. "Now, let's press our advantage. Rhom, fire magrails as soon as we're in range. Target their damaged ships first."

"Aye, sir. Firing solution locked. Magrails hot in three… two… one… firing!"

The ship simulated a shudder as the magrail rounds were launched, streaking across space at near-relativistic speeds.

Rhom kept his eyes on his screen. "Impact in one point six seconds."

The rounds found their mark. The tactical display showed several direct hits on the already damaged Zodark vessels.

"Two enemy ships disabled, sir!" Rhom said. "A third is showing critical damage to its propulsion systems. Friendly forces are reporting multiple successful engagements across the AO, as well. Intel confirms enemy fleet suffering significant casualties and degraded combat-effectiveness. Multiple hostile vessels show reduced maneuverability and diminished offensive capabilities. Stand by for updated battlespace assessment."

"Excellent work. Sato, have Sierra group focus fire on that crippled ship and Echo group spread their fire across the hostile's flanks. Let's keep them off-balance."

As the orders were relayed, the Zodark fleet returned fire. Brilliant beams of energy lanced out across space, some finding their marks on the Republic ships.

"Lasers impacting on Deck Six, Section Two, and Deck Seven, Section Three. Minimal damage reported."

The Zodarks' laser weapons were instantaneous, giving them a slight edge in terms of targeting. "Have those ships fall back and rotate fresh vessels to the front. Reynolds, execute random vector changes every five seconds. Don't let them get a solid lock."

"Aye, aye."

The battle continued to rage, with both sides exchanging fire at long range. Lee's strategy of keeping the engagement at maximum distance started to pay off.

"Sir," Sato said, "Sierra group reports they've taken out three more Zodark vessels. Our casualties are light. Minor damage to two frigates and one cruiser."

Lee's eyes never left the tactical display. "Good. Have Echo group shift twenty thousand kilometers to starboard. I want to create a cross fire with Sierra group."

As the minutes ticked by, the tide of battle turned in favor of the Republic fleet. The Zodark forces, unable to close to their preferred engagement range, were being systematically picked apart by the combined firepower of Lee's ships.

"Commander," Rhom called out, "enemy fleet is showing signs of disorganization. Their formation is breaking up."

Lee saw his opportunity. "All ships, concentrate fire on their flagship. Let's cut the head off this snake."

The Republic fleet responded with a devastating barrage of magrail fire and missile salvos. The Zodark flagship, already damaged from earlier exchanges, stood little chance against the concentrated assault.

"Direct hits on enemy flagship!" Rhom exclaimed. "She's breaking up, sir!"

That was almost too easy. "Don't let up. Pick your targets and finish them off. I want this simulation ended decisively."

As the last Zodark ship fell to the Republic's guns, the simulation faded away, leaving the bridge of the RNS *Poseidon* in its normal state.

Lee looked around at his crew. "This was the final exercise before our deployment to the Intus Campaign. Your execution against a numerically superior enemy force was nothing short of exemplary."

Yet it was too easy, he thought. *Maybe our scenarios are still based on the capabilities of our old Republic warships.* With these high-power technological advances, the game really had been upped.

His steely gaze fell on his XO. "Commander Sato, compile full after-action reports from all department heads. I want a comprehensive debrief with lessons learned in one hour."

I think we are ready. I hope I'm right.

He planned to review everything down to the letter. If he was going to bring his people into battle, he was going to do it with the confidence that he had done everything he could to prepare them for it.

Chapter 43
Accept Nothing Less

Year 2096
RNS *Gallipoli*

Chief Petty Officer Brian Ford's face dripped with sweat as his feet pounded hard on the treadmill. Its surface absorbed the impact and redistributed the energy to propel him forward. Unlike the ancient models, this one adapted to his stride, minimizing joint stress and maximizing efficiency. It was everything Ford needed. After training long hours, there was nothing like exercise to get your brain clear again.

Twenty-five minutes earlier, the interface had blinked to life. It projected a holographic display at eye level. "Pull up that show… about ancient aliens," Ford said.

The hologram shimmered. Footage from a century-old program appeared. A host with an outlandish hairstyle moved his hands wildly, his voice filled with excitement.

"These elongated skulls found in South America defy explanation," the host said. "And nearby, the Nazca mummies—three-fingered, three-toed beings with long feet and humanlike features. Standing at five foot five, they've baffled scientists for years."

Ford chuckled, shaking his head. The world had changed so much since then. He wondered what these TV personalities would think if they could see the galaxy now.

They'd think, "Zodarks? Hyper-killing warriors with blue skin, three meters tall, and three eyes to boot? Nah. And advanced tech? No way! Hell-bent on throwing everyone into subjugation under their watch? Run for the hills!"

"DNA analysis from four universities concluded they weren't human," the host continued. "So where did they come from? The stars?"

Ford's mind meandered. Had the Republic encountered beings like the Nazca mummies? Were there secret negotiations happening behind closed doors? Probably. Why wouldn't they? What, maybe a handful more aliens spoke with them, and on how many occasions? The idea wasn't backward-thinking. The government hid a lot, and this was most likely another one of their secrets. He bet they'd been talking for years—maybe hundreds of years, and various governments, from the old Soviet Union to maybe even the Caesars in Rome.

Nah, maybe not that far back.

His musings were interrupted by a woman's voice.

"Hey, Chief. Mind if I join you?"

Ford glanced over to see Lieutenant Love approaching. He nodded and switched off the hologram. Although she did her best not to be too annoyed with Ford's ancient alien obsession, he knew she detested it, never wanting to discuss let alone see any information on the subject. "Be my guest."

Love hopped onto the adjacent treadmill and matched his pace. "One day until we ship out. You nervous?"

"Not really. Which actually makes me nervous."

"How's that work?" Love asked.

"They say you're more focused with the right amount of nerves. Too calm, and you might miss something."

"Huh," Love said. "I don't get nervous much. Worry I might get a bit emotional sometimes, though. Not great when you're hauling troops into the pits of hell."

Ford nodded, understanding. "Gotta keep a level head out there. Trust me when I say this, Love. You always do."

Love glanced at him. "Y'know, Chief, I tend to run my mouth around you."

"No kidding." Ford smirked. "I was starting to think you had some kind of verbal diarrhea. Should I requisition some Imodium for you?"

"Ha… ha. Very funny," she retorted. "I'll have you know my verbal emissions are top-notch."

"Oh yeah? Is that why the comms always crackle when you're on frequency?"

"That's just my magnetic personality, Ford. Can't help it if I interfere with electronics."

They continued their banter for a few minutes, and then Love's expression turned serious. "Hey, you hear about the new Altairian-human hybrid ships? Scuttlebutt says they're having major malfunctions. Might not deploy when we do."

"Altairian," Ford mused. "You get the… memo?"

Love nodded. "A while back. You?"

"Yeah. Not much talk about it, which is surprising."

"A few people brought it up around me. We're in an alliance. Was wondering what the Altairian part meant in the hybrid's name. Couldn't figure it out until that all-hands bulletin."

"Maybe everyone just figures I know about aliens, so I somehow knew about this?" Ford asked, almost to himself.

"Or you're the weirdo who won't shut up about it, so they avoid you at all costs." She winked at him.

Ford grinned. "Hey, low blow. Way low. What you think about the alliance?"

"The more, the merrier," said Love.

"You trust it?" Ford pressed.

"I trust other species hating the Zodarks about as much as we do, so… yeah, I don't find it too hard to believe."

"How many are in the alliance?" Ford asked.

"How would I know? We got the same communication, didn't we? I think the Altairians and the Primords for sure, but I'll bet there are a few others they haven't told us about yet. They probably told us about these two because these are the races it appears we're going to be interacting with right away. I'm sure that'll change if the mission requirements change."

"Sounds about right. Semper Gumby, right? I mean it's not like we humans tend to shoot first, ask questions later. It rings true that it's just the Prims and Altairians."

"Shooting first and asking questions last reminds me of the Zodarks," Love said. "I don't want to put us on their level, in their category."

"We're not. Don't worry about it."

Ford paused. "How are you holding up, Love?" he asked. "Everything OK?"

Love's stride faltered for an instant. "I'd appreciate it if you didn't ask me that again, Chief."

"My apologies, Lieutenant," Ford said. "Won't happen again."

"Good, 'cause I don't want to keep talking about it."

A long holowindow stood in front of them. It showcased New Eden's beauty. Mesmerized by the planet's glow, Ford marveled at how far they'd come. He maintained his pace. "I understand."

"Do you, really?"

The intensity in her tone caught Ford off guard. A twinge hit his gut, as if he'd been sucker punched. He swallowed hard. "I don't. But I know what loss is. It's not fun. I'll leave it at that."

Love studied him for a second. "Ford, what's your story? Why is your past such an enigma?"

Ford's chest tightened. "Now I get how you feel, Love. I'd rather not discuss it. Let's leave it be."

"Fair enough."

They ran in silence for another long while. The only sounds were their breathing and the treadmills' whir. Sweat beaded on their foreheads, trickling down their faces.

Ford cleared his throat. "So, about Cooper. Think you've got a secret admirer there."

Love rolled her eyes. "Wouldn't be the first time. It'll blow over. Always does."

"How do you handle it so well?" Ford asked. "You're cool about the whole thing."

"Practice." Love shrugged. "Plus, I've got more important things to worry about than some pilot's crush."

"Yeah," he said, staring out the holowindow, the planet in full view, "can you believe how fast New Eden's developed? Just five years and look at it now."

"It's something else. The Sumerians have been a big help with that."

Ford recalled what he knew about the Sumerian race. Discovered on New Eden, freed from Zodark enslavement by Earthers, with more of their kind still held captive on other worlds. Their home planet, Sumer, remained under Zodark control to this day.

"It's wild," Ford said. "A whole race that looks just like us but didn't come from Earth. Still can't wrap my head around it."

"Real head-scratcher, that one. Maybe it's how humans developed everywhere. Same perfect conditions on different planets."

"Could be. You know they're talking about liberating Sumer, right? Just like we're doing for the Primords on Intus."

"Yeah," Love said. "Got major resources there, too. At least, that's what I hear."

Ford wiped perspiration off his brow. "One of the main reasons to help the Prims get that world back, I'd say." For a few minutes, all they did was try to outpace each other. "When did you first hear about them?"

"Are you trying to slow me down?" Love asked.

"Yeah… but, no… seriously. When did you hear about them?"

Love shrugged. "Not too long ago. You?"

"Same here."

"Heard they're tough SOBs in a fight, though."

Love grinned. "That's the rumor. Hey, you catch those images of the Altairians? They flashed on my personal display in my quarters."

Ford nodded. "Affirmative. They're… different, to say it bluntly."

"You're telling me. Slap some glasses on 'em and they'd look like the eggheads in Research and Development."

Ford burst out laughing, almost losing his footing on the treadmill. As they continued their run, their breathing grew heavier. When Love increased her speed, Ford, not to be outdone, matched her pace.

"Trying to keep up, Ford?"

"I've been running longer than you today, Lieutenant. But nice try," Ford countered.

Love's expression tightened. "Kinda can't wait to get into the fight. To surprise those bastards on Intus."

"Yep." With a quick sigh, Ford slowed his treadmill until it stopped. "You win this race, Love. Even though we both know you didn't."

"Whatever helps you sleep at night, Chief."

Ford stepped off the treadmill, stretching his muscles. "I'm off to hit the showers. See you first thing tomorrow when we jump to Intus. It's gonna be a long ride."

"Get some rest, Ford."

"Will do."

"I'll accept nothing less," Love said.

As Ford walked out of the gym, he passed several staff members exercising. A woman lifted weights, performing bicep curls. In another corner, a pilot executed thigh curls, his muscles straining with each repetition. Life before combat—sometimes it was as normal as life without continuous war.

Ford had put himself in this situation to defend humanity for the Republic. It was the single greatest thing he'd ever done. Before that, he was a nobody. In fact, he'd call himself a loser, though he used that term lightly. Nowadays, he was determined to do anything to fight the threat aiming to enslave humanity across the stars. Would they really put humanity in shackles if they could? There was no doubt in Ford's mind. Anyone who thought otherwise was clearly hard of seeing. Nonetheless, with another major battle looming, even the smallest contribution he could make held significance. Like Love, he'd accept nothing less than giving his all, fueled by a drive to make a positive change, no matter how small his impact might be.

Chapter 44
Nothing and Everything

Year 2096
RNS *Poseidon*
FTL Transit to Intus

Lee was pulled out of a daydream when a knock at the door pulled him back to the present.

"You wanted to see me, Cap?"

Boyd MacGregor stepped in without waiting for a response. Grease smudged his coveralls, and he smelled of metal shavings. He kept his hands in his pockets until Lee stood and gestured to him.

"Come. Sit, please."

MacGregor lowered himself into the chair across from the desk. The seat's springs groaned. He leaned back and eyed the cross and Bible with a look of curiosity, though he didn't mention them. His face held a placid kind of knowing, the unspoken acknowledgment between men who'd not had much time for religion in their lives as of late, other than the silent prayers most people in war spoke when all hell was breaking loose around them.

"You're not much for calling engineers in unless something's burning." MacGregor tilted his head. "What's on fire?"

"Nothing. This time." Lee lowered himself back into his seat. "I just wanted to talk. Perhaps about... you?"

"Talk about *me*?" MacGregor let out a half snort, half chuckle. He rubbed a hand over his jawline, leaving a streak of reddish grime behind. "Not much to know there. I've told you about enough, I think. I like to fix things; I keep things running."

"I know that."

"Well, I'm not exactly memoir material."

"Sure you can manage a couple of highlights, Mac." Lee folded his arms. "Throw me something here."

"You bored, Cap?"

"Do I look bored?" Lee pressed.

MacGregor looked him up and down. "Negative, sir. May I be frank with you?"

"You always are," Lee replied. "That's why you're here right now."

"You look like crap. Your hair's a mess, and those dark circles under your eyes make you look half dead. When's the last time you looked in your shiny mirror?"

"OK, maybe you're being too frank."

"Sorry, sir."

"I'm fine with it, Mac."

MacGregor rested his elbows on his knees and leaned forward, hesitating for a moment. "Well, I grew up in a scrapyard. Brooklyn, middle of nowhere. My old man ran a parts shop—called me in every time a circuit board fried, or a rotor got stuck. Not because I was a prodigy or anything—I was just cheap labor."

"You do all right with that cheap labor?"

"Paid my way into a vocational school. Got a certificate with the change I wasn't spending at the pool hall or on bad decisions." MacGregor grinned. "Then I got lucky—Navy snagged me before I fell into something worse."

The room quieted.

"Cap, I thought you called me for something… official?"

"I did, Mac." Lee gave him an almost tired smile. "Just for company. We exit FTL tomorrow. If I could think about anything else for a while—this seemed as good a distraction as any."

MacGregor gave a nod. "Well, I'm happy to oblige." He shifted in his chair. "You know, most COs don't do this. Call someone in just to chat."

Lee remembered Oldendorf's words from years ago, spoken over a glass of bourbon in his office after a particularly rough deployment. "Being a captain is the loneliest damn place on Earth, Lee," the old man had said, eyes distant. "Sometimes you need one or two people you can just… talk to. About nothing. Everything. Doesn't matter what. Problem is, no one wants to talk about nothing with their captain. Ever. Sometimes you have to force it, even when it feels awkward as hell. It's to keep your sanity."

Lee pushed away the memory. "Well, Mac, most COs aren't sitting on top of experimental tech about to emerge into the biggest space battle in Earther history. Besides, I've learned from experience that isolation makes for poor command decisions."

"Fair enough." MacGregor's eyes drifted to the cross again. "You religious, Cap?"

"More than most." Lee picked up the cross. "These days... I believe more than ever."

"Not me." MacGregor scratched his stubbled chin. "My ma was Catholic. Dragged me to mass every Sunday until I was sixteen. Then one day, I just stopped going. Never said why. When things get dicey in Engineering, I still find myself making the sign of the cross."

Lee smiled. "Old habits."

"Yes, habits," MacGregor said. "Cap, since we're being honest here—the crew's noticed you walking the decks at odd hours. They worry."

"They shouldn't."

"With respect, sir, they will anyway. That's what happens when you've got good people under you. It's what happens when you've got a crew that actually cares about their captain as much as he cares about them, you know?"

Lee considered this, remembering more of Oldendorf's advice. "Tell me something, Mac. What keeps you up at night?"

MacGregor was quiet for a long moment. "The sound of the engines," he finally said. "Not the actual sound—I know every hum and whine by heart. It's the sound they might make when something goes wrong. The ones I hear in my dreams. Sometimes I wake up convinced something's failed, and I have to check the diagnostics three times before I can sleep again."

"That why I sometimes catch you walking the decks at odd hours?"

"Guilty." MacGregor shrugged. "We all carry our ghosts, Cap. Some of us just hide them better than others."

"Tomorrow... you think we're ready?"

"Engineering-wise? Yes. The rest?" MacGregor stood, stretching. "That's more your department, isn't it?"

"Suppose it is." Lee rose as well. "Thanks for the talk, Mac."

"Anytime, Cap. And, sir? Try to get some sleep. Those ghosts will still be there tomorrow."

After MacGregor left, Lee stood at his viewport, watching the FTL distortions ripple across space. Oldendorf had been right—

sometimes you needed someone to talk to about nothing. Sometimes nothing was everything.

He picked up the cross, then carefully placed it in his desk drawer. Tomorrow would come soon enough. For now, the quiet company of memory would have to do.

Chapter 45
Opening the Gate

RNS *George Washington*
Intus System

The moment the *George Washington* exited the Solblight Stargate, the ship jolted as its systems realigned with local gravity and electromagnetic fields. The void of the Intus system unfolded before them—black and cold, but already on fire.

"Sensor sweep!" Captain Fran McKee snapped from her chair. "Full passive, then active. Get me a picture of this damned system."

"Spinning up all arrays now," her sensor chief replied. "Infrared, LIDAR, multi-band radar, neutrino and magnetometric feeds coming online… beginning active sweep."

Static flared across the main viewscreen as the *GW*'s targeting systems recalibrated. Outside, a growing number of warships materialized—burning engines, shifting formation, dozens of enemy signatures lighting up one after another.

"Multiple hostiles at two-ten mark five," Lieutenant Keene, her operations officer, called out. "Looks like one Orbot battleship and a full Zodark fleet grouping—battleships, cruisers, frigates. They're already in firing range."

"Of course they are," McKee muttered. "Weapons hot. All ships—prepare for immediate engagement."

"Ma'am!" her EW officer shouted, "Enemy targeting signatures spiking—Zodark plasma torpedoes in the tube… lasers warming. They're locking us up."

"Here we go," McKee said grimly. "Comms—fleet-wide alert. Defensive wedge, staggered spacing. Bring the fleet into formation and return fire at will."

Outside the bridge viewport, the *George Washington* began maneuvering on attitude thrusters, her hull bristling with weapon turrets and launch ports as they rolled to broadside position. All around her, the first-wave Republic fleet was emerging from the stargate—eight battleships, twelve cruisers, eight destroyers, and eight frigates fanning out into formation.

The first enemy barrage came in hard and fast.

Beams of focused light from Zodark lasers sliced through space, striking the Republic line. Plasma torpedoes followed—slow but deadly—glowing with unstable energy, spiraling toward their targets like miniature suns. A pair of torpedoes slammed into RNS *Topeka*, a first-gen cruiser, peeling open its midsection in a fiery rupture.

"Holy crap! We just lost the *Topeka*—she's gone!" shouted someone from the CIC pit.

"Return fire—now!" McKee angrily replied. They'd been in system less than a few minutes, and they had already lost a cruiser.

In seconds, magrail slugs roared from the *GW*'s turrets, the twenty-four thirty-two-inch and twenty-four sixteen-inch guns thundering in sequence. The slugs tore across the void at hypersonic velocity, each one packed with a high-explosive payload designed to crater armor and rupture bulkheads.

The *GW*'s heavy plasma cannon—mounted centerline—charged and fired, sending a bluish-white bolt screaming toward a Zodark cruiser. It struck amidships, exploding in a flash that sent debris spiraling into the black.

McKee glanced toward her flight operations controller. "Launch all drone squadrons. I want a defensive screen up and Raiders targeting those battleships."

"Aye, ma'am. Orion and Raider squadrons launching now."

From the *GW*'s belly, squadrons of P-97 Orion fighters and B-99 Raider bombers shot out like a storm. The remotely piloted fighters arced into position, forming a spherical perimeter around the fleet. Within seconds, they began intercepting incoming enemy squadrons—Vulture fighters and Glaive bombers that were streaming toward the Republic force from the flanks.

The battlespace exploded into chaos.

Zodark fighters clashed with Orions in a dizzying ballet of turns, burns, and flashes of light. Raiders broke off into attack groups, accelerating toward enemy capital ships, evading fighters and laser sweeps trying to blot them out of existence.

The blackness of space around the Republic warships filled rapidly with red tracer fire. The volume of fire from the 30mm point-defense batteries increased exponentially as they tried to intercept the oncoming swarm of enemy bombers, fighters, and plasma torpedoes streaking through the darkness toward them.

"Damn it, two frigates down," Ops reported. "One destroyer taking heavy fire—a laser penetrated through its mid-deck section. It's venting atmosphere and fluids."

"Hold formation!" McKee directed the ships of her fleet. "If we break now, we lose the gate, and we can't lose it. Keep your sectors locked and keep firing!" The enemy had been waiting. But now that McKee's fleet had fully arrived—the real fight had begun.

The bridge of the *George Washington* shook as another wave of Zodark plasma torpedoes detonated near her forward hull. Shrapnel and molten debris pinged off her reinforced prow. Somewhere below deck, the sound of rupturing bulkheads groaned like a beast in pain.

"Status on turret seventeen?" McKee barked as the damage control board lit up like a Christmas tree with yellow and red flashing lights at various points across the *GW*.

"Still offline—initial damage assessment shows the hydraulic return circuit's fried. It's immobile right now until they can repair it," LaFine explained as he read aloud the report forwarded to him. "Turrets fifteen through twenty-four are active. We've still got teeth."

"Good, then bite already."

Outside, the *GW* surged into the thick of the fight, flanked by three *Ryan*-class battleships. The *GW*'s twin-barreled thirty-six-inch magrail cannons unleashed hell with every synchronized salvo, the recoil shuddering down the spine of the ship. The massive slugs—each weighing nearly three tons—screamed across the void, their superdense tungsten cores punching through hulls like they were designed to do. Moments after impact, the single ton of high explosive packed into the center of each shell exploded, further ripping apart the decks inside the enemy vessels.

As the barrage of slugs from the Republic ships relentlessly pounded the Zodark ships and the lone Orbot battleship, the enemy was beginning to feel the sting of each salvo.

A Zodark battleship attempted to cross McKee's formation and direct fire toward the vulnerable cruisers screening behind her. The *GW*'s fire-control system calculated the intercept in a split-second. "Target acquired—turret twelve, fourteen, and sixteen firing—"

The shots hit amidships with devastating results.

Two slugs smashed through the modulated armor like paper, the third entering just above the engine core. A split second later, the HE charge detonated inside the enemy ship's spine. The Zodark vessel cracked wide open from a series of secondary explosions. In the blink of an eye, a molten vent of gas and flames erupted from the newly created holes in the ship's armor. The vessel began a rapid disassembly, with its deck plating peeling outward from the pressure of internal explosions.

As the Zodark battleship blew apart, some of the crew aboard the *GW* erupted in spontaneous cheers.

"Confirmed kill on Zodark Battleship Gamma-3," Keene announced as soon as the bridge had quieted down.

The victory was short-lived. Four cruisers approached the *GW*'s port flank in a tight formation, their laser turrets stitching glowing scars across her hull. One beam struck just aft of the bridge tower, burning a six-meter-long furrow down the upper decks. Fires flared in section D-17 from the intense heat of the laser against the ship's hull.

Interior alarms wailed.

"Damage control to decks sixteen through eighteen—double up fire teams," McKee ordered, her voice firm. "LaFine, bring the portside secondaries to bear and hammer those bastards."

"Aye, Captain. Turrets five through ten—fire!"

The sixteen-inch secondaries spun and roared. Smaller than the primaries, but no less deadly, the slugs shredded one cruiser's bow in a concentrated volley. A follow-up salvo struck a second ship directly across its command section—detonating inside where Republic intelligence believed the Zodarks' CIC and bridge sections were located. The ship's lights flickered, then went dark. It slowly listed out of formation.

McKee watched as her bridge monitor showed the tiny figures of Zodark crewmen being sucked into space. The images were intermixed with sporadic flares, burning away the last remnants of the ship's atmosphere. Immediately afterward, McKee knew that its crew had been suffocated to death because the ship began to drift.

All around the Republic ships, the enemy resistance stiffened. From the edge of the Republic formation, two destroyers were torn apart under concentrated laser fire. Another cruiser, RNS *Kansas*, took a broadside of plasma torpedoes—its hull buckled, split, then vanished in a cascade of secondary explosions.

McKee's fleet was hurting—but there was nothing more she could do other than keep fighting and hope they took out more enemy ships than she was losing.

"We're down six ships," Keene announced grimly. "Another four are reporting moderate damage but still fighting. Damage reports coming in from a dozen more—our frigates, though, they're being chewed up by the Zodark bombers."

"Have the drone pilots tighten their formations," McKee ordered. "Get the Raiders to use our ships as shields until they're in position to hit those Zodark cruisers—we don't want them to circle around and hit us from the flanks again."

"Yes, ma'am. Relaying the instructions now."

Outside, the Orions and Raiders adjusted to the changing tactics of the Zodark ships. They shifted into tighter coverage as Glaive bombers tried to punch a hole through the Republic battleline. Interceptor missiles fired in overlapping arcs, slicing through Zodark wings, while 30mm rotary guns ripped fighters apart like paper.

Then, suddenly, there was an opening.

"Captain, we have a clear shot on the Orbot battleship. Recommend primary turrets, concentrated fire."

"Do it."

All remaining thirty-six-inch turrets oriented toward the massive Orbot vessel.

"Six turrets, twelve-barrel salvo, centerline fire—*firing*!"

The deck of the *GW* shuddered as six twin-barrel turrets unleashed a wall of kinetic death. The slugs struck seconds later. One embedded deep into the port engine housing. Another detonated inside a launch bay, obliterating fighters and rupturing its missile magazine. The Orbot ship reeled, trailing debris and a ribbon of vented coolant that froze into crystal across the starscape.

But the Orbot vessel didn't explode. Instead, its FTL drive ignited. The massive ship vanished in a burst of light, spinning up and jumping away from the battle.

"What the hell... where did that ship go?" LaFine asked, confused.

"Who cares?" McKee muttered. "It's not here, tearing our ships up. Let's focus on the remaining ships left."

A moment later, one of the Republic battleships, the RNS *Resolute*, took a direct hit from three converging plasma torpedoes. The forward hull crumpled. Fires flared across its length before the ship drifted out of formation, venting debris and comm chatter.

McKee's jaw clenched. The fight was far from over.

Another Zodark cruiser broke formation, attempting to sweep around the Republic battleline. At that moment, the *GW*'s plasma cannon, which had already been cycling, reached full charge.

"Firing plasma cannon!"

The plasma bolt lanced out—striking the cruiser dead-center. It detonated violently, folding in on itself before shattering like glass. A cheer broke out across the bridge. A single shot had blown the enemy vessel apart.

"All Republic ships—tighten the net. Let's finish this line," McKee ordered.

A coordinated push followed. Battleships focused their fire, knocking out two more Zodark cruisers. The destroyers surged forward, launching plasma torpedoes into weakened targets, while drone bombers peppered the flanks with saturation strikes.

Then the remaining Zodark vessels began to pull back— fractured, burning, but not broken. They spun up their FTL drives and leapt away in the direction of the planet Intus, disappearing in streaks of light.

Silence returned to the bridge—not peace, but the cold vacuum that followed chaos. The last of the Zodark warships had jumped away, trailing wreckage and damage toward the far side of Intus. The space around the stargate was a graveyard of twisted debris and drifting hulks. Fires burned out slowly from ruptured ships, their atmospheres venting into the darkness in shimmering clouds.

Captain McKee sat back in her chair, eyes scanning the main tactical display as her fleet began to regroup. Her voice cut through the quiet.

"Begin damage assessments. All ships report status and casualties."

"Aye, Captain," Keene acknowledged. "Fleet-wide status request transmitted."

Screens around the bridge lit up with returning signals—some full reports, others fragmented by damaged comms arrays. The *George Washington*'s own CIC was already processing incoming damage.

"Decks sixteen through eighteen suffered hull penetration," the engineering officer reported. "We've sealed the breaches, but we lost twenty-seven crew and two drone relay nodes. Portside magazine for turret nine's offline. Damage control teams are already rotating through power relays and life support redundancies."

"How long to restore full combat readiness?" McKee asked without flinching.

"Six hours for mag relays. Drone node swaps in two. Hull patching is underway—non-critical for now."

McKee nodded. "Make it happen. Prioritize critical weapon systems and drone control interfaces."

She turned toward the tactical station.

"LaFine, rearm all functioning magrail turrets. Plasma cannon too. I want to be ready to fire again at a moment's notice."

"Aye, Captain. We're already recycling the loader arms."

Below decks, McKee knew that teams moved in coordinated rushes—fire suppression crews dragging hoses through scorched passageways, engineers prying open buckled plating to bypass failed power runs. Drone technicians would replace scorched control conduits and re-sync surviving Orions and Raiders with fresh relays. The *GW* had taken hits—but she was still standing, still deadly.

On the main view, shattered Republic hulls drifted silently through space. A handful of cruisers and destroyers were too damaged to continue. Others were limping along, patching breaches and tending to their wounded. Twenty percent of McKee's original force was gone. Fifty percent more bore heavy scars of the engagement.

But the Zodark fleet at the gate had been broken.

"Status of the comms probe?" McKee asked.

"En route through the stargate now, ma'am," replied the comms officer. "ETA for bounce-back signal is six minutes."

"Very well. Begin rotating fleet-wide repair protocols. Anyone still combat-capable will rearm and reorient toward the next vector—planetary orbit around Intus."

A soft chime sounded a few minutes later.

"Signal received. Probe confirms success. Stargate is stable. Eight orbital assault ships are preparing to transit."

"Bring up the feed."

One by one, the massive gray silhouettes of the Republic orbital assault transports emerged from the Solblight stargate. Designed for planetary drops and troop deployment, they were armored, bulky vessels, bristling with anti-missile guns and maneuvering thrusters. Even as they cleared the gate, their escorts began falling into protective formation.

A slow exhale left McKee's lungs. Phase one was complete. The gate was secure. The hammer was ready.

She stood.

"Transmit orders to the fleet. Begin FTL sequence for all operational vessels. Our destination is orbit over Intus. Let's finish this."

"Aye, Captain," Keene replied.

Across the fleet, fusion drives flared to life as surviving warships aligned for short-range FTL jumps. Engines rumbled with energy as countdowns began. The blackness above the stargate flickered with burn trails.

Captain Fran McKee watched it all unfold from the bridge of her battered flagship.

"Time to remind the Zodarks why we're here."

Year 2096
RNS *Gallipoli*
Intus Orbit

The invasion—no, the counteroffensive—had already begun. Captain Fran McKee led the fleet against the Zodark forces orbiting planet Intus. Her warships thundered through space like a stampede, heading toward the green world.

With weapons fire abounding, two fleets engaged head-on—Zodark cruisers and battleships guarding their world, while the Republic, Primord, and Altairian forces meant to take it.

Coop tapped several buttons on the holodisplay on his control panel to initiate the Combat Space Patrol sequence. Systems came online. His drone pod whirred to life. Through the neural link, he felt the actual Orion starfighter stir to life as well. Its sensors became an extension of his own senses.

No matter how many times it happened, it still felt weird to Coop. One day, he'd get over it… he hoped. Thankfully, the sensation wasn't there during flight and combat.

"Coop here. Orion Five prepped and ready for launch," he said.

The *Gallipoli* shook from a direct hit. Klaxons blared as the operator at the flight deck replied, "Launch Control to the Jolly Rogers, all systems green. Commence launch sequence."

A lurching sensation hit Coop as his Orion propelled out of the RNS *Gallipoli*'s hangar bay. Space enveloped Coop's screen. Stars shined against the endless black. Before him, planet Intus floated, a sphere of vibrant greens and deep blues. The planet's dark green aura gave Intus an almost magical appearance.

Coop maneuvered his craft into formation with the rest of the Jolly Rogers. The other Orions fell into place around him. No sooner had they cleared the *Gallipoli*'s defensive perimeter than Coop's HUD lit up like a Christmas tree. Red dots swarmed across his display. Each one represented a Zodark starfighter, one of the venerable Vultures.

"Holy hell," Coop said under his breath. The swarm was massive—easily three hundred strong and closing fast. His HUD indicated the Vultures were still two hundred thousand kilometers out, but at the speeds they were traveling, the distance would close in no time.

The comms crackled to life. "Jolly Rogers, this is Strike. We've got a storm incoming. Form up defensive formation Delta-Seven around the *Gallipoli*. I want a tight screen, people. Vector assignments as follows: Coop and Raven, you've got the starboard bow quadrant. Wraith and Ghost Dog, take port bow…" Strike continued, rattling off assignments in rapid-fire.

From within his drone control pod, Coop glanced at the tactical display. It showed his wingman's Orion fighter positioned off his own craft's wing as they moved into formation. "Hey, Raven, try to keep up this time, yeah?" said Coop. "Don't want to have to save your butt again."

Raven's voice crackled through. "Muzzle it, Coop. We're on mission. Stay focused."

I was just kidding, man. Relax, Coop thought. *Great-Great-Gramps would have handled that better.*

The squadron spread out. They formed a protective screen around the *Gallipoli*. Coop had to admit, the Jolly Rogers made a damn fine team. Out here with dozens of other Orion squadrons protecting the other ships, including the *Gallipoli*, his squadron might be the best. For himself, he'd be nowhere else but with the best. The best with the best, they say.

In a short span, space erupted into a blurry version of Armageddon with the speed of the starfighters, both ally and foe. The Vultures' formations broke apart as they engaged the Republic fleet. Magrail fire from the Republic frigates, battleships, and cruisers lit up the darkness and downed several Vultures in quick order. Still, it wasn't even close enough to stem the tide.

"Incoming," Strike's voice cut through the comms. "Multiple torpedo launches detected. HUD says… we've got over two hundred inbound."

Coop's holodisplay lit up with target locks. He didn't wait for orders as he knew what needed to be done. He fired his lasers, the shots lancing out to intercept the torpedoes. Flashes erupted as the lasers found their marks, detonating the projectiles before they could reach their targets.

Ahead, the battleship RNS *Georgia* dominated the view. Behind, the *Gallipoli* maintained its position. Between these two naval titans, the void was alive with hell. Scores of Orion and Vulture fighters flew in a dogfight, their weapons fire illuminating the black.

The comm channels erupted.

"Got three! No, make that four!"

"Watch it, they're coming in hot on vector two-niner-zero!"

"Crap, we've got leakers! *Gallipoli*'s taking hits."

"Banshee here, I'm hit! Repeat, I'm…" The voice cut off. "Banshee back. Drone's toast. Linking up to a new Orion now. Be back in the fight ASAP."

Coop gritted his teeth, focusing on the task at hand. He didn't have time for chitchat or congratulations. Every second counted.

Laser fire moved through space. Torpedoes exploded. Through it all, Coop remained hyper-focused on the battle.

"Wraith, two bogeys on your six." The warning cry burst into the comms.

On Coop's tactical display, the holo showed a cluster of friendly green dots—the Jolly Rogers squadron. Among them, he spotted Wraith's identifier, with two red triangles closing in fast from behind. The enemy fighters were mere seconds away from optimal firing range.

Coop broke formation. "Raven, on me. We're going to clear Wraith's tail."

"Copy that," Raven said, falling in behind Coop's Orion.

"Raven, you flank left and cut off their escape vector. Watch for crossfire."

Coop pushed his Orion into a port turn, lining up behind the two Vultures harassing Wraith. His magrail guns spooled up, and he let loose a burst of fire. The first Vulture exploded. The second broke hard to starboard, and right into Raven's line of fire.

Perfect, Coop thought. *Damn, I'm good.*

In seconds, the Vulture erupted into flames, debris flying everywhere.

"Nice shot, Raven."

"Thanks. Let's get back in formation before—"

Strike's voice interrupted Raven's words. "All units, be advised. Ospreys are launching, operating under Talon Force designations. They need cover. Phantom, Specter, you're on Osprey One, designated Talon

Force One. Wraith, Ghost Dog, take Talon Force Two. Raven, Coop, you've got Talon Force Three. These birds need protection. Form up and clear them a path."

The Ospreys would be carrying ground troops for the ground invasion. Those assault transports were also vulnerable with limited firepower out in space, so failure to keep them safe wasn't a choice. To Coop, success was the only option.

"Roger that. Raven, let's move." Coop banked, heading toward the transport. They now flew parallel to the massive *Gallipoli*. The orbital assault carrier loomed so close, he felt he could touch it. "Talon Force Three, this is Coop. We've got your back. Stay tight to our formation and follow our lead."

As they moved to escort the Osprey, the battle raged on. Coop's world narrowed to his pod's controls, his HUD, and his wingman's voice.

"Coop, bogeys on approach!" Raven said.

A fresh wave of Vultures bore down on them. The enemy fighters sliced between the *Gallipoli* and the RNS *Georgia*. Both allied capital ships opened fire, but their response was limited to point-defense weapons. The big RNS ships had to be cautious. If they weren't, a more powerful volley risked friendly fire, potentially striking Orions darting between the larger vessels.

Despite the restrained defense, the space between the two ships became a kill zone, orange-and-red explosions flashing, only to be sucked up by the vacuum of space. All around, Vultures succumbed to the weapons fire. Many pushed through, their own blasters blazing. Coop calculated vectors and probabilities in an instant, searching for a path through the combat.

"Talon Force Three, full burn on my mark," Coop said. "Raven, we're going to split their formation. You go high, I'll go low. Hit 'em hard."

"Copy."

"Three… two… one… mark!"

Coop spun his Orion into a tight corkscrew. Two Vultures gave chase, their energy beams sizzling past his craft. He cut thrust, letting them overshoot, then fired his ventral thrusters. The Orion flipped end over end, and suddenly Coop was behind his pursuers.

His targeting system locked on. "Eat this." He fired magrail rounds. The first Vulture flared, then exploded. The second jinked hard, nearly colliding with its disintegrating wingman.

Coop continued. He matched the survivor's evasive maneuvers, anticipating each turn. A quick burst from his laser blasters sheared off one of the Vulture's wings, sending it into an uncontrolled spin, where it slammed into the *Gallipoli*'s thick hull.

"Bandit down," Coop reported, scanning for his next target.

Three Vultures had Raven pinned down, peppering his armor. Coop dove into the fray, barrel-rolling between two of the attackers. He fired off a spread of tactical missiles, not aiming to hit but to scatter the formation. It worked, the missiles flying toward Intus's atmosphere. The Vultures broke off from the chase and banked away, giving Raven the opening he needed to escape.

Alarms blared in Coop's pod. Quickly, he found himself sandwiched between two hostiles. He killed his main engines and fired maneuvering thrusters in rapid succession, making his Orion "hop" erratically. The Vultures' shots went wide, vanishing into the darkness beyond. In a split second, Coop ignited his main drive. He flipped over his craft, getting a perfect shot at the underbelly of a Vulture. His magrails tore through its vital systems, and the enemy fighter erupted. No way the Zodark pilot had survived.

As he celebrated the kill and his fast reflexes, Coop's cockpit brightened with warning lights. A third Vulture had latched onto his six, matching his every move. Coop's stomach tightened, this bandit following every maneuver like it was glued to his tail. His monitor flashed red—weapons lock. He veered, but the enemy stayed close.

"Come on, come on," Coop muttered. Losing a drone wasn't just a tactical setback; it meant he wouldn't be there to continue flying cover for the Osprey he was assigned to protect.

Just as Coop was about to attempt a risky maneuver, a streak of light blazed past his cockpit. The pursuing Vulture shattered in a yellow flash.

"Tango down," Raven said. "You can unclench now, Coop."

Coop let out a breath he didn't realize he'd been holding. "Raven? Cutting it a bit close there, weren't you?"

Shut your trap, Coop! he thought to himself.

"That's a roger on your six being clear," Raven said. "You're welcome for the assist, sunshine."

That's what I get, Coop thought. "Copy that, Raven. Solid hit."

The remaining Vultures, their cohesion broken up, began to retreat. Coop's adrenaline was still pumping as he lined up another shot. "That's right. Run!" he shouted as his guns burst forth once more.

As they tucked into formation on either side of the Osprey, Coop smiled. They'd cleared a path for the Osprey, the planet growing larger in front of them.

"Talon Force Three to Coop. We're clear and on approach. Thanks for the assist."

"Anytime," Coop said.

After the Ospreys flew into Intus's lower atmosphere, Raven and Coop formed back up to return to the *Gallipoli*. As Coop moved his Orion through the battlefield, the massive RNS *London* and RNS *Napoli* floated on either side of the *Gallipoli*, their lasers blasting at Vultures.

Warnings erupted on Coop's HUD. Crimson lights flashed as enemy fire struck his Orion. Coop assessed the hit on the display. The enemy shot had pierced the Orion's hull just aft of the cockpit, striking the main power distribution node.

In an instant, the spacecraft's systems began to fail. The primary power core shut down to prevent a catastrophic overload. Coop's control inputs became sluggish, then unresponsive as the flight computer and maneuvering thrusters lost power.

The HUD blinked off. Died. That left Coop with only the dim glow of emergency lighting in his pod. Without power to the inertial dampeners, the Orion would drift, spinning slowly as momentum carried it forward.

This, Coop thought, *is not good.*

****

The emergency interface blinked on. Coop punched in commands, accessing the restart sequence. Nothing. He tried again, this time bypassing the main power grid. The pod remained dark. Cursing under his breath, he initiated a hard reset—something they taught you never to do midflight unless you were desperate. He was desperate.

Three seconds passed. Five. Eight. The longest damn seconds of his life.

Then a whir. Lights flashed on. The HUD sputtered back to life. Systems returned one by one. Coop let out the breath he'd been holding as the Orion's engines growled to life.

"Damn," Coop said. *I got lucky. Good*, he thought. Still, it stung his pride. He'd been careless.

Pushing aside his frustration, Coop veered toward a trio of Vultures who'd broken through the Orion's defensive perimeter, harassing *Gallipoli*. He primed a salvo of JATMs and moved the crosshairs over the enemy fighters. The targeting reticle pulsed as it tried to find a lock.

Three rapid beeps sounded. The reticle turned red, confirming target acquisition. *Double good.*

The words "LOCK ACHIEVED" flashed on the screen. The weapons status indicator switched from amber to green.

"Let's see how you like this," he said, pressing the trigger.

The JATMs streaked from his Orion, leaving trails of blue fire. They homed in on their targets. From his perspective, he'd caught the hostiles off guard. The first Vulture broke apart in a mess of fire, its hull fracturing into a thousand shards. The second and third followed, blasted apart.

Coop grinned.

"Eyes on your backside, Coop!" Raven's transmission sliced through the static. "You've got an ace on your tail!"

Sure enough, a Vulture closed in fast behind Coop. "I see him." Coop jerked his Orion, initiating a split-S to drop below the pursuer's line of sight.

Raven's voice came again. "Bank hard right, then engage bow thrusters. I'll come in from above and we can—"

"I've got this," Coop said. *This Zodark's flying textbook. I can read him like a nav chart. Too predictable.*

Before Coop could implement his plan, detonations lit up the starfield. Through his pod's camera feeds, multiple torpedoes slammed into the *Gallipoli*'s hull. His virtual drone pod cockpit, housed within the massive *Gallipoli* itself, shook with each impact. Outside, flames erupted from the strike points before being extinguished by the vacuum of space. They left gaping wounds in the *Gallipoli*'s exterior.

The distraction cost him. His pursuer seized the opportunity, blasting away and nearly smoking him.

"Coop!" Raven shouted. "Listen! Straighten out! I've got a clear line on your bogey, but I can't take the shot with you flying so erratically."

Coop grimaced. Anger boiled inside him. He was better than this. He should be able to shake this bastard on his own. Still, no matter what he tried, the Vulture shadowed his every move.

"Cooper!" Raven's voice was blunt now. "Cut right, thirty-two degrees up, then engage bow thrusters for two seconds. Do it now!"

"Trust me on this one," Coop replied. He threw his Orion into a bunch of wild maneuvers, trying to break free.

"Damn it, Coop! We're a team. Now do what I say before we both get vaped!"

Why can't I shake this bogey? Cooper thought. *One more try.*

Despite evading the Vulture's weapons lock, Coop's latest maneuver failed to lose his pursuer. He swallowed hard, realizing his options were dwindling to nothing. Zip. Zilch. Zero. "All right," he said. "On your mark, Raven."

"Now!" Raven said.

Coop followed Raven's instructions to the letter. He banked hard right, climbing thirty-two degrees, then initiated the thrusters beneath his craft's nose. For two heart-stopping seconds, his Orion drifted, completely vulnerable.

Raven's voice rang louder. "Aft engines, full burn!"

Coop slammed the throttle forward. His Orion leaped ahead just as Raven's craft dove from above. The enemy veered hard to port, finding himself in the wrong spot at the wrong time.

Raven opened fire. His magrail guns lit up the void, catching the Vulture. The hostile died in a mushroom of fire, reduced to space debris in seconds.

Silence reigned over the comms. Coop cleared his throat. "Thanks. Nice work." The words felt more than strange in his mouth.

"You too. That was some fine flying at the end there."

Coop blinked, taken aback. There was no gloating in Raven's tone. *And he actually gave me credit? The guy flew like a pro, giving orders with the precision of a seasoned combat instructor.* Who knew Raven had this much talent, let alone such a wealth of tactical knowledge, crammed inside that compact cranium of his?

"Respect," Coop said.

"Say again? Didn't copy," Raven responded.

Coop shook his head, realizing he'd spoken out loud. "Negative, Raven. Disregard last transmission."

"Roger that. Maintain radio discipline. Over."

After he glanced at his tactical interface, Coop absorbed grim data. The holographic display showed a sea of red icons where green had once dominated; nine of his twenty-four Orion squadron starfighters had been knocked out of the fight within a matter of seconds. As he watched, one of the remaining green icons fluttered, its status uncertain. Another section of the display showed a welcome sight of drone pilots receiving launch clearance from Flight Operations Control. Soon, fresh unmanned fighters would join the fray. Seconds after, his HUD lit up with new contacts. Another wave of Vultures flew toward them, their weapons already charging.

"Raven," he called out, "you ready for another dance?"

"Always," Raven said

Chapter 47
The Gate

Year 2096
RNS Poseidon
Solblight System

Lee was beginning to feel nervous as the countdown clock continued toward zero. Soon, they would drop out of FTL to arrive at the jump point near the stargate that would transport them to Intus. He had trained his crew hard and felt they were as ready as possible. Still, this was the first time he would be going into battle with one of these hybrid warships. In theory, his heavy cruiser punched well above its weight. The blending of the best of human and Altairian offensive and defensive weapon systems should give the Republic and their alliance an edge it didn't previously have.

"We are almost there," Sato said softly as she stood next to Lee, also watching the clock continue to move toward zero.

"Yeah, things are going to move quickly once we reach the gate," Lee replied. He did his best to project calm confidence.

"We're ready for it," she assured him.

Lee returned to his seat as the ship neared the point where they would drop out of FTL.

"Helm, prepare for transition to real space. Comms, the moment we exit FTL, I want communications established with the *Aussie* and the rest of the fleet. Tactical, get our sensors up and make sure we're seeing what's happening around us—let's make sure we didn't just land in the middle of some Zodark ambush around the gate. Eng, I'll need those MPD thrusters online ASAP, so we can get the ship underway toward the gate."

A chorus of acknowledgements rolled in rapid succession as the various sections of the bridge prepared the ship and the crew for a return to normal space, and hopefully, an uneventful arrival. Seeing his crew in action like this, issuing orders and running through procedures like a well-oiled machine made Lee's swell pride. Months of hard drilling and training was paying off.

Reynolds announced loudly, "All stations, exiting slip space in three…two…one…and we're out."

The lights swirling around the *Poseidon* flicked off like a switch, and the ship emerged from the FTL bubble into the blackness of space. The ship shuddered briefly as the Ark-Fold FTL drives disengaged and transitioned to the MPD thrusters that would propel the ship forward. This was the part of FTL travel Lee disliked the most—the momentary sense of vertigo as the ship reentered normal space.

The moment they were out, Lee heard Sato snapping off commands as she whipped the bridge crew into action. It took a moment for the bridge to adjust the situation around them, but as more sensor returns fed into the ship's navigation and tactical systems, they began to reveal a picture of the stargate not too far off in the distance. An armada of ships was steadily building up around the jump points and the gate itself.

"Captain, we're being hailed by the *Australia*," announced Rodriguez.

"Patch them through," responded Lee.

The image of Captain Rodney appeared on the monitor. "Commander Lee, it's good of you to join us," Rodney began, sarcasm dripping from his voice. "I need your ship to catch up with the rest of our task force. The first wave has already jumped into Intus. Admiral Halsey wants the lead elements of the second wave to get into the system ASAP—that's us. We're to clear the other side of the gate of any hostiles and then link up with Captain McKee and the *George Washington* near Intus, so hurry up. Out." The salty Irishman ended the call before Lee had a chance to acknowledge the orders.

"Reynolds, you heard him. Plot us a course to join the rest of our task force and get in range of the gate to jump," directed Lee before turning his attention to his tactical action officer, Lieutenant Rhom. "TAO, we're still a little way from reaching the gate, but I want our gun batteries ready to engage the moment we are through."

"Aye, Captain. I'm getting the gun crews spun up and ready for action," Rhom acknowledged.

All around the *Poseidon*, a mass of warships advanced toward the stargate. It was a sight to behold, with the lumbering *Ryan*-class battleships and the dozens of troop transports nestled safely in the center of the fleet. Lee even spotted the Primord ships beginning to arrive and joining them. He was impressed by the size of their vessels. Even a handful of Altairian battleships were present—their massive vessels bristling with guns were a sight to behold.

Lee saw the gate activate as several corvettes and similar size destroyers crossed the gate's event horizon and disappeared. He suspected they were part of the scouting element for the main element of the second wave. Situated not far from the gaggle of troop transports was the fleet commander's ship, the RNS *Voyager*, Admiral Halsey's vessel. It was from her ship that the majority of the battle would be directed.

"Captain, we're nearly caught up to the *Aussie*," informed his helmsman.

"Copy that," Lee responded.

"Sir, we're receiving a message from the *Aussie*. They're directing us to follow them through the gate and prepare to fight," Rodriguez announced, a hint of excitement in his voice.

"Acknowledge the message and let them know we're proceeding through the gate," Lee directed before shifting his focus to Reynolds. "Helm, you heard the order. Take us through the gate. It's time to get in the fight."

As the *Poseidon* neared the gate, it activated, drawing Lee's ship through it.

Chapter 48
Into Hell

Above Planet Intus
RNS *George Washington*

Captain Fran McKee ran her fingers nervously through her hair as she read the battle report. The initial arrival of the fleet at Intus had been met with heavy losses. She knew they needed those new warships the Altairian warships to hurry up and join the fight in the second wave.

Until Admiral Halsey showed up, however, McKee was the acting operational fleet commander, so she straightened herself and went to action. Turning to her XO, Commander Yang, she directed him to assign a pair of corvettes to shadow the Zodark ships that were withdrawing. "I don't want them regrouping on the far side of a planet without us knowing about it," she explained.

"Yes, ma'am," Yang replied, sending her orders out the fleet.

She turned to her operations officer next, ordering the flight deck to launch their fighters so the Deltas on the ground could finish their mission sooner. The faster they took out those ion cannons, the faster they'd be able to begin hammering the locations of those Zodark facilities the Primords had provided the coordinates of.

"Aye, captain. I'm on it," came the quick reply.

McKee turned her attention back to the *GW*'s damage control board. Three sections that had been red had turned yellow.

McKee sighed in relief. *The fires are under control now*, she realized.

The hull breach in section two alpha had also been sealed up. Unfortunately, though, they'd lost six primary turrets and fifteen secondary turrets in the action thus far. It would definitely take a while to have all of the weapon systems back in the fight.

At least we still have our superweapon, McKee thought. Their plasma cannon could certainly dish out a lot of hurt on the Zodarks.

"Coms, how long until Admiral Halsey's group arrives?" McKee asked.

"Five minutes," Lieutenant Branson replied.

McKee nodded. *Things are moving right on schedule*, she realized.

Her task force had jumped into the system three hours ago to begin clearing a path for the ships carrying the Republic Special Forces soldiers who were going to conduct a high-risk, high-reward HALO insertion from low orbit to land the first wave of ground forces on the surface. This was crucial to the entire plan. Those ion cannons had to be taken offline—otherwise the orbital assault ships couldn't ferry in the thousands of soldiers that would be arriving with Admiral Halsey's fleet in the second wave.

The Prims had kept their promise and jumped in their fleet to support the Republic. Although they had fewer ships, their vessels were more capable than the Earthers'—at least for now.

McKee's operations officer announced that Admiral Halsey's fleet was arriving, and Captain McKee watched with pleasure as dozens of ships appeared on the monitor on the bridge. There were so many of them—forty transports and orbital assault ships.

This is definitely the largest human fleet that has ever been assembled in one place, McKee realized.

Lieutenant Branson relayed a message from Admiral Halsey. It was time to break off from their current position and establish a screening position for the transports.

Captain McKee acknowledged the order and sent directions to her task force to move to Beta formation. She would keep the *GW* near Intus, in the middle of the fleet. This would maximize their strategic advantage if the Zodarks suddenly materialized.

Like a well-coordinated colony of ants, the ships moved with purpose—McKee's task force shifting to the outer edge of the cluster of transports, and the orbital assault ships closing in on Intus.

McKee relaxed into her seat. *The next phase of operations is in Halsey's hands*, she thought.

Just as she was settling in, alarm klaxons interrupted the very temporary peace.

McKee's weapons officer, Lieutenant Commander Cory LaFine yelled out, "We've got a wormhole appearing!"

Her operations officer, Lieutenant Arnold, explained that the Orbot battleship they'd spotted earlier had returned, bringing eight Zodark cruisers with them. "They're emerging one million kilometers from the transports!"

McKee was in shock. She didn't know how this could possibly be happening. She'd been sure they'd incapacitated that Orbot ship.

Having no time for self-pity, McKee stood and issued a series of orders. Her task force needed to lock onto those Zodark cruisers. Meanwhile the *GW* would focus everything they had on that Orbot battleship.

We're not going to let it escape this time, she thought angrily.

While they were moving into a blocking position to protect as many of the transports as they could, Admiral Halsey sent a flash message from the *Voyager*. She was ordering the transports to FTL out of the battlespace. They would head to the stargate to buy some time until McKee's task force could clear the area of enemy ships again. McKee could see veins pulsating on the side of Halsey's neck—she must be as angry as McKee felt in that moment.

"We're on it, Admiral," McKee replied quickly. She explained that this was the same Orbot ship they had fought earlier, and that it had already been severely damaged. She also suggested that the transports should try to position themselves behind the *GW* until they could jump away.

"Good idea, McKee. I'm ordering the transports to move behind your ship until their FTL drives can charge and they can fall back to the gate," Admiral Halsey replied before ending the transmission to get back in the fight.

Captain McKee swiveled toward her weapons officer. "Weps, how many of our primary and secondary turrets are still operational?"

Lieutenant Cory LaFine checked his console before answering. "Captain, damage control got turrets twelve, fourteen, and seventeen back online. That gives us eighteen of our twenty-four thirty-six-inch magrail guns. But we're still down fifteen of the sixteen-inch secondaries."

McKee exhaled sharply, muttering a curse under her breath. "Then concentrate the sixteen-inch turrets on those Zodark cruisers. I want the plasma torpedoes split—half to the cruisers, half to that Orbot battleship. They're slow, but they'll break anything they hit."

"Aye, Captain," LaFine replied, spinning back to his station and relaying fire orders across the network.

Space outside the *George Washington* lit up in streaks of coherent light—Orbot lasers slicing toward the fleet's lead ships. The Zodark cruisers joined in, loosing volleys of plasma torpedoes that glowed like miniature suns. Two of them streaked in and slammed into the *GW*'s starboard hull. The bridge shuddered under the impact. Warning lights flared—no penetration, just scorched armor.

"Return fire—full battery," McKee snapped.

Across the *GW*'s hull, magnetic capacitors screamed to life. The thirty-six-inch turrets fired first.

Each magrail slug—six meters long and forged from depleted uranium—launched at over Mach 20. The rails crackled with blue-white arcs as they spat out slugs with explosive bursts of electromagnetic fury. Thunderous recoil thudded through the ship's frame, as if a god had struck an anvil in the void.

The slugs tore across space faster than the eye could follow. One of the Zodark frigates never stood a chance. A dozen hits ripped through its hull in rapid succession, breaking its spine before it detonated in a blossom of fire and twisted alloy. The second frigate banked hard to escape but veered into a cluster of plasma torpedoes. The impact tore the vessel in half—the bow continued on in a silent drift while the aft section vaporized in a chain-reaction blast.

Then the big guns found their true mark.

Three synchronized volleys from the thirty-six-inch turrets struck the Orbot battleship broadside. The slugs punched through its outer hull like needles through cloth, carving glowing tunnels hundreds of meters deep. One round penetrated all the way to its central reactor stack. Internal systems flared and shorted out. Vents blew wide. Clouds of frozen gas and Orbot drone components spilled into space.

The Zodark cruisers twisted and rolled, trying to dodge the incoming storm. The *GW*'s sixteen-inch slugs slammed into their flanks like battering rams. One cruiser lost half its propulsion grid in an instant. Another's dorsal section erupted in a plume of superheated metal, spinning the ship off-axis.

The *GW*'s less powerful pulse beam arrays joined in—faint compared to Altairian or Primord tech, but enough to score deep gashes across the cruisers' hulls. Damage mounted. Fires erupted inside pressurized compartments, only to be snuffed out by explosive decompression.

McKee watched the carnage unfold on the tactical display.

"Keep up the pressure," she ordered coldly. "We're not done yet."

Lieutenant LaFine barked, "I need those missile batteries back online now!" LaFine cursed before responding to whatever was being said to him over the comms. "Petty Officer Oats, I don't care if your lieutenant's dead—if you're the highest rank left in that bay, then *you're* in command. Get me a firing solution on the Orbot battleship and those cruisers."

He didn't wait for an answer. "Figure out what missile pods are still hot. Next, split the remaining Havocs evenly to target those six Zodark cruisers and that Orbot battleship. After you're done, repeat the process with the torpedoes. Understood? Good. Make it happen."

LaFine turned to McKee to explain what had happened. "Sorry about that, Captain. Those Zodark torpedo hits we just took appear to have hit the missile control center on deck two, Section Charlie-One. It wiped out the section's leadership down to the sixth person in line. I just ordered a gunner's mate second class to take charge of our remaining missile pods and get 'em back in action."

"Geez, make sure damage control knows what's going on and get another officer sent over there to take charge of things," McKee directed, a bit surprised the missile command deck had been wiped out.

Warning—Missiles inbound! Warning—Zodark fighters and bombers incoming!

"All PDG stations, stand by to intercept inbound targets!" Commander Yang shouted.

Outside the *George Washington*, the space above and around the Primord planet Intus continued to devolve into a chaotic conflagration with bursts of multicolored laser fire intermixed with a fury of missile trails and streaking plasma torpedoes. The Earther battlegroups pressed the attack, unleashing a storm of firepower on the enemy formation. Magrail slugs tore through the void, hammering Zodark cruisers, while salvos of Havoc anti-ship missiles arced toward the massive enemy vessels.

Captain McKee did her best to remain calm at the center of the commotion. Her gaze locked on the main display, but the range and motion distortions were blinding—too much light, too much movement. She needed clarity.

Then she remembered something Miles Hunt had told her once.

Sliding back into her command chair, she flipped open the foldable monitor and began tapping. Surveillance drone feeds flowed into a custom 3D rendering interface—an old app Hunt had built during his tour in command of the *GW*. The tactical sphere resolved around her, transforming the chaos into something she could read.

Now we're in business.

Her fleet's cruisers and battleships were closing hard, pressing into the Zodark line. Railgun salvos struck like war hammers, breaking up their formation. The enemy hadn't adapted—at least, not yet. The Republic was lethal up close, and the Zodarks were learning that too late.

But the Orbot ship—that beast—wasn't so naive. McKee watched its projected course bend away from the cruisers. It was diving, dropping low, angling to bypass the Republic screen entirely. McKee's eyes narrowed as she watched its plotted trajectory arc beneath the *GW*—right toward the outbound transports.

"No. Not today."

"Donaldson," McKee snapped, "match their vector. I don't care if you have to use docking thrusters—stay between them and our transports. They're trying to slide underneath us and line up a shot. Deny them that opportunity."

"I'm on it, Captain." Donaldson's hands danced across his console, rerouting thrust and flipping vector nozzles as the *GW* shifted position. The massive ship responded with a slow, deliberate glide—a wall of armor and firepower repositioning to block a juggernaut.

"Brace for impact!" someone shouted.

A second later, the Orbot battleship's main beam sliced through space. The *GW* shuddered violently as the laser bit deep into its hull, vaporizing armor and shearing into the lower decks. The ship pitched hard as Donaldson kicked the *GW* into a banking maneuver, throwing everyone sideways.

McKee gripped her seat, jaw clenched.

Countermeasures deployed in a crackling burst. Anti-laser SW pods detonated, flooding the battlespace with metallic aerosols and water vapor. A shimmering cloud bloomed across the laser's path— dispersing, refracting, distorting.

The Orbot beam flickered, degraded.

"Where's my jamming?!" McKee barked.

"Working it, ma'am, but they're burning through fast!" her EWO shot back. "Too close—signal interference is overlapping. We can't isolate the frequencies!"

McKee's knuckles whitened. The Orbot ship was forcing them into a knife fight—where its systems had the edge.

She stared at the display, watching the enemy try to press the flank again.

"Then screw their precision," she muttered. "Let's show 'em what mass and momentum can do."

McKee leaned toward LaFine. "Weps—I think it's time we begin rotating those Hellpiercers into the mix. Order the primary gun crews to replace every third shot with a Hellpiercer. We need to finish this battleship off before it can do any further damage to us or the fleet."

LaFine's eyes widened slightly. "Understood, Captain."

Before he could relay the order, Commander Yang turned sharply in his seat. "Ma'am—are you sure about that? If one of those slugs veers off-target or strikes an ally—Primord, Altairian—it could destroy them. That gelatin incendiary crap clings to everything it touches."

McKee didn't answer right away. The Hellpiercer was the Navy's latest experimental projectile they were testing against the Zodarks. It was a blended version of napalm, thermite, and white phosphorus the lab coats had engineered to cling to the internal surfaces of an enemy warship. Once the core detonated, it dispersed the sticky substance everywhere, burning at thousands of degrees Kelvin to destroy a ship from the inside out. It was the ultimate horror weapon for internal destruction—a ship-killing psychological terror weapon.

Her eyes stayed fixed on the tactical sphere—on the transports still trying to escape, and the Orbot battleship maneuvering for a kill shot. Every second counted.

She weighed the risk. Friendly ships were tight in the battlespace. Accidents could happen. But if the Orbot got through? Everyone burned.

She turned back to LaFine. "Do it. Load the Hellpiercers."

LaFine nodded and keyed the fire control net.

Yang exhaled, tension in his jaw. McKee kept her voice cold and steady. "We stop that monster now… or we bury half our army in orbit."

The *George Washington's* thirty-six-inch turrets rotated in sync, elevation gears locking as the fire-control system recalculated trajectories.

With a shriek of magnetic discharge, the next volley launched.

Three massive slugs tore through space—two standard penetrators, and the third: a Hellpiercer.

The air on the bridge seemed to hum with residual tension as the rounds streaked toward the Orbot battleship.

Then came impact.

The first two slugs slammed into the Orbot's lower hull, punching clean through the forward weapons deck and venting atmosphere in an instant.

The Hellpiercer struck a moment later—center mass. A microsecond after penetration, the warhead detonated. The result was cataclysmic.

A blinding white flash burst from deep inside the Orbot ship's superstructure. Armor plates the size of small buildings buckled outward. A geyser of debris, plasma, and shattered composite surged from the rupture point as internal decks collapsed inward. Entire sections of the ship lit up as secondary explosions rippled across its spine. The battleship lurched from the force, its port stabilizers flickering as it drifted off course—wounded, but not yet dead.

"Holy hell…" someone muttered on the bridge.

Before the awe could settle, a warning tone sounded across the command deck.

"Captain," said Lieutenant Commander Keene, the ops officer, "we've got movement—Zodark cruisers on approach. Five of them, coming in high and fast on an intercept vector. Same ships that withdrew earlier. Looks like they're coming back to box us in with the Orbot."

McKee's jaw tightened. That damned battleship just wouldn't die—and now the Zodarks wanted more blood.

"Open a tight beam to Captain Rodney aboard the *Australia*."

The connection buzzed once, then stabilized.

"Rodney, this is McKee. We've got Zodark cruisers inbound on our six. They're trying to trap us between them and that Orbot battleship. I need your squadron to intercept and finish them off— now."

Rodney's voice came back cool and confident, his Irish accent thick. "Understood. The *Australia* is on the move. We'll cut them off before they reach you."

McKee watched the 3D battle display as the RNS *Australia*, a *Ryan*-class battleship, pivoted sharply and surged forward. Six Altairian-human hybrid cruisers flanked her—sleek, crescent-shaped vessels bristling with both kinetic and laser weaponry.

The group accelerated in unison, forming a spearhead aimed at the approaching Zodarks.

McKee narrowed her eyes as the tactical symbols converged.

"Let's see how they like being the ones boxed in."

"Stand by—plasma cannon charging," Lieutenant LaFine announced. The *GWs* special weapon was finally joining the fray.

The deck trembled as the ionized gas continued to build. Lights flickered as power surged into the centerline cannon. A high-pitched hum soon filled the bridge.

"Firing now."

A white-hot bolt of plasma erupted from the *George Washington*, streaking across the void like a lance of lightning. It struck the Orbot vessel just forward of the stern.

The effect was immediate. The bolt bored straight through the rear section of the ship, vaporizing armor and internal decks. Atmosphere and fluids vented in a violent burst, scattering debris and hundreds of Orbot bodies into space.

The *GW* shook violently a second time as the Orbots' primary weapons struck the ship again. The *GW* rattled so hard, everyone grabbed for something to keep from falling. McKee checked the damage control board; red and yellow lights flashed on different sections of the ship, reflecting the serious damage from this last hit. They had a hull breach on decks six and seven, just above the hangar deck.

Just then, McKee caught a glimpse of two Republic destroyers as they swooped in and unloaded a barrage of plasma torpedoes and Havoc antiship missiles into the Orbot ship before they were both blotted from existence.

The Orbot ship maneuvered out of the way of the plasma torpedoes heading its way. It managed to evade six or seven of them, but another dozen slammed into various sections of the vessel. The battleship was too close to the human fleet to allow it much time or space to get out of the way of the devastating weapons.

When the destroyers' Havoc missiles closed in on the battleship, all but one of them were intercepted. However, the one that got through slammed into the outer hull of the Orbot vessel, its five-hundred-kiloton warhead detonating against its armor. The brief, mini-sun-like flash whited out the bridge monitors as the external cameras adjusted to the flash and the return of the void.

As the cameras readjusted, McKee and her crew saw a series of explosions begin to ripple through the enemy ship before another flash temporarily blinded the cameras once more. When the image returned, they saw the giant Orbot vessel breaking apart. Debris from the explosion flew out in many directions as nearby ships scattered to avoid colliding with wrecked chunks of the destroyed vessel.

Across the bridge, the crew erupted in spontaneous hoots and hollers as they celebrated the destruction of the first Orbot vessel they'd ever encountered.

McKee stood from her chair, raising her arms. "OK, settle down," she said. "We scored a victory taking that ship down, but this fight is far from over. Comms, redirect the task force to engage those two remaining Zodark cruisers. We need to finish clearing the battlespace so assault ships can deploy their troops to the surface."

The battle raged a bit longer as the rest of the task force made short work of the remaining Zodark ships. As the conflict drew to a close, McKee shook her head in dismay. Surveying the wreckage of the battle, she saw dozens of destroyed and now derelict hulls floating in the void, surrounded by the frozen bodies of their crew. The enemy had caught them off guard when they had jumped into the middle of their fleet, slashing and dashing as much as they could before her task force of battleships and cruisers could stop them.

"Ops, how many ships did we lose?" McKee asked, dreading the answer.

Before her ops section could answer, the video display next to her captain's chair popped on, and Admiral Halsey's face appeared. "Captain McKee, that was some quick thinking and good shooting. I'm ordering the fleet to begin the ground operation to neutralize those ion cannons on the surface. We need to begin offloading our forces as quickly as possible. Once those cannons are offline, I need your ships to begin hitting the designated targets the Primords gave us. Hopefully, we can weaken the Zodark forces on the planet before the majority of our ground forces begin to arrive."

McKee nodded in acknowledgment. "Yes, ma'am. Do you still want my space wings to support the orbital assault and the RA landings once they get started?" she asked. "We sustained some heavy casualties, but we can probably take on wounded from the surface should the need arise."

A short pause ensued as the admiral gazed off in another direction, calculating her response. Finally, Halsey replied, "Yeah, that sounds like a good plan, Captain. Have your fighters and bombers do what they can to support the ground assault. Halsey out."

The screen went black, leaving McKee with her new orders.

Seeing her bridge crew intently focused on their tasks, McKee stood up and walked over to her operations section. "Ops, send a message down to Flight Operations," she directed. "Tell them to reposition our fighters and bombers to support the Deltas and the RA as they land. Tell the medical transports that once it's safe to begin picking up the wounded from the surface, they are to commence medical evacs as soon as possible."

"Yes, Captain, right away," Lieutenant Arnold replied.

McKee used her communicator, pinging her chief engineer. "Commander Lyons, how bad is the damage?" she asked. "How soon can you complete repairs?"

A long moment went by before she got a response. "Captain, we took some hard hits. The starboard launch tubes on the flight deck are offline. Decks six and seven have a hull breach in sections H, J, and K. I'm trying to get that area sealed up and repaired as we speak. We also lost five more of our primary turrets during this last fight, along with three more secondary turrets, and the starboard torpedo tubes. It's going to take some serious time and likely a port call to a shipyard to get everything back online." McKee could hear a lot of shouting and alarms going off in the background as Lyons spoke.

Captain McKee sighed. She knew the damage was bad, she just wasn't sure how extensive it was. "OK, Commander, keep me posted on that hull breach, and do what you can," she replied.

"Will do, Captain. But please do keep in mind, this is going to take days to repair, not hours. Lyons out."

Lyons was clearly busy, and a lot was going on. McKee knew he was probably deploying his small army of synthetic repair workers to the hull breach. The team of Synths could operate on the outside of the ship and throw together some temporary patches. Those humanoid repair workers had saved many-a-ship during this war.

Using her communicator to contact the medbay, McKee asked, "Dr. Michaels, what's the situation like down there?"

"How do you think it's going, Captain?" the doctor responded sharply. "We've been in a battle. I've got casualties. People are dying down here."

Dr. Lane Michaels was the lead doctor on the *George Washington*. He was a brilliant surgeon and medical practitioner, but he was also a staunch pacifist. After being drafted a couple of years ago, he'd begrudgingly accepted a posting to the *GW*. He'd been selected to be the lead doctor on the ship because of his experience as an attending physician at the University of Chicago Hospital. Despite his position at the famous teaching hospital, his prominence within the community, all the work he was doing in Chicago, and his position as a pacifist, he had been unable to avoid the draft. He was often unable to hide his bitterness at the position he'd been placed in.

"It's bad up here too, Doc," McKee answered calmly. "How many casualties do you have down there?" she pressed.

A moment went by before he replied, "Roughly two hundred and thirty injured. Another three hundred or so were either killed or spaced during the hull breach."

"Just do your best, Dr. Michaels. The ground force is going to begin their operation shortly. Once they begin to take casualties, their critically wounded will be evacuated to the *GW*. They are likely to take hundreds, if not thousands of casualties during the first day. Until the hospital ships are in position, we are the best hope these soldiers will have of surviving their wounds. I'll alert you the moment they're inbound, but for now, you probably have a few hours to stabilize the wounded you have and prepare to receive more."

He grudgingly acknowledged. Then she cut the transmission, not wanting to hear his further complaints of being overwhelmed. He had a job to do, and so did she.

Chapter 49
Sweet Jesus

RNS *Gallipoli*

Lieutenant Naomi Love felt a strange sense of calm, despite knowing that her small crew aboard the *Jack* was about to see its first real combat. Time slowed down as they waited for the *Gallipoli* to come out of FTL. It wouldn't be long now until her Osprey joined the first wave bringing Deltas to the surface of Intus.

Just have to get them down there to the upper atmosphere without getting blown up.

Love had aced every sim she'd ever been in, but there was no substitute for the real thing. She knew that the minor incursions she had experienced putting down the last throes of the Zodark insurrection on New Eden would seem like child's play in comparison to the gauntlet they were about to go through.

She turned to her copilot, Lieutenant Caleb Green. "You ready?" she asked.

"Not sure anyone can be ready for this, but I'm as ready as I'm going to be," he replied.

"Ford, how is our cargo doing back there?" Love asked over the comms.

"Pumped and ready for action," her crew chief replied.

"Well, they'll certainly have plenty of that," she answered. "I guess we'll see who has the strongest stomachs."

Green laughed.

"You all right back there, Williams?" Love asked.

"Weapons are ready to rock," he responded. "Just stretching my arms to keep those trigger fingers ready."

"Good deal. Wouldn't want you getting carpal tunnel back there," Love teased. In truth, she knew Williams was going to be insanely busy in just a few moments.

The timer in her HUD counted down. She closed her eyes and took a deep breath, letting it out slowly.

Three, two, one.

"*Gallipoli* coming out of FTL," she announced as the ship shook. "Standby for launch."

As soon as she got the all-clear from the flight operations control deck, Lieutenant Love pulled the *Jack* out of the hangar and launched them into the most unbelievable chaos she could imagine.

Zodark Vultures had risen from the surface of Intus and were racing about, firing their lasers at whatever Republic vessels happened to be in their path. Red and blue streaks of light flashed all over the space around them. The lush surface of the green and blue planet below was hardly visible with all of the activity before her.

"Ford, Williams, hang on to your britches—it's going to be a wild ride."

She dove, ducking and weaving the entire time. Love wasn't about to make their Osprey easy prey. Then a giant beam, wider than any lightning bolt Love had ever seen, shot up from the planet's surface towards one of the Republic ships above her.

Holy hell, she thought. *That has to be the ion cannon.* It was no wonder they needed that thing taken out.

The Orion starfighters had joined the Ospreys, keeping the Zodark fighters off their trail as much as possible. Love pulled the *Jack* toward Intus as fast as she dared descend.

The quicker we get out of here, the more likely we are to survive, she realized.

Above her, Love was aware that the larger space vessels were engaged in their own melee. A Zodark cruiser was taken down by a Prim destroyer, only to have a huge gash ripped into its side by the ion cannon a moment later.

When the *Jack* pulled into the upper atmosphere of Intus, Love felt like her stomach dropped into her knees. Out of the clouds, small Zodark vessel suddenly emerged, firing lasers directly at them. She swore under her breath, then pulled the *Jack* into a series of evasive maneuvers that would have surely made anyone with any hint of motion sickness lose their last meal.

"Williams?" she yelled.

"I'm on them, LT!" he bellowed back, clearly in the middle of returning fire.

"We're sixty seconds away from jump altitude!" Love shouted over the radio. "Be ready to get the hell off my bird!"

****

Chief Brian Ford was grateful for his magnetic boots. Without them, he was quite certain he'd have been tossed into a wall like a ragdoll by now.

The Deltas they were transporting clutched their rifles with white knuckles or grabbed at any nearby handle or bar to stabilize themselves. Despite their hard-charging personas, these Special Forces soldiers were human enough to show some concern over all this laser fire.

Ford pulled aside the master sergeant in charge of the Deltas. "This is going to go fast," he explained. "I need you to make sure everyone is ready to go, because when I turn that light green, we won't be waiting around for long."

"Roger that," the man confirmed. Less than thirty seconds later, he gave Ford a final thumbs up to let him know that all systems were go.

As they neared the jump location, Ford migrated to the rear ramp of the *Jack*. The red light was still on, and they twisted and turned as they continued their descent.

Suddenly, the Osprey pulled up hard. Ford and the Deltas grabbed for something to right themselves as they tried to stabilize and fight the inertia that drove them into the floor.

When the *Jack* finished leveling out, Ford lowered the ramp and switched the jump light from red to green.

"Go! Go! Go!" he yelled.

"Let's do this!" roared the master sergeant as he led the charge, running straight out of the back with reckless abandon.

Any nerves the Deltas had been feeling apparently disappeared the moment they could actually do something other than sit around hoping not to die. The Special Forces soldiers raced out of the back of the Osprey with practiced precision, pulling their arms in tight and straightening their legs to make themselves more aerodynamic as they dove towards the surface of Intus.

That's something I don't think I'd ever have the guts to do, Ford thought. It was a realization he decided to keep to himself.

As soon as the last operator had cleared the ramp, Ford closed the back of the bird up.

"All clear!" he told Love.

"Let's get out of here!" she replied, pulling the *Jack* upward rapidly.

"Fine by me," he answered.

As they bobbed about in the most absurd patterns to avoid near-certain death, Ford thought about the Deltas who were falling from an astronomical height, using special masks to keep them sufficiently oxygenated.

"God speed," he muttered.

Williams growled. "There's so many of them!" he yelled. Ford hadn't paid much attention to his crewmate until this moment, but Williams had gone full Rambo, firing at a rate he didn't think the *Jack* was capable of.

"Hang tight," Love said over the radio. "We've got an Orion coming to assist."

Just as she finished her announcement, their Osprey shook, hard. Ford immediately went to see what the damage assessment was.

"LT, I sure hope you were right about that Orion giving us backup," he said over the radio, "because you aren't going to be able to pull your turns quite so tight until we get back to the *Gallipoli* and I can patch a few things up."

There was a moment of silence. Green was actually the one to respond. "I won't assault your ears with Love's original response," he said with a laugh, "but our friendly Orion has arrived just in time to save our hides from the brutal tongue-lashing."

Ford smiled. *Come on* Jack, he thought, willing the Osprey to safety. *Take care of me, and I'll take care of you.*

Chapter 50
Protect the Transport

RNS *Poseidon*
Orbit of Planet Intus

Lee took a breath as he prepared himself for the coming battle. He had just been given an opportunity to lead a small squadron of vessels, and he was determined not to buckle under the pressure. While he knew the fate of the battle wouldn't hinge on the calls he made, its outcome would certainly be influenced by them. There was no room for error, no passing the buck. It was now on *him* to make the tough calls.

As Lee looked at the navigational display of Gamma Task Force and the approaching Zodark cruisers, the distance between their forces continued to shrink. The time until battle was counting down. The distance now stood at a mere two hundred and ninety-six thousand kilometers—a span that would be covered all too quickly given the speeds their forces were traveling at.

I guess it's time to address the ships now under my command, Lee realized.

"Rhom, open a channel to the ships of our Gamma Task Force," he ordered.

"Aye, sir," Rhom hastily replied. "Channel's open."

Lee cleared his voice before depressing the talk button. "This is Commander Lee aboard the *Poseidon*," he began. "By now, you should have received the order from Captain Roberts, placing your ships temporarily under my command. Our task force has been directed to intercept a squadron of Zodark vessels attempting to attack our troop transports. I'm here to say we're not going to allow that to happen. As we approach optimal weapons ranges, you are cleared hot to engage. Let's show the rest of the fleet what these ships can do. Out."

Within minutes, the void ahead of them bloomed into a burst of light as Lee's small force unleashed their weapons on the enemy. Soon, dozens of magrail rounds streaked from the Republic ships. They were quickly joined by volleys of Havoc antiship missiles, their engines flaring as they accelerated toward their targets.

The Zodarks reacted rapidly, responding in kind. Their weapons joined the fray, firing volleys of plasma torpedoes toward Lee's task force. They were less maneuverable and not as quick as the Havocs, but when they hit, they caused considerable damage—they were definitely a weapon to avoid being hit with, if at all possible. As volleys of torpedoes headed toward Lee's task force, the Zodarks' formidable laser beams lanced out, their reddish hue illuminating the darkness around them as they connected against the hulls of Lee's vessels. The Republic ships responded by initiating their electronic warfare tools, which would attempt to disrupt the Zodarks' targeting sensors. Clouds of sand and water mixture exploded as well, defraying the effectiveness of the lasers.

"Sir, Zodark cruisers at bearing zero-four-seven, mark zero-one-six," announced Rhom from tactical. "I could be wrong, sir, but it looks like some of those cruisers are attempting to form a screen between us and a few of those faster moving Zodark frigates heading for our transports."

This had caught Lee by surprise. "Rhom, direct our frigates, *Dagger* and *Vigilant*, to continue pursuing and engaging those enemy frigates," he directed. "Tell the cruisers to stick with us as we go after the rest of these Zodark vessels."

Lee addressed his helmsman. "Reynolds, bring us to heading zero-four-eight, mark zero-one-nine and begin to turn the ship to port, so we can bring our full starboard side turrets to bear."

He turned back to comms. "Rhom, if you're done relaying those instructions to the others, I need you to start targeting that lead cruiser with the gun crews. Let's start pounding on them with our magrails."

"Aye, sir," both officers responded in unison.

The *Poseidon* shifted, maneuvering into position.

"Targets locked, gun crews ready," Rhom reported.

"Fire," Lee said excitedly, itching to start delivering some Republic love in the form of a three-ton slug with a one-ton high-explosive warhead.

The *Poseidon* shuddered as its main guns fired; the force of the projectiles leaving the barrels could be felt throughout the ship. As the first volley left, the fire-round cylinder rotated, the autoloader pushing the next slug into the firing chamber. As each round was fired and the cylinder rotated, the empty slot would be reloaded by another autoloader, allowing the magrails to fire round after round in quick succession. In short order, they had sent a storm of tungsten rounds hurling toward the enemy.

Lee ordered the magnification on the main viewscreen increased so they could better see the impact or misses against the lead Zodark cruiser they were targeting. He watched in awe like the others as slugs began punching holes through the cruiser's armor before exploding inside the guts of the ship. Within moments of the first slugs hitting the cruiser, the enemy vessel began making slight modifications to its trajectory, causing multiple volleys of slugs to sail harmlessly by.

"Wow, direct hit with that first volley," Sato exclaimed. "Unbelievable—that ship is hardly any showing signs of significant damage, despite the multiple hits."

"Sir, the Havocs are closing in—approaching terminal speed to impact," the sensor officer called out. "We're detecting some unusual power fluctuations in the Zodark formation," he added. "It looks like they might be activating some sort of point-defense systems of their own and deploying countermeasures to try to spoof the missiles before impact."

"Huh, that's interesting," said Lee. "EWO, what's the status on our jamming attempts?"

"Right now, ineffective, sir," replied Lee's electronic warfare officer, Lieutenant Jakub Witkowski. "Our two forces have closed the gap too much between us. Their sensors are able to burn through our jamming at these closer ranges."

Crap, Lee thought to himself as he considered what to do next.

"Witkowski, if they're burning through our jamming, see if you can boost our jammers by redirecting power from our secondary systems and non-essential systems. If we can concentrate more energy on a narrower band of frequencies, we might get lucky and throw their targeting sensors off a little longer."

"Ah, yeah. That's a good idea, sir. I'll start doing that now."

"Good, Witkowski, and keep at it," Lee replied. "Even if we don't break through immediately and disrupt the targeting sensors against this particular cruiser, we might be able to scramble their ability to communicate and coordinate their actions with the rest of their force," Lee explained.

He tapped his comm button, connecting him to engineering. "Mac, I need more power. We need to boost our jamming signals as much as possible right now. We need to blind these Zodarks' targeting sensors or at least disrupt their comms and navigation sensors."

"Roger that. Consider it done," MacGregor replied. Lee heard him shout orders to his people before he returned to his conversation with Lee. "You should have the extra power in few seconds, sir."

"Ah, what the hell?" exclaimed Rhom. "That grouping of four cruisers we've been barreling toward just separated into four more. I don't know how we missed it, but it looks like they were hugging each other from aft to forward, making it appear like a single ship."

"Wait, you're saying this group of four cruisers is now eight?" Lee felt his pulse quicken at the sudden turn of events.

"Affirmative, sir" Rhom confirmed.

Lee cursed at not seeing through their trickery sooner. They were now in a real bind and totally outmatched in firepower. He needed to act quickly if he was going to save his force. He turned to his XO. "Sato, open a channel to Captain Roberts. We have to inform him of the situation."

"Yes, sir. Channels open."

Lee took a breath before he spoke into the comm. "*Poseidon* to *Aussie*. The enemy force of four cruisers at grid zero-four-six-zero-one-two is now eight cruisers," he explained. "It appears they pulled some trickery on us and spoofed our sensors by hugging their ships tightly together until they got closer to us. We're heavily out gunned, sir. If there is any way possible to have additional ships sent our way, we could really use them right now."

Captain Roberts's gruff voice came back seconds later. "They spoofed us, eh?" he said. "Well, we were bound to experience it ourselves at some point. Give me a moment to contact McKee and see what additional ships she can send. While I'm doing that, I'll direct *Thunder* and *Oceanus* to you. Stand by."

Roberts had accepted the information a lot better than Lee thought he would have. He turned to Sato. "Roberts is sending the *Thunder* and *Oceanus* to us immediately while he contacts McKee about the change in the situation," he reiterated.

"Well, that's good. At least we have another pair of heavy cruisers headed our way," Sato replied, sounding a bit more optimistic than Lee felt.

Minutes ticked by as Lee waited for Roberts to give him an update. In the meantime, his ship and the others with him continued to engage the enemy force closing in on them.

"*Aussie, Poseidon*. The cruisers I'm sending your way should be at your position in eight mikes. McKee acknowledged the change in the situation and is dispatching the battleships RNS *Idaho* and *Stonewall* to your position. These are *Ryan*-class ships. They're going to be a bit slower in getting to you. Their ETA is four-four mikes. You're going to have to figure out how to outmaneuver these guys to keep 'em at arm's length until additional help can arrive. How copy?"

Damn, eight and forty-four minutes till help arrives, Lee thought to himself. That could be both an eternity and lightning quick in space warfare.

"*Poseidon, Aussie*. Solid copy. Thank you for the additional support," replied Lee. "We'll figure it out, sir. *Poseidon* out."

As the realization set in that they'd have to make do against a superior force until additional help arrived, another volley of magrail slugs struck the starboard side of the lead Zodark cruiser. Lee watched the penetrators pierce into the ship along multiple points until an enormous flash erupted, temporarily whiting out their cameras. When they readjusted moments later, Lee was as shocked as the others to see one of the slugs must have detonated near its engineering section—exploding its reactor core. The blast was so powerful, it broke the ship apart, sending shattered sections of the enemy ship in multiple directions.

The bridge crew cheered excitedly at scoring their first kill. Lee let them celebrate for a moment before reminding them the battle was far from over. "We aren't out of danger yet," he reiterated.

"Rhom, excellent shooting by your gun crews," Lee praised. He directed, "Shift fire to the next cruiser in line," he directed. "We still have seven to go."

"Reynolds, I need you to bring us to heading zero-five-four, mark zero-two-seven. Let's keep them off-balance and buy ourselves more time until the calvary arrives."

As the battle continued to rage around them, Lee was beginning to feel a bit more confident about their situation. The other cruisers on their way were now two minutes out. For now, his ships were holding their own as they continued to maneuver in various ways to keep the Zodark vessels from getting too close, negating the brunt of the enemy's electronic warfare jamming against their targeting sensors.

While Lee's cruisers were heavily engaged, his pair of frigates had managed to intercept the Zodark frigates—*before* they could slice their way through the formation of troop transports still heading toward Intus. Reynolds's idea of trying to get the Zodarks to react and engage their frigates and not the transports appeared to have paid off. A trio of Primord cruisers and a single battleship had moved into a blocking position, protecting the convoy. The transports were safe for now, but they still had seven more cruisers to deal with.

The Zodarks continued to try and close the distance between them and Lee's ships. The *Poseidon* executed another maneuver to try and evade. As they did, Lee spotted a possible gap in the Zodark battleline that he might be able to exploit.

He turned to his XO. "Sato, get me the *Hydra*. I've got an idea that might help us."

Moments later, the face of Commander Walsh appeared on a side screen. "*Hydra, Poseidon.* What can we do for you?"

"Commander, I'm seeing a potential weak spot in the enemy lines," Lee began to explain. "If you look at the last ship in the Zodark battleline, it appears to have fallen further away from the rest of them. What I'd like you to do is try to thread the needle between them and the other ships, allowing you to bring to bear both sides of your weapons at the same time to hammer two of those ships. You think you can handle that?"

Walsh nodded slowly. "Yeah, we can handle that. It's going to place us in knife range, but if you guys are able to keep up the jamming and continue pounding them from afar, we can probably score some solid hits, maybe knock another cruiser or two out of the fight."

"Good, we'll keep the pressure up on our end," Lee replied. "Good luck, and we'll see you on the other side." Then he ended the call.

Moments later, the *Hydra* peeled off from the main group, its engines burning bright blue as it accelerated toward the gap in the Zodark line. As the *Hydra* closed in, Lee stared at the tactical display, watching the subtle shifts in the enemy formation as they began to react to the *Hydra*'s new heading.

Is it possible the Zodarks planned this gap? he wondered. *Did I just send* Hydra *into a trap?*

Suddenly, the Zodark cruisers seemed to anticipate Lee's changing strategy. They adjusted their battleline and shifted their fire to the approaching Republic vessel.

The *Hydra* banked slowly, releasing countermeasures to avoid the first salvo of Zodark fire, while Lee's ships continued to try and jam their targeting sensors. In minutes, the gap in the enemy line began to close and transformed into a pincer move that would bring to bear the maximum amount of laser turrets on the *Hydra*. As the enemy maneuvered to bracket the *Hydra,* it exposed the starboard side of the vessel closest to the *Poseidon*. Seeing an opportunity to strike a quick blow and aid one of his ships, Lee ordered his ship to engage.

"Hammer it! Fire everything we've got!" Lee raged excitedly.

The *Poseidon*'s weapon systems roared as they fired a broadside of weapons against the exposed cruiser. Volley after volley of slugs sailed toward it like a surprise meteor storm. They also fired a dozen Havoc missiles, hoping to add to the damage they were about to deliver.

In less than a couple of minutes, the hail of slugs tore into the enemy Zodark cruiser, lighting it up. As the third volley hammered the ship, four of the twelve Havocs slipped through the enemy's point defense—their explosive charges riddling the already heavily damaged ship. By the time the fourth volley of slugs ripped into the cruiser, a cascade of secondary explosions rippled across the ship, until its reactor exploded in a brilliant flash that tore the vessel apart.

Despite the destruction of another cruiser, the Zodark vessels maintained their firing on the *Hydra*, energy beams lashing out and scoring its armor as it approached their battleline.

While Lee's two other cruisers were filling the battlespace with their own volleys of magrail slugs and Havoc antiship missiles, a lucky round shot from the *Argo* managed to score a critical hit to one of the cruisers. Lee wasn't sure exactly *what* it hit, but whatever it was, it caused an avalanche of explosions across the aft section of the ship. While the attack didn't destroy the enemy ship, it appeared to have knocked out their propulsion. The Zodark cruiser was now adrift, and its weapons fell silent.

Three down, five to go...

"Sato, is it me, or does it seem like those remaining ships are continuing to ignore us while they keep their fire trained on the *Hydra?*" Lee asked. He grew more and more concerned.

"No, it's not you, sir. They seem pretty intent on hammering the *Hydra*. I'm not really sure what more we can do to change that right now."

Lee watched in horror as the *Hydra* crossed the battleline, placing them dangerously close to the enemy ships. The *Poseidon*'s sensors were barely able to track the return fire from the *Hydra* before their engines went offline and they appeared to have lost power. Lee wasn't sure what the status of the ship was, but one thing clear—the *Hydra* was out of action. The remaining five Zodark cruisers now shifted their fire at the *Poseidon.*

Turning to his comms officer, Lee said, "Rodriguez, see if you can hail the *Hydra.* God only knows if anyone is still alive, but we have to find out."

"Already ahead of you, boss. I've been trying to raise them on the backup comms system that we use in situations like this. I don't know what to say right now other than I'm not receiving a reply to any of my hails."

"Damn it. Keep trying. Make sure to tag their location, speed, and direction they're drifting so a rescue ship can try to board them once it's safe to do so," Lee directed Rodriguez. It was about the only thing left he could do for right now.

Lee shook his head as he glared at the tactical display. He had made a fatal decision. Had he ordered them on a suicide mission? Or had he made the right call, and the enemy just got lucky? He pushed the thoughts out of his mind and returned his focus to the fight still at hand.

Lee directed Rodriguez to open a channel to the two cruisers he had and the *Thunder* and *Oceanus*, which had just arrived. "All ships, this is *Poseidon*," he began. "We can't do anything to help the *Hydra* right now, and we don't know if anyone is still alive after the pounding they took. But we still have five enemy cruisers left to finish off. We need to focus our efforts on taking them out. To that affect, I want everyone to concentrate your fire on the cruisers designated Zulu-Two and Zulu-Three. Let's make them pay for the *Hydra*."

The four remaining ships of his temporary command responded swiftly. Volleys of magrail slugs and Havoc missiles raced across the expanse toward the pair of cruisers he'd identified. As the minutes to impact ticked by, Lee watched as the enemy battleline shifted their positions once more. The Zodarks evaded the brunt of the storm headed their way, and realigned their ships to bring more of their laser batteries against the *Poseidon.*

Lee grimaced as the first three volleys of slugs passed harmlessly by their intended targets. However, more than half of the fourth volley scored multiple hits. Only a pair of the thirty Havocs they fired managed to get past their point defense weapons and plowed into one of the vessels. While they didn't appear to have landed any kill shots or crippling hits, they did succeed in silencing multiple laser turrets, which cut down on the intensity of fire being aimed at them.

As Lee glanced at the clock to see how long until the pair of battleships would arrive, he saw the time had whittled down to less than a few minutes. *Yeah, we can survive a bit longer,* he thought hopefully.

The *Poseidon* shook violently from multiple laser strikes. The enemy ships were rapidly closing in. While this gave Lee's ships a better chance of scoring some devastating hits, it also placed them in better range of the Zodarks' hard-hitting plasma torpedoes, which they now appeared to be flooding the battlespace with.

"We have multiple torpedoes inbound. Interceptors are engaging, PDGs are standing by!" Rhom hastily announced.

As the count of torpedoes directed at them rose above fourteen, Lee hoped like hell the interceptors could thin them out before they came into the effective range of their PDGs. While he couldn't feel the shudder of interceptors being fired from their VLS pods like he could when the magrails fired, Lee could see the growing number of interceptors being directed at the incoming threats. He cursed under his breath as multiple interceptors missed their marks, sailing harmlessly past their intended targets. It was now in the hands of the second and third wave of interceptors to take out or at least reduce their numbers before the PDGs would have to engage.

Only three of the interceptors hit. Now they were down to the third and final wave before it would fall to their PDGs to save them. *Come on, eleven more to go.* He silently willed the remaining interceptors to hit. Five more of the torpedoes were taken down. That left six remaining for the four of their ships' point-defense guns to deal with.

"Here they come," Rhom announced. "PDGs engaging! Oh, crap—brace for impact!"

Chapter 51
Mother of all Battles

RNS *Poseidon*
Above Planet Intus

Lee gripped the sides of his chair as the ship was rocked by a torpedo hit. Alarms sounded and the power to the bridge momentarily flickered. He glanced at the damage control board and saw they had taken a hit to starboard near the forward section of the ship. His turbo laser turrets two, four, and six showed red, and so did his magrail turret two. He'd just lost half of his offensive weapons along his starboard from a single hit.

"Damage report! How bad are those turrets? Is it possible we can get them back in action?" Lee shouted to be heard over the klaxons still blaring. "And turn that damned alarm off. I can't hear myself think."

The bridge fell silent as the alarm turned off.

Sato took over relaying information to him. "Sir, reports are still coming in. I just did a visual check from an exterior camera—it's not good."

Lee bunched his eyebrows. "What does that mean, XO? Give me details. How bad is it?"

"Sir, the torpedo hit deck nine, section one bravo, upper gun deck," Sato began. "It tore a gash into the hull, venting part of the deck and sucking gun crews out of the breach. The bulkheads in sections one alpha and two alpha appear to be holding. Turret two on deck seven, lower gun deck lost power. That torpedo must have severed a main powerline for the magrails. As to time to repair and whether we can return those guns to action—engineering will give us a better read on that."

Damn it! The whole crew got sucked out of the ship. Lee tried to remain calm and think. The ship shook hard again from another laser hit. They were still in the thick of the battle, and he had to get back to fighting the ship if they were going to make it out of this alive.

"Sato, coordinate with engineering to get the power restored to the guns ASAP," instructed Lee before pivoting to Reynolds. "Helm, half our starboard guns are offline, and obviously, we need guns to fight. I want you to angle us up thirty degrees as you turn the ship starboard toward the enemy battleline. We are going to pass overtop of them before realigning our portside guns on them."

"Whoa, that's going to take us dangerously close to them as we cross over, showing our belly," Sato interjected with concern.

"I get it, but what choice do we have if half our guns are offline?" Lee countered. "We have to reposition the ship to the side that has operational guns." He paused. "I don't know if you remember from our tour of the *Poseidon* at the shipyard when we took possession of her—the shipbuilders made a point of highlighting the reinforced hull and added armor along the belly of the ship. They did this to give us the ability to support a ground force with more accurate strikes from low orbit or even the upper atmosphere. If we're going to absorb more hits, I'd rather have it against our strongest section of the ship."

Sato nodded slowly. "OK, if this is the plan, I recommend we make full use of the situation and fire our remaining Havocs from the belly VLS pods one and two. At that close range, they'll be hard-pressed to take 'em out before they slam into the top of their ship."

Lee smiled at the possibility of nailing the cruiser that had just cost him a pair of gun crews and mauled his ship. "I like it. How many Havocs do we have left?"

Sato looked at her station before responding, "Of the hundred and sixty-eight we started with, we've got sixty-two left—almost all of them in the lower VLS pods."

"Outstanding! Then that's exactly what we're going to do. Make sure the lower PDGs are ready to intercept any torpedoes they might launch at us and have our remaining interceptors ready to fire," Lee ordered. "We're about to enter a knife fight, and time will be of the essence."

"Sir, I'm receiving a damage report from the *Duncan*. They took two torpedo hits from that last volley," Rodriguez cut in. "One hit deck three, section four alpha, and the other hit deck five, also section four alpha—propulsion. The reactors are stable, but they've lost the starboard side engine. It's gutted, non-repairable. They said they're losing speed and won't be able to stay in formation with us."

Lee was about to ask a follow-up question when she further added, "Sir, I'm receiving a message from the *Idaho*. Captain Mensah is requesting to speak with you."

About time the calvary got here, he thought.

"Put him through to my station."

A second later, the image of Captain Mensah appeared on his screen. "Commander Lee, *Idaho* and *Stonewall* are on station. We can see you guys are in a tough fight with multiple ships heavily damaged. How can we best help you?"

"Captain, you have no idea how good it is to see you right now," Lee expressed. "I've lost half my guns on the starboard side. We're attempting to cross overtop of the Zodark battleline so we can realign ourselves to use our portside guns. If you're able to position yourself on the portside of their line with us and have the *Stonewall* support my other ships *Argo, Thunder,* and *Oceanus*, we can probably create a hell of crossfire between our two lines, with them in the middle."

Mensah looked off screen for a moment before returning to Lee. "I was about to ask you what the hell you're doing charging their line, but it makes sense now. We can see your other cruisers are adjusting their position to angle their guns downward along with yours, so you guys don't end up shooting each other if a barrage misses its mark. Our ships aren't quite as quick as yours, but if you can maybe slow your pace down, we should be able to catch up and join your battle."

"Consider it done, sir," replied Lee. "We took out three of their cruisers so far, but we have five to go. I think this plan is going to work, and we're going to nail a few more now that you're here."

Mensah nodded approvingly before he ended the call. For now, all Lee could do was continue to rely on the half of his weapons that still worked, until they finished crossing the enemy battleline. As his squadron continued to pound the enemy, Lee's ship continued to close the gap between their lines. It wasn't long before the lead vessels must have figured out what he was doing, and began to turn to starboard. Within minutes, the others began to follow suit, trying to keep him pinned to using the weapons of his battered side.

Aw, damn it! This isn't going to work, he realized. He cursed under his breath. *We're going to make it work!*

"Reynolds, they're on to our plan and trying to negate it, but we have momentum and speed on our side. I want you to turn ship harder to starboard and push the engines to max power. We're going to try to counter their move," Lee order.

While the *Poseidon* began to turn harder, Rodriguez updated the other ships to what they were doing. Lee directed them to match the

Zodark moves and continue to hammer their lines. As Lee continued to watch the battlespace between them close, the intensity of enemy fire directed at his ship increased dramatically. Then the rear vessel in the Zodark lines did something totally unexpected—it began to break off from their line and turned hard to port, angling their cruiser to deliver a near head-on drive-by at dangerously close range.

Rhom saw the change to the situation immediately and shifted the focus of his gun crews to target the vessel closing in on them. Lee was beginning to sweat profusely as the vessel converged on them. Then he got a call that changed the equation yet again.

"Bridge, Engineer, I've got some good news to report," Mac exclaimed. "We just finished rerouting a power line to turret two on deck seven. I can't guarantee how well it'll hold up if we take another hard hit, but for right now, you should have another pair of magrails to use."

Lee could practically cry in relief at the news. "Mac, you may have just saved our asses," he replied. "We're in a tight spot up here, and we're likely to take a few more hits, but this is huge. We needed that extra firepower right now."

"That's good to hear, Skipper. We're still working on trying to patch the hole so we can get the other two turbo lasers operational again. I'll keep you apprised of our progress. Engineering out." Mac disconnected the call as the shouting and alarms in his background intensified.

"Rhom, get turret two back in the fight," Lee directed as he saw the approaching cruiser closing in on them. "Oh, and Rhom—let's hit this guy with half of our Havocs. We might get lucky and score a critical hit."

"On it, boss! Turret two engaging. Locking target for Havocs one through thirty-one—missiles firing," Rhom confirmed.

Lee watched the volley of magrails fire at near-pointblank range. The barrage of six slugs was quickly followed by six more. The captain of the Zodark ship apparently saw the error of his way, getting too close to a Republic warship—the cruiser tried to turn to evade, but it was too late. The spread of penetrating slugs scored direct hits along the centerline of the top of the ship. As the warheads began to explode inside the vessel, the second volley crashed into the cruiser near the aft section of the ship. A whole series of explosions rippled across the enemy cruiser just as the Havocs began to arrive.

Within seconds of their impact, the ship exploded, ripping it apart in a giant blast. The crew cheered wildly with excitement. They had scored another ship kill, and Lee decided to let them have a moment of jubilee before he reminded them that they had four more to go. By now, they were beginning to close the gap, and the *Poseidon* neared the moment when it would pass over top of the lead enemy ship.

As Rhom was reorientating the guns, the four remaining Zodark cruisers fired a volley of plasma torpedoes at them and snapped quick shots off with their lasers. The *Poseidon* shook violently from the laser hits. Alarms blared and sections of the ship blinked yellow on Lee's display.

"Fire the interceptors and go active with the PDGs *now*!" Sato shouted over the noise and chaos.

Lee watched the tracks of the torpedoes bearing down on them and knew they were in trouble. Unlike previous torpedo attacks, the range to impact from when they were fired was too short to get off more than a single volley of interceptors.

Just as he was about to give up hope, Lee had a sudden realization. *Wait, those things have to convert to plasma before they're dangerous…yeah, it just might work.*

"Helm, turn us into the torpedoes *now*!" Lee ordered forcefully.

Reynolds, to his credit, didn't hesitate for a second and turned the ship head-on into the wave of torpedoes. Of the sixteen heading for them, the interceptors knocked five of them out before the point defense guns went active. The entire battlespace around them came alive with brilliant streams of red tracer fire. A few torpedoes exploded as they flew into the hail of gunfire.

"Brace for impact!" shouted Rhom as Lee gripped the armrest of his chair.

The bridge shook as the first three plasma torpedoes impacted—there was a sickening, deep thud that echoed up from the ship's belly, like a hammer striking bone. Then came the fourth and fifth—these had converted into flaming plasma sticks of death as they drove through the deck. Bulkheads groaned. Lights flickered. Acrid smoke flooded the air, thick with the stench of scorched metal and burning insulation.

Alarms screamed. Sparks rained from overhead panels. On the tactical board, deck one in sections two and three lit up in a wash of red. Then, in section four, decks two and three, propulsion flashed in bright crimson. Lee's gut sank. The engines were gone. They were still at near-maximum velocity, but now they were tumbling forward without control, unable to steer or slow—like a rudderless ship.

"Firing Havocs thirty-two through sixty-two!" Rhom roared above the chaos.

Lee gripped the armrest, knuckles white, eyes locked on the forward monitor. A burst of static obscured the image—then cleared just in time to catch the magrail volley. Slugs screamed past the enemy's bow—so close, but they missed. The second wave hit. Six of the magrails smashed into the Zodark cruiser's spine. The explosion was immediate. Fire bloomed across the enemy ship's centerline, like a string of solar flares. Then came the Havocs—dozens—raining down like an exploding hailstorm across the top of the ship—bursting with chain-linked detonations that shredded armor and tore into the structure.

A flash of white consumed the screen. Cameras scrambled. Then…clarity.

The enemy ship was gone—torn in half, its forward section spinning wildly while the aft tumbled away, bleeding gas and molten debris. Lee's breath caught in his throat at the thought of victory.

Then, at this zenith of glory, someone yelled, "Incoming—brace for impact!"

The lasers hit from point-blank range before anyone could react—three beams tearing into the *Poseidon*'s starboard side. One sliced through the superstructure like a scalpel, while another punched through to the bridge's bulkhead. Steel screamed and popped from the heat. The wall to the left of Lee glowed orange before violently exploding inward—showering the crew with molten shrapnel and a rush of superheated gas.

Jagged shards tore through his left side. The pain hit like a freight train.

Oh my God, it hurts!

That was the last thought Ripley Lee had before everything went black.

Year 2096
RNS *Gallipoli*
Intus Orbit

Naomi Love sat in her Osprey's cockpit. She looked at the picture of Jack on the dashboard. "Keep us safe," she whispered.

Green occupied the copilot seat. "That last troop drop did a number on the starboard thruster."

"How bad?" Love asked.

"Nothing the deck gang couldn't handle. Patched it up good as new."

"Deck gang?" The term brought a faint smile to Love's lips. The mechanics, known as aviation support equipment technicians, were the unsung heroes keeping their birds in the air.

At the rear of the Osprey, Ford and Williams settled into their jump seats. Ford checked the magrail systems. "Magrails are primed and ready," he called forward.

Williams adjusted his helmet, scanning the readouts. "Ammo reserves are full. We're good to go."

"Roger that," Love replied.

A flick of her wrist brought up the cabin monitor. Regular Republic Army soldiers filed in, each touching the plaque on the wall. "Vivere Pugnare Alium Diem," she murmured, watching as they took their seats.

"Second drop today," Green noted, staring at the interface attached to the dash.

Love raised her helmet's visor and rubbed the tired out of her eyes. "Yeah. Let's make it count."

The journey to Intus had been grueling. Two months with the Intus Task Force, led by Captain Fran McKee aboard the RNS *George Washington*. Twenty-three hours ago, they'd entered this system. Almost a full day of relentless combat had left both fleets battered and scarred.

The initial assault had been comprised of a HALO drop—High Altitude Low Opening. After the Ospreys had reached the upper extremes of the atmosphere, the Deltas, wearing their specially configured exoskeleton combat suits, began their high-stakes missions by jumping from the Ospreys. As they approached the surface, their suits would deploy a parachute to slow them down before landing, and then they'd immediately jump into whatever fight they found themselves in. It was the only way to deploy a combat force to the surface until the planetary defensive weapons could be taken offline and additional forces brought to the surface.

Hours into the fight, they had largely succeeded in taking down several of the enemy ion cannons, creating a large enough gap in the enemy defenses to allow for more follow-on forces to reach the surface. Now they were bringing in the regular troops—landing at drop zones instead of performing aerial insertions.

"All systems go, Green?"

"Full operational readiness, Lieutenant."

In the back, Ford gave a thumbs-up on the screen. "All subsystems operating within parameters."

Williams chimed in, "Turrets calibrated and synced. We're set."

The comms crackled to life. "Wolfpack Squadron, this is Wolfpack Actual, call sign Hawkeye. Sound off for preflight check."

Love listened as Wolfpack Two responded, then keyed her mic. "Wolfpack Three, all systems go. Troops secured."

Hawkeye's tone burst through a second time. "Roger that, Wolfpack. All birds reporting ready. Be advised, we're flying into an active combat zone. Maintain tight formation and be prepared for evasive maneuvers. We'll have Orion escorts."

"Copy that, Lead," Love said.

The radio buzzed with chatter as Hawkeye requested clearance. Love waited as the tower responded. This was it—time to go.

"Wolfpack elements, on my mark, engage thrusters and follow in formation. Three, two, one… mark."

With a nod, Love eased the Osprey off *Gallipoli*'s deck. The moment she and the rest of the troop transports cleared the bay and exited into the void, combat erupted around them. Love was hoping for a smoother ride the second time around, but it looked like they would have no such luck.

Republic ships clashed with Zodark vessels, kinetic and energy weapons blasting through the expanse. Explosions sprouted like burning wildflowers, silent in the vacuum but no less lethal.

"Tally ho, Wolfpack." Hawkeye's pitch was tense. "We've got Republic and Zodark ships exchanging fire at two o'clock. Stay low and fast. Our fighter escort will try to keep them Vultures off us, but be ready for anything."

Love scanned for threats. "Green, keep an eye on our six. This is going to get hairy."

As if on cue, a stray energy blast rocked the formation. Love wrestled with the controls, keeping the Osprey steady as they plunged into the heart of the battle. She wove through the melee, following her Wolfpack lead.

An Orion fighter screamed past, locked in a dogfight with a Zodark Vulture. The two craft spiraled away, spitting weapons fire.

"Incoming!" Green warned.

Love juked hard. The Osprey shuddered as debris from a nearby eruption peppered its hull. "Damage report!"

In the back, Ford's voice came over the intercom. "No damage showing as of yet."

"Damn, we got lucky," Love acknowledged.

Two Orion starfighters swooped in, taking up flanking positions on either side of Love's craft.

"Wolfpack Three, this is Bear. We're your escort to the planet's atmosphere. Ninja and I are on your tail."

"Roger that, Bear," Love said. "Appreciate the company."

"Be advised," Bear replied. "No enemy Vultures detected planetside, but we're picking up active anti-aircraft fire intensifying and expanding rapidly. Looks like the Zodarks are ramping up their ground defenses. Proceed with extreme caution."

"Understood, Bear." Love scanned the turbulent space around them. "What's the SITREP on our exfil?"

"We'll get you to the upper atmosphere, but after that, you're flying solo. Triple-A is too hot for us to push further."

"Acknowledged. We'll take it from here once we hit atmo. Again, thanks for the escort, gentlemen."

Weapons fire crisscrossed their path as they rolled, the two Orions providing cover when needed. In three short minutes, they approached the planet's outer atmosphere.

Bear came through the comms once more. "Wolfpack Three, this is your stop. Good luck down there."

"Roger that, Bear. Ninja. Wolfpack Three out," Love said, her ship along with the other Ospreys in Wolfpack Squadron breaking away from the escorts and diving toward Intus below. The planet's atmosphere reached up to embrace them. Love's Osprey bucked, rattling her teeth. Flames licked at the viewports.

"Status on ground defenses?" Love called out, keeping the craft steady.

Green read the data on his console. "Ion cannons off-line. Deltas did their job. We've got scattered ground-to-air emplacements, but nothing we can't handle."

Love appreciated Green's calm demeanor. "Engine status?"

"Holding steady. That patch job's working."

They broke through the cloud cover, and Love's breath caught. The lush forests she remembered from her last trip were now scarred with battle. Smoke rose in thick columns, the ground littered with the aftermath of conflict.

"Two klicks to drop zone," Green said.

Love guided the Osprey lower. Craters and explosions dotted the landscape, some worryingly close. The craft shuddered as a nearby blast sent a shock wave through the air.

"Talk to me, Green."

"Starboard engine's running hot. Nothing critical yet, but keep an eye on it."

Anti-aircraft fire was minimal. Love's eyes narrowed. "This is too easy. Why is this so easy?"

They descended farther, the jungle canopy closing in fast.

In the back, Ford studied the tactical holo. "Lieutenant, looks like they're concentrating their fire at grid reference Lima-Echo-Three-Seven."

Love pressed her comm unit. "Wolfpack Lead, this is Three. We're seeing minimal Triple-A at our approach vector. Possible concentration of enemy fire at Lima-Echo-Three-Seven. Over."

"Roger that, Three. All units be advised, possible trap at the primary LZ. Shifting to alternate drop point at coordinates Tango-Whiskey-Five-Two. Acknowledge."

A chorus of acknowledgments came through as the squadron adjusted their flight paths.

"Three copies. Adjusting course now," Love said, banking the Osprey.

"LT," Williams said. "I've got movement in the canopy at our two o'clock, range six hundred and fifty meters."

"Wolfpack, this is Six," another pilot cut in. "Confirming visual on ground movement. Possible infantry or automated defenses."

"All units, maintain current altitude," Hawkeye ordered. "Prepare for hot drop. Troops, stand by for green light. T-minus ninety seconds to LZ."

"All right, team," Love said. "This is where it gets interesting. Ford, Williams, ready the guns. Green, eyes sharp on the instruments."

The jungle rushed up to meet them as the Ospreys lowered toward the new landing zone—a large glade full of vibrant grasses and surrounded by woodlands. Love eased back on the throttle. Her troop transport's descent slowed, and she felt the familiar tension coiling in her gut. This was always the most vulnerable moment.

"Ramp down in three… two… one…"

The rear of the Osprey yawned open. Love heard the soldiers in the cargo compartment stirring. On her monitor, she watched them rise, weapons at the ready. When the Osprey touched down with a slight bump, Ford shouted, "Go, go, go!"

On Love's screen, the troops poured out of the transport, fanning out to secure the immediate area.

"Last one clear!" Ford reported from the back.

"Roger." She lifted the craft, hovering just above the ground.

"Hostiles incoming!" Williams shouted. "Eleven o'clock!"

The camera zoomed in, revealing Zodark soldiers charging across the battlefield. Standing over three meters tall, these aliens sported three eyes and four powerful arms. They wielded blaster rifles and swords, their massive forms kicking up dirt as they rushed toward Love's Osprey with earth-shaking strides, closing in fast.

Love's jaw clenched as she swiveled the Osprey, bringing its arsenal of weapons to bear on the approaching horde. "Engaging chin gun." The blaster came to life, spitting bolts at the advancing enemy.

In the back, Ford manned the starboard magrail gun. "Targets acquired. Engaging!"

Williams took the port side. "I've got multiple hostiles at zero-four-four degrees. Firing!"

The rotary five-barrel magrails roared, projectiles tearing through the air and into Zodark ranks. The battlefield was a maelstrom of weapon fire, flames, and smoke. An RA soldier scaled a nearby tree, settling into a sniper's perch. In quick succession, Zodarks crumpled to the ground.

"Ford, Williams, how's our ammo?" Love asked, unleashing another barrage from the front turret.

"Running low," Ford replied. "Maybe enough for a few more bursts."

"Fuel's not looking great either," Green added. "We need to bug out soon."

Love pressed her lips into a thin line. "Affirmative. We're going for quality over quantity now. Time to make every round matter."

She brought the Osprey around, lining up a final run on a cluster of Zodarks attempting to flank the RA soldiers' position. The magrails burst out rounds one last time, cutting down the alien soldiers in a hail of projectiles.

"That's it," Ford said. "We're dry."

"Alpha Six," Love said, "this is Wolfpack Three. All deployed, LZ secure. Ready to RTB."

"Copy that, Wolfpack Three. RAs are groundside and moving out."

"Affirmative, Alpha Six. Show them what Big Army can do." Love switched channels. "Wolfpack Three to *Gallipoli* Control. Mission complete, returning to ship for reload and refuel."

"Roger, Wolfpack Three. Docking bay four is prepped for your arrival. Tech crew standing by."

"Copy, *Gallipoli* Control. Beginning ascent. ETA to docking, seventeen minutes." Love patched into her ship's comm. "All right, let's make this turnaround count. We've got more soldiers to deploy."

Love's Osprey rose fast, climbing away from the battlefield. She allowed herself a moment of relief as they gained altitude.

Without warning, the viewscreen filled with a mass of black shapes. Love's eyes widened. "What the—"

It was a flock of creatures, their wingspans enormous, bodies thick and black, with long, sinuous necks ending in beaks resembling serrated blades.

"Evasive maneuvers!" Love said.

The flock slammed into the Osprey with incredible force. Alarms blared as the craft trembled. Love fought the controls, struggling to keep them airborne as warning lights flashed across her console.

"Status?" she asked.

"Port engine's damaged," Green said. "We're losing altitude!"

"We're going to lose the engine. You need to find us a place to land, so I can figure out what needs fixing to restart the engine!" Ford shouted above the sounds of alarms blaring.

Love gritted her teeth, knuckles white on the control yoke. "Hang on!"

The Osprey plummeted, smoke trailing from its damaged engine. Love's world narrowed to her instruments and the rapidly approaching ground. She managed to find a spot with minimal trees as they rapidly approached the ground.

"Brace for impact!" Love yelled.

They hit the ground with a crunch. Love muscled the steering, fighting to keep the Osprey upright as they plowed through the underbrush. Dirt kicked up everywhere.

"Come on, come on," she urged, willing the craft to stay together. With a final heave, the Osprey skidded to a stop.

For an instant, all was silent save for the hiss of escaping steam. Love stirred, shaking her head to clear it.

"Everyone OK?" she called out.

"Been better," Ford groaned. "But I'm in one piece."

"Same here," Williams said. "A few bruises, nothing major."

"Green?" Love glanced at her copilot.

He nodded, rubbing a welt on his forearm. "I'll live."

"We need to get her back in the air. Now."

I can't believe I did this! Love thought. *We need to get out of here, quick-like.*

She pushed the ignition. Nothing happened. After another try, still nothing.

"Running diagnostics on my handheld," Ford informed. "It's the starboard repulsor. The impact knocked it out of alignment, or worse. We're not going anywhere until it's fixed."

Love swore under her breath. In the distance, the sounds of battle drew closer. "All right, let's move. Green, stay with the ship and monitor comms. Ford, Williams, you're with me. We need to patch her up before those Zodarks find us."

They rushed to the rear of the craft. Love slammed her fist on the ramp release. As it lowered, she grabbed a rifle from the weapons rack, tossing another to Ford. Williams was already strapping on his sidearm.

"Green, get the engines going as soon as they are ready, and watch the sensors for activity," Love ordered.

"Roger that, LT," Green replied.

Love stepped onto the jungle floor while Ford hefted the emergency repair kit, scanning the damaged repulsor.

"Let's make this quick," Love said, setting a perimeter with motion sensors.

Williams took position, rifle at the ready. "Lieutenant, I've got movement on the eastern flank."

Love's heart pounded. "Ford, how long?"

He pried open an access panel. "Couple of minutes, if we're lucky."

The rustling grew louder as something approached the clearing from the edge of the trees nearby.

"Multiple signatures incoming!" Green's voice crackled over the comms. "At least a dozen, closing fast!"

A towering figure burst into the clearing, its twisted features illuminated by the dappled sunlight. It stood like a blue giant with its four muscular arms, two clutching blasters, the other two gripping wicked looking swords. The Zodark's mouth stretched open, revealing jagged fangs as it let out a guttural roar.

Love squeezed the trigger

Chapter 53
Hold Them Off

Year 2096
Jack
Intus

Love's rifle bucked against her shoulder as she unloaded on the Zodark soldier. The giant alien's chest erupted in a spray of dark blood. Its shriek was cut short as it toppled backward, blades clattering across the forest floor.

From her periphery, another Zodark lunged out of the dense foliage. Before Love could react, a burst of gunfire tore through the alien's side. Just behind her, Petty Officer Williams's rifle was trained on the falling creature.

"Got your back, Lieutenant," Williams said.

"Appreciate it," Love replied.

Her heart pounded a bit too hard. *This was a bad idea*, she thought. With the Osprey's weapons systems out of ammo, they had no choice. Keeping Ford covered while he made repairs was their best shot at getting off this rock alive.

Another Zodark came through the undergrowth, its blaster raised. Love fired a burst. The alien's weapon shattered in a shower of sparks. Weaponless, it charged forward, its four arms flexing.

Love's next shots punched into its chest. She sent more bolts, and more. *Take that, you prick!* The creature stumbled but didn't fall. Love's heart sank as she emptied her magazine.

"Williams!" she yelled.

"I'm blasting it. It's not going down," Williams said.

The Zodark faltered. Blood oozed. Still, it came.

With a guttural roar, the alien raised one of its swords, ready to cleave Love in two. Time slowed as Love's rifle clicked repeatedly. In that frozen moment, she stared into the Zodark's eyes, drew her sidearm, and fired three rapid shots. The rounds found their mark, slamming into the Zodark's third eye. The alien's head snapped back. A geyser of gore erupted from the ruined socket. The monster swayed before it crashed to the ground.

"Green, status update!" Love said into her helmet comm.

Static crackled as her copilot's voice boomed through. "Lieutenant, we've got company closing in fast. Multiple heat signatures from the west and south."

"Terrific," she muttered.

Williams took a step closer, scanning the tree line. "Looks like they're trying to flank us."

"Not if we can help it," Love said. "Ford! How much longer?"

The crew chief kept his focus on his work. *How does he do that, even under heavy fire like this?*

"Couple more minutes, Lieutenant!" Ford said. "This bird took a real beating."

"We don't have a couple minutes." She swapped out her magazine.

Heavy footfalls resounded from all directions. A group of Zodarks dashed into the clearing, weapons raised and ready to fire.

Love's muscles constricted with shock. "There's too many. Ford, we need those systems online now!"

"Almost there."

"Just get it done!"

Too many Zodarks stood before her. "Looks like this is it," she said. "We don't go down without raising some more hell!"

All around, rifles cracked. And they didn't come from her team. Those were Republic rifles. The Zodarks jerked and fell.

From the jungle emerged a squad of Delta operatives. Their battlesuits shined. The lead soldier, his armor marked with the insignia of a sergeant, headed toward Love.

"Lieutenant Love? Petty Officer Williams? Chief Ford?" the sergeant asked. His voice was a bit distorted by his helmet's speaker.

Love breathed for the first time in a long time. "Damn glad to see you."

The sergeant motioned to his squad. "Bravo Two, secure the north. Charlie Five, take the south. Delta Three and Four, watch our six."

The Deltas spread out, forming a defensive perimeter around the downed Osprey. Their weapons swept the tree line, ready for any threat.

"More hostiles inbound, Sarge," one of the Deltas said. "Reading multiple heat signatures closing fast."

The sergeant turned to Love. "We'll hold them off. Get that bird in the air ASAP. Not a request. Get airborne."

"On it, Sergeant," Ford said. "I'm hurrying with repairs."

Blaster fire erupted around them as the Deltas engaged the oncoming Zodarks.

"Echo Six, contact left!" a Deltas yelled. "Tango Seven, suppressing fire!"

Magrail rounds pierced through hazy smoke, their orange detonations illuminating the area. The shriek of dying Zodarks mingled with the controlled bursts from the Deltas' weapons. Combat reverberated from all directions.

"Come on, come on," Love murmured to herself.

Ford worked fast, perspiration covering his brow as he realigned the repulsor array. "All right, let's see here. Bypassing the… and shunting energy from the auxiliary cells… gotta get the harmonics…"

Love backed up and hunkered down beside the man, weapon at the ready. Ford could talk a Zodark's ear off, even during combat.

"Diverting thruster output to compensate for the imbalance," Ford continued, pulling a set of tools from his belt and making small adjustments. "That should stabilize the field and… this should do it. It's not pretty, but it'll fly." He twisted a knob, and the Osprey's engines roared to life. Ford emerged from the access panel. "We're good to go, Lieutenant!"

Love rushed toward the ramp. "Sergeant! We're prepping for takeoff!"

The Delta sergeant nodded. "Affirmative. We'll keep these uglies off you." He turned to his team, barking orders. "I want interlocking fields of fire. Nobody gets through!"

"Give 'em hell, Sarge!"

"With pleasure, ma'am. We'll make these bastards wish they'd never set foot on this rock. We're giving them a master class in warfare."

The Deltas continued to fire, their rifles reverberating through the jungle. An explosion sounded. Dirt flew everywhere.

Love, Williams, and Ford sprinted up the ramp. The deck plates vibrated beneath their feet.

"Green, get us in the air!" Love said, sliding into the pilot's seat.

"Already ahead of you," Green replied.

The Osprey lifted off the ground. Green didn't wait for full stabilization before pushing the throttle forward. Blaster fire pounded the hull as Zodark soldiers engaged from below.

"Armor's holding, but we're not out of the woods yet," Green said.

"I'm taking over the controls." Love grabbed the yoke and guided the damaged craft upward.

The sky opened up before them as their engines roared to full power. As they climbed, the atmosphere thinned the higher they climbed, stars piercing the twilight.

"Lieutenant, multiple bogies at twelve o'clock," Green announced.

Love's eyes narrowed. A squadron of Zodark Vulture fighters bore down on them.

"Coop, we could use some air support," Love said into her comm.

"On my way," came the reply. "Hold tight."

A sudden explosion rocked the Osprey. Warning lights flashed across the console.

"Ack, we're leaking atmosphere in the troop bay!" Ford shouted from behind.

"Coop, anytime now!"

"Hang in there," Coop said. "Engaging the Vultures."

Through the cockpit window, a squadron of Orion fighters swooped in, magrails blazing. The vast expanse lit up as Coop's team engaged the enemy, drawing their fire away from their damaged Osprey.

"Path is clear, Lieutenant," Green said.

"Let's not waste it." Love pushed the throttle as far as it would go.

The Osprey limped toward the safety of the fleet. Behind them, the battle raged.

As they sped toward *Gallipoli*, Love allowed herself a moment to breathe. They weren't out of danger yet, but with her crew and a bit of luck, they'd make it.

"Lieutenant," Green said, "I think we just pulled off a minor miracle."

Love nodded. "Let's hope our luck holds." The orbital assault carrier loomed before them.

"Love," Coop said. "You've got more incoming—"

Chapter 54
Bringing Them Home

Year 2096
RNS *Gallipoli*
Intus Orbit

Inside the virtual cockpit, Coop manipulated the holographic interface. He switched between multiple screens displaying various aspects of the ongoing space battle. From what he could see, the conflict had reached a stalemate. The Republic forces needed the arrival of their second wave, which included several Altairian-Human hybrid vessels.

Until then, this first wave would continue to exchange fire with the enemy. More damage would be sustained on both sides. Both fleets would make push here, a nudge there, a retreat over yonder, only to find themselves back where they'd started.

A stalemate.

Coop wondered how much longer they could sustain such intense combat. The balance was precarious, and without reinforcements, their position could deteriorate. The Zodarks had lost two capital ships, the Republic only one.

Coop adjusted the thruster controls and flew his Orion drone through the debris-filled battlefield. He avoided incoming fire while tracking enemy movement, simultaneously coordinating with his squadron.

A lot of work, shuffling a hundred things at once, but all pilots did it, and he did it better.

Strike had ordered Coop and several other pilots to assist the Ospreys ascending from the planet's atmosphere and support them through space combat. He had tasked Coop with escorting the last ship to exit, which happened to be Love's. Her ship lagged drastically behind, a lone straggler in the wake of the Osprey transport formation.

Coop's heart fluttered at the mere memory of her. He quickly chided himself, forcing his focus back to the mission. There was no time for silly infatuations. Still, he couldn't shake the sensation. What was this emotion? He berated himself again, pushing away the distracting thoughts.

Strike had designated Coop as the patrol lead, as well. This position put him in charge of the small team escorting the Ospreys to the RNS *Gallipoli*'s landing bay.

Why did he put me as lead? Coop thought. *I must have impressed him. Thing is, I bet Raven impressed him as well.*

It was the first time Coop had thought anyone even came close to his skill. During this engagement, he had learned that he and Raven made a good pair in a fight.

The battle raged in Intus's thermosphere, one hundred kilometers above the planet's surface. This region—the boundary between the atmosphere and space—was a tactical sweet spot. It was high enough for spacecraft to maneuver with great effect, and low enough to maintain a fixed-point position over the ground forces on the planet below.

Coop's squadron were navigating through this engagement zone. Beside them loomed the *Gallipoli* and *Georgia*. The two capital ships maintained a close formation, separated by a mere three kilometers—a hair's breadth, but necessary for mutual support in the heat of combat.

This proximity allowed for overlapping point-defense systems and rapid deployment of support craft like Coop's Orion drones. From this vantage point, the curvature of Intus was clearly visible, its atmosphere a thin glowing line separating the planet's surface from the dark expanse of space.

"Tally ho, bandits at two o'clock high," Coop said. "Raven, form a fighting wing. We've got incoming bogies."

"Acknowledged, Coop. Velcroed to your rear, out."

Through his neural link, Coop felt the Orion's engines thrum as he pushed the drone into a tight turn. A Vulture's laser bursts missed him, singeing *Gallipoli*'s hull. Coop didn't know how long the battle had raged today, but the fatigue was setting in and his vision began to blur. He'd watched too many fellow pilots' drones get vaporized, only to see them jump back in with fresh Orions minutes later.

"Ghost Dog, give me a tail sweep," Coop said, the oncoming wave of enemy fighters heading their way.

"Clear for now, boss. But I've got a pair of bandits breaking off—looks like they're making a run for that damaged Osprey."

The Osprey in question was the *Jack*. It had struggled to ascend through the planet's upper atmosphere. The damage to its hull was visible on Coop's zoomed-in cam feed, no doubt sustained during its escape from the surface.

"All right, team," Coop said. "Multiple friendlies in front of the *Jack*. I've got visual on sensor array. Strike's already assigned flight leads and wingmen, so stick to your designated roles. Form up in your elements and stand by to receive."

"Roger that, Coop. Bear here, forming up with Phantom now."

Coop continued, "Each element will escort one transport to the *Gallipoli*. Remember your intercept protocols and keep those bogies off our birds at all costs."

"Ghost Dog checking in. IFF locked and loaded. Ready to play shepherd."

Coop nodded. "Aye, Ghost Dog. Everyone else, check your IFF tags for your assigned Osprey. As they continue to exit the atmosphere, lock onto your troop transport and guide them home. Maintain tight formation and keep comms open. Any enemy gets within weapons range, you're cleared hot."

"Ninja here. Weapons systems primed and itching for some action. Let's bring our boys and girls home."

"Phantom confirming visual on Ospreys. They're looking a bit roughed up but still kicking."

As they sped toward the Ospreys, Coop's HUD lit up with new targeting information. Love's Osprey limped along, slowing down. A plume of smoke followed, flowing out one of the vectoring engines on its wingtip.

"It's bleeding speed," Coop said. "Raven, we're gonna clear a path for Love. The rest of you, maintain your assigned positions. Form up on your designated Ospreys and provide cover. These fellas are limping home. We're their shield. Let's bring 'em in safe."

"Wilco," came the chorus of acknowledgments.

Coop pushed his Orion to full throttle, engines flaring as he rocketed toward the vulnerable transport, planet Intus in full view. "Lieutenant Love, hang tight. Almost there."

"Copy that, Coop," Love said. "Much obliged. Our engine's shot to hell."

As they closed the distance, Coop's tactical display lit up with the bogies converging on the Osprey. "Several hostiles on intercept courses."

"I see 'em," Raven replied. "What's the play, boss?"

Coop's mind spun, assessing angles and vectors. "Ninja, play dead. Bear, get ready to strike when they bite."

"Roger that," Ninja said, his drone's power signature immediately dimming.

One of the Vultures broke formation, angling toward Ninja's apparently crippled Orion. "Bear, you seeing this?"

"Affirmative. Target acquired. Waiting for the green light."

The enemy fighter closed in on Ninja's "helpless" drone, its weapons ready for the kill shot. Coop held his breath, waiting for the perfect moment.

"Now, Bear! Light 'em up!"

Bear's Orion changed trajectory. Its targeting systems locked onto the distracted Vulture. A volley of hypervelocity rounds tore through the enemy ship, turning it into an expanding cloud of superheated gas and charred metal.

"Splash one!" Bear said. "That's for my friends, you Zodark bastard!"

Two more Vultures closed in fast on the Osprey's nine. "Raven, break ventral. I'm going dorsal. Let's scissor these guys."

The two Orions split apart. Coop's drone accelerated dorsally, thrusters firing, while Raven pushed his craft into a steep ventral vector. Their simultaneous movements created a three-dimensional crisscross pattern in space. This rapid divergence in opposite directions—Coop's craft moving "up" and Raven's "down" relative to their starting position—seemed to confuse the enemy's targeting systems.

Perfect. Exactly what Coop wanted.

"Fox three!" Coop released a salvo of antifighter missiles. The projectiles streaked toward the lead Vulture, forcing it to break off its attack run on Love's Osprey.

Raven guns bore down on the second Vulture. "Scratch two!"

Coop's sensors screamed warnings as more Zodark fighters joined the engagement. "We're outnumbered here, people. Somebody call for the cavalry!"

As if on cue, a new voice blasted through the chatter. "This is Reaper Lead, call sign Boomer. We heard you boys could use a hand."

Coop's heart soared as a squadron of heavily armed Reaper drones emerged from the *Gallipoli*'s launch bays. "Boomer, this is Coop.

You're a sight for sore eyes. We've got damaged Ospreys trying to make it home. Could use some cover."

The Reaper drones were ground support combat ships, made for both space and atmospheric operations. Each unmanned craft carried a devastating arsenal: a chin-mounted magrail gun for precision strikes, thirty-six smart missiles for multiple targets, and a choice of either four one-thousand-pound or two two-thousand-pound guided bombs. These drones could provide the all-too-important fire support for infantry. Their ability to transition from orbit to planetside made them invaluable in complex combat scenarios, and right now, they were more valuable than ever.

"Copy that, Coop," Boomer responded. "We're inbound to clear you a path. Just point those transports toward the *Gallipoli* and don't stop for anything."

In seconds, the Reapers unleashed their firepower on the Zodark Vulture formation, overwhelming the lighter enemy craft. Seizing the opportunity created by this sudden onslaught, Coop and his team moved into position and formed a protective escort alongside the damaged Ospreys.

"Lieutenant Love, this is your escort home," Coop transmitted. "Stay on this vector and don't deviate. We'll handle any further party crashers."

"Understood, Coop," Love said.

The transport's damaged hull loomed large in Coop's rearview display. "Just stay on me."

Raven fell into formation. His drone flanked the battered Osprey. "Sensors lit up. Hostile cluster detected at coordinates zero-four-five by two-seven-zero." Raven's voice resonated through the link. "Vector change advised."

Coop spotted the approaching Zodark fighters. "I see 'em. They're not getting anywhere near these transports." He switched channels. "Boomer, this is Coop. Hostiles closing in on sector three-seven-nine. Can you spare Reapers 3, 4, 7, and 9 to engage targets at the specified coordinates?"

An instant later, smart missiles streaked across the expanse, finding their marks. The Vultures erupted.

"Nice shooting, Reapers," Coop said. "All right, everyone, let's lock this down. Bracket those Ospreys. I want a continued shield around each transport. Adjust your vectors as needed, but keep those Ospreys in your bubble.”

A cascade of confirmations filled the comm link while the Orion drones executed their maneuvers.

“How’re you holding up in there, Love?” Coop asked.

“Systems stable, but she’s handling like a drunk elephant,” Love said.

“Copy that.”

“Wolfpack Squadron, you’re clear for approach,” came the voice of *Gallipoli*’s flight control. “Orions, stand by for new orders.”

“Roger that, Control,” Coop said. “Love, you’re all set. See you on the inside.”

“Thanks for the ride, gentlemen,” Love said. “Drinks are on me when we’re back on solid ground.”

As the Ospreys glided into *Gallipoli*’s landing bay, Coop and his team broke formation. “All right, let’s get back out there and keep our big mama bird safe. Form up on me—we’re heading to sector five-one-three.”

The Orions swung around in perfect unison, their engines flaring as they moved to take up defensive positions around the massive carrier.

A tremor rocked through the *Gallipoli*. Coop squinted as warning klaxons began to blare throughout his cockpit pod.

“What the hell was that?” Raven asked.

Coop’s pod’s systems blinked on and off, failing. The holographic displays sputtered, plunging him into darkness. A lurch hit his stomach as his neural link to the Orion was abruptly severed.

“Mayday, mayday!” Coop shouted into his now-dead comm. “All systems down! I’ve lost control of my—”

His words were interrupted as another massive impact shook the *Gallipoli*. Coop was thrown against his restraints.

All the lights in the room went dark.

Chapter 55
Into the Darkness

Year 2096
RNS *Gallipoli*
Intus Orbit

Chief Brian Ford sprinted down the ramp of the *Jack*, Love, Green and Williams hot on his heels. Pungent smoke billowed from the damaged section of the ship, obscuring their vision. He needed to fight the flames before one of the engines completely melted down. Two petty officers wielding fire extinguishers rushed past, foam spraying as they battled the blaze.

Ford watched the damaged section as the fire control teams completed their tasks, drowning out the fire and making sure it couldn't spread any further.

In the next second, the landing bay plunged into darkness. Ford waited for the emergency lights to activate. A few of the ones that ran on a separate battery system from the ship's main power lines kicked on, but not the main relay of emergency lights needed to keep the flight bay operational. Thankfully, the artificial gravity and life-support systems stayed on, so whatever it was it didn't seem critical just yet.

Love stood next to Ford in the dark as a few deckhands dished out orders and others with flashlights ran in different directions to fulfill them.

"The ship must have been hit," Love said as she looked around for visible signs of further damage.

Ford squinted, his eyes adjusting as he unhooked a flashlight from his belt and powered it on. "Yeah, I think so. It looks like the power to the flight deck is out. It could be worse, I guess—we still have active life-support systems."

"How's that possible?" Love pressed. "Shouldn't the backup generators have kicked in by now?"

"They should have. This isn't a simple power outage."

Ford spotted a junior engineer nearby. "Lieutenant! Why isn't this fixed yet?"

The young officer grunted. "Sir, we're working on it. Engineering's stumped. Nothing like this in the manuals."

Ford frowned. "It shouldn't be this complicated. What's the current theory?"

"They think it might be a cascade failure in the primary power distribution node."

A thunderous impact caused the ship's frame to jerk.

Ford kept his balance, his mind on overdrive. He tapped his skull, Love staring at him. She usually kept quiet when he went into this state, and for good reason. When he concentrated on something this hard, a solution usually arose. But... now... nothing.

Lieutenant Love clapped her hands together, breaking him out of his anxious thought spiral. "Ford, Green, Williams—I can see your minds racing down rabbit holes. This may not be a situation we've trained for exactly, but we need to focus on what we know to do. It's *our* job to get the *Jack* repaired as quickly as possible, so we can be prepared to get back out there when we are called upon. It might be a little harder without the lights and without some of the tools, but we have flashlights and limited emergency lights we can use. Let's do what we can. The rest of the ship's crew will do *their* jobs and get the *Gallipoli*'s power situation sorted. But we are right here, right now—understood?"

"Aye, LT," they answered in unison.

"Ford, you're the boss right now," Lieutenant Love continued. "Tell us what we can do to help."

Ford had needed that reset. He couldn't focus on the bigger picture right now. Even if he could come up with a solution, it wouldn't be in his power to fix it. But there was something he had control over—the *Jack*.

"Right," said Ford. "The first thing I'll need to do is get a good look at the engine now that the fire is out. Green, go grab one of those rolling ladders. Love, see if you can locate any lighting bigger than a flashlight, so I can see what I'm doing. I'll gather the tools I'm sure that we'll need, Williams can help me carry them, and we'll go from there."

"On it," said Green.

"We've got you, Ford," Love confirmed.

"Let's do this," said Williams.

Ford straightened his shoulders and made for the tools, Williams in tow.

We've got this, he reminded himself.

RNS *Gallipoli*
Intus Orbit

Commander Leo Nilson's mind whirled like a turbine as he bent over the computer terminal. The ship shuddered under another Zodark onslaught of torpedo detonations.

"Need to bypass the main fail-safe protocols," Nilson told Lieutenant Park Bora as he looked over the holo interface. "The computer thinks it's protecting the ship, but it's killing us. Need to access the override somehow. Doing so without main power will be tricky."

"I don't know, Nilson," Lieutenant Park said. "That circuit was designed for emergency life support, not weapons systems. Power output is nowhere near what we'd need. Plus, it bypasses all the safety interlocks and could overload the conduits. We'd risk blowing out half the relays on this deck. Not to mention, the phase variance might be too high for weapons-grade energy transfer."

Nilson opened his mouth to respond, but Park held up a hand.

"But you're right," she admitted. "We gotta try it. It's our only shot."

Nilson turned to a couple of nearby engineers. "Slovok, Kalani, you're with us. Grab every portable power pack and toolbox you can find."

The team scrambled to comply as Nilson led the way through the depths of engineering.

"Where exactly is this backup circuit?" Lieutenant Kalani asked.

Nilson pointed ahead. "Lower maintenance shaft, Section 31-Alpha. It's a tight squeeze."

They pressed on and weaved through debris-strewn corridors. The ship lurched, nearly throwing them off their feet. A horrifying screech of metal tore from somewhere above them.

Finally, they reached the access hatch to Section 31-Alpha. Nilson wrenched it open. Before them was a cramped crawlspace barely large enough for a single person.

"This is it," Nilson said, gesturing Park forward. "The circuit panel's about ten meters in."

Park nodded, steeling herself. She grabbed a flashlight and squeezed into the claustrophobic tunnel. The others followed, passing tools and power packs along the line.

As they neared the panel, another blast rattled the ship. Park's flashlight illuminated twisted metal where the access cover should have been.

"Damn it," she muttered. "The panel's jammed shut. We'll have to force it open."

One of the engineers passed forward a pry bar. Park wedged it into the warped seam and heaved with all her strength. The metal groaned but held fast.

When the vessel convulsed, Park lost her grip. The pry bar went spinning out of her hands. It clattered down a deep service shaft.

"Well, great," Nilson said. "Kalani, do you got another pry bar?"

"Negative, sir."

Park wiped her brow. "Welding torch?"

Kalani shook his head. "Left it back there."

"We'll have to do this the hard way," Nilson said. "Everyone, grab an edge and pull."

They wedged fingers into the seam. They pulled and pulled, grunting. The panel mocked their efforts.

Lieutenant Park rummaged through her pack. "Wait." She fished out a compact vibration hammer. "This might work."

She pressed it against the panel's edge, activating it. The tool buzzed, sending vibrations through the metal. They waited. Little by little, the panel moved. A portion of the metal bent more.

Park killed the hammer. They all grabbed hold again, exchanging quick glances. After one collective breath, they pulled. Metal screamed as the panel gave way. Before them stood a nightmare of blackened circuits and melted wire bundles.

"Well, hell," Nilson muttered. This was bad—worse than he'd hoped. "Wire cutters. Splicing kit. This is gonna be fun."

He dove in as soon as the tools touched his hands, stripping damaged sections. Sweat stung his eyes. Each impact against the hull made him work faster. They were running out of time.

"Almost—" The words caught in his throat as he reached for the neural interface connection. "Just need to—"

The crash came without warning. Nilson looked up to see a chunk of metal falling toward him. He jumped back just before it slammed into his head.

"Holy hell, that was close!" Nilson exclaimed. The stakes were already high enough, but this just flooded his system with adrenaline.

Hands shaking, he turned back to the mess of wires. He twisted the final connections together, muttered a prayer he hadn't used since the Academy, and held his breath.

Nothing.

Ten seconds crawled by. Then a weak whir, growing stronger as systems came back online. The overhead lights surged as the reactors spun up. Nilson was in a hurry and squeezed past Kalani, Park, and Slovok. He practically fell out of the access tunnel.

His boots slapped against deck plating as he sprinted to the nearest terminal. Data flooded the holodisplay. It was too fast to read, but he didn't need to. He typed across the interface, muscle memory taking over as he rewrote fail-safes. The code flowed, messy but functional. No time for elegant solutions.

The deck vibrated as weapons came back online. Lieutenant Park had caught up to him.

"Main systems are stable," Nilson reported. "But we need to watch those fail safes. They're held together with spit and wishful thinking."

Park smiled and clapped her boss on the shoulder. "You did it, Commander. We'll hopefully live to fight another day now."

Chapter 56
What Happened?

Year 2096
RNS *Poseidon*
Medbay

Lee awoke to pain.

It wasn't sharp, not exactly—it was more like someone had laid bags of gravel across his body and told him to move. Every breath felt thick. He groaned, his low rasp drawing someone's attention.

A shadow leaned over him—it was someone in a white coat with tired eyes. "Easy, Skipper."

Lee blinked, squinting against the ceiling light. "What... the hell?"

"Don't move too fast," the ship's doctor said, already loading a hypospray. "You've got enough shrapnel in your leg and arm to decorate a Christmas tree. And whatever hit you in the head nearly cracked your skull. Hang on a second. I'm about to top off your pain meds."

The hiss of the injector kissed Lee's deltoid muscle, and within seconds, the pain dulled into a heavy numbness.

His vision cleared. The ceiling sharpened into focus. The hum of medical equipment filled the silence between slow beeps of a heart monitor. Lee turned his head slightly, winced, then pushed through it.

"What happened?"

"You got thrown like a ragdoll when the bridge took that final laser hit. Shard of metal tore into your left leg just below the knee— nasty gash. Multiple tiny fragments peppered your left arm. As for your skull..." The doc gave a dry smile. "You caught a glancing blow from what we think was a loose console brace. Knocked you out cold."

Lee let that settle. "How long?"

The doctor checked his watch. "Sixteen hours."

Lee exhaled. Then, reflexively, he started to say, "Status report. Damage. Crew—"

"Not from me," the doc interrupted gently. "But your XO's on her way. She's got the full SITREP."

As if summoned, the medbay doors slid open and Commander Sato stepped through—her uniform singed, one arm in a sling, a bandage across her jaw. She looked tired but alive. Her expression softened when she saw him conscious.

"Rip," she said, managing a small smile. "Good to see you still breathing."

"Mostly," he croaked. "How bad?"

"Bridge crew got banged up. A lot of burns, some broken bones, shrapnel—Rodriguez, Reynolds, and Rhom survived. They'll be back on duty soon—days to weeks, depending on the injury." Her smile faded. "We did lose four others from the bridge. Concussion and plasma flash from the wall breach got them instantly."

Lee's chest tightened. He closed his eyes, just for a second. "Damn."

She nodded. "Yeah."

There was a pause before she stepped closer, lowering her voice. "MacGregor's got propulsion coming back online any minute. Swears he fixed the primary conduit with duct tape and superglue. His words, not mine."

Lee actually laughed—then immediately regretted it as pain bloomed in his side. "Sounds about right."

"It's not pretty," she continued, "but we'll have enough control to rejoin the Fleet in orbit around Intus."

He exhaled in relief.

"Now," she said, gesturing to the IV line feeding into his arm, "you're going to rest. That's why you have an XO. I've got the ship."

She turned to go, paused at the door, and looked back once.

"You did good, Rip. We're still here, and so is the *Poseidon*."

Lee didn't answer. The exhaustion surged again, heavy and irresistible. He let himself sink back into the bed, eyelids pulling shut as the soft hum of the medbay faded to quiet.

Then sleep took him.

Chapter 57
Time to Hunt

Year 2096
RNS *Gallipoli*
Intus Orbit

The pod room reeked of burnt circuits. The power on *Gallipoli* had come back on not long ago. Still, there was a problem with the drone pods. What exactly, Coop didn't know, and engineers swarmed the area, working on whatever they could to get things right because at the moment, all Jolly Rogers' Orions were floating without a controller. Who knew how many had been blown out of space? They would be easy pickings for the Vultures when the AI-assisted auto-pilot software took over until they could reestablish a connection.

Worse off, without drone control, the *Gallipoli*'s defense screen had a massive hole in it. The Vultures would exploit that weakness, probably already were. Each Orion could handle maybe two enemy fighters at once—multiply that by dozens of off-line drones, and it meant at least fifty to sixty Vultures free to harass the fleet's support ships.

Coop sat in his pod. The formfitting crash webbing pressed against his flight suit. Condensation beaded on the inside of his visor. He breathed rapidly.

He pressed and tapped over controls. They didn't respond. Around him, the other pods thrummed. Tech crews scurried between them as they rushed to restore power. Coop's pulse thundered like it belonged to someone else, his chest tight with the absence of action. *I need to get out there! Need to help the Republic!*

"Damn it!" Bear's voice surged through the comm. "This is worse than waiting in line for chow knowing the cook's burned the stew again."

"Bear, maintain comm discipline," Raven cut in from his pod. "Priority is drone status. Need to calculate potential losses and remaining combat-effectiveness."

"Yeah, good luck with that," Ghost Dog muttered. His voice sounded distant, like it was being filtered through exhaustion. "The way those Vultures were swarming? We'll be lucky if we find enough pieces to fill a cargo container."

"Your statistical analysis is appreciated as always, Ghost Dog," Ninja replied, his words coming fast. He always talked faster when systems were down.

Bear laughed. "You're one to talk, Ninja. What is it you always say before launch? 'Try not to get me killed today, guys'? Very inspiring."

The group's faint snickers felt forced. Coop caught himself smiling behind the visor of his helmet. The thought of his drone floating powerless—or worse, already gutted by a Vulture—gnawed at the edges of his composure and his grin dropped. The guys were trying to make light of things. Coop wanted to join, but words caught in his throat. His heart kept pounding too loud, kept reminding him of everything not happening. Every second in this pod was another second the enemy gained advantage. He'd seen too many battles turn on smaller margins than this.

"We're missing the fight," Coop finally said. "They're out there getting hammered, and we're stuck here, waiting for the pods to come back on. Useless."

"Mister Obvious," Bear said.

"Ease up, Coop," Raven said. "It's being handled. Strike will work this out. We'll get back out there."

"Good thing you're here to play coach," Ghost Dog said.

"You good over there?" Bear's voice cut in, firm. "Doesn't sound like it."

"Just don't like sitting on my hands. They need us in the fight, not… whatever this is," Ghost Dog replied.

"Relax." Ninja sounded like he was trying to convince himself more than Ghost Dog. "If our Orions are gone… well, not much point thinking about that yet. One way or another, we'll be back in soon. New Orions or not."

"Shut it," Strike's voice came over the group channel. "You get paid to fly, not to moan. My Jolly Rogers don't whine."

Everyone fell quiet. Bear eventually broke the silence, speaking low enough it almost didn't feel like he was addressing anyone in particular. "Man, it's real satisfying, sitting here listening to nothing."

A laugh bubbled up from Ninja, shaky but genuine. Even Ghost Dog chuckled, though it was cut off when Strike spoke again. "Quit it.

We're working on restoring control to the pods. Shouldn't be much longer. Stay sharp."

Coop fidgeted with the dead controls, running over toggles and switches without pressing any of them. He resisted asking Strike for updates—the harsh tone in his last order made it clear that silence was preferred. The stillness pressed in on him. Nothing moved except for the ragged rise and fall of his own chest.

"Hey, Bear," Raven started. "If your drone's toast, you think they'll let you pilot by… what'd you call it last time? 'The seat of your oversized pants'?"

Bear laughed again but softer this time. "Say the word, and I'll strap you to my back and fly us both out there."

"I'd like to survive this war. Thanks, but no thanks," Raven said. Silence crept back in, the weight of what was happening—or not happening—dragging down their brief humor.

A second after, like breath returning to lungs on the brink of death, power surged back through the pods. The equipment glowed to life, consoles coming awake, pods whirring as they reconnected with systems. Coop's head snapped to his display.

"Here we go, ladies and gentlemen," Bear said. "Time to see if Murphy's Law is still in effect. Wouldn't be the first time I've lost a bird—lost three during the New Eden campaigns alone."

One by one, telemetry readouts filled the monitors inside each pod. On Coop's screen, lines of static scrambled before settling into something clearer. His gut sank. His Orion's feed showed… nothing. Not the empty void of space, but shredded wreckage drifting in an uneven spiral away from the combat zone. The high-resolution display made every shredded piece of his drone painfully clear—the jagged edges where Vulture fire had torn through composite armor. Parts of wings, a portion of the tail. He gripped the controls anyway, willing a response from a drone that no longer existed.

Bear's voice crackled over the tactical frequency. "Bird's down, Command. Confirm total system failure."

"Status report, Bear?" Raven transmitted on the squad channel. "Your QLink readings match mine?"

"Confirmed kill. Direct hits to the core and primary systems," Bear said. "Orion Seven-Alpha is combat ineffective."

"Ninja reporting complete systems failure," Ninja called in. "All critical subsystems nonresponsive."

Ghost Dog's status light blinked red on the tactical display—standard combat protocol for total drone loss.

"Raven, report combat status," Strike demanded.

A three-count of dead air before Raven responded. "Raven maintaining marginal drone control, sir. Multiple systems compromised. Operating at thirty percent combat effectiveness."

"Thirty percent exceeds zero, Lieutenant. Maintain position," Strike said. "Coop, status?"

Coop eyed his tactical readout. The debris field that used to be his Orion spun through the void. "Coop reporting complete asset loss, sir. Drone destroyed."

"Copy all," Strike responded. "All pilots, initiate Emergency Protocol Seven-Charlie. Submit replacement requisitions through Command. Priority clearance authorized. Acknowledge."

"Acknowledged," Coop transmitted, thumb pressing the emergency replacement beacon. His eyes never left the wreckage signature on his combat display, memorizing the kill zone coordinates.

Shutting the feed off, he let out another breath, slower this time. The *Gallipoli*'s systems buzzed around him now, the pod room warmer with sound.

The replacement requisition pinged confirmation in his HUD. T-minus sixty seconds until drone reassignment. The last pieces of Coop's Orion disappeared from his feed as his pod synced up with a fresh Orion.

Soon he'd be back in the fight. And this time? This time he'd make damn sure the Zodarks learned why you don't piss off a Jolly Roger pilot.

The interface began its warm-up sequence.

Time to hunt.

Chapter 58
Echoes on the Bridge

Six Days Later
RNS Poseidon
Orbit above Intus

Captain Ripley Lee sat back in his chair for the first time in nearly a week.

The medbay haze was gone, replaced by a dull ache in his leg and a slight throb behind his left eye that hadn't faded since he'd woken up. But he was here. Back on the bridge. Back in command.

He scanned the room slowly, taking in the state of things.

The console banks had been reassembled in a patchwork of scorched steel and riveted plating. Wiring snaked along the walls like arteries beneath the skin of a healing wound. Some stations still flickered. Others had fresh panels with mismatched interface fonts—hastily installed replacements salvaged from the ship's spares or fabricators.

It worked. Somehow, it all worked again.

But what caught Lee's eye—what *held* it—was the hole.

The wall that had once housed bridge, section three, was gone. In its place, a temporary pressure screen shimmered faintly, holding the void at bay. The twisted remains of the hull and bulkhead had been sealed, but the absence lingered like a scar.

Over there was the place that Ensign Trammel had stood. Nearby, Chief Goral had run for the manual override.

Gone, both of them.

Lee exhaled slowly, his hand resting on the armrest as if to ground himself.

He had made the right call. Tactical doctrine said as much. So had Sato. The ship's AI combat log was also on his side. But none of that silenced the whisper at the back of his mind.

What if you'd done something different? he asked himself. *What if you'd seen it faster? Chosen another vector? Held fire for two more seconds?*

More than a hundred names had been added to the casualty ledger. Their sacrifice had saved the ship, saved their task force…won the battle.

But they weren't here to see it. And he was.

Lee clenched his jaw and forced his eyes back to the forward screen, pushing the thoughts aside—for now. Duty didn't care about guilt. It only cared that you showed up and made the next right call.

Behind him, the bridge buzzed with quiet efficiency—less chaotic, more focused. Everyone moved a little slower, spoke a little softer. The ghosts hadn't left. They just stood behind every empty chair.

Lee sat taller in his seat.

They were still in the fight.

****

Captain Ripley Lee sat in silence in the briefing room, his chair rigid beneath him, hands folded over his still-healing leg. The remote fleet conference was being broadcast in real time from the *Voyager*, patched in across secure comms channels to every surviving ship captain and executive offer of the Republic, Altairian, and Primord warships in the Intus system. The holoscreens lining the room flickered, each bearing the insignia of a task force and its commanding officer.

Lee's screen showed the sharp, tired face of Captain McKee in her command seat aboard the *George Washington*. Beside her was Captain Roberts—proud, uniform crisp, face all but glowing under the attention.

"Let's begin with the damage report," Halsey said, her voice taut but composed.

The first reports came from the Primord fleet. Admiral Stavanger's voice was gravel over static. "The Primords lost two battleships, seven cruisers, and five frigates. Damage across another nine vessels—moderate to severe. We're initiating temporary repairs in orbit until reinforcements can cycle in."

Lee felt his stomach twist.

The Altairians were next. Admiral Pandolly, ever the pragmatic commander, reported with clinical precision. "Three cruisers destroyed. Two frigates lost. Six others undergoing system triage in orbit. Our technicians are sharing schematics for temporary stabilization fields with Republic engineers."

Then came McKee. Her tone tightened as she listed the Republic toll.

"We lost four battleships, three of the ten hybrid heavy cruisers, twelve first-generation cruisers, four of the ten hybrid frigates, nine of our older first-gen frigates, and eight missile and torpedo destroyers."

Lee's throat went dry. He knew the numbers were bad, but hearing them laid out like that felt like a punch to the gut. Each ship wasn't just metal and mass. They had crews—voices, faces…friends.

One hundred and forty-seven ships had jumped into Intus as part of the invasion. Sixty-three were either destroyed or too damaged to fight again for months.

The room was quiet.

And then the mood shifted.

Admiral Halsey's voice resumed across the main channel. The sharp edge in her tone softened, just a little. "Despite our losses, our enemies' are far worse. The Orbots lost one of their battleships. The Zodark military presence in this system has been essentially gutted. We count one Zodark star carrier destroyed, ten battleships, twenty-three cruisers, twenty-nine frigates, and thirty-three assorted cargo vessels, freighters, and troop transports, most of which were caught in orbit around Intus or docked at the comms relay station near the Rass gate."

Lee blinked. He'd expected a fight. Even a win. But that? That was annihilation.

A part of him wanted to feel triumphant. But all he could think about was the wall that was no longer there on the bridge.

"Captain Roberts," Halsey continued, "your task force accounted for eleven of those cruisers, eight frigates, and six cargo vessels destroyed. That's one hell of an accomplishment."

Lee's eyes shifted to Roberts's image on the screen. The man didn't gloat—but there was pride. Justified pride.

Halsey wasn't finished. "As such, I am awarding both you and Captain McKee the Navy Cross for your leadership during the Intus campaign. You may each recommend up to five officers or enlisted personnel for the Silver Star. I will approve those without question. Additionally, you may recommend up to two hundred Bronze Stars with valor devices for spacers under your command. Commendation and achievement medals can be issued at your discretion."

Lee was already thinking of names—people who'd stood when everything fell apart, people who'd died on his bridge.

Then Roberts said something Lee would never forget.

"Admiral, if I may… I'd like to recommend an additional Navy Cross…for Commander Ripley Lee."

Lee's head snapped up, eyes widened.

Roberts went on, calm and sure. "It was his ship and crew that destroyed four Zodark cruisers. I saw it on the fleet feed. He realigned his cruiser mid-battle to bring his portside weapons to bear after his starboard side was rendered inoperable. I thought he'd lost his mind turning headlong into multiple waves of plasma torpedoes. But several of those torpedoes failed to convert before impact due to proximity—and they bounced off. His maneuver saved his ship and allowed him to finish the attack run."

A moment of silence passed.

"Four cruiser kills," commented Halsey. "For a brand-new commander… of a newly fielded hybrid warship."

Another pause.

"OK. I'll approve it."

Lee sat motionless. His mind spun, numb with disbelief. He didn't know what shocked him more—being recommended for the Navy Cross, or hearing Roberts speak about him with genuine respect.

The man who had once seemed like a tyrant now looked like a mentor. Maybe there was more to him.

The meeting moved on. Halsey outlined the next steps. "The Primordian government has offered access to their shipyards in the Kita system. It's three stargate jumps from here—about seven days travel for most ships. I want all damaged Republic and allied ships rerouted there immediately. McKee, Roberts—you'll organize the deployments. We need these vessels repaired and ready to rejoin the Fleet as soon as possible. The next campaign is already in motion."

The briefing ended a few minutes later.

Sato's voice chimed in. "Sir, we've just received our redeployment orders. We're being routed to Stavros Naval Shipyard, orbiting Helios Forge in the Primord system of Kita. The Altairians have a facility there too, apparently—specialized for their platform maintenance."

Lee nodded, pulling himself back to the present. "Understood."

He shifted in his chair, feeling the ache in his healing ribs and leg.

"Lieutenant Reynolds," Lee called out. "Set course for Kita. Best possible speed."

Reynolds turned from his console, his expression uncertain. "Sir… with our propulsion still running at thirty-two percent… this is going to be a long one."

"How long?"

"Eighteen days minimum. That's if MacGregor's duct tape holds."

Lee let out a long breath, then cracked the faintest smile.

"Then let's start praying."

Chapter 59
Trust Me

Year 2096
RNS *Gallipoli*
Intus

Coop's fingers cramped around the stick. Hours and hours of combat had taken their toll—so many hours he'd lost track. His squadron, pilots like Raven, Bear, Ninja, and Ghost Dog, had held together better than he'd expected. Hell, better than anyone had expected. In truth, Coop was impressed.

"Raven, bandits at two. Watch your six."

"Got 'em."

Strike's gamble, giving Coop his own team, was paying off. They'd kept the Republic's transports intact. Coop's team had become the go-to escort for critical missions, their reputation growing with each successful run.

He finally gave me my chance, Coop thought. *Maybe I should thank him later.*

The comm crackled. "Coop, Wolfpack Actual. Got a situation. Incoming."

Coop's eyes moved to his radar. Lieutenant Paul Randolph's signature appeared on screen. "Reading you. CSAR run?"

"Affirmative. Delta-Nine protocol."

"Raven?" Coop said.

"Five-by. Prepared for engagement. Better yet, ready to dance."

The past day had been a marathon of combat. They'd screened the *Gallipoli*, shielding the orbital assault ship from wave after wave of Zodark attacks. Coop had cycled through a couple of Orions, losing two to enemy fire. The longer they kept these starfighters in the fight, the more Zodark ships they could send to the scrapyard.

Debris cluttered Coop's scanner. The *Gallipoli* loomed to starboard, her hull scarred from repeated Zodark attacks. Vulture wreckage drifted past his viewport. Their ranks were thinning, but plenty remained. Randolph's Osprey cut through the maelstrom. Ahead of them, planet Intus, its swirling atmosphere all different kinds of greens, filled the viewscreen.

"Thirty seconds to atmo," Raven said.

"Randolph, we're riding this down with you. Intel shows Vultures planetside."

"Confirmed." Something in Randolph's voice made Coop check his scanner again. "Keep it tight."

The Orion shuddered as they hit atmosphere. Warning lights flashed—heat dispersal working overtime. They punched through a layer of clouds, the world below coming into focus.

"Raven, status?" Coop asked.

"Transport's locked in. Wait—" Raven's tone changed. "Contact. Three bogeys, zero-four-seven. High."

Coop's HUD lit up. "Randolph, hang back. Raven, we're going high."

His Orion climbed. The Vultures emerged from the cloud cover, sun glinting off their hulls. Too damn close to the transport.

"Weapons hot," Coop said, thumb finding the trigger. The targeting reticle pulsed red. No matter what, this Osprey had to land.

"Fox three!" Coop launched a group of multipurpose smart missiles. "Chaff, chaff, chaff!" Metal particles burst behind them as the Vultures scattered, their formation breaking apart as they evaded. Coop's HUD lit up with warnings as the enemy ships returned fire, lasers slicing through the air.

Raven's voice cut through static. "They're targeting the transport."

Coop yanked the stick hard right, tracking the nearest Vulture. The .50-cal magrails thundered. "Hit 'em with ECM, scramble their sensors. Do it, now."

The electronic countermeasures started jamming the enemy's targeting sensors. Raven took advantage of the opening—one clean shot, and the Vulture became a fireball.

"Nice work, Raven. Their weapons array is—"

Everything went sideways. A blast caught Coop's peripheral vision just as Raven's signal vanished from his scanner.

"Raven, report!"

Static answered.

"Damn." Coop wrestled his Orion level, scanning his sensors. Where Raven's signature had been, there was nothing but debris.

After five seconds, the comm sparked to life. "Coop, this is Raven. A Vulture toasted my bird. Bastard got me good. Requesting clearance for a fresh Orion. I'll be back ASAP."

Coop banked hard toward Randolph's position. Two Vultures still harried his Osprey, their shots getting too close for comfort.

"Could use some help here, Coop." Randolph's voice stayed steady... somehow.

"Coming in hot." Muscle memory took over. "Break left on my mark."

The Osprey's rear turret spat fire, keeping the Vultures at bay. Coop lined up his shot, breathing slow. "Three... mark!"

Randolph's ship rolled left, clearing Coop's line of fire. He unleashed magrail rounds, shredding one of the Vultures. The craft exploded, and Coop rocketed through the burning cloud.

"We've still got one more on your tail and—" His words were interrupted as warnings flashed across his HUD. "Damn it! Weapons systems are off-line!"

One Vulture left, closing fast on Randolph's six. No weapons, no time.

"Randolph, I need you to trust me. Cut engines when I say."

A beat of silence. "Copy that."

Coop pushed his thrusters to redline. "Now!"

The Osprey's engines went dark. The troop transport plummeted into a nosedive. At the same instant, Coop gunned his thrusters, hurtling toward the Vulture at breakneck speed.

"Come on, you Vulture prick," Coop said under his breath, the distance closing. "Just a little closer..."

At the last possible second, Coop jerked his controls hard. His Orion clipped the Vulture's wing, sending both craft into a spin. The Vulture, thrown off course, careened past the falling Osprey, heading toward the surface below.

Coop's world turned black as his control pod shut down, the link to his soon-to-be-destroyed Orion severed. He hoped Randolph had made it safely to land.

After a moment of darkness, Coop's systems burst to life. He keyed his comm. "Wolfpack Actual, status?"

"On the ground. Delta team's moving. Nice flying up there."

"Just doing my job." He checked his scanner to plot his route back to the fight.

"Coop, you crazy son of a—" Raven cut in. "That wing clip was something else."

"Look who's talking. You're not so bad yourself."

"Hell's frozen over," Ghost Dog broke in. "The infamous Cooper giving compliments?"

Coop snorted. "Don't get used to it, Ghost Dog. That was for Raven, not your sorry butt."

Ghost Dog laughed. "Got a sense of humor, huh? I like that. And, whatever you say, boss man. Now stop lollygagging and get back in the fight. We need you out here."

"Roger that," Coop said, initiating the start-up sequence for another Orion. "Requesting clearance now. I'll be back in the black before you can say 'Zodark scum.'"

Chapter 60
Welcome to the Forge

Twenty-Four Days Later

RNS *Poseidon*
Stavros Naval Shipyard-Helios Forge
Kita System

"Three breakdowns, two propulsion failures, one flaming coolant line, and a partridge in a pear tree," Lee muttered as he finally saw the vast structure of the Stavros Naval Shipyard come into view.

It had taken them twenty-four days to limp across three jumps. The last one had nearly ended in disaster when the main propulsion system sputtered to a full stop just shy of the Kita gate. They'd been dead in space for three full days, drifting quietly and praying the fishing line and chewing gum MacGregor had used to keep the ship running hadn't finally given up for good.

Luckily, the Altairians had sent help—a repair barge with the needed parts, a few brilliant engineers, and one very sarcastic logistics officer who, upon arriving, asked, "So, how exactly did you break *everything?*"

Lee's answer had been short: "Talent."

Now, as *Poseidon* entered the Kita system proper, Lee stood silently, hands clasped behind his back, taking it all in.

"Busy system," he muttered.

That was putting it lightly. Hundreds—no, maybe thousands—of ships buzzed between the system's three major stargates and its four visibly inhabited planets. He counted nine moons hosting light-to-moderate orbital traffic, plus what appeared to be dozens of asteroid outposts and mining facilities interlaced through the belts.

"Sir," Sato said, stepping up beside him. Her tone was half-wonder, half-awe. "Are you seeing this? That has to be the largest station I've ever laid eyes on."

She wasn't wrong. The Stavros Naval Shipyard made the Republic's biggest orbital yards look like playground jungle gyms. Enclosed drydocks, lattice-ringed construction slips, kilometers-long factory arms—all orbiting a central superstructure that must've been over ten kilometers in diameter.

Rodriguez piped up from comms, eyes wide. "Message from the Altairians, sir. Welcome packet received. We're cleared for Slip 32-Delta on the outer repair ring."

Lee nodded. "Send our regards. Reynolds, guide us in. Let's not ding their paint job on the way in."

"Aye, Commander," Reynolds replied, hands already gliding over the controls.

The closer they got, the bigger the station seemed to grow. And then they saw them—rows upon rows of laser batteries, mounted across every exposed surface, overlapping fields of fire covering every possible approach angle.

"Whoa," Rhom said, whistling through his teeth. "Someone's either *paranoid* about security… or seriously compensating for something."

Laughter rippled across the bridge.

Lee grinned. "Hey, I'm just glad the Death Star is on *our* side."

That earned a chorus of chuckles and a few nods.

Then Reynolds turned in his chair. "Whoa there, 'Skipper. If *that's* the Death Star… doesn't that make *us* the baddies in this story?" he asked, completely deadpanned.

Lee froze mid-laugh and blinked at Reynolds. "Shut up, Carl. You're ruining the story," he replied with all the seriousness he could muster.

The bridge erupted—genuine, cathartic laughter echoing off the patched walls. For a few moments, the tension of the past month lifted. They might be limping, scorched, and down a few decks, but they were alive. And they had made it.

Helios Forge loomed ahead, waiting. And with it, a chance to rebuild.

2097
Three Months Later

Three months—that's how long the shipyard estimated for full repairs.

The list of damage was long enough to fill a tactical scroll: multiple hull breaches, crumpled bulkheads, and a completely gutted and rebuilt bridge, CIC, and command deck. The hangar bay had to be stripped bare and re-outfitted from the deck plating up.

But the real nightmare? The Cyclone MPD thrusters.

The propulsion system had overheated so badly during their limp to the gate that portions of it had fused to the hull plating. The engineers had no choice but to cut the ship open, section by section, just to extract the ruined systems. Welding her back together had taken nearly a month—sealing the cuts, aligning the armor plating, and rerunning structural integrity matrices. Lee joked once that they'd performed major surgery with a blowtorch and rebar.

As if that weren't enough, the main power conduits between sections one and two had to be rewired entirely. Decks seven, eight, and nine were stripped bare to rerun the power capacitors that fed the starboard weapon systems. Whole teams rotated in shifts around the clock, rebuilding the ship's nervous system from the bones out.

It had been a giant, flaming cluster from the moment they'd arrived.

The one saving grace? The work was so technical and advanced that most of MacGregor's team couldn't even assist—or the rest of the crew, for that matter. They were placed on shore leave down on the planet for the duration of the repairs.

That didn't stop *Mac*, of course.

He shadowed the Altairians like a starstruck apprentice, bouncing between decks, spewing engineering jargon, and watching every wire run like it was a masterpiece. He called it his "doctorate in hybrid ship repair and construction." Somehow, he even convinced a few of his engineering team to give up the lion's share of their shore leave just to shadow the Altairians alongside him.

Lee had walked in on one lesson—Mac passionately arguing with a pale-skinned Altairian over the optimal cooling dispersal methods for next-gen capacitors. Neither one noticed him standing in the doorway for nearly five minutes. It was the first time in weeks Lee had seen Mac look truly happy.

The actual invitation to the surface came with little fanfare, but the implications were clear: they were not merely welcome—they were honored guests.

Lee and his senior officers were invited planetside to Valdrakar—not for a simple debrief or diplomatic dinner, but as guests of the Primord government, recognized as instrumental heroes in the liberation of Intus. The sheer number of Zodark vessels destroyed had shattered a regional command structure that had stood for generations. And when word spread that Lee's crew had personally accounted for four warship kills, and that he'd received the Republic's second-highest medal, the response was nothing short of royal.

The Altairians pulled out every stop.

From the moment they stepped off the transit shuttle and set foot inside the orbital elevator terminal, they were treated like rock stars. Flags bearing the Republic and Primord emblems flew side-by-side. Honor guards in gleaming armor saluted them as they passed. Locals lined the landing concourse to catch a glimpse. Some clapped. Others bowed. All cheered.

And then they arrived at the hotel…if it could even be called that.

The towering spire of crystalline glass and carved stone stretched more than a kilometer into the sky. Suspended gardens floated on platforms outside the upper floors. Inside, the architecture defied physics—sweeping staircases that twisted in midair, walls that shifted hue with the day's light, and waterfalls cascading through transparent tubes that threaded through the entire atrium.

Their rooms? Luxurious didn't do it justice.

Each suite had floor-to-ceiling windows overlooking Valdrakar's luminous skyline, rainfall showers with programmable scents, gravity-adjustable beds, and furniture that seemed to mold itself to their bodies. Even the room service menus came on soft holographic scrolls, read aloud by politely voiced AIs in whatever accent one desired.

They were waited on, hand and foot—every whim anticipated, every need met before they even voiced it. And they weren't charged a single credit.

Sato had summed it up best when she'd dropped into a plush couch and muttered, "If this is what victory feels like… I could get used to it."

Lee wasn't sure if it was the luxury or the warm, genuine gratitude of the Primords that touched him more. But for the first time since Intus, he allowed himself to breathe—really breathe—and enjoy the peace.

Even if only for a moment.

Chapter 61
Iron and Fire

Year 2097
Republic Embassy, Naval Liaison Office
Valdrakar, Primordia
Kita System

Commander Ripley Lee had been expecting the summons.

With the repairs to the *Poseidon* nearing completion, it was only a matter of time before orders started flowing again. MacGregor had been keeping him up-to-date with the yard's progress, and despite a few setbacks, they were ahead of schedule.

Three months—that's how long it had taken to bring their battered cruiser back from the brink. It wasn't half bad, though, considering the ship had nearly come apart at the seams.

Lee made his way through the polished corridors of the Republic Embassy in Valdrakar, the newest outpost of diplomacy in the Primord home system. The location seemed both sleek and efficient. Lee was directed through security and down a side corridor into a far more spartan building labeled Republic Naval Liaison Office.

The NLO wasn't designed to impress. It was functional to a fault. And that was exactly how Roberts liked it.

Lee knew this conversation was coming. The downtime after Intus had been both a blessing and a curse. Too much time on their hands made people restless. It had only taken three weeks for the first casualty—a spacer who took his own life.

That hit Lee hard.

He immediately recalled the crew, restricting shore leave and restructuring their schedules. Four days on duty, three off. Mandatory physical training every morning. Every crew member, from enlisted to officer, was required to attend a 90-minute personal counseling session. Once a week, they'd sit in ten-person group therapy sessions. No topics were off the table. Lee wanted his crew to cope, to adapt, and above all, to trust each other—to lean on one another. He had a feeling this was going to be a long, brutal war, and he was determined to try and get as many of his people through it alive as possible.

Sato had taken the lead on organizing weekly team-building exercises—some physical, some intellectual—but all centered on building grit, perseverance, and unity.

If one of his crew needed professional advancement or training, Lee personally worked through McKee's office or Captain Roberts to get them into the right courses.

When Admiral McKee was promoted and got wind of the *Poseidon*'s program, she decided to see it for herself. And she brought Roberts with her. That part had been... tricky.

Roberts hadn't known about the training program. Lee had taken the initiative, wanting to give his crew structure in a time of chaos. McKee had assumed it was a task force initiative.

Lee had to think fast.

When McKee asked if the rest of the squadron was running the same program, he jumped in before Roberts could speak.

"Actually, Admiral, Captain Roberts had me test this concept with my crew first—see what worked and what didn't before rolling it out more broadly."

Roberts didn't miss a beat. He didn't blink or contradict him. Just nodded slowly, playing along. McKee bought it. She was impressed.

After lunch at the newly commissioned NLO, McKee left with a final request: a report on their recommendations for future downtime training between deployments. She wanted it by Monday.

As she walked out, Roberts turned to Lee. "Commander Lee, walk with me back to my temporary office."

Lee followed, mentally preparing for the ass-chewing of a lifetime. But when they arrived, Roberts sank into his chair, waved for Lee to sit, and surprised him.

"That was quick thinkin' back there," he said, voice low and even. "Appreciate you not hangin' me out to dry in front of the Admiral."

Lee straightened. "Just didn't want the Admiral to think the program lacked oversight, sir."

Roberts grunted. "Truth is, I gave you all a long leash on purpose. Wanted to see how my commanders handled downtime. Some buried their heads in the sand. Some vanished into shore leave. But you? You trained your crew, kept 'em sharp. Cared for them. That tells me a hell of a lot more than a stack of eval reports."

Lee blinked, surprised by the rare praise.

Roberts leaned forward. "So, tell me, Lee—what makes you different? What lit a fire under your ass when others spent their time sunbathing and boozin'?"

Lee hesitated, choosing his words carefully. "I guess...I grew up different. Faced different challenges."

"Yeah?" Roberts cocked an eyebrow. "Like what?"

"I grew up in a small Mennonite community—in Wyoming," Lee said.

Roberts's eyes narrowed. "Seriously?"

"Yeah, but I didn't exactly share their pacifist worldview. My dad taught me how to hunt and shoot, live off the land. But he hated the idea of violence—didn't want me going anywhere near the military."

Roberts snorted. "So naturally, you joined anyway."

Lee smirked. "Not exactly."

Roberts squinted. "There's more to this story."

Lee played coy. "Maybe."

"Spit it out, Commander. I've read your file. I know about the Olympic medals. I know you joined the Academy late. You aren't some black-bag intel spook planted in the fleet, are you?"

Lee laughed. "No, sir. Not unless they forgot to tell me."

"Because if you are, I'll personally toss you out the nearest airlock. I've had enough of intel operatives trying to play fleet commander. It was a nightmare back in the early Republic days."

"No spook here, sir. Just a messed-up kid who got a second chance."

Before Roberts could push further, a knock came at the door. Master Chief Marks poked his head in. "Captain, Admiral McKee needs to see you immediately."

Roberts stood. "All right. Tell her I'm on my way." He turned back to Lee. "We'll finish this later. Get that report on my desk by Monday."

As the door closed behind him, Lee muttered under his breath, "There goes my weekend."

****

One Week Later
Republic Embassy, Naval Liaison Office
Valdrakar, Primordia

Kita System

The meeting room looked like it had been carved from obsidian and steel—sleek, silent, and cold. Walls hummed with embedded shielding tech. The air was sterile, and not a single window overlooked the city outside.

Security badges had to be triple-verified just to enter. Inside, a large holotable dominated the center of the room, flickering with system maps, troop deployments, and still-classified after-action footage from the Intus invasion.

Captain Roberts stood at the head of the table, arms crossed, jaw clenched. His dark uniform looked pressed within an inch of its life. The expression on his face? Not so much.

"Right, you bunch of primped-up peacocks," Roberts began, voice as grating as a belt sander. "I know you've been livin' it up like holovid stars the past months—sippin' whatever fermented starlight the Primords pour in their crystal goblets, gettin' fat off golden shrimp, and floppin' your arses into gravity-adjustable beds with views of the damned spires of Valdrakar."

He paused, letting the silence settle.

"But what you didn't know is that this was a test—a real one. And most of you failed."

A few officers exchanged uneasy glances. Lee remained still, watching.

Roberts continued, "Some of you used this time as an excuse to disappear, party, or just slack off. Maybe you thought the war was over. It isn't. This is going to be a long, long war. You are the commanders. These crews live or die by your leadership. If you can't own that, then step aside for someone who can."

He jabbed a finger toward the table. "You want to know who didn't waste this time? Commander Lee. While the rest of you were gettin' massages and drinking top-shelf scotch, Lee had his people on a hard rotation: PT, counseling, team-building—hell, even professional development. They got better while the rest of you got soft."

There were a few stiffened backs and red faces in the room now. Roberts let the silence stew.

"Now I expect every damn one of you to take a good, hard look at your command logs and ask yourselves how you let a rookie commander outpace you all. Because he did."

Master Chief Marks entered the room, a satchel slung over his shoulder. Without a word, he began distributing sleek handheld devices to each officer seated at the table.

Roberts held one up.

"Gentlemen, meet your new lifeline—the Qpad. Think of it like your old data pads got into a bar fight with a quantum computer, and this is what limped out of the alley."

There were a few low snickers.

"Everyone—and I mean *everyone* across the Republic—is getting issued one of these. This is how we'll communicate from now on. Mass messages, secure data, orders, logs—you name it. This replaces the outdated crap we've been stuck with for the last decade."

Lee turned the device over in his hand. It was sleek, about the size of a large, modern phone, with a matte black finish and faintly etched Republic insignia.

"Now, for those of you wonderin' how this is all supposed to work," Roberts continued, "Space Command is implementing something called the battlenet. It's a satellite-delivered comms net that'll operate on two channels—a secure net and a monitored, non-secure net."

He stepped to the holotable and flicked a control. A schematic of the Republic systems blinked into view.

"Battlenet is already live across the Republic core worlds and expanding across the Intus system as we speak. It's built to eventually support near-real-time system-wide communications via comm relays and satellites. Will it reach Kita? Probably. Eventually. But for now, you'd better learn how to use these."

A few of the commanders were already tapping through their devices, scrolling through the interface. They were clean and responsive. They were truly a military-grade user-interface, with priority comms channels preloaded.

Roberts crossed his arms again.

"Don't lose it. Don't break it. And don't forget to charge it. This thing is your new heartbeat."

He let that settle in before moving on.

"Now, let's talk about what comes next. You boys are officially being attached to a new joint task force—JTF-10. Before you ask—we didn't name it. Someone told me back-in-the-day that the Americans called their first Special Forces group, 'Group Ten.' Why? Because if the Soviets ever found out about it, they'd think there were nine others just like it—real Cold War mind games stuff."

He snorted. "Well, I guess the same logic stuck."

He turned to the holotable again and brought up a star map, zooming in on the Rass system.

"Here's the rub. We're heading into the Rass system. It's the next target on the liberation list. The Zodarks took it from the Primords decades ago. Now we're taking it back. But listen closely—this one's going to be deep behind enemy lines. No friendly bases. No fallback points. No cavalry waiting in the wings."

The map zoomed out again, highlighting several green icons orbiting a gas giant.

"What the Primords *do* have are a few retrofitted transports they've turned into expeditionary bases. Mobile supply depots, munitions bunkers, fuel stores—you name it. They float these things in together like a little nomadic cities; they're support ships clustered like barnacles."

A hologram appeared above the table, showing four massive transport ships docking in formation, surrounded by smaller utility craft. Defense corvettes and shuttle traffic weaved between them.

"They may look clunky, but they work. They'll be our logistical lifeline during this op."

He turned back to the room, tone dropping.

"Our task is to deploy with a Primord recon team and begin prepping the battlespace. We're talking surveillance, early strikes, softening targets, and setting the board. My role will be Deputy JTF Commander, and I'll be the ranking Republic officer in theater.

"As the Republic's senior officer, I get the inglorious job of playing house maid and protecting this little piece of heaven for us," Roberts said, his voice thick with sarcasm. "That means I need to assign two of you to become our eyes and ears in the Rass system. You'll be scouting the area, conducting hit-and-run attacks on Zodark convoys, and taking advantage of any target of opportunity that presents itself."

He glanced around the room before locking eyes with Lee. "Lee, I'm placing you in charge of Blue Team."

Then his gaze shifted across the table. "Commander Jay Tulip—JT—you're taking Red Team."

The two officers nodded, the weight of the assignment already settling in.

"Each of you will have a pair of frigates assigned to your team. I'll keep a quick reaction force with the rest of the cruisers in case you run into more trouble than you can handle. But don't count on much more than that. We're going to be deep behind enemy lines, gentlemen. Very deep."

The Qpads in every officer's hand buzzed, almost in unison.

"Your new orders are being uploaded now," Roberts said, tapping his own device. "Review them. Digest them. We ship out in three days. I expect every one of you to get your ships and your crews ready for action. No excuses."

Chapter 62
Behind Enemy Lines

Mid-2097
Stargate 352-NHW
RNS Poseidon

The past seventy-two hours had passed in a blur of checklists, last-minute system diagnostics, and deep anticipation. Commander Ripley Lee stood in the center of his bridge, boots planted, arms crossed, watching his crew move like muscle memory incarnate. If there was one saving grace about running his crew ragged during shore leave, it was how quickly they'd snapped back into fighting shape. The *Poseidon* was sharp again—maybe sharper than ever.

Lee didn't ask how the other captains were doing. He didn't want to know. After Roberts had used him as an example in that closed-door meeting, the room's temperature had dropped by ten degrees. That kind of spotlight burned in all the wrong ways. He wasn't here to make friends. He was here to win.

Still, it felt *right* to be back in his seat—back aboard his ship.

"Commander Lee, we've received the order to jump." Sato's voice cut through his thoughts like a calm blade.

"Very well, XO. Acknowledge the order," he said, rotating toward the helm. "Lieutenant Reynolds—take us through the gate."

"Aye, sir. Initiating gate sequence now," Reynolds replied, hands dancing across the console.

The *Poseidon* surged forward, slotting into position with the rest of the squadron. There were ten ships total, with Blue and Red Teams flanking one another. The Primords had jumped ahead of them, their formation barely a flicker in the gate's ripple as it collapsed behind them.

Lee hoped they arrived undetected. The Rass system was vast and unruly—home to abandoned mines, derelict stations, and a hundred places for Zodark patrols to be lurking.

As the ship approached the gate, Lee turned his head. "Rhom, the moment we clear the event horizon, I want local sensors up and weapons ready. If the Primords are already in a firefight, we move to support. But whatever you do—do *not* go active with the primaries. I don't want to light us up like a damned fireworks display."

"Understood, sir," Rhom said crisply. "Guns are spooled, crews are locked in, and local sensors are standing by for passive sweeps. We're ready."

Lee gave a short nod. That was why he liked Rhom: sharp, dependable, and tactical to the bone. Sato was much the same now—anticipating his commands before he even gave them.

Am I that easy to read? Lee shook the thought loose.

The gate flared around them.

Stars bent and twisted as if caught in a whirlpool, and with a low hum of inertia buffers kicking in, the *Poseidon* slipped into the swirling blue light of the jump corridor. A heartbeat later, the stargate swallowed them whole.

The moment they exited, the Primord fleet transitioned to FTL, vanishing into the darkness of the Rass system. They were headed toward a predetermined hideaway—coordinates unknown, even to the rest of the Republic squadron. Once they'd landed and confirmed the area was secure, a Primord frigate would return to relay the location.

In the meantime, Lee and the rest of the Republic ships were stuck, waiting at the stargate.

Privately, Lee couldn't help but feel the whole situation was backwards. Sitting still, exposed, near the one point in space everyone in this system would know to watch? It was tactically unsound at best—and suicidal at worst.

"Sir, we're being hailed by Captain Roberts. He wants to speak to you," said Lieutenant Lucia Rodriguez.

"Put him through to my station," Lee replied, bracing himself.

Captain Eamon Roberts's face appeared on screen, red-faced and seething.

"Lee, something got screwed up with the timing of our arrival," Roberts growled. "The Primords were supposed to be *at* the hideaway before we jumped. Their frigate was supposed to be waiting here to pass along the coordinates. But surprise, surprise—they're not. And I'll be damned if we're going to sit around at this stargate like a bunch of targets, waiting for a Zodark patrol to tear us apart."

Roberts tapped something off-screen. "I just confirmed with the Primords—they're diverting a frigate to Moon XF752. I'm sending you the coordinates now."

The coordinates appeared on Lee's Qpad.

"Lee, I want Blue Team to jump now. Get on station with weapons hot and your *local* sensors up. If we land into a mess, I want eyes-on right away. As soon as we clear FTL, transmit your sensor package to the rest of us. Then shut it down, go dark, and hold. We'll wait for the Primord ship to show up with our new coordinates."

Lee sighed. *So, someone* did *screw up.*

"That's a good copy, sir. We're on the way. *Poseidon* out."

The screen blinked black.

Lee turned in his seat. "Reynolds, set a course for the coordinates the *Aussie* just sent. Comms—send the FRAGO to the *Dagger* and *Vigilant*. Tell them we're jumping in sixty seconds. We need to get out of here and find the squadron a place to land that isn't a damned target painted in space."

A minute later, the *Poseidon* surged into FTL, her escorts close behind. Lee sat motionless in his chair, eyes fixed on the stars streaking across the monitor. He couldn't shake the unease coiling in his gut. *Please don't be occupied,* he thought, fingers tightening around the armrest.

"Exiting FTL in five... four... three... two... exiting now," Reynolds called out.

The ship jolted gently back into normal space. The forward monitors flickered, recalibrating.

"Rhom, get local sensors online. I need eyes—now," Lee ordered.

"Aye, sir. Local sensors coming up," Rhom replied, already hunched over his console.

Sato was ahead of the curve, syncing comms with the *Dagger* and *Vigilant*, issuing standby protocols. The bridge was dead silent, save for the low hum of systems spinning up.

Seconds passed like hours. "Oh crap," Rhom muttered, his eyes widening. "We've just landed in front of a Zodark gas mining op—two frigates on station. One's already turning toward us. The other... just jumped away."

Lee's stomach dropped. *Of all the coordinates in the system...*

"Reynolds, engines to fifty percent. Match our heading with the moon's orbit. Let's drift into position like we belong here," Lee snapped.

He swung toward Sato. "Get the *Dagger* and the *Vigilant* moving. Have them pursue the remaining frigate—disable it if possible. Rhom, hit the closest frigate with our turbo-lasers the moment you've got a firing solution. As soon as we're angled in, bring the primaries online and start sniping those mining vessels. Let's make this hurt."

The ship groaned softly as her engines ramped up, angling the *Poseidon*'s portside weapons toward the targets. Sato routed the external cameras to the main monitor, magnifying their view.

There it was—the enemy frigate, closing fast. Four bulbous gas miners drifted behind it, tethered to a collection array glowing with processed gases.

"Primaries locking," Rhom said. "Turbo-lasers engaging!"

Streaks of plasma shot across space. The Zodark frigate jerked hard to starboard, thrusters flaring. The *Dagger* and the *Vigilant* swept in on its flanks, hurling kinetic slugs and plasma torpedoes.

One of the gas miners erupted into a fireball—brilliant, chaotic, and sudden.

Then Captain Roberts's face appeared on Lee's monitor, still red, and now sweat-slicked with frustration.

"Lee, what the hell happened?"

"I don't know, sir," Lee replied quickly. "We exited FTL right into the middle of a gas mining site. Two Zodark frigates were present— one bolted instantly. Probably ran for reinforcements. Until the Primords pass us the real hideout coordinates, I figured we'd knock out targets of opportunity."

Roberts swore under his breath and shook his head. "What a SNAFU this is turning into. The moment the Primords—"

"You've got to be kidding me!" Rhom shouted. "Sir, we've got new contacts—just exited FTL. Aw, crap… Enemy battleship—make that *two* battleships, and four cruisers."

Lee's heart thudded against his ribs.

He turned back toward Roberts, voice level despite the spike of adrenaline. "I'd take a SNAFU right now. Things just went FUBAR. We've got enemy battleships and cruisers inbound."

Roberts didn't say anything for a second. He let loose a torrent of obscenities.

"Engage! Take evasive maneuvers, and let's hope that Primord ship gets here with our new jump location before these Zodarks catch up to us!"

"Copy that, sir. Aw, crap—there's more jumping in!"

****

From the Authors

Brandon and I hope you've enjoyed this book. If you'd like to preorder book two of the Battles of the Republic series and continue this action-packed military sci-fi series, please visit Amazon.

If you would like to stay up to date on new releases and receive emails about any special pricing deals we may make available, please sign up for our email distribution list. Simply go to https://www.frontlinepublishinginc.com/ and sign up.

As a bonus, if you sign up for our mailing list, you will receive a dossier for the Rise of the Republic Series. It contains artwork of the ships we've written about, as well as their pertinent stats. It will really help make the series come to life for you as you continue reading.

As independent authors, reviews are very important to us and make a huge difference to other prospective readers. If you enjoyed this book, we humbly ask you to write up a positive review on Amazon and Goodreads. We sincerely appreciate each person that takes the time to write one.

We have really valued connecting with our readers via social media, especially on our Facebook page https://www.facebook.com/RosoneandWatson/. Sometimes we ask for help from our readers as we write future books—we love to draw upon all your different areas of expertise. We also have a group of beta readers who get to look at the books before they are officially published and help us fine-tune last-minute adjustments. If you would like to be a part of this team, please go to our author website, https://www.frontlinepublishinginc.com/, and send us a message through the "Contact" tab.

AC	Air Conditioning
AI	Artificial Intelligence
AO	Area of Operations
ARCOM	Augmented Reality Combat Operations Module
ASAP	As soon as possible
CONOP	Concept of Operations
CSAR	Combat Search and Rescue
ECCM	Electronic Counter-Countermeasures
ECM	Electronic Countermeasures
ETA	Estimated Time of Arrival
EVA	Extravehicular Activity
FOB	Forward Operating Base
FTL	Faster-than-light
GE	Galactic Empire
GMM	General Command Communication
HALO	High Altitude, Low Opening
HUD	Heads-up Display
JATMs	Joint Advance Tactical Missiles
JTAO	Junior Tactical Actions Officer
LZ	Landing Zone
MIA	Missing in Action
MRE	Meals Ready to Eat
NEOS	New Eden Orbital Station
NORDO	No Radio (out of communication)
PA	Public Announcement
PTSD	Post-traumatic stress disorder
RNS	Republic Naval Ship
ROE	Rules of Engagement
SUV	Sports Utility Vehicle
TAO	Tactical Action Officer
VBC	Victory Base Complex
VIP	Very Important Person
VLS	Vertical Launch System
VTOL	Vertical Take-off and Landing
XO	Executive Officer

www.ingramcontent.com/pod-product-compliance
Lightning Source LLC
Chambersburg PA
CBHW070204310726

48976CB00001B/212